AN ANCIENT HOPE

By the same author

THE STANDING HILLS

A HOUSE OF CLAY

THE DARKNESS OF CORN

AN ANCIENT HOPE

Caroline Stickland

St. Martin's Press
New York

ISBN 0-312-10929-6

First published in Great Britain by Victor Gollancz.

First U.S. Edition: May 1994
10 9 8 7 6 5 4 3 2 1

To my aunt,

Agnes Hendry

AN ANCIENT HOPE

Chapter One

It was widely considered by her acquaintance that Theodosia Farnaby should not have been brought up by her aunt. Her friends did not agree and the young man now strolling by her side in the warm September sunlight could see no fault in her at all.

They were making their way down a mossy path that led through the flower garden to the summerhouse, where Theo's easel had been carried before her visitor arrived. The pavilion had been built as a Greek temple by her grandfather, but his son, a man with no illusions about the English climate, had had its columns incongruously glassed in with Gothic folding-doors. It was a building that suited Theo for, though she appeared as serene and dark-haired, as upright and graceful as any well-brought-up Athenian maiden, there was a piquancy in her eyes that is not often to be found in classical statuary.

The path was narrow and the young man, who enjoyed looking into those eyes, was close enough for his fingers to brush hers as if by accident. Finding no withdrawal of her hand, he took it in his with the firmness appropriate to the successful merchant that he was and to the strong beating of his heart.

'Are you glad that you've come back?' he asked.

'Yes.' She smiled into his face. 'I am. Can you tell me why? Is it the fine weather?'

Drawing her fingers slowly out of his, she lifted her skirts to climb the two steps to the summerhouse. The folding-doors had been opened but the heat inside smelt of having been trapped behind glass. A jug of lemonade had recently been placed on the round table and Theo removed its muslin cover to pour tumblers for them both, before taking one of the seats.

The young man placed his chair close to hers and, leaning forward, traced an R in the dew on the side of the jug then, piercing it with an arrow, put his hand to his breast in anguish.

'Ralph,' said Theo, 'if your father could see you so foolish – and on a working day.'

'He knows that I work towards the merging of two mills. What stricter attention to business could there be?'

'So,' she took the fan that was hanging from her waist, 'it seems that the longer the other party takes to agree to contract, the more afternoons you must sit in the sun?'

'A sad arrangement,' he agreed, 'but we all have our duties to perform.'

They sat together looking at the garden with the appearance of idleness but with all their senses alert. Although cousins, they were not so much alike as to make strangers realize their relationship, and the year Theo had spent touring Europe with her aunt had served to introduce an unfamiliarity between them that had added an attraction to the eight weeks of her return.

Had a stranger passed before them at that moment he must have thought them blessed. To be young, prosperous and loving in a golden hour in 1850 was to feel the world before them scattering its riches at their feet. If the stranger had known that each was heir to a mill, whose ropes and nets were cast out across the continents to bring wealth to this pleasant Dorset town of Bridport, he would have walked on secure that for them, in all this flower garden, there could be no worm in the bud.

It was true that these secluded walks had seen them more often in happiness than sorrow. The house whose side they could glimpse across the rose trees and trellises had been Theo's home all her life. A plain, white, four-storied building, tall enough not to seem dwarfed by the high walls that enclosed its grounds or the hills that rose behind, it had been built by the grandfather whose desires, whether for a thriving business or a Greek temple, were simple and always attained. It was here that her father's sister had come to take charge of the motherless infant she had been and here that Aunt Louisa had taught her the independent habit of mind that so outraged those who were born to be sheep.

The house lay at the edge of Allington, on the outskirts of Bridport, and from its upper windows Theo had an unimpeded view across the water-meadows to the village of ropeworks, warehouses and cottages that was her uncle's property and, by common usage, bore the family name of Carnow. Her mother had been Sarah Carnow and would have been glad to know how often the mile that separated their homes had seen her daughter and her brother's sons travelling to meet one another.

The two boys had known the Farnaby mill and home as well as they knew their own. Their uncle's stables and orchard were as much their growing place as Carnow was Theo's. There was such a constant, easy intercourse between the families that, although the fathers were agreed that a union between Theo and either Charles or Ralph was to be hoped for, it was felt the domestic intimacy they shared would serve to bar romantic inclinations. Louisa had been twenty, elegant and clever, when she had been handed the bundle of lace and long-clothes that was Theodosia and for years the only sentimental attachment that had arisen was a brief court paid her by Charles. The elder of the two boys and precocious, he was only five years Louisa's junior and devilment drove him to hint a desire that was proscribed by the Book of Common Prayer. Louisa was never one to mistake fool's gold for the genuine metal nor had she any wish to marry and she quelled his mischief with words that were absorbed painfully into his secretive nature.

The startling event that occurred ten years before the afternoon on which Theo and her admirer strolled in the garden had not surprised Louisa, who saw in it the advantage that could come to Ralph. Charles, always his father's darling, had long preferred money to work and had persuaded Mr Carnow to allow him to renounce his future claim on the mill in exchange for the value of what would have been his inheritance. Had his wife, Ann, still been well, Mr Carnow would have been prevented from following this course but, though an astute man in other matters, he was besotted by Charles and, against all advice, agreed. It was fortunate for the firm and the younger son that Mrs Carnow had brought so substantial a dowry to her marriage that she had been a financial partner in all but name and had always insisted that Ralph should have an equal share in the future of the mill.

The loss of capital involved in the transaction had been worsened by a blow which fell before Mr Carnow had properly understood that Charles had cut the lines that bound him to his home. Five hundred pounds was drawn from his depleted bank account on a forged cheque. Edward Trent, his trusted chief clerk, was convicted of the theft but the money was never discovered and for some time, despite all the aid that Mr Farnaby could give his brother-in-law, it seemed that the business must fail.

Young as he was, Ralph proved to be the mainstay of his father. Released from the shadow of his brother's presence, his conscientious and level-headed application to all aspects of the works gradually re-established their standing and brought trade from those who had begun to look on Carnow's as suspect. Now, at twenty-nine, he was justifiably proud of the part he had played in recovering the prosperity of the firm.

Nor was it only his professional achievement that was warming his spirit. He had watched Theo's growth with friendship and interest. Although nine years older than she, he had always been prepared to give her his time because she had never been a simpering miss. From the days when her leading-strings had had to be tethered to a post to prevent her frequent escapes from the confines of this garden, she had been of a determined and adventurous nature. It was a pleasure to play at croquet or archery with a girl who did not feel it incumbent upon her to lose if she were playing against a young man. When he had walked beside her goat-cart she had always preferred to hold the reins herself and when she had graduated to the saddle she had been as ready to take a fence as he. It was not that she was a romping girl. She was not unruly or unmindful of her neighbours' sensibilities but she had been encouraged to a liberty of thought that was unusual even for this notoriously unorthodox town.

There had been a time when Ralph was so enmeshed in the struggle to save the mill that he felt that he had become separated from social life and had not an hour to give to anything that was not business. It was only as the pressure upon him decreased and success returned that he realized that his continual visits to the Farnabys' house had not been to consult his uncle but to be solaced by Theo.

When he was keeping up a public front of confidence in the firm, he brought his worries to her. When he sat late at his desk, tired and dispirited, he thought of her. When he sailed to the Grand Banks of Newfoundland to sell his lines to the fleets, he brought back furs for her. When he had news of each step gained towards prosperity, he brought it first to her.

He was so used to thinking of her as a friend that the realization that he was in love came upon him gradually. The conversation of those who had not Theo's intelligence made him impatient, her appearance became the yardstick by which he measured and condemned womankind, he grew bad-tempered whenever she and Louisa talked of leaving the town for a few weeks of change of air but it was only when thoughts of her began to deprive him of sleep that he understood his symptoms.

His affliction was apparent to Theo and her aunt long before the revelation came to him. Theo had not been brought up to shy away from the idea of love. Louisa had taught her to enjoy this laudable emotion but to approach it with open eyes and an awareness of its complications. The belief current among sentimentalists that a girl should be unaware of her feelings until a declaration was made to her was despicable to these two warm-hearted women, who had witnessed the false innocence and mercenary courtships it encouraged, and for this reason they were often thought immodest. In her immodesty, Theo, with her open manner, her quick mind and sensual nature, looked on Ralph's love and saw that it was good.

There was only one doubt about the rightness of the match in Louisa's reckoning. Theo had seen so little of the world that it was possible she favoured Ralph because he was the best of the young men she had met and not because her own love was deep. Since the death of Theo's father three years before, Mr Carnow had been her guardian but he had such faith in Louisa's judgement that he did not interfere in their arrangements. When Louisa decided to take Theo abroad for a year to widen her experience and test her attachment, he put no obstacle in her way. Ralph had been against the scheme but admitted that his motives were selfish and his reluctance to lose her did him no harm in Theo's eyes.

Throughout their absence, there had been a constant correspondence and the letters sent from Paris, Naples and Rome, from Florence and Lausanne, showed a lively appreciation of travel but no hint of amorous intrigue. Both father and son awaited the women's return with a growing confidence that Ralph would have his desire.

Their expectation was not disappointed. Theo was plainly enriched by her travels and had matured to a fascinating degree.

She seemed eager for Ralph's attentions and he, who had never spoken plainly to her of his feelings, began to woo her in earnest. Aware of each other as they had never been before, the pair dallied together in the late summer weeks yet did not quite come to the point.

This afternoon had been one of unblemished pleasure. There was a delicious anticipation between the two. The brief touches they exchanged, the words they did not say, the meaning in their eyes made the sun warmer and their seclusion more complete. Theo fanned herself slowly. It excited her that the year they had spent apart had made them strangers.

There was in this man beside her all the qualities with which she was familiar but changed and made more alluring by the difference in his way of seeing her. A year of fearing her loss had burnt all cousinship from his mind. Memories of easy days of childhood with the girl that she had been were separate now from his need of her as a woman that he wanted for his own.

I don't congratulate myself, she thought, but I want this change. I want a fierce, possessive love. I feel my pulse beat faster when he takes my hand. It is luxurious.

Outside, the afternoon sun shone full upon the peach trees cordoned against the garden walls. Bees, heavy and foolish with heat, made soft uncertain flights between late-season flowers. Beyond the house, the woods upon the hills had not begun to turn and were dense and green against the sky. I am completely glad, thought Theo, yet cannot recognize myself.

She rose from her chair and went down the pavilion steps to the round pool that the path skirted. Sitting on its rim, she trailed her fingers amongst the yellow water-lilies and dropped palmfuls of water into their waxy cups. The air was laden here with lavender planted to be brushed against and with the too-sweet scent of carnations. She felt that she could weep but did not know why.

Ralph followed her and brought the hat that she had cast aside. He placed it gently on her hair so that the shadow of its wide brim veiled her face. Laying his hand against her cheek, he said, 'I wouldn't have your skin less pale.'

She turned her head to touch her lips to his wrist. 'Would you think less of me?' she asked.

He sat beside her on the stone rim. 'I think of you at every moment of the day,' he said. 'Whatever I'm doing I think of you. I want no change in you or in my thoughts. I have perfect happiness – why do you smile?'

'Because I was taught Greek. The gods are jealous of human happiness and punish those who boast of having it, yet we sit here quite unafraid.'

'What courage we have.'

'Yes,' she smiled again, 'but then, I think that we've nothing to fear.'

Chapter Two

The October winds of Newfoundland blew coldly about the man now walking along the harbour at St John's. His city clothes and soft hands marked him out from the sailors and fishermen working on the quay but his air of self-assurance and purpose protected him from open insult. He was looking intently across the water at a brig, which was riding at anchor at a distance too great for him to see its name. There was activity on its deck and a boat which had taken provisions to it was now being rowed back to the shore.

The man waited by the steps to which the boat was returning. He was not pleased by his surroundings. The white, northern light and the grey waves did not suit him. He had no objection to gulls circling in a warm Mediterranean air but here their bitter cries as they fell upon discarded fish reminded him too forcibly of his position. In his view he was among savages.

He disliked the silence that was behind the noise of the harbour. It seemed to him as if beyond the surge of the sea, the creak and slap of resting vessels, the shouts of orders and repartee, a great quietness lay ready to descend. He felt it to be more than the end of the fleets' season. Winter would come and ice hold the North in stillness. For one such as he, it would bring desolation.

The boat had reached the steps and its oarsman tied it to an iron ring. The man stepped closer to the edge of the quay and called down to the rower.

'Do you come from the *Bridport Maid*?'

The sailor looked up and, in the broad West Country vowels that his questioner had not heard for so long, said that he did.

'Where is your captain?'

'In the lading house, sir, unless his business is done. I'm bid to fetch him back.'

'Where is this house?'

The sailor climbed the steps to point out the office. A labourer, thought the man wryly, in canvas stinking of fish-oil, turns me into a boy again because I hear his voice. I must be growing soft-hearted.

'Do you sail on the tide?' he asked.

'Ay,' the sailor smiled, showing a gold tooth. 'The last run. There's wives who'll be counting the days.'

The man took a pair of doe-skin gloves from the pocket of his greatcoat and began putting them on. He was elegantly dressed but it now needed some contrivance to keep him so.

'I'll seek out your master,' he said. 'What name will it be?'

'Moore. Captain Moore.'

The man raised his eyebrows slightly. 'Indeed? Yes, it would be. How time passes.'

He left the sailor without thanks and made his way through the crates of salt cod waiting to be shipped to Europe, the coils of rope that pointed to his past and future, the drying seaweed that was so offensive to one who liked to walk the soft carpets of a casino, until he reached the lading house.

Entering the hall, he looked about him. There was a room to his left with a window and a hatch in the wall. Through the glass, he could see two clerks seated on high stools at their desks, and, talking animatedly to an official with whom he seemed to be on familiar terms, Philip Moore. He moved back, out of the direct sight of the occupants of the room. I would have known him anywhere, he thought, that tedious good humour, that practical look. He won't want me on his ship but he'll take me for my father's sake. I needn't offer to pay.

The door opened and Moore came out, folding papers into a leather satchel.

'Good day, Philip.'

Moore turned to see who had spoken to him. It was unusual for him to be addressed by his Christian name on this side of the Atlantic. He saw a man who seemed familiar and yet to whom he could not put a name. For a moment there was puzzlement on his alert, observant face and then a look of distaste replaced it.

'I see you recognize me.'

'Charles Carnow.' Moore's tone was cold. He'll want something from me, he thought, he has that same amusement, that calculation in his eyes that was always there. Ten years have not improved him. In this place, at this time, I think I know what he will ask.

'The last person you would expect to meet here?' said Charles. 'Not the most agreeable location but I was born in the trade and what's bred in the bone will out, don't you find?'

Moore fastened the straps of the satchel.

'I daresay you want a passage home,' he said.

'Home,' said Charles. 'There are times in one's life when that word is profoundly dull and others when it has a most satisfactory ring. This is one of the latter.'

If I don't take him aboard, thought Moore, he'll come by another ship. He won't hesitate to tell old Carnow I refused. Poor Ralph, this won't please him.

'Come with me to an inn,' he said, 'and tell me your arrangements.'

They went out of the hall and Moore led the way to a tavern in a side street nearby. Although they had grown up in the same town as sons of prosperous businessmen and had only a year between them in age, their different ways of living were so stamped upon them that a good judge of character would hardly have considered them of the same species. A bad judge would have marked Charles's manner and appearance and decided in his favour. There being more bad than good judges in the world, Charles was able to live without fear of anything more than temporary interruptions to his comfort.

The inn was warm after the harbour winds and the lamps on the shelf around its wooden walls made the afternoon seem dark outside. Seeing Charles's eyes flicker towards the stove, Moore took a table beside it and ordered hot brandy. Two men were eating chicken stew, dipping bread into the gravy, and, from a corner where he sat with his feet on a settle, another nodded at Moore without breaking off a slow conversation with a serving maid who was polishing glasses. Despite himself, Charles felt a pathetic relief to be sheltered and paid for with the prospect of safety before him.

The brandy was brought immediately and the girl passing the time of day as she set out the spirits, the jug of hot water, the lemon and sugar, delayed the necessity for conversation between the reunited men. Moore was a decisive thinker and was a captain at the age of thirty-four through his own merits and not because his father had built the brig he sailed, but his long dislike of his companion held his tongue. His mother had been a friend of Charles's mother and was now of Louisa Farnaby. He himself was close to Ralph. The families were bound together by the strong social and business ties of a community where grandfather had known grandfather. He had considered the Carnows well rid of their elder son and when, after Ann Carnow's death, there had been no more news of Charles, had hoped that Ralph might never be disturbed by the reappearance of his brother. He knew Charles to be unscrupulous, selfish and idle, and the cleverness and charm which deceived many had no virtue in his eyes to soften these faults. There must be a self-seeking reason for Charles wishing to return to Bridport and, bearing in mind Carnow's old preference for his worthless boy, it would undoubtedly be to Ralph's detriment. It angered Moore that Charles should be returning to succour himself with any part of what Ralph had worked to recreate. Already, he felt irrationally responsible for any distress that might be caused his friend by the brother's return.

'Did you think me dead?' asked Charles. 'Or should I say did you hope?'

'You can say neither. I haven't spared much time these years for thoughts of you.'

He spoke calmly. Often as a boy, he had been ruffled by Charles's jibes but now they were nothing to him. He wondered how much Charles knew of his family. There had been no word from him since a letter telling him of his mother's death had been sent to Baden-Baden in forty-two. The addresses on the few notes she had received from him were various and told the searching father only that the son was travelling from one pleasure-resort to another. There had been no plans mentioned in these communications and, no reply being received to the letters sent to Charles's last-mentioned lodgings, it had not been clear whether he had even known of his loss. The possibility that he would shock Charles with the tidings did not perturb Moore. He was curious to hear where Charles had been concealed during his years of absence and was sure that whatever he had been about it would not be to his credit.

'Will you give me a passage?' asked Charles.

'Yes.'

The thought of Charles's company for the weeks of the voyage did not put warmth into Moore's voice. He had a reason of his own for looking forward to a season in port and had expected a journey made short by anticipation. The crossing now lengthened remarkably in his mind.

'I thought you would,' said Charles, 'but don't feel you must. I can go south and sail by another way. Do you still carry my father's lines?'

Moore twisted a piece of lemon until the last of the juice was in his glass. The citrus oil was as sharp as sea air as it rose from the hot spirit.

'You know that I do,' he said. 'You must have found me by making enquiries on the matter.'

'Is business as prosperous as ever?'

Moore gave him a wry look. 'As ever?' he said. 'It's better than when you left if that's the time you mean. It fell away almost to nothing after you'd taken the capital but Ralph has risen like a phoenix from the ashes.'

Charles poured more brandy on to his dregs of sugar.

'I thought he would,' he said. 'I had every faith in my little brother. He'll never cause any excitement in the world but he plods here, he plods there. It gets the job done.'

'Your memory's at fault. Ralph achieves his ends without any parade about it . . . You haven't asked of your father.'

'If he were dead you wouldn't accept me on your ship.'

The answer gave Moore reassurance. It was inconceivable that one so cold would not be seen through, however doting the parent.

'Did you hear of your mother's death?' he asked.

'I did.'

'Yet you sent no regrets.'

Charles shrugged. 'Death is final. There's nothing to say on the subject.'

The door opened and three officers entered. They were talking and laughing amongst themselves, questioning each other on where they should sit and what they would have. The serving girl crossed the room to take their order and, as she passed, Moore saw that her glance slid to Charles.

'So,' Charles said, 'when I return it will be to a diminished household – or is Ralph married?'

'No.'

There was an instant's hesitation in his answer which made Charles raise his eyebrows.

'Ah,' he said. 'I recognize your "no" as "no, but – ". It would seem that Ralph is on the brink. Would I know my sister-in-law?'

'There's nothing certain as yet but he has an understanding with Miss Farnaby.'

Charles put his glass down suddenly. 'Miss Farnaby! Good God! She must be forty if she's – No,' he tapped his fingers on the table as though he were counting. 'You must mean the chit. Well,' he considered the possibilities of this. 'That will give Ralph another mill when she comes into her own. How is my uncle?'

'He died four years ago.'

'Did he? More luck for my dear brother. And what of my cousin? Is she worth looking at?'

'She's reckoned handsome by those who talk freely of a lady,' said Moore. 'Miss Farnaby has all the qualities of a gentlewoman.'

Charles drew down the corners of his mouth. 'Then she should suit the earnest Ralph. She can beguile his evenings with tea and needlework and may God have mercy on his soul.'

Moore stood up and placed some coins by his glass. 'Have your trunk brought down to the quay,' he said. 'I'll send the boat back for you. If you aren't there you'll have lost your chance. I'll give orders not to wait.'

Towards midnight Charles was in his cabin on the *Bridport Maid*. He undid his cravat and lay on his bunk in his shirt with his arms crossed over his eyes. Putting the sole of one foot to the heel of the other, he dragged off his boots and kicked them on to the floor. The excessive care he had taken over his appearance was no longer necessary; there would soon be new boots for the asking.

The swell of the open sea lifted him in strong, rhythmic rolls and the lantern hanging from the low ceiling shone a dim, steady flame on walls that rose and fell in a regular flow of shadow and light. There was a vitality and confidence about the ship and its master that was unlike anything Charles had encountered for many years. However much the crew might wish for more pay and leisure, there was not a man amongst those sailing who would not have thought Charles contemptible had they known his way of living. Indeed, he found himself secretly intimidated by Moore as a captain, so at home with the obedience of his men.

It was not only the change in Moore that daunted him. A long road had taken him from the triumph of his departure from the town to which he was now returning and it was a road that had become increasingly stony and forlorn. On the morning that he had left, with thousands to his name and his father weeping, it would have been unimaginable that he could ever come to this. To be young, heartless and rich is a heaven of a kind and it is the tragedy of those who inhabit it to have too little wit to see that it is transient. He had set out confident that he had the means for a life of indulgence and ease. His intention was to exert himself only to increase his wealth by the most pleasurable methods. He began to live as he thought a gentleman should.

The Channel behind him, he had travelled from one resort to the next, hiring the best of rooms, ordering the rarest of wines, strolling the promenades with the weariest of airs and finest of coats. He had gambled upon his father's fondness to achieve his early inheritance and it was gambling which was to be his future resource. The time when he would be in need of money seemed very far away and at first he played the tables simply for pleasure. He found the company in casinos congenial and the atmosphere stimulating. It excited him to lounge in a close, scented room watching masked women cut and deal cards with white, be-ringed hands. The hushed, indolent world of rouge-et-noir suited him and its atmosphere of languid monotony, in which all emotion whether at gain or loss was suppressed and even the change from night to day excluded in its draped and gilt interiors, acted upon him like a soporific drug. Before a year was out he awoke to the stark realization that he was left with a financial need to win.

Abandoning the wheel, he turned to games of skill. He had his brother's aptitude for figures and the diligence and ambition that Ralph was directing into rescuing the Carnow works, he applied to cards. His winnings were enough to keep him in plenty if he cultivated his talent for befriending the rich. His ability to fall into what seemed to be uncontrived conversation with naive newcomers to a town, combined with his amiable willingness to introduce them to the amusements to be found, his protectiveness, his good-natured acceptance of his losses when he first played with them and his appearance of wealth beguiled his new acquaintance into familiarity. Invitations to winter in Italian villas, to cruise in yachts, to summer as the guest of those taking a house at spas cut his expenses by a welcome degree. Gradually, however, the hospitality fell away. His hosts found themselves poorer for his acquaintance and warned others against him. In time, he felt that Europe should rest as fallow land and he took ship for America.

The east coast and southern states became his hunting ground and New Orleans saw much of him but somehow he did not prosper as he had done before. Years of deception had made his charm wear thin and scorn of those he cheated showed through the threadbare places. He never lived without comfort and was certainly never near despair but he grew tired. Each new venture upon the pockets of the affluent required more thought and effort. His confidence in himself did not lessen but he became aggrieved. It did not seem proper that he should have to strive for a luxury which should be his by right. He began to think that Ralph had had the best of the bargain and, as he sat on verandas taking glasses from the trays of slaves, as he shot game never seen in Dorset, as he travelled amongst those who were not always as conscious of his superiority as he was himself, he began to be sour.

There had come a time, several months before, when his disdain for his victims led him astray. He was staying with a family in New York, whose own distant English ancestry made them too ready to trust one from the old country. A cousin of his hostess, a young married woman, bored by her life, was spending the summer with her relations while the house being built for her was finished. Her husband's days were spent in his office and her eyes turned to Charles. He had always had a policy of not soiling his own nest but, in this case, ennui and over-confidence weakened his resolve. A brief flirtation led rapidly to afternoons in which each was believed to be alone in their room overcome by the heat. The young woman was excitable, careless and dramatic – a bad choice for a clandestine affair – and Charles soon found it expedient to depart hurriedly by the servants' entrance, leaving most of his luggage and no forwarding address.

The element of farce did not appeal to him. He had no sense of the ridiculous when it was he who was made to look foolish and, while the pain caused to the family who had sheltered him did not disturb him at all, his vanity was wounded. His resources were also low. He'd had to flee his haven while still at the stage of losing at cards to prove his probity and what possessions he had thrust into his valise were all that remained of his wealth. The sale of a gold watch and seals and several rings rescued him from penury and he marshalled himself for recovery.

Fearing that he was being sought by the wronged husband, he did not think it wise to return to known haunts where enquiries might be being made. He had never tried his luck in Canada and journeyed north, amusing himself with thoughts of the pioneer life. It did not answer. He found no openings for his peculiar talents and his arrogance and nationality did not endear him to the inhabitants of Quebec. He was not downhearted but he wished for a time of security in which to recuperate. It occurred to him that he had been away from Europe long enough for there to be a new harvest there for him to gather and, as he dwelt on this, a scheme evolved in his mind that would replenish his stores, give him rest and satisfy his growing enmity for his brother.

He would go home. He had every confidence that the puritan Ralph would have repaired the damage his premature inheritance must have done to the business and was equally sure that he could soon reinstate himself in first place in the affections of the doting father he had ignored for so long. A dutiful contrition for his neglect would make a touching beginning to a reunion which could provide great financial advantage. To this end, he spent what was almost the last of his money in taking passage on a cargo boat up the St Lawrence to Newfoundland. The river had begun to ice and he ran the risk of being stranded, penniless, in St John's for the winter if the last ship had sailed for Dorset, but his memory for the boldness of the English captains had served him well and fortune offered him the vessel which was most convenient for his needs.

Lying in his bunk as the ship surged forward, he smiled at his situation. Above the enveloping sounds of the brig's movement, he could hear footsteps passing his cabin and the calm, firm call of an order aloft as an adjustment was made to the sails. Already, as he rested in this place where he need wear no disguise, he felt invigorated by the purposeful nature of his surroundings. He was not a man much given to laughter but a sudden excitement at his prospects almost made him laugh aloud.

There was an aspect of the domestic life to which he was voyaging which it amused him to think of and which he was curious to see in operation. The infrequent letters he had sent to his mother were not written from family feeling nor was the date of the last haphazard. He had kept up the correspondence only because he knew that amongst the news Mrs Carnow would send would be the consequences of the theft of the five hundred pounds from his father's bank account, which had occurred shortly after his own departure.

So large a sum being lost, just as his share of the worth of the business had been withdrawn, was a matter of moment and his mother's letters were full of the detention, trial and conviction of Edward Trent, their trusted chief clerk, for the forging of a cheque. Had Trent taken to forgery ten years before he would have hanged for his crime but instead – and to Charles's satisfaction – he was sentenced to twenty years transportation.

It was a result which caused great grief to Mr and Mrs Carnow. Trent had been their right arm for half a lifetime and, although they considered that it was just that he be severely punished for so vile a betrayal of their belief in him, their hearts ached for the path he had taken and they could not find it within themselves to visit his sins upon his wife and child. They did not need to. The young Mrs Trent, crazed with shame, swallowed arsenic and, after days of torment, removed herself forever from the sorrows of the world, leaving nothing for her daughter but a sealed packet, to be opened on her coming of age, and the prospect of destitution.

She had been a favourite of Mrs Carnow and the news of her death was conveyed to Charles together with the information that the five-year-old Ettie Trent, now destitute and, to all intents, orphaned, was to be taken into the Carnow household out of pity for her mother.

It was this last intelligence that was amusing Charles and causing such a quick interest in seeing for himself how the ménage had developed with the years. He had a double reason for his curiosity. It was Charles who had stolen the money and it was Charles who was as likely as Trent to be the father of the pardoned Ettie.

The situation of the child – brought up as the object of magnanimity in a house to which she might belong by blood – was just such as to divert Charles. He had had no fondness for her when she was an infant but he wondered now whether the remaining Carnows were beginning to discern a family likeness in her face and whether her character followed her mother's or his. He was inclined to think that she was his daughter for, although Mrs Trent had genuinely never known, he was convinced that his own line must rout that of a quiet, cuckolded clerk even in the womb.

Poor Helen Trent – he was glad that he had given her some of the inspiration she could never have had from her husband. He remembered her well. Above the tar and salt of the ship, he could almost smell the violet pomade she had always worn and which he had been forced to wear to prevent anyone noticing he had been with her. Altogether, she had been an astonishment to the people of the works from the day that Trent had brought her home. It was common knowledge that Trent had been conducting a written courtship with a woman he had met at a chapel tea-drinking while visiting relatives in Devon, but it was assumed that the lady could match his own forty years. When he had returned from his wedding with an eighteen-year-old bride who was softly spoken, grateful and flawlessly beautiful, his friends and employees could hardly believe their eyes. While Trent's good humour, intelligence and responsibility were then still admitted, these did not seem to be attractions that would draw so lovely a girl away from younger men.

Her reason for the marriage was easily discerned. She was the daughter of genteel parents who had recently died leaving nothing but debts behind them. She had no income, no trade and, without these, no prospects. It had been a relief to her that Trent had wished to make her his wife and she had accepted him for the sake of a home with no stronger feelings than gratitude and liking. She had intended to be loyal and true but it was her misfortune that the first of her bride-visits should have brought her the love of her life.

Mr and Mrs Carnow had wished to show their respect for Trent by being quick to pay a call. They had presented themselves at their clerk's house the day after his return and with them, ready to look more closely at the interesting Mrs Trent, had gone Charles.

She had been his from that day. A consuming love had overtaken her and held her in its bondage until she was released by death. She was capable of hiding her obsession from all except its object, but beneath her demure exterior she was passionate and immature. Charles was only two years her senior, ardent and compelling, and her seduction by him was achieved with ease. She recognized her wrongdoing but could not stop herself and, when a daughter was born to her before she had been married a year and she could not tell who the father was, she had begun to grow unbalanced. She was torn by guilt at having betrayed her husband yet could not give Charles up. She was jealous of his attentions to other women but pathetically thankful for the care he took not to arouse any suspicion that could tarnish her good name. The occasions they could be together in safety were not frequent but their affair continued until Charles had left for Europe, promising to send for her when he had decided where to settle.

He remembered how completely she had trusted in his love and how sure he had been that he could rely on her silence. It had never been his intention to have her join him abroad but he had been so confident of her devotion that he had entertained himself by hinting at the extra sum that would be his above his inheritance – hints that would come together in her mind after the theft and tell her the truth of it. After the event, such teasing had seemed rash and it was to discover whether Helen, realizing that she had been abandoned, would take her revenge that he had kept up the correspondence with his mother. He regretted that Helen, with her dark, scented hair and the quick rustle of her skirts as she ran to him, should have come to such an end but it was flattering that a woman would die for him and convenient that she could no longer reveal his secret. The necessity for writing home was gone and he put away his pen.

There was a peculiar pleasure in thinking that Trent still suffered for another's crime. He was the type of man – scholarly, dependable and unable to guard his wife – that Charles despised the most. Knowing that it was Trent who would bear the blame had added a special enjoyment to planning the forgery. It had not been hard to carry out. His father banked in Bristol and, every quarter, would send Trent to cash cheques and bring the ready money back to the mill. If he had been methodical enough to write a single cheque for the amount he needed, Charles would not have been able to take his chance without his unwitting accomplice being suspected but Mr Carnow would draw one sum for wages and others for various expenses arising and the bank was used to several cheques being presented at once.

Taking advantage of this habit, Charles filled his bedroom fireplace with the ashes of practice signatures and departed from his grieving parents with a blank cheque, removed from his father's desk, in his pocket-book. He appeared to have left for London but had, in fact, retired to rooms in Bristol. An advertisement was placed in a local newspaper asking junior clerks wishing to fill a vacancy in a country business to apply to a box number. A candidate was selected and invited for an interview in a coffee house on the same day that Charles knew Trent would be collecting his father's monies. The applicant was just as Charles had judged him from his letter – a stolid, unobservant lad eager to be obedient. A few questions were followed by Charles handing him a cheque and instructing that it be taken to a nearby bank, cashed and the five hundred pounds brought back. The junior – sure that this was a test of his honesty – did exactly as he was bid, was waylaid in an alley close to the coffee house by Charles, was congratulated upon his dispatch and ordered to report for work in a fortnight. His employer then removed to France, richer and more content.

The scheme had been so simple and effective that it caused Charles pride even now. He took his arms from his eyes and linked his fingers behind his head. There had been times in the past when he had regretted not having stolen more but he appreciated that he had cut the family finances to the bone and if the damage had been worse all the efforts of the tedious Ralph could not have revived them. Had he killed the goose that lays the golden eggs, he would be spending a lean winter. Instead, the brig rolled beneath him and carried him forward to strengthening powers and home.

Chapter Three

They had been cantering along the wide grass verge of the lane but where they turned west on to the track to the wood the ground grew stony and they reined in to a walk to protect their horses' legs. Theo turned in her saddle to look back at Ralph as he came close beside her. The blood had come into her laughing face and her pale skin was flushed.

'I love to ride fast,' she said. 'I love the feeling of the speed.'

'It suits you. It makes your eyes shine.'

Ralph leant over and gently pushed back a tendril of hair that had fallen on to her forehead. He used every excuse to touch her and she did not prevent him. Her left hand was resting on the leg that gripped the horn of her side-saddle and he took it and held it in his as they rode slowly between the banks of thorns. The movement of their horses rocked their arms – now extending, now closing – so that they were always conscious of the firmness of the grasp needed to keep them together and the warmth it engendered through the thin leather of their gloves.

It was the first week in November but the afternoon was of such soft clarity that someone looking at the blueness of the sky from a heated room would have said it was summer. Here, on the track that led down into the valley, the air was crisp and cold with a faint tang of the sea. There was no breeze to stir the withered leaves and the stillness of the landscape seemed to emphasize the vitality of the riders.

They were not yet promised to each other. If betrothal had been a matter of decision on the part of the man and not of petition, their marriage would be a settled thing but although Ralph was almost sure that Theo would answer his question with 'yes' there was a restlessness about her that gave a possibility of refusal. He no longer understood her. Impatient for the end of their courtship, he found himself making free with her – as he was at this moment – in a manner that he knew to be impertinent, yet it was not at these times that she drew back from him. In public, he was more delicate for her reputation than she was herself and it was then, in the midst of his care for her name, that she seemed to look at him from beyond a barrier.

They were not together in the day as often as they had been when Theo had first returned to England. He could no longer spare so much time from business but today he had left the mill at noon to be with her and had found the barrier in place. It was an afternoon for the open air and Theo had wanted to ride. It seemed obvious to her that they should enjoy what fine weather the year had left for them and she had not expected an objection. They had always ridden together and it was a surprise to her that Ralph should suddenly feel they should not be seen alone in such an activity. He knew they would be observed leaving for lonely haunts and, now that it was plain he was paying her his addresses, speculation upon what could occur between them before they returned would be in the mouth of every gossip. It offended him that Theo's character should be on the world's lips but to Theo herself there seemed something coarse and hypocritical in his attitude.

Despite his increasing inability to hide his desire for her, she trusted him to behave as a gentleman. She was not concerned with appearances and, if their relations were fundamentally pure, it did not trouble her that the small-minded should think her indiscreet. Her aunt agreed. Louisa did not think Ralph a dishonourable man and saw no reason to treat him as though he were. She knew perfectly well that an afternoon with Ralph, in however secluded a place, would not leave Theo a disgraced and ruined wretch and could not give weight to his scruples.

The women and his own real inclinations were too much for him. They had ridden out as Theo wished but for the first miles there had been a reserve in her manner. For Theo, autumn brought anticipation and a feeling that the year was not dying but beginning. She wanted to marry the exhilaration of love to the excitement of wind and speed and the sight of grey waves being driven to the shore. It spoilt her mood to share the freedom of the afternoon with one who was looking over his shoulder for fear someone should think badly of her, but her coldness did not last. If nature was not turbulent enough to suit her, it did give her mellow stillness; if Ralph was over-conscious of her repute, he was so from the strength of his emotions and a possessive chivalry which was tiresome in its practice but altogether flattering in its intent. Her eyes, which could be so hard, were soon soft enough to encourage him.

The track they had taken was leading them down into the valley in a long, slow curve that opened the view to the west. They were far from any village and even the farmhouses nearby were few and hidden in the folds of the coombes and spinneys. At the top of the slope they could see along the ridge of the hills to the cliffs that swept in muted colours to the Devon coast but as they rode on their sight was led inland. There were stubble-fields showing yellow-brown on the downs and the hedgerows had lost the freshness of their leaves but the valley was mainly meadowland and the rich green of the grasses beneath the brilliant blue sky gave the effect of being far from winter. This was a favourite place for Theo in every season. There was a wood where the track began to rise again which was a particular delight to her and which she could not pass on horseback without pausing to walk amongst its trees.

They approached it in country that seemed more secret than any they had yet ridden through. Gorse, still in flower, dropped its golden petals on dew-ponds that reflected the silent riders on waters as tranquil as if they were already ice. Nuts hung in the hazels that edged the woods and thrushes fluttered and swung amongst the half-stripped elderberries, too eager for the fruit to be afraid of hoof-beats.

The wood bordered the track on their right. A narrow stile, concealed by bushes from those who did not know it was there, led into it and they pulled in their horses as they reached the posts.

'You must let go of my hand,' Theo said.

'I always have to: I never want to.' Ralph lifted her fingers to his lips and she drew her hand slowly out of his. The intimate nature of their ride was making her conscious of her pulse. It did not please her to put an end to his touch but the voluptuous pleasure it gave her was a reproof to her indecision. She slid down from her saddle and, tying her reins to the stile, went into the wood.

The path was narrow and she led the way. Is this coquetry? She thought. I scorn his delicacy for my name, then draw him on to acts which would be to my detriment if they were known. I know that he loves me yet cannot bring myself to take that step which would secure us to each other. He wants me for his wife. What better husband could I have? But the risks for us are so different that I cannot give myself easily. There are constraints in marriage for a woman. I fear subservience. He has never treated me as if my sex makes me his inferior but if he should ever wish for mastery the world and the law will let him take it. I am not yet of age. I have not come into my inheritance and if I marry him I will never have the independence it would give me. My mill and all its income will be his. I trust him to deal fairly but there will be a difference, however subtle, between being the mistress of my fortune and one who is allowed its benefits.

Yet I wish for marriage. I wish to love and be loved. I wish to see his face at the rising and the setting of the sun. I wish to hear the tale of his day as he sits tired in the room that is ours. I wish to hear his breathing in the darkness as he lies beside me in nights that have always before been silent. I wish for a lover and a child. Is this the way or am I lost in the wood?

Behind her, Ralph said, 'Why are you hesitating? Don't you know your path?'

She stopped at a cleft in the earth where a shallow stream ran noisily over a stony bed.

'I'm not sure,' she said. 'It divides here. This one runs straight but crosses the brook and looks too steep to be easy; that one – I can't see where it goes.'

'Then let's take the straight and steep and know where we're going. Hold my arm and the bank will be no obstacle.'

'You're right. I remember now.' She gathered her skirts and crossed alone. She had been this way a hundred times; she could not think why it had suddenly seemed strange.

Ralph followed her amongst the trees. It was an oak wood and though it was so late in the year autumn had barely touched it. 'Laggard to come and laggard to go' is said of the oak, and the leaves above them, hardly tinged by decay, gave the truth of the saying. The sunlight fell in startling brightness through branches of mature summer growth and the air was green and sea-like around them. The sound of the stream running through trees unstirred by any breeze was loud in their ears and where the slanting sun was unimpeded on its course the water glinted and shone beneath the dying ferns. The moss on the broad trunks, the layers of other years upon the ground where bluebells came, the gleaming brook, all gave out a damp scent of fertility and nurture.

I watch her walking, thought Ralph, and I love every movement she makes. The soles of her boots, so narrow and neat, show themselves as she raises her feet to step over stones and it excites me. She holds the loose of her habit in a bunch of skirts behind her hip and I love the curl of her fingers about the cloth. A branch hangs low over the path and she dips beneath it gracefully, fluidly, just as she dances. A dove calls from deep in the wood; she lifts her head to look for it and the curve of her neck makes my breathing quicken. Am I mad? I know her to be a pearl among women, but no witch. How can she enchant me so? I think I am a fool but I would rather have this foolishness than all the sobriety my life has had to offer.

His reputation was for coldness. He was not a playful man; he smiled enough and no more at the pleasantries of social intercourse. Even amongst the aristocracy of trade in Bridport – a group not noted for its eagerness to become the idle rich – the hours that necessity had driven him to work were a byword of industry. It was assumed by those who did not know him well that business filled his needs and that he would take a wife when he considered it time to sire an heir. The dislike between the Carnow brothers had been well known but Ralph had never given the world a clue that animosity would have been the truer word. His calm acceptance of the burden of recovering the stability of the mill reinforced the belief that he did not have strong feelings for anything beyond his work. There was no display of resentment or jealousy from him; no sullenness in his demeanour to his father and how could any man hide these things if he felt them? Perhaps, it was said, he had always been aware of his commercial talents and knew, in the long run, which side his bread would be buttered.

His few intimate friends had known another man and could have told that self-discipline preserved his dignity. He had a warm and loyal heart and was too intelligent not to have been sensitive to the injustice of his upbringing. The death of his mother and uncle had been bitter to him. To have been loved is a precious burden; it gives the loved one strength and out of the strong comes forth sweetness but its loss brings a thirst for its return which can never be quenched in this life and a hunger to share the talent for affection it has created. He felt the sting of knowing that he would always be second-best for his father and he wanted Theo for his own the more because of this. His home had been lonely since Mrs Carnow's death, and though Theo and Louisa had always welcomed him, he yearned for the closeness of marriage. He had grown impatient; the warmth of his love was not fraternal and he followed Theo along the sunlit path with fervent eyes and the breath caught in his throat.

Theo walked firmly but the hand she used to put aside stray branches shook as it grasped them. With every step, she grew more conscious of Ralph behind her. He did not disguise his longing and his need seemed to reach about her, hampering her going and bidding her to return. She felt it binding her to him and her heart and most of her mind consented. This covetousness was what she craved for; it fascinated and transported her. She was afraid of the familiar and routine; she ached for foreignness. This ardent man was a stranger and to be here with him excited her.

Her concentration upon the path failed. She did not notice where she was walking. Turning quickly to avoid collision, she jerked her head and the muslin veil bound about her hat flew out and became entangled in a wild rose that climbed a dogwood tree. She stood, unnaturally alarmed by the check, and Ralph reached up to pull the veil from the thorns. Her face was close to his; her eyes were wide and dark and did not drop their gaze as he looked into them. He put one hand on her back and one at her neck and kissed her.

She held his arms, her fingers tightening. There was no roughness in him nor was he more urgent than herself but as she thought – this is what I would have – she felt herself ensnared. She leant back from him and their hands fell together. It was hard to tell whether there was more intimacy or diffidence between them. A taboo had been broken and in the confusion of their spirits they did not know how to behave.

'"Once he drew with one long kiss my whole soul thro' my lips."' Theo's voice was low; a grave, bewildered whisper.

'Did I? Did I?'

He was too avid for her. She dropped his hands and started away, the thin veil tearing on the rose. Some animal in the undergrowth took fright at her movement and she, in turn, flinched at its escape. She regained the path and followed it deeper into the wood, the green air around her dim and glowing in her unfocused sight. Ralph followed her but did not come close enough to touch her trailing skirts. He did not know whether he should be ashamed. His action had been spontaneous and uncontrolled; it disturbed him; perhaps it had disgusted her. He did not want to soil or corrupt her but so plain a demonstration of carnal desire must be an affront to a maiden. It could not be base, arising as it did from his love, but to a woman its physical expression must seem insulting.

Theo went ahead. Her heart beat with such force that she felt it would injure her. 'My heart, pierced thro' with fierce delight.' The poetry came to me before any other thought. It comes again. I am alive with feeling. I want to turn and hold him to me but I cannot. I entered this wood afraid of giving myself to domesticity and habit – now I am afraid of the depth and nature of the commitment he has shown me I must make. And he walks behind, near but not too near, afraid that I will reject him because of what he has done. What fools we are. I could end our foolishness with just one word.

The ground had been rising gently, unnoticed by them both. Ahead, on a spur of land given height by the steepness of the drop to converging streams, the ruins of a chapel stood like a symbol of the peace they had broken. A perfect archway in one wall of crumbling lichened stone curved over the path and Theo led through it and waited for Ralph. There were no other signs of what used to be except fragments of a line of stones that showed where one other wall was built. A carven face watched from beside the arch and she looked up from it to the canopy of oaks that was the roof. An age of her life had passed away since she had entered the wood but the sun was as bright and the leaves above her as still and translucent as when she had come in. She thought how often she had sat here dreaming of romance and sensation and how she stood now, afraid of her wish being granted and of it being denied.

'Did I offend you?'

At the sound of Ralph's voice, she withdrew from her introspection. She could not understand her own reaction nor the contradictions in her mind but she was sure that she did not want to hurt him for what, after all, had been a simple action.

'No.' She smiled, but not in an inviting manner. 'You've never offended me. I don't think you could. I know you too well.'

'To know all is to forgive all?'

'I don't have enough experience to say.' She went forward a few paces. 'The altar must have been here.' Musingly, she stared at what had been. 'I heard of a ruined church in Wales where a man married a wife. Years later, a widower, he came again to marry a different bride. There was a handkerchief on the altar. It was the one his young wife had lost at his first wedding. What do you think the second bride thought?'

'That life is full of chance and sadness and that we must not let slip what joy comes in our way.'

'Do you think so? She would have been a sensible woman.'

'Theo.' He took her hand and she let it rest in his. Finding that he had not angered her, he could restrain himself no longer. It was the time and place to make his offer. 'Theo, my Theo, my own—'

She put up her free hand and laid it on his lips. 'Please,' she said, 'not yet. Let us be private a little longer.'

They walked their horses home through the twilight, taking the back lanes to avoid the town. The evening was cold and the westerly wind that had been blowing that morning returned to bring gusts of soft, salt air that tasted of autumn. Ralph was not unhappy. She had not accepted him but neither had she refused, and her behaviour made it seem that he had only to be patient and he would have his desire.

They rode side by side, without speaking. There was candle and lamplight in the houses they passed and in the cottages, where day must linger, the fires made rooms glow in the gathering darkness. Theo was tired but it was the weariness of physical exertion and did not trouble her. There was much in her mind. She remembered the boys she had seen on her travels, poised on rocks to dive into the warm Italian seas. It was her own position. She stood upon the brink of giving her pledge to Ralph, entrusting herself to him in the most dangerous of life's adventures. Like the divers, she had risen and leant to cast herself into the waters and was balanced in the last instant in which she could change her mind. The fears for her independence had not died but, as they rode through the grey lanes, the reddening sunset before them, the slow hoof-beats, the creak of leather, the distant caw of rooks the only sounds, they were overlaid by the comfort of companionship and the warmth of emotion that was the residue of the vehement afternoon.

It was later than they thought when they reached Carnow and the mill was closed and quiet. Ralph pulled his watch from his pocket and remarked that they had not kept dinner waiting. The relations between the cousins' households were so easy and accommodating that the families dined with each other as a matter of course. Invitations were sent only if there were to be other guests and the Farnaby women kept evening gowns in a bedroom, which had gradually become known as theirs, so that they could arrive as Theo was now and still be presentable at table. It had been agreed at noon that Louisa would be driven over to join the Carnows for dinner and that Theo should arrive with Ralph without first going home.

They turned left at the millpond and rode slowly through the warehouses and offices towards the house. There were some dwellings for employees scattered amongst the business buildings and a handsome, severe terrace for spinners at the far end of the village but most of the hands had returned to the town and there was no one else on the road.

The Carnows' home was a plain and imposing Georgian house set in a garden at the heart of the works. Stables, orchard and vegetable beds were ranged about it but it left no doubt that its principal purpose was to shelter a family that had not yet decided to be ashamed of trade.

Entering the gates to the stableyard, they noticed that Louisa's carriage was already standing without horses in its shafts. Ralph considered the time again.

'If you give me your reins,' he said, 'I'll see that she's put up for the night. You'll just have time to dress.'

Theo dismounted and handed over her mare. She would rather not have the evening before her. The most conversation that she would welcome was the exchange of the day's news as she and Louisa sat in their dressing gowns, brushing each other's hair late at night. She was still wrapped about with tenderness from the afternoon but being in these familiar surroundings was bringing pinpricks of impatience.

Going through a door in a high wall, she walked along a path bordered with yew to the side of the house. She did not ring or go around to the front but let herself in through a room lined with boots, walking sticks, umbrellas, croquet mallets and the impedimenta a passing Carnow might feel necessary to an emergence from the house.

Reaching the hall that ran centrally from front to back door, she heard voices from the drawing room. Thinking that she would look in to tell her aunt and uncle that she and Ralph had returned, she laid her whip on a chair and went into the room. An unusual tableau was before her. Aunt Louisa and Mr Carnow occupied their customary seats, Ettie Trent, her thick, fair hair over her shoulders and her sharp eyes alert, sat on a footstool clasping her raised knees, and a stranger, leaning back with his legs crossed and a demeanour of being very much at home, watched her come in with an air of expectant confidence. He rose to his feet and, as she waited to be introduced, she thought that what had made the assembly so strikingly different was nothing tangible. It was not the presence of an unknown man but the atmosphere of intense emotion that pervaded the room.

Mr Carnow had also risen. He came to Theo and took her hand, drawing her towards the visitor who came a pace forward to meet her.

'My dear,' said Mr Carnow. His voice was excited and childish, quite unlike its usual tones. 'You won't remember – you were too young. My dear – this is Charles.' He put her hand into the stranger's. 'Charles – little Theodosia.'

Theo was made no wiser by this exchange. She found her hand bowed over by the unexplained Charles and looked at her uncle with a hint of displeasure in her eyes. It was some years since her Christian name had been used freely when being introduced. Mr Carnow, however, was occupied in gazing at his guest with a vapid smile upon his face.

The clear, dry voice of her aunt added detail. 'The gentleman is your cousin, Charles, who left us so long ago. He gratifies us by his return. Come, Theo, you must be tired. Sit down.'

Theo withdrew her hand and took a seat on the sofa beside her aunt. Her astonishment was too great to conceal and she felt gauche and unkempt. The men returned to their chairs.

'Will you drink a cup of tea, Theo?' asked Louisa. 'We won't stay to dine. Charles has had an exhausting journey and has much to tell his father.'

Theo said that she would and Ettie left the footstool to pour from the silver teapot that was normally locked in the glass-fronted cabinet in the dining room. There was a deftness and precision in Ettie's movements. A cup of tea provided by Ettie would be exactly tailored to its recipient's taste, not because she wished to earn approval but because she saw no point in second-best. She was a private, quick, observant girl with a memory so good that Mr Carnow called her his memorandum-book. Inclined to give people a start by appearing noiselessly and staring with a piercing directness, she convinced them that they had been summed up and seen through. They were right. Her judgement was remarkable. She had never believed in her father's guilt and had remained loyal despite their separation yet she did not bear a grudge against the Carnows for his conviction. The evidence had been strongly against him and she understood how it had persuaded those who were not his daughter. She appreciated her good fortune in being taken in by the Carnows and was fond of Ralph, as she had been of his mother. It was as well for the errant, a magistrate had once remarked, that she was a female for if she had ever come to sit on the Bench her justice would have sent shivers down the spine.

Ettie carried the cup to Theo and returned to her former position. Her skirts were long but her hair was not yet up, as befitted one who seemed neither child nor adult. Charles watched her with interest. He had expected her to resemble one of the three participants in her creation but found that she was not like either her mother, Trent or himself. The sport there would have been from observers gradually noticing a similarity between Ettie's features and his own was lost but life would be more peaceful without it and he could not decide whether to be relieved or disappointed. He was, however, gaining considerable amusement from seeing how much she had been accepted as one of the family and, when a moment arose, intended to congratulate his father upon his charity.

Theo sat regarding the company with open curiosity. Drinking the tea gave her an excuse for not joining the conversation until she had collected herself. It was plain to her that very different reactions to the wanderer's return were in progress amongst them. She knew better than to expect any physical clue to her opinion from Ettie and, as the girl was not pert, it was unlikely that she would speak unless spoken to in a situation such as this. It would be when Charles was elsewhere that Ettie would deliver her verdict and then only if asked.

Her aunt was another matter. Louisa was angry but her face was so guarded that only those who were most intimate with her could read it. She was not making a pretence of any gladness at the sight of her nephew but she was behaving with a cool civility which neither man seemed to feel was less than was required. There was nothing sentimental in Louisa's character and Theo did not anticipate any show of affection for one who had been the instrument of such a burden of responsibility falling upon Ralph at so young an age, but the degree of reserve in evidence told Theo that her aunt felt a strong dislike for Charles.

Louisa was a graceful, indomitable woman. She was strong-minded and loving and neither brandished these qualities at her acquaintance nor hid them from those who could recognize their presence. Never having met a man she wished to marry and having been equipped by providence with a child, a private income and an independent temperament, she had turned down the many offers she had had in favour of being mistress of her brother's home and raising Theo as her daughter. She was not against marriage and believed that Theo would be the happier for having Ralph as her husband, but her remarks to those who had the impertinence to tell her that without being a wife and mother she was not fulfilling the role of her sex were incisive enough for the ignorant to think her severe and cold-hearted. Theo knew otherwise and was more ready to trust Louisa's judgement of Charles than that of his father, who had proved his infatuation for his elder son ten years before and was demonstrating it again at this moment.

At sixty, Mr Carnow was still a vigorous-looking man. His colour was high and he had a tendency to run to flesh but his upright figure caused him to carry his weight well. The breathlessness that was gradually coming upon him, he put down to the enfeebling nature of the warm summer and he was confident that the bracing effect of winter would rout this trivial but irritating ailment. Theo was so used to him and to the oddity of it being the son who guided the father in business that she had not thought of her uncle as either old or weak. Now, as she watched him sitting forward in a chair pulled close to Charles, pleating the skirts of his frockcoat, ever and again reaching to touch his son's arm as if he could not believe that he was really there, she was fearful of the consequences for Ralph. The nakedness of the father's joy was disquieting and, after so long a silent absence on Charles's part, seemed foolish and demeaning. She did not want her uncle lowered in her estimation; the suspicion that he was ridiculous made her uncomfortable.

Mr Carnow's folly lay all in one direction and this was the first occasion Theo had seen it in play, since before she had been too young to understand its importance. Her uncle was a naturally level-headed man but he had an Achilles' heel. He had been violently smitten with paternal love at Charles's birth. The boy had been the first-born of a wife married for love and it had seemed to Mr Carnow, then a young man in the bloom of cherished domesticity and engrossing industry, that he could ask no more of life for perfection was already his. He was a doting father and his care for Charles was intensified by the deaths of two subsequent children. By the time Ralph was born, he had learnt to distance himself from offspring that he considered bound to die and concentrated abnormally upon Charles. A still-born girl and a boy who lived three months followed Ralph and when it was clear that Ralph had stamina enough to flourish, Mr Carnow could not readjust his expectations and give his sons an equal share of his love. He liked Ralph and approved of his achievements but his devotion was all for Charles and he was quite unable to see his favouritism. His wife was a sensible, strong-willed woman and was able, with her dowry as a lever, to ensure that

Ralph, who she recognized as the more capable of the two, was acknowledged as a future joint owner of the mill but she never succeeded in making her husband understand that he was unjust in his valuation of his sons. Generous and charitable in all other matters, fair to his workers and kind to his dependents, Mr Carnow remained besotted by the one person close to him who did not deserve his adoration. That he had felt pain at Charles's loss was known to his family but the depth of his yearning to be reunited with his son was revealed only now as he sat by the revenant, a look of pathetic bliss lighting his eyes.

Charles was well pleased with his welcome. He could not deny that his sleep the night before had been disturbed by misgivings. Despite his outward confidence, he admitted to himself that it was possible that his father would greet him with the same lack of enthusiasm that Moore had shown. He could not think what he would do if he were turned away from his old home. Once he had allowed himself to consider that this might happen, he found that he was too exhausted in mind to form any plans. He must be in even more need of a refuge in which to recover his cunning than he had imagined.

Uncharacteristic anxiety had so grown upon him, that when Moore had told him that morning that the wind was dying and they might not put into harbour today after all, he had felt a secret relief. He had despised himself for the weakness of this emotion and, finding that they were standing offshore in the afternoon close enough for familiar sights to bring back his youth, had hailed a returning lerret and was rowed to the coast his feet had not walked on for a decade.

The same wryness that was in his thoughts when he had first spoken to the sailor in St John's came back to him as he made his way from the sea. Just as the sound of the half-forgotten Dorset accent had twisted his heart, so the haunts that had been too customary for him to notice, except with impatience for change, brought an acute nostalgia that was like a weight upon his chest. The long weeks aboard ship made walking agreeable and he did not look for transport but strolled beside the harbour, where the shipyards were sweet with the scent of Norwegian pine, and along the estuary that narrowed amongst its reed-beds towards the town, as if he had no object but mild exercise.

The alterations in Bridport moved him in a manner that made him irritable with himself and induced an aggressive resistance to the peculiar softness of his feelings. Here the old bow-front of a shop had been replaced with plate-glass; there a dwelling-house had become an office. Fences were now railings; a barren mulberry tree that had crowded a small garden had been cut down; brass plates held different names. He was angry that it was not only he who had kept pace with the world and it hurt him strangely that things were not as they were.

As he walked through the open country that separated Carnow from the town, he found his skin clammy and his pulse pounding in his veins. He had passed the Farnabys' house with his hat pulled to hide his face. Until he was with his father, he did not want to meet anyone he knew. Nearing the mill, he had made a deliberate effort to subdue the surprising emotions that he felt were unmanning him.

As he drew close to his home, the prosperity that was apparent in the energy and activity of the works went some way to restoring him to his usual tone of thought. The laden carts that made the streets busy, the roar of the machinery from the ropewalks, the women glimpsed braiding nets at kitchen tables awoke his avarice. He began to calculate what the family income might be and wonder whether it might be more than rest that he could obtain here.

On opening the gate to the house, his cupidity was interrupted for a moment by an irrational expectation of being received by his mother. He did not know the maid who answered the door and the sight of a strange face steadied him. A messenger was sent to the counting-house summoning Mr Carnow. Charles waited in the drawing room; his father came – and all was exclamation, tears and welcome.

The first disbelief and agitation of reunion were now over. Father and son had sat together as the afternoon darkened and Charles knew he had nothing to fear. There was no reproach from Mr Carnow, who could see only his good fortune in the blessed restoration of his boy. After the struggles of the past years, it gratified Charles to learn how much his father appreciated his worth. He relaxed and confidence flowed back into him like a spring-tide. It would not be prudent to show how sure he was of coming to take first place with his father and profiting greatly from the mill but he allowed himself to be at ease in his home.

He was considering the room as they drank tea. There had been changes but much in it was the same as when he had left. The mirrored over-mantel in its ornate gilt frame still reflected the portraits of his grandmother and her sister, in the startlingly inadequate dress of the early century. The french windows in the bay still led down stone steps to the lawn but they and the two sash-windows were hung with muslin caught up in a different style and enclosed with curtains, not of crimson moreen, but fringed blue velvet. The Pembroke tables and the great globe, on which his father had shown him their trade routes, were in their places and the fire-screen of roses and doves in faded silks, that his mother had worked as a girl, still stood by the hearth. The sofa where his aunt and cousin sat and the armchairs he and his father had taken were those he had climbed upon as a boy but were differently covered in bottle green plush. The walls were now papered in alternate stripes of red and blue leaves on a white ground but the bookcases, which had never been locked, still held the familiar titles amongst the new spines. The plaster bust of Abraham Derby, whose chipped ear he had blamed on Ralph, was there amongst the Chinese jars and scrimshaw boxes. The effect was both disorientating and reassuring. It reminded him of leaving a ship by the gangplank, walking a board that swayed and gave glimpses of deep waters but which led to solid ground.

The two women seated amongst these half-familiar objects surprised him. He had thought of Bridport as a place of rustic stagnation for so long that he had expected dull-wits and dowdy provincialism. Instead, he found elegance and an independence so strong that it travelled round Europe without a male protector. He was intrigued and diverted but did not quite approve. Looking at Louisa, with her white shoulders sloping to her low, violet gown, her dark hair dressed with burnished gold, the garnets at her slender neck, he admired her appearance and commended himself for having chosen her to tease with his flirtations when he had wished to hide his affair with Helen Trent. She was handsome, he thought, but cold. It was his cousin, once a schoolroom girl he had ignored and now so struck by his presence, who had the warm blood in her veins. He wondered whether those large eyes could be made to turn from Ralph to him.

There was the sound of footsteps in the hall and the door opened again. Ralph, coming straight from the stables, looked in, as Theo had done, to say they were home. Like Theo, he was immediately conscious of unusual currents of tension in the room. His first glance had not fallen on Charles but his brother's rising drew his attention. For an instant that was magnified by the silence of the watchers, he did not know Charles, then recognition came to him. He stiffened and antagonism was plain in his eyes before he could conceal it.

Mr Carnow was standing beside Charles and without making a greeting Ralph turned to him for an explanation. His father was smiling at him, with an expression of tremulous, shamefaced coaxing. He had taken hold of Charles's sleeve above the elbow and was holding the arm a little forward, as a mother will pull a child who is reluctant to join a gathering. No one spoke and Ralph regarded Mr Carnow with anger and disgust in his gaze. His quick intelligence surveyed the future and gave him no false hopes. The favourite had returned and the cruelty of his desertion would be as little accounted as the loyalty of the son who had stayed. The reunion would cost them dear but in what ways Ralph could not yet tell.

'Won't you shake hands?' Charles's voice was composed. He had made the first gesture and, whether Ralph agreed or refused, the credit for proffered friendship would be his in Mr Carnow's mind. His brother took his hand. Using the motions of courtesy, Ralph began to construct a barrier that would hide his true feelings while he felt his way forward, but as they touched neither could prevent old rivalries showing. Enmity flared and was subdued by both for expediency's sake. It was only as the boy was thus revealed in the man that Louisa realized how far they were from childhood.

Beside her, Theo stirred and moved closer to her aunt. This hostility was beyond her experience and it roused and excited her. There was fear in her feelings, although she could not tell of what she was afraid. It disturbed her that, having decided that she resented routine, this change should make her doubt whether it was an aversion to the familiar that held her back from Ralph. Her heart was beating now as it had in the wood. Was it from the primitive desire to see her own man defeat an enemy? Or from something she did not understand?

Louisa rose and Theo, flushed and startled, followed her example.

'It's growing dark,' Louisa said, 'and we must leave. Don't ring for the maid. We can give our own instructions outside.'

'Aren't you staying?' asked Ralph, sharply. 'I thought you were.'

'I think it better not to tonight and your father has plans for tomorrow.'

Ralph turned to Mr Carnow, who, again, had a look of childish pleading in his eyes.

'We'll give a dinner, Ralph,' he said, 'just for our closest friends. A celebration for being a family again.'

'Ralph.' Theo, who had been lingering over her preparations for going down to dinner in order to waylay him, took his hand as he passed along the landing and drew him into the room where she and Louisa left their wraps. 'Tell me how the day has gone. I've thought of nothing else since last night.'

She could feel by his grip that he was tense. Sore at heart, he was comforted by her voluntary touch and continued to hold her fingers as they stood behind the door she had pushed to. He gave a short laugh.

'Can't you imagine? The beloved has returned and joy is unconfined.'

'Is Uncle Carnow so pleased to have him back?'

'If Charles had saved the queen from drowning he couldn't be more fêted. It's all smiles and tender reminiscences.'

'What's he been doing all these years? Where has he been?'

Ralph stared at himself briefly in the looking-glass. 'Now that's something on which he's rather vague – but, oh, so charmingly. Yes, indeed. In Europe and America, certainly. Where? Why, everywhere. And doing what? Living as a gentleman, of course. What else should his father's son do? It's taken all his money – he makes no secret of that. I suppose he was afraid that we'd ask for some if he pretended he had any. But it's not poverty that's brought him back. Oh, no. He's been pining for his dear father and wondering if he'd be welcome until he could stay away no longer. The touching scenes there've been in this house should be written up in verse.'

Theo had never heard him in this mood before. She sympathized with his acrimony but the scorn and suspicion he showed increased the strange agitation she had been suffering since the night before. It was oddly enjoyable.

'How have you and Charles —?' As she spoke, the ringing of a handbell downstairs interrupted her.

'We're late,' said Ralph. 'Everyone must be here.'

He blew out the candles on the chest of drawers and held the door open for her. As they came out on to the landing Charles, who had returned to his room for his pocket-book, was approaching them, walking towards the stairs. He glanced from them into the darkened bedroom and back to their faces. Although there was nothing offensive in his manner, Theo suddenly became conscious that her behaviour must seem indiscreet to a stranger and, flushing, she turned and moved away. When her back was towards him, Charles looked at his brother and raised his eyebrows mockingly. Ralph, now also aware of the unsavoury interpretation that could be made of their situation, bit back his anger and followed Theo down to the hall.

Mr Carnow and his guests were leaving the drawing room. They were all well known to each other and there was little ceremony in this progression towards the table. Ettie, whose precocious character had led to her early inclusion in adult entertainments, was helping Mrs Parris, the wife of Mr Carnow's estate manager, to untangle the chain of her fan from where it had caught on her lace mittens. Mr Parris, an able organizer of the fields of flax and hemp grown for the mill, was in conversation with his employer. Louisa was talking over Mrs Parris's shoulder while Maud Parris, lively, eighteen and the reason Philip Moore had been eager to reach England, was leaning on Moore's arm and laughing.

The three cousins reached the dining room as the others were still being allotted their seats. Louisa, noticing that something was wrong, gave Theo an enquiring look. Theo shook her head quickly and took her place to one side of Moore. It was the habit of the house for Mr Carnow to sit at the head of the table with

Ralph at its foot. Ettie, Louisa and Theo would take the sides. Automatically, Ralph went to the chair opposite his father and was drawing it out when Mr Carnow noticed him.

'Ralph,' he said, 'you won't mind I'm sure. Charles is the elder. He should have that place.'

The guests fell silent. Ralph, arrested with his hand on the back of his chair, could feel Charles watching him. His hand tightened on the wood.

'Ralph,' repeated his father. 'Will you keep your brother standing?'

There was no sound in the room.

'I'm convinced,' said Louisa, 'that Ralph would keep nothing that isn't rightfully his and would lend even that to make Charles comfortable on what, no doubt, will be a short visit.'

Her eyes met Ralph's in perfect understanding. He left his chair and sat at Theo's free side. Under cover of the white cloth, she touched his wrist and the fleeting gesture told her the rapid throbbing of his pulse. Charles took the seat that faced his father. Mr Carnow, made oblivious by his bliss to the tension in the room, smiled across the staring company.

'Now,' he said, 'we can all be merry. Things are again as they should be.'

Chapter Four

'And it's been the same ever since. The novelty isn't wearing off. You'd imagine that it was Mr Charles who had had the running of the works.'

Ettie broke off to blow on the cup of chocolate that had been given to her on her arrival at the Farnabys'. Theo was preparing a canvas and had painting and sketching materials scattered over the table and the scrolled sofa on which she sat. Louisa had been writing letters at a rosewood escritoire but had laid down her pen when Ettie was shown in. Theo looked across at her.

'Exactly as you thought it would be,' she said. 'Do you think it'll last?'

It was late morning two days after the dinner party that had celebrated the prodigal's return. There had been a night frost but, although the first distinct winter coldness was in the air, the sun was shining with a cool brightness that was interrupted at intervals by the clouds that were passing rapidly across the sky. Ettie, sent to Allington with a message from Mr Carnow, had found her walk fresh and exhilarating and was sitting by the fire with her face made highly coloured by the wind.

'I'm afraid that it will,' said Louisa. 'I'm reluctant to speak harshly of your uncle, Theo, but I'll take the privilege of one who is his old friend. The man is a fool where his sons are concerned. He always has been and always will be. We can only hope that Charles is not planning to stay.' She turned to Ettie. 'Has he said anything of what his intentions are?'

'Nothing at all. There hasn't been a hint in his conversation and, judging from the way Mr Carnow's on tenterhooks, I'm sure he hasn't given himself away in private. He won't want to. It would spoil his sport with Mr Ralph if we weren't all wondering.'

She drank her chocolate in a decisive manner while Theo and Louisa considered her point. The drawing room was on the first floor and was not conducive to pessimism. Lit by four windows in two adjoining walls, it was bright, elegant and charming. The ceiling and marble fireplace were white, the walls pale pink, the curtains apple-green but although the colours were modern there was an old-fashioned appearance about it.

The grandfather, who had supplied Theo with the improbable Greek temple in her garden, had equipped the house for his bride with the most simple and well-made of Regency furniture. It had put him to considerable expense at the time and was much frowned upon by his older relations who felt that what had been good enough for his father should have been good enough for him but, as with all his purchases, it had proved its worth with the years. There were now more objects in the room than its previous owners would have thought suitable but, apart from a modern bookcase, all the furniture now gaily upholstered in pink or narrow white and green stripes would have been recognizable to them. The effect was more simple and alluring than rooms decorated with the heaviness that was growing popular, and the curiosities that it contained only added to its attraction – the principal amongst these being a narwhal's horn that Ralph had brought Theo from Newfoundland when she was still of an age to believe that it was lost by a unicorn.

Theo rose from her seat and went to a window. The rose bushes in the flower garden, where she had so often walked with Ralph, were sheltered by the high walls and were almost still in the sunlight but the taller trees that bordered the long lawn behind the house were being tossed by the wind. In her fancy, the scene reminded her of herself. There was a part of her that stood firm in the warmth of her love for Ralph but in the past two days a strange wind had arisen. Her cultivated garden was besieged by nature. She could not sleep soundly at night. The afternoon in the wood and the arrival of Charles had become entangled in her emotions. Distress for Ralph was mingled with a shameful, excited desire to witness the spectacle of the men's rivalry.

Ettie put down her cup. Theo's suppressed agitation was not unnoticed by her but, judging that it did not arise entirely from sympathy for Ralph, she made no comment.

'No, the reason that I was sent,' she said, 'was to tell you that the schoolmaster will be arriving today. Mr Carnow thought you'd like to know.'

Theo left the window and, picking up a paintbrush that had fallen to the floor, returned to the sofa. This should have been important news for her. Although there were few children employed inside either her own mill, her aunt's or the Carnows', all those born to ropeworkers were taught at their mother's knee to braid nets from the firms' yarn and were expected to add to their families' income by this home industry. Feeling a responsibility for them, Theo had persuaded Louisa and Mr Carnow that a school should be set up at which they could take turns in learning to read and write. As her scheme was not so ambitious as to deprive the families of money they required by taking too much of their children's time, it had not been difficult to achieve her end and a schoolroom had been erected at the Allington edge of Carnow beside a cottage which was to be for the use of the tutor. While the Farnabys had been in Europe, the building had been completed and a teacher engaged. As the position had been offered and accepted by letter, the appearance of the young man who was to put her project into practice would normally have had Theo's attention. This morning it did not intrigue her.

'I admit,' she said, 'that at this moment I feel a strange lack of interest in good works.'

At Carnow, the arrival of the new teacher was occupying only a small part of Ralph's thoughts. He had been in the mill since eight, two hours after the day's work had begun, and although he was appearing to concentrate on the business in hand his mind was equally divided between it, Theo and the behaviour of his father and Charles. It irritated him that he was distracted in this way. He was aware that the correspondence that had filled the morning could have been done in half the time it had taken and the loss of efficiency annoyed him.

Early responsibility had given him a gravity beyond his years but today tiredness made his directions sharper and his face more grim than was usual. He had slept little for the past two nights. The afternoon in the wood with Theo would not let him rest. To have held her as he had made celibacy a torment to him. To have seen the strength of her reaction, her flushed skin, intense eyes; to have heard her first words, her quickened breathing; to have followed her flight through the trees, unsure if she was insulted by him; to have had the question that beat in his heart postponed in a manner that promised much; these things were like thorns in his flesh. His impatience to be her husband was almost more than he could bear yet it must be borne until she would say one word. He had waited long for her to return his love and it hurt him that she did not need him as he needed her. His nature made him want to protect her from the world but he was conscious that she was threatened by no one but himself. He was afraid that delay might bring a sourness and impurity into his feelings for her and he struggled with his disquiet.

That the shock of his brother's return and the jealousy and resentment it had engendered could be poisoning his thoughts and drawing fears from his imagination that had no real basis, was accepted by his reason but did not calm his emotions. The presence of Charles unsettled him. Childish reactions leapt in his breast at each sign of his father's preference for his brother and had to be constantly suppressed. If there had been a limit set upon Charles's stay, he could have endured the slight upon him better but he suspected his brother of having designs upon the mill once again. He did not believe that a man capable of such separation from his family would return to it unless he were a broken man or audacious enough to make another play for its wealth. Charles, it was obvious, was neither broken nor penitent and audacity had always been his second name.

Charles and Mr Carnow were alone together now and Ralph did not like it. There had been a slyness about Charles at the breakfast table that had warned Ralph to be on the alert. Their father and Charles were to drive out together that morning to old haunts that Charles professed an interest in revisiting. Ralph had grown used to loving his father despite his shortcomings and it was as painful to him, though not as surprising, as it had been to Theo to see him dote so pitifully on his errant son. It disappointed him that Mr Carnow's favouritism should be as flourishing now as it had been in earlier years. He did not want to feel contempt for his father but he knew that whatever plan Charles intended to use to fill his purse, Mr Carnow would fall for with subservient joy. So strong were Ralph's suspicions, that he was constantly mindful that the works were still in his father's name and could be disposed of as he chose. It was true that a will, drawn up when

Charles was given his share of the inheritance, had left everything to Ralph, but a will may be changed at any time.

He got up from his desk and stood at the window that looked out on the entrance to Carnow that he and Theo had ridden into two days before. The bright cold sun that was filling the drawing room at the Farnabys' with winter light fell here on to austere white walls and dark, polished wood. There was no disorder in this room. Every detail from the shine on the brass lamps, that had often burnt midnight oil for Ralph, to the carefully drawn-up projection of future production and sales were evidence of conscientious industry. In this office his young adulthood had been consumed by dark struggle and gradual triumph. Despite his father's name on the deeds, this mill was Ralph's domain and he intended to defend it.

A consignment of Italian hemp was being delivered that morning and he decided to walk to the warehouse to see it unloaded. Physical activity might clear his head. He disliked having to buy in hemp to supplement what was grown in their own meadows but it was necessary only because the demand for Carnow rope had risen. If the land at Loders that he was negotiating for became theirs, they would soon have no need of outside crops.

Going out through the counting-house on the floor beneath, he crossed the passageway and passed the line-walks. These were in a long two-storied stone building, severe and impressive, erected by his grandfather and with the innovation, ordered by himself, of glass in its windows. The Carnows' manufactory was a mixture of old methods and new, out-work and production on the premises. Ropes of all lengths and thicknesses were made in these walks beneath the net-fitting loft but a regular flow of carts carried twine into Bridport and out to the villages, where braiders netting in their homes worked Jumper looms or plaited by hand. It was an industry familiar to all who had inhabited the district over the centuries. Even the design of the town with its deep, straight side streets that were the ropewalks before there were great mills and the wide pavements for the braiders who looped their twine to the house walls told the story of the local trade. Its fame was such that a hanged man was said to have been stabbed with a Bridport dagger, and to those in the area who had other yearnings it must have seemed that they had been born with a rope around their necks, but to Ralph there was romance and ambition twisted into the threads.

He was proud and possessive amongst the workings of the mill. The sounds of activity were about him as he passed the weir and spinning-sheds and walked down the road towards the warehouse, where the delivery was being made. A subdued roar rose from the sheds when the machines were in motion but it was so regular that it became unnoticed by the people of Carnow and it was the noises that varied that caught the attention. The iron-bound wheels and horses' hoofs, the shouts of the men loading and unloading carts, the women who had come to collect their twine exchanging greetings and calling to their children, the rattling wheelbarrow of the hackler, the mill-bell punctuating the day – these gave vigour to the scene.

It enlivened Ralph to walk amongst the stir and clatter, aware that it was he who had brought the mill to this stage of prosperity. He knew the name and ability of everyone he saw and, though he did not have the warmth of interest in their lives that would have made him start a school without Theo's prompting, he was just enough to have agreed to her suggestion even if he had not loved her. It did him credit that through all the difficult years that had followed Charles's departure, the hands had never been paid in the salt cod brought back from Newfoundland as they were at other firms. He was civil to their employees but, despite being approachable on matters of dispute and, unlike many masters, trustworthy amongst the women of the mill, he was not on such terms with the workers that there was banter in his presence and he sometimes envied his father's easier ways of speech.

A wagon was drawn up outside the warehouse and bales of Italian hemp, wrapped in matting, were being carried from it through the wide doors. The thick, heavy smell of flax and hemp met Ralph before he was inside the building. In the dimness of the barn-like store he made his way through the stacked materials, examining the quality of this package and that. Bundles of long stricks that had already been hackled and were waiting to have their second, refining combing by machine lay next to the raw stems of the plants. Amber Russian hemp and the silky Italian, whose whiteness drew what light there was, were piled, faintly shining, amongst the native crops. In his mind, Ralph did not see only the contents of the warehouse. He saw the foreign lands they had come from and the ships that brought them here; he saw the cleaning, spinning and braiding that turned them to rope and net; he saw the many who did this work, the fishermen who trawled the nets, the sailors who hauled the ropes; he saw the generations of his family who had built this trade and the children he and Theo would bring up to it; and there was one other thing he saw as he walked at the heart of the hive – he saw no place for Charles.

The young man who climbed down from the hired gig that afternoon and stood looking at the school and house that were to be his domain would have been glad to have faced life with half the confidence of Ralph. Barclay Hyde at twenty-two had not yet learnt to value his talents as much as he despised his failings. Orphaned when he was nine years old, he had been put in the charge of his only relative, his father's cousin, and from that day had had none of the affection for which his gentle soul yearned. His guardian was not an unkindly man but he had no wish to have a child under his feet and no understanding of anyone who did not share his own interests. Had Barclay been able to join him in his wholehearted enthusiasm for destroying wildlife by the various seasonal means open to the English gentleman, he might have grown attached to the boy but it was beyond his imagination to be fond of a dreamer and he gladly passed the care of his ward into the hands of headmasters.

The schools to which Barclay was sent were good of their kind and he grew to be a young man in surroundings which were as congenial as they could be for a boy who would have been happier at home. At the end of his schooling, when he had proved to be an able scholar, Barclay was sent to Oxford by his guardian, who, though without tender feelings for him, was willing to do his duty and provide him with every opportunity he could. College life was a mixed blessing for Barclay. It was a pleasure for him to study without being hedged about with the petty regulations of schools but he could join in neither the religious excesses of many of his fellow undergraduates nor the rowdy, drunken practical-joking of others and being odd-man-out worsened his natural shyness. He was awkward, unpractical and given to blushing.

Lonely and unused to social gatherings, he did not know how to comport himself at the occasional tea-drinking and smoking concert to which he was invited.

Since the death of his mother, he had rarely spoken to a woman who was not a servant and the presence of ladies caused him acute discomfort. It was his most fervent wish to be married and have a home, but even if he were ever to be able to afford to keep a wife, he did not envisage being capable of steeling himself to a proposal. Nor could he picture any girl wishing to have him as a husband and when he became a Bachelor of Arts and took up a post outside Southampton in an academy for the sons of gentlemen, he thought that he would grow old, unloved and solitary, in a room set aside in that or a like establishment for the use of single masters. He was himself the son of a gentleman but although he had inherited a small, private income it was not enough to keep him in idleness and it was fortunate that he turned out to be a patient, gifted teacher. His memories of his own youth made him sensitive towards the needs of the boys and slow learners blossomed under his eye.

Teaching was a talent that he enjoyed but he did not feel that it compensated for his lack of social graces. He was aware that the daughters of the older masters giggled over his deficiencies and deliberately asked him to fetch food and drink at gatherings, knowing that he could not so much as carry a cup without spillage. The joys of the football and cricket pitches were as foreign to him as those of the hunting-field and gun-room and he could not join the staff in their muscular team spirit. It had seemed to him that he was doomed to be an outsider but he was not resigned to his fate and when an opportunity to change had arisen he had not hesitated to take it.

The uncle of one of the pupils was an old friend of Mr Carnow. On his visits to treat his nephew to beer and pie, he had listened to the boy's tales of academy life and, after observing Barclay for himself, had recommended him to Mr Carnow as the master for the mill children. He felt that the young man would flourish away from the trammels of communal living and Mr Carnow and Barclay were both desirous of proving him right.

Now, as he stood before the gate of the house, whose red bricks were starkly new, and looked at the schoolroom beside it, his character revealed itself in his thoughts. He was full of trepidation at the task before him but it was not a reluctance to face his pupils that made him anxious. The warmth of his eagerness to open mental doors for the unknown children caused him to doubt his own abilities and fear that he would fail in them. There was nervousness in his anticipation of the strangers he must meet and a hope that here, at last, he would find friendship.

His apprehensions about his employers had been eased by the treatment he had already received. It had been an additional annoyance to Ralph that morning that his father and Charles should announce that they would drive out in the trap, despite it having been arranged that this vehicle was to meet Barclay at Dorchester Station. As Mr Carnow agreed with Charles that the teacher could surely find his own transport on finding himself alone, it had fallen to Ralph to fulfil their obligations. Feeling that the young man was of the type to be alarmed by the formality of a carriage, he had hired the gig. A cart was to follow with the trunks. A note had accompanied the driver of the gig, welcoming Hyde and inviting him to wait on the Carnows that evening when he had begun to settle in. The effect on Barclay was an appreciation of the thoughtful kindness behind the deeds.

The cart, which had been rumbling at a discreet distance behind the gig, drew up to the house and the two drivers began to unload the luggage. As he opened the unlocked door for them and returned to the road, Barclay was aware of the scrutiny that accompanies any activity in a village. Although his house and school were on the edge of Carnow, facing open meadows and the river, they were in full view of the handsome terrace of cottages further up the hill, where women and children were sitting outside in the cold sunshine, netting. He was thankful that they were not so close that he must acknowledge their presence if he were not to be thought uncivil. Nevertheless, the consciousness of their eyes made his feet larger and his hands uncontrollable.

It was a pity that he could not hear the comments being made about him for, despite a certain scathing humour, they were not malicious. His appearance, which was pleasant but not inspiring, his three trunks, portmanteau and a curious object wrapped in rugs, his pretence that he did not know he was being watched and his dropping of the coins as he tipped the drivers were all discussed with interest up and down the line of netters. It did not worry the women that their children were to be taught by such an awkward young man, for they thought it only to be expected that a life devoted entirely to book-learning would naturally produce a creature as doe-like and helpless as Barclay appeared to be. They were amused by the spectacle of his arrival but the reappearance of Charles, with all its possible complications, and the news of what was occurring between the masters that day took more of their attention and distracted them from ribaldry.

An hour or more after Barclay had seen his belongings carried in, the watchers were gratified by the sight of Theo riding up and tying her mare to the schoolhouse gate. It was not her call upon the tutor which enlivened the conversation of the women, although Barclay's startled demeanour as he greeted his visitor was something to behold, but the question of whether Miss Farnaby would become Mrs Ralph now that the elder son was home.

Inside the schoolhouse, Barclay, his ears as red as his face, was removing an assortment of belongings from a chair, so that Theo could sit down. Having had the note from Ralph asking him to visit the Carnows in the evening, he had not expected to meet any of the other participants in his appointment until then and was considerably embarrassed by the lack of order in his unpacking.

He transferred two cups and a clock to a precarious position on the edge of a table and moved the chair an inch as an invitation to Theo. She sat and, laying her whip on the floor beside her, folded her hands in her lap.

'I'm afraid that I've come at an inconvenient time, Mr Hyde,' she said.

'Oh, no,' said Barclay. 'No, indeed. No.'

'My aunt, Miss Farnaby, would have accompanied me but she had an engagement elsewhere.'

'Miss Farnaby? Miss Farnaby?' said Barclay and wished himself dead.

Theo, rightly interpreting this question as a confusion about the number and relation of those involved with the school, explained the family connections which had led to her project. She had come to welcome the new teacher as a penance for her lack of interest about his arrival that morning but what had been begun as a duty was turning into a pleasure. It seemed to her that Barclay was a most likeable young man and his bashfulness did him no harm in the eyes of one who had suffered the attentions of many arrogant puppies eager for her face and fortune. It occurred to her, as she thought this, that she had seen no one to equal Ralph but, while granting herself the credit of this reflection, the dissatisfaction of the last few days remained.

'Then,' said Barclay, 'it is really you, Miss Farnaby, who I should thank for my position.'

He was in an agony of shyness at being so close to Theo, who was not only a gentlewoman but lovely to look at, yet, at the same time, he recognized that she wished him well.

'You should rather take me to task for not having thought of it before,' said Theo. 'Education is such a precious gift. Those of us who've been given it should be prepared to share what we have.'

'You're most altruistic, Miss Farnaby,' said Barclay. 'If more masters felt as you do – ' He lost himself in fear that he had offended her by including her in this masculine assembly or by an implied criticism of her class.

Bowing her head to the compliment, Theo took the opportunity to change the subject. She was reluctant to be praised for her motives at a time when she was ashamed of her indecision and restlessness. It had come to her, as she had ridden to Carnow, that part of her aversion to the commitment of marriage was caused by jealousy of Ralph. She envied him the active part that he played in the world. Although she knew that the success of the mill was due to his efforts and valued him for them, she had been too much of a child during the hardest years to understand what a prisoner of circumstance he had been. Despite an awareness of how many yearned for her own life of wealth and leisure, she resented being restricted by her sex to the roles of idleness or Lady Bountiful. She suspected that there was an element of spite in her demurring and a greed to have mastery over Ralph for as long as she was able.

'Do you think you'll be comfortable here, Mr Hyde?' she asked. 'If there's anything else you need, please say so.'

'I believe,' said Barclay, overcome by a desire to express his gladness to a friendly listener, 'that I'll be happier here than I've been since my mother died. I've lived in dormitories and study-bedrooms since I was nine years old, Miss Farnaby, but this will be a home.'

He looked about him with a glowing face and Theo was smitten by guilt for being discontented with her lot when so little could put such gallant hope into another's eyes. They were sitting in the parlour of the small house, with the kitchen and scullery to be seen through an open door. Steep stairs in the hall led to three rooms above and a wash-house and coal-house stood in the garden behind. It would have maddened Theo to have lived in these cramped conditions but to Barclay it was paradise.

Thanks to Louisa's interest, the house was not without objects both practical and attractive. There were good wooden floors in the living rooms and brick in the offices. A modern range, mysterious to Barclay in its workings, stood in the kitchen awaiting a guiding hand. Decorative cast-iron fire surrounds were upstairs and down and water was piped to the scullery. The barest of furnishings had been provided but beyond cooking utensils, tables and chairs, a bed and its coverings and curtains at the front windows, the equipping of the house had been left to its future occupant. Its austerity made Theo think of the dormitories which Barclay had talked of as in the past and she looked curiously at the scatter of his unpacking to see whether his possessions would be able to soften the effect.

One of his three trunks stood open and revealed itself to be entirely full of books – the result of Barclay's own purchases and the remnants of his parents' library. Another must have had its lid lifted and lowered again for the sleeve of a greatcoat was hanging outside. The third, from which Barclay had been excavating packages when Theo arrived, was providing a clutter of china, engravings, ornaments, candlesticks, embroidered cushions, footstools, figurines of lovesick maidens and busts of prominent men which Barclay had gradually been acquiring against the day when he would have a home. The only piece of furniture which he seemed to have brought was the rug-wrapped object the watchers had seen carried in from the cart. Freed from its protection, it was revealed to be an unusually fine worktable of an old-fashioned design in walnut.

Seeing Theo gazing at it, Barclay displayed its compartments with innocent pride. It had been his father's first gift to his wife and had been of such fond value to its user that, even as a bereaved boy, Barclay had thought to plead for its retention. He did not tell Theo of his yearning for other female hands to know its ingenuities but she could read his soft heart, and again her guilt was awakened. She rose from her seat to admire it the better and as she turned away she noticed a young woman waiting at the gate.

'If you've business with Sadie,' she said, 'don't make her stand outside on my account. Pray ask her in.'

Thrown into confusion by the assumption that he was expecting the girl and searching his mind for any mention that might have been made to him of a domestic, Barclay went to the door and invited her to enter. His nervousness when with women was never far away but he immediately felt more at ease with the newcomer than he did with Theo. Her lack of gentility was a comfort to him and as she went past him into the room, lowering her shawl from her head, he felt that a protective force had been thrown about him.

Sadie Holman had lived all her nineteen years in the terraced cottage from whose doorstep she had watched Barclay arrive. Her father was the hackler Ralph had heard rattling his wheelbarrow of hemp that morning and her mother had made a capable netter of her, before dying of the scarlet fever that had also killed two of Sadie's sisters. She was sturdy, fair-haired and fresh-faced, with a ready smile and a nature that led her neither to think it hard that she should be left as housekeeper to a father and three younger children nor to succumb to a fatalistic belief that this and no other was to be her lot in life. A keen curiosity about the world invested all her actions, and her optimism encouraged her to look about for opportunities to improve herself.

From the time that she had heard of the school, she had had a plan in mind. She was too old to join the classes but her thirst for instruction prompted her to be ready to offer to cook and clean in exchange for lessons. Nothing had been known of the prospective teacher but watching his arrival had confirmed her decision by adding an unexpected element. She did not realize it but the independence of her family left part of her unsatisfied. If she died tomorrow she would be sincerely missed by her father and the children but they would manage on their own. Their resourcefulness was admirable but part of her yearned to succour helplessness. The sight of Barclay acting with such dreamy incompetence had caused a warmth to rise in her breast which she could not fully explain. It became imperative that she should offer her services to him before he hired someone else.

There were, however, prominent in her thoughts other matters of keen concern to those whose livelihood depended on the Carnows and meeting Theo brought them forth. The afternoon had been one of news and rumour of the masters' activities and, aware that Theo would be as interested as she, Sadie made her curtsy and began her tale.

'Have'ee been up to the mill yet, Miss Farnaby? Or the house?'

'No,' said Theo, catching the implication in Sadie's tone, 'I came first to greet Mr Hyde. Has anything happened?'

'The works are all abuzz, Miss, we can't hardly do our tasks for talking on it. Mr Charles be coming back into the mill. The old master settled it with him this morning.'

A sensation of sickly heat began to flood Theo.

'What do you mean?' she asked. 'Into the mill? As a partner?'

'That I couldn't say, Miss. I d'just know it's to work alongside the family. There's to be a sheep-roast this evening to honour Mr Charles and old Mr Carnow's sent out for cider by the barrel but I don't know if that b'aint counting his chickens afore they're hatched.'

Theo gripped her hands together.

'How so?' she said.

'There's more than one master at this mill,' said Sadie, 'as it's only fair to say, and one might be more master than t'other. Old Mr Carnow wanted everything comfortable for Mr Charles and he give orders for an extra desk put in Mr Ralph's office. No sooner than t'were in than Mr Ralph comes and orders 'er out again.'

'And was it taken away?'

Sadie laughed shortly. 'That it were. I heard that Mr Ralph were as white and quiet as death – the way he d'go when he's real angry – and nobody says him nay then.'

*

The night was cold. Stars were sharp in a clear, dark sky and frost was stiffening leaves and grass. Theo walked behind her aunt, who, in her turn, was following Mr Carnow and Charles. They had left the house to go to the celebration in the meadow behind the cottages and in his excitement and pride Mr Carnow had fastened himself to Charles, oblivious of the discourtesy of not offering their arms to the women.

Theo was glad to walk alone in the darkness. Veiled and wrapped in a fur-lined cloak, she carried with her a private fever that was emotional as well as physical. A prickling of her skin told her that the air was cold but she felt hectic and alien to the winter night. Her breath misted on her veil and when she held it away from her face the chill was like the stroke of a knife against her cheek.

The party at dinner had been tense and brittle. There had been no one there except the family and the currents of strong feeling had been like winds crossing the room. She had had no chance to be alone with Ralph and he had not mentioned the episode of the desk. Beyond the statement that Charles was to take an unspecified position in the mill, there had been no mention of the day's happenings. Ralph's silence and Louisa's dryness did not encourage Mr Carnow to expand upon his hopes but it was plain from his nervousness and inability to look Ralph in the eye that there had been a scene of some magnitude that afternoon.

Charles gave no sign of being affected by the atmosphere and what conversation there was had been chiefly between him and the two women, concerning their travels. He had exerted himself to be entertaining and Theo had found herself more amused by him than she cared to admit. His lightness and cosmopolitan manner and the inexplicable attraction of a man who had devoted his life to pleasure fascinated her. She was proud of Ralph's strength and his open but unspoken contempt for the decision of his father and brother yet, perversely, she found Charles's hedonism alluring.

She looked behind her now to see whether Ralph was joining them but he had been absent while they were robing themselves and had not reappeared.

'We can hardly blame him,' said Louisa, noticing Theo's

movement and speaking in a low voice. 'I'm of the same mind myself. Such nonsense.'

'Perhaps he'll come later,' said Theo.

'It's more than I would do. We'll leave as soon as we can.'

They had made their way past the warehouses and were crossing the footbridge by the weir that would bring them into the meadow. There was firelight before them and the sound of laughter. A fiddler was playing at the far side of the field and snatches of song and the cries of dancers carried clearly in the still air. Two sheep had been roasted over fires begun that afternoon and the smell of mutton-fat from the stripped bones was heavy and cloying in the freshness of the night. Barrels of cider had been brought in a cart and a man lying open-mouthed against its wheel had had a full tankard upturned over his head so that his hair clung wetly to his glistening face. There were fewer people than Mr Carnow had expected and the glowing windows in the terrace confirmed that many had preferred their homes.

'This wasn't wise,' said Louisa, seeing Mr Carnow press forward to a group of drinkers, who raised a rowdy cheer at the sight of Charles. 'Wait here and I'll tell him that we'll take our leave.'

She walked purposefully towards him. He and Charles were now shaking hands and exchanging greetings in the midst of an increasing crowd of revellers, apparently quite forgetful of herself and Theo. Standing watching her aunt cross the grass, Theo felt a distaste for the proceedings which seemed to be attended only by those who wished for free drunkenness. A race had been begun. A celebration for the returning son had been announced and those whose livelihood was bound up in the mill had divided into two camps. Dark figures whirled in their dance back and forth behind the rising flames and the music shrilled in the late hour. Footsteps approached her, crisp on the encroaching frost.

'Have they left you alone here?'

Ralph was beside her. In the uncertain, red light his face was set and bitter. She could feel anger like ice about him.

'We won't stay,' she said. 'Aunt Louisa is saying so.'

They stared together at the charade before them.

'The fatted calf,' he said, fiercely. 'Tell me. What use is there in acting decently in life?'

She put her arm through his. Her heart had again the strong, shuddering beat it had had in the wood and at the brothers' meeting. His hand closed on hers and she returned his grip but, as their fingers locked, her eyes followed Charles and were dazzled by the glare of the flames.

Chapter Five

The progress of the attachment between Theo and Ralph seemed a private matter to them but was being watched with much interest and criticism by their acquaintance. Theo was not the most popular young woman in Bridport and it must be said that envy and disapproval played a part in the discussion of her affairs. Her independence and travels were frowned upon by those who would have liked them themselves and her lack of that demureness it was the fashion to display made matters worse than if she had been adept at casting down her eyes. Although gossip had not gone so far as to say that she would come to a bad end, it was thought that her obvious reluctance to give up her spinster freedom might lose her an excellent match. The annoying aspect of this was that, being an heiress, the single state would not bring her to see the error of her ways. She might yet live to be as wealthy, content and forthright as her aunt.

Helpful neighbours, who thought her upbringing lax, had not hesitated in the past to attempt to remedy her failings and there had been a period in those awkward adolescent years when Theo had let her sharp tongue retaliate. It had been necessary for Louisa to teach her that even the most foolish have feelings that can be hurt and that to react hotly to their insults is always undignified and often unkind. As Louisa did not invariably follow this advice herself, Theo did not feel that the standard she must reach was frighteningly high and her manners improved. The damage, however, had been done and forever after these were people who were outwardly friendly but who would be glad to see her fall.

One of those who had suffered from Theo's comments was entertaining Mrs Parris and Maud to tea on the Thursday afternoon following the sheep roast. Mrs Horn had the comfortable assurance of one whom fate has showered with good things without giving her a mind likely to wonder why it should be she who was so fortunate. She was a few years older than Mrs Parris and because of this and the fact that her spouse had an income without the trouble of an occupation, she felt able to take a faintly patronizing attitude to the wife and daughter of the Carnows' estate manager. Mrs Parris, secure in her own good opinion of her husband, did not feel it necessary to take a stand against this but Maud, her wits already slightly astray after having been accompanied through the town by Philip Moore, was not so patient. It was an irritation to her to have to sit making polite conversation when she could have walked on to the harbour with Philip and she was finding it increasingly hard to keep her remarks commonplace.

The tea was drawing to a close. Mrs Horn was still absently lifting sweet biscuits and eating them with nibbles and wide gestures that were strewing fine crumbs about her person and floor, but Mrs Parris and Maud were merely waiting for an opportunity to take their leave. The room was well-proportioned but was so crowded with objects, over-heated by coals and darkened by the laurels pressing up to the windows that it seemed claustrophobic and both guests were eager for fresh air. The visit was ostensibly caused by an invitation issued as part of the usual social round but Mrs Parris was well aware that it had been prompted by curiosity about the family relations at Carnow. She had been responding blandly to inquisitiveness since they had arrived and was weary of it. The need to make their journey home before the early dusk overtook them was an excellent excuse to be gone and she was about to make it when Mrs Horn introduced the subject of Theo.

'I suppose,' she said, 'the events at Carnow must have pushed aside the marriage plans. Perhaps the diversion will mean there'll be second thoughts.'

'I'm not aware that there was to be a wedding,' Mrs Parris replied. She spoke as if the matter were of no interest but her hostess was not so easily to be deterred. Reaching forward for an almond finger, she waved it knowingly at her guests. Maud moved her feet restlessly but the volume of her skirts hid her desire to run from the room.

'Come,' said Mrs Horn. 'We're all perfectly aware of which way the wind's been blowing. And, though I'm not one to praise myself, I must say that if I'd been asked to prophesy how things would turn out this is just what I'd have said. Theodosia has always had far too high an opinion of herself and that's a fact. You won't find many better matches in this town than Ralph Carnow. I don't say he doesn't have his faults. There's sometimes a lack of graciousness in his manner in company which isn't quite pleasing. As if he'd rather be adding up his accounts than talking to you, but that's no bad thing in a young tradesman.' She leant back and bit a morsel from her biscuit. 'Of course, he isn't a gentleman; he works for his livelihood but Mr Farnaby was the same so Theodosia can't use that as an obstacle. No, it's sheer wilfulness. She's been reared with no sense of duty and this is the end of it.'

Maud took a harsh breath and turned her head sharply as if drawn by an irresistible force to examine the wallpaper.

'Yes,' said Mrs Horn, with amused decision. 'You don't like to hear it, do you, Miss Maud? Young women today have no liking for responsibility. When I was a girl there was none of this keeping a good prospect on tenterhooks while we thought will we, won't we? Our parents saw to that. There was none of this gadding off to foreign parts either, consorting with who knows who and filling giddy heads with ideas. If Theodosia misses her chance it'll be no more than Miss Farnaby deserves for bringing her up to self-will.' She gave a derisive snort. 'Mind you, now that Charles Carnow's home we may see a change. She may set her cap at him.'

'But, Mrs Horn,' said Maud, 'he is the elder son. Surely it would be her duty.'

There was an instant's pause while this remark was digested by its recipient and then she turned an indignant face upon the speaker.

'Were you taught— ' she began but Mrs Parris interrupted.

'My dear Mrs Horn,' she said, 'you will allow me to order my family.'

The calm authority with which she spoke surprised Mrs Horn, who had believed that it was she who could dominate, and Mrs Parris took advantage of the silence to stand up.

'May I ring for our shawls to save you any trouble,' she said, doing so. 'I think we must leave. I feel the darkness gathering.'

Mother and daughter walked side by side up South Street without speaking. Maud's face was like a violet, cool and sweet. She was wearing a bonnet with hanging blown-glass tear-drops which gave her even more the appearance of a dew-drenched flower. That the drops were shaking with her rage only added to the effect. As they approached their turning into High West Street, she could contain herself no longer.

'I'm sorry for my words, Mama,' she said, defiantly, 'but not for my thoughts.'

'That,' said Mrs Parris, 'is exactly as it should be.' She smiled and the knowledge of being in accord with her mother flattered Maud, who had not been entirely transported to adulthood by eighteen years and the admiration of a sea captain.

They walked companionably through the town, exchanging greetings with friends and glancing into lighted windows. It was not yet dusk but the afternoon had sunk into that quiet, heavy grey that makes the fireside beckon. The coldness was enough to make home seem welcome but not so severe that travellers would put down their heads and hurry. To Mrs Parris it was refreshing. Although she found petty gossip tiresome she did not give it much importance and a little exercise was sufficient for her to shake off the effect of Mrs Horn. She thought of the people passing in the street, of the dinner for that evening but most of all she thought of her daughter and Philip Moore.

Maud's thoughts were also of Moore. They twined themselves around her indignation on Theo's behalf but each defence of her friend served to emphasize how satisfactorily her own attachment was progressing. She had believed last winter that she had cause for hope with Moore but it was a hope brought out by such subtleties that she had tried to persuade herself that she would not care if she were mistaken. Her hair had only just been put up and her school-books shut away. There had been more about her of the child than there had been in Theo at seventeen. She had always been petted by her parents and, although she was not spoiled, she was less independent than Theo and had a greater need of approval. Her parents had plainly not thought her ready for marriage and Moore, recognizing this and accepting that his own burgeoning feelings might not be as strong when she had discarded her girlishness, had not committed himself in words.

His return this season had brought them closer together. As she grew into a woman, Maud was no less lively and loving. She had always been fascinated by the sea and Moore could fasten her eyes upon his by recalling episodes of his sailor's life. They would walk beside each other as decorously as a pair of nuns but their talk would be of storms and glaciers, of nails ripped out by wind-torn rigging, of the death-throes of whales and the northern lights. It was her most fervent wish not simply to be his wife but to travel with him to imagined shores and as she moved through the streets of Bridport, where quiet lives were supported by the trade of far continents, her mind reached to the sunset and the green waves of Newfoundland.

It was as she and her mother crossed the bridge and turned into Allington, that Barclay Hyde first saw Maud. He had come into town to place orders with shopkeepers recommended by the invaluable Sadie and was stepping out of a grocer's, when he had seen the pair. Mrs Parris had called on him the day after his arrival and he guessed immediately that the vision of gentle maidenliness at her side was her daughter. Maud was so perfectly the image of delicate femininity of which he dreamed that he retreated out of their sight to avoid an introduction, and finding himself once more at the counter was obliged to ask for a damson cheese he did not require to cover his confusion. It said much for the success of his time at Carnow that although it did not occur to him to fall in with Mrs and Miss Parris, he followed their path later that afternoon with cheerfulness and a speculative warmth in his heart.

If Mrs Parris and Maud had stopped to visit the Farnabys on their way home, instead of quickening their pace to avoid the dusk, they would have found it more difficult to defend Theo against the strictures of Mrs Horn.

Louisa was spending the afternoon at her mill. Her father had left the smaller of his two ropeworks to his daughter with the condition that, while the majority of the income derived from it would be hers, it was to be in the charge of his son. The portion of profits that was not for Louisa was to be his as the reward for his responsibility. Louisa had always taken an active interest in her possession and was as well-versed in its processes as any master. During his life, her brother had overseen its progress and had the final say in disputed decisions but in effect, it was run by the manager he had appointed. Mr Wykeham, now in his late fifties, was portly, asthmatic and capable of recognizing an intelligent woman when he met one. He and Louisa were excellent friends and, to the scandal of the rope industry in general, were often to be found closeted together in his private office with two small glasses of Madeira and the account books.

They were so at this moment, with the result that when Charles called on his relations he found Theo alone in the drawing room, roasting chestnuts at a smouldering fire. Inside the house, the hour seemed later than during his ride. Theo had been sitting day-dreaming and had not rung for candles. The curtains were still drawn back to show the lowering sky and the warm light from the coals filled the room with a slumberous glow.

As Charles was a family member, the maid had shown him upstairs without first asking whether Theo was at home and he came upon her suddenly as she was thinking of him and Ralph. She was seated on a low stool as he entered and she laid the roasting-pan in the hearth and rose with consciousness in her face. Her handsome image, as she stood with her head held proudly to disguise her emotion and her hands twisting her heavy bracelets, appealed to Charles. He had not yet worked a full week at the mill but, despite his elation at the ease with which he was wooing his father, he was already finding it tedious that he was no longer a man of leisure. Drawing rooms inhabited by attractive women who flushed at his approach were more to his taste than offices and if he could confound his brother by becoming intimate with Theo it would make the afternoon still more enjoyable. It had not escaped him at the dinner table on the night of the sheep-roast that she had found his company entertaining nor that it had been against her will. If she was reluctant to be friendly towards him for Ralph's sake, it would be stimulating to persuade her to eat out of his hand.

'I've interrupted your reverie,' he said.

'I'm glad that you did. I'm too idle for my own good.'

'Beautiful women were made to do nothing.'

His remark did not please Theo. She did not agree with it but could not argue freely without accepting a compliment she felt to have been too forward. Her annoyance gathered her enough to control her first discomfort and offer him a seat. Charles, seeing that he had been too precipitate, took a chair beside the fire and prepared to be less hasty. The maid's return with cake and wine smoothed the awkwardness of the moment and when they were alone again, knowing that it was a subject which interested her, he began to talk of his travels.

He had been away from Bridport for so long and his life had been so different from Ralph's that, although she knew the history of his departure, Theo could not hold it in her mind that his pleasure had been bought at great cost to his father and brother. With him before her, she saw only a man of wide experience of the world, whose journeys had been for culture and the study of mankind and whose anecdotes did not include the price of hemp. Her own expedition filled him with questions, and resorts with which she was familiar brought tales from his store of memories. She had never had to think about what she could afford and she did not wonder how he had financed so many years of indulgence. Gambling did not occur to her and he did not mention it. Ralph had told her that Charles made no secret of being penniless but this was a description people were apt to apply to themselves without justification and she did not take it seriously.

As the evening darkened outside and the shadows deepened in the corners of the room, they sat together in the firelight as he drew her closer into comradeship with reminiscences which they shared but which were unknown to the rest of Theo's friends. It enthralled her to have an understanding in common with a man who was so unlike those she had grown up amongst. She was lulled by his easy flow of conversation and ashamedly amused by his occasional pitying jibes at stay-at-homes. They seemed to be united by a sophisticated vision of life not dreamt of by the people who surrounded them. This hour was so distinct from other calls she had received that it did not seem disloyal to Ralph to slide into sympathy with Charles. She relaxed, sitting half-turned in her chair, her face resting against its wing, her feet crossed on the stool, sometimes watching her visitor, sometimes gazing into the flames.

After a moment of quietness in which there was no striving for words to break the silence, Charles leant forward and picked up the roasting-pan she had been using when he arrived.

'I don't remember when I last tasted a chestnut,' he said, holding it towards the fire. 'May I?'

She nodded and he went down on his knees in front of the hearth but was so clumsy in trying to open the pan that she laughed and knelt beside him. Taking it from him, she said, 'The catch is difficult. You turn this – there, it's open.'

She tipped out the nuts she had been warming when he had arrived, which were now too dry to be worth eating, and he reached behind her for the dish she had been using to fill the pan. He put in a dozen and, at his request, she showed him how to master the obstinate catch and how near the flames to raise the pan. They were so close that her skirts lapped over his legs and their hands touched as she showed him what to do.

There was nothing impertinent in his manner and his whole attention seemed to be upon his task but the agitation that had troubled her since the day of his return thrust her peacefulness aside. She tried to subdue it, castigating herself for an unchaste reaction to an innocent amusement but, despite her efforts, her breathing quickened and she felt colour come back into her face. She wanted to flee from him as she had from Ralph in the wood. The heat of the fire was engulfing and she looked aside to reach for the handscreen to shield her skin. Away from the flames, the room seemed dark and cavernous and the rich scent of the roasting chestnuts reminded her how cloying the smell of the mutton had been on the night of the celebration and of the figures dancing in drunken licence.

Alarmed, she raised herself from her knees and tried to go back to her chair but her bunched gown caught under its seat and she subsided on to the stool.

Charles turned from the fire. 'Is it too hot for you?' he asked.

She stared at him, wide-eyed and unable to answer.

He busied himself with shaking the roasted nuts as if he were oblivious to her distress but inwardly he was triumphant and contemptuous. Ralph should have married her before this, he thought. She's ripe to be a wife and so bored that a stranger can excite her with a look. Her hands are trembling. Now she twists her bracelets again.

'Ralph should be here to do this with you,' he said.

'Yes.' Her voice could hardly be heard.

He moved around to face her. 'Does he neglect you?' he asked.

'No.' Her fingers stretched to pull her skirts from where they were now trapped beneath him but closed without touching them.

He opened the pan and tipped the chestnuts into his palm.

'No!' she said. 'You'll hurt – ' but he did not flinch.

'You shouldn't be anxious,' he said. 'I've never been afraid to be burnt.'

That Charles did not have his heart in the work he had shown such eagerness to take up, had not escaped Ralph. He was fair-minded and would grudgingly have given Charles credit if he had exerted himself but it was already apparent that he intended merely to coast through his duties. It exasperated Ralph that Mr Carnow could not see through his eldest son.

It was true that the work Charles was to undertake was not yet clearly defined. The episode of the desk being placed in Ralph's office had revealed that Mr Carnow had intended Charles to occupy a senior position but the nonsense of this had been forcibly put to him by Ralph who refused to countenance such a move. It was so ludicrous that a man who had almost shipwrecked the mill and who had been absent from the business for ten years should take a leading part in its running that even Mr Carnow was obliged to admit it. He would not accept, however, that there was no unfilled place which had been waiting for Charles and Ralph was made to conjure a role for him out of thin air.

As a result, Charles was now installed in the counting-house, with private instructions given to the chief clerk that no task allotted to him should be passed without minute scrutiny. It was Ralph's intention that not only would the supervision by a trusted employee keep Charles from causing mischief but that the type of work would prove so uninspiring to a dilettante that he would soon wish to leave Bridport. Indeed, Charles had already become cavalier in his attitude towards timekeeping, preferring to stroll about the works getting, as he put it, the feel of the place, or inventing errands in town rather than sitting with a ledger. Naturally, the owner's son had more leeway in these matters than the hands and could not be called to order by the clerks, but the freedom he allowed himself was surprising to the senior employees who had expected at least a show of perseverance in his early weeks.

This afternoon Ralph was tired but well pleased with his day. He had just returned from Loders where he had completed the negotiations for the farm along the river valley. Contracts had only to be exchanged and land perfect for the growing of hemp would belong to the Carnows. When the beds were established, the expense and complications of importing hemp would disappear until, he thought happily as he sat at his desk making optimistic calculations in his pocket-book, production had increased enough to make a still greater supply necessary. Satisfied by his achievement, he indulged himself with dreams of riding out with an admiring Theo to see his purchase, of pandering to her desire for change with travels to the source of their materials, of Theo in the shade of old Italian gardens, of Theo rapt and loving, standing beside him as their ship sailed into the soft, white nights of St Petersburg.

He was agreeably occupied in this manner when the door opened, interrupting him. The only person who would enter his office without knocking was his father and, despite their recent differences, Mr Carnow's appearance at this moment was welcome to Ralph. He rose and crossed the room to draw a chair to the other side of his desk and put a shovel of coal on the fire, while they greeted each other.

Mr Carnow subsided into the chair. He was disappointed that the breathlessness that had been growing upon him during the summer had worsened instead of being routed by the cold weather as he had hoped. Climbing stairs was beginning to be something to be avoided and it annoyed him that something so simple should have to be thought of at all. He sat grasping the arms of the chair and sucking in deep breaths to steady himself. Ralph handed him a glass of sherry and went back to his own seat.

'I'm glad you've come,' he said. 'I would've told you at once but I didn't know where you were.'

'Told me what?' Mr Carnow, his breathing becoming easier, laid his hand on his chest. 'Lord, I'm not as strong as I was. I'll take a draught of porter in the mornings.'

'About Steegan Farm. You remember I was going out there today. We discussed it last night.'

It irritated Ralph a little that he should have to explain. He had assumed that his father had come expressly for news of the transaction. The proposed purchase had been of concern to them for several months during which the owner of the land, a man of a vacillating temperament who could afford to hold on to meadows he wished neither to possess nor to put to good use, had blown hot and cold over the sale. It was to the glory of Ralph's powers of persuasion that he had not only brought the deal to a conclusion but that he had succeeded in paying no more than a fair price. He was justifiably proud of his day's work and, while being too old to wish for praise, would have liked Mr Carnow to have shown enough interest not to have forgotten what he had been about.

'Ah, yes. Did it go well?'

What was obviously merely a polite enquiry, curbed Ralph's enthusiasm to pass on the glad tidings and his reply was less exuberant than it would have been if he had expected a reciprocal relish of the victory.

'We shook on the payment I wanted to give,' he said. 'The contract's being drawn up and the land's ours.'

Mr Carnow nodded and set his glass down on the desk.

'Charles is visiting your Aunt Louisa and Theo,' he said. 'It's touching to see him with such a fondness for the family again. He was so anxious to learn to know them better that I told him to take the afternoon off. Of course, he didn't want to do it but we can't have him adding his figures all day long. It's too hard on a man who's led such a life as he.'

The opportunities for disagreement contained within this speech were so numerous that Ralph hardly knew which to choose. He was hurt that his news should have been passed over with such a lack of attention but he recognized this was immature and tried to master it. He did not master another emotion.

'My aunt is at her mill,' he said. 'She told me yesterday she would be. I mentioned it at dinner to you both.'

'No matter,' said Mr Carnow complacently, 'Theo can entertain him.'

'I daresay it slipped Charles's memory that his aunt would be away.' Ralph began to play with the pen he had been using but his eyes were on his father's and his tone was dry.

'Charles and Theo are cousins,' said Mr Carnow, stiffly.

'As indeed, are Theo and I.'

Mr Carnow stared at the wall and fidgeted with his watch-chain. He was no less delighted by Charles's return but, now that he was becoming used to it, he was less absorbed in the novelty and was beginning to suspect that others did not view the reunion with the favour it deserved.

'I haven't wanted to say this to you,' he said, looking back at his son, 'but I feel that I must. I've been displeased by your attitude towards Charles from the start.'

'When you say from the start,' asked Ralph, 'do you mean from the start of our childhood, the start of his departure with his inheritance or the start of his penniless arrival at the address he had not written to for nine years?'

Mr Carnow stood up and clasped his hands behind him. It was a posture Ralph knew well from upbraidings as a boy and he derived some bitter amusement from seeing his father resume it. The child we have been remains with us and the child in Ralph yearned for his father's approval but his adult self was stronger and he was not to be intimidated.

'I believed that I had taught you to be Christian,' said Mr Carnow with a severity that caused Ralph to raise his eyebrows. 'I don't say that Charles has been prodigal but we can look to the Scriptures for guidance upon how we should behave when a long-lost son finds his way home.'

'But we have.' Ralph was sardonic. 'We may not have killed the fatted calf but there are sheep who may no longer safely graze.'

He could feel himself moving towards the sarcasm that drives reason from an argument but he saw nothing except humbug in his father's recourse to religion and the temptation was there.

Mr Carnow flushed. 'Can you not be charitable?' he asked. 'Is it beyond you to be hospitable to your own brother?'

Ralph leant back in his chair. His inclination was to rise to his feet but he did not trust himself.

'Is it beyond you,' he said, his voice hard, 'to understand what is being done? Do you think affection has brought Charles back? He has no money and he knows he can persuade you to anything. He's come to fill his pockets at our expense. Fill them and he'll leave you again.'

Mr Carnow was shaking. 'It's untrue. He has genuine – he feels – ' he pointed his finger at Ralph. 'This is jealousy,' he said. 'Since you were boys you've never given him his due. If he leaves he'll have been driven away by you – by your spite – and I will never forgive you. If he needs money who should he come to but me? And if I give it who can say no? I will do as I please with my own.'

Chapter Six

Theo did not recover easily from her hours with Charles. He had not left the house before her aunt had returned and Louisa's cold civility towards him had made Theo feel that she had indeed been disloyal to Ralph. Her intimacy with Charles had made her ashamed and excited. Louisa was not a woman to dislike a man without good cause and her attitude reminded Theo that it had been love of selfish pleasure that had taken Charles from England. She admitted to herself that it was Ralph who had played the more manly part and she was humiliated by her lack of control in Charles's presence. Although a sly and luring voice within her defended Charles, she accepted that Ralph was the better man and it mortified her that she should be swept into tremulous shyness by one who had nothing to recommend him but an easy manner, a past with room for mystery, and his being a stranger with a relation's right to close connection with her.

Throughout the evening, she strove to calm herself. In her mind, she ridiculed the strength of feeling the afternoon had aroused. She reviewed the events and words that had arisen and told herself that nothing had occurred, but she was not so young and inexperienced that she did not realize that it is the undercurrent in a quiet sea that drags the swimmer beneath the waves. The look in Charles's eyes as he had made an innocent remark, the pull of her gown trapped beneath him as she tried to move away, the touch of his hand as he opened hers to put chestnuts into her palm – these things came back to her and sent the blood into her face. Despite her shame, she had enjoyed the sensations that had shaken her, just as she enjoyed the tensions between the brothers when she was in their company. She believed that her character must be base to find pleasure in rivalry and the regard of an indolent man, and she struggled to suppress her agitation as she went about the occupations of a domestic evening. Her appetite was small enough to be noticed disapprovingly by Louisa at dinner, her chess-playing was without concentration, her embroidery silks snapped as she drew them through her work, the novel she took up lay unread in her lap. At last, complaining of tiredness, she said that she would retire early and went to be alone.

Her bedroom seemed a haven of solitude. The maid unlaced her and was sent away without any of the small talk there was usually between them. Left to herself, Theo relaxed into a voluptuous languor that yet had a taut chord of perturbation running through it. Her fire was burning high, filling the room with a dancing ruddy light. The lamp was not lit and she blew out the four candles so that she could enjoy the colour of the flames. She lay on her sofa, a cushion held to her chest, her hair loose and trailing to the carpet, whose arabesques had been the paths she had led her Noah's animals, two by two, as a child. It had been simple then to save her charges from the flood. She had not questioned that the lion and lioness should walk willingly into the Ark. Now, as she watched the shadows moving on the walls, she wondered how each pair had been chosen. Had the unicorn hung back unable to decide upon a mate until the waters rose and her chance was gone? She reached down as if she held the old wooden shapes and rocked her hand to give them their stiff-legged walk. Lifting her arm again, she looked at that hand. The small fingers that had coaxed the herd aboard had grown long and white; a gentlewoman's hand that had been gloved throughout all her travels to preserve its pallor, with skin as soft as the creams smoothed on it. She felt a sudden revulsion at the sight. It seemed to her to have done nothing useful and to be condemned to do nothing until it was folded across her at its end.

Was it this, she asked herself, that drew her to Charles? He, too, had lived in idleness and with him there could be none of the jealousy she realized she suffered for Ralph's more active life. It was women's role to be passive but, having caged its birds, the world despised them for not flying and only with another lotus-eater could she feel unreproached.

She left the sofa and went to a window, pulling the curtains behind her so that she could not be seen from outside. The night was dense and dark. No stars shone through the unbroken layer of cloud. At intervais, lanterns shed circles of misted light on doors and kerbstones. A shaft of dim yellow came from the rear of the house and ribald voices followed a man-servant, unidentifiable in a maid's cloak, as he hurried to lock the gates. A carriage passed, driving towards Carnow, sprays of yesterday's rain arching from its wheels. On the leaves of the ivy that climbed about the windows, she could see the first, faint powder of frost.

It was cold in this recess where the fire did not reach. She sat on the window-seat, wrapping her arms around her drawn-up knees and laying her cheek on her hand. At this moment, with her resentments and petty reasons for disaffection plain in her mind, she longed for Ralph. The ways of the world were none of his making and, if they prevented the woman he loved accepting him, he was injured by them as much as she. Alone in this corner, it came to her how often he must have suffered loneliness and her heart ached for him. His father, who had weakly risked their livelihood for the sake of the favoured son, had been no companion for him; the friends he had grown up with were his competitors and could not be told his confidences; she had been too young to hear them. He must have a hunger for the loving attachments of life that business could not satisfy and without which there was no point in gaining wealth. Man cannot live on bread alone; if he is asked to labour so hard to earn his bread that his spirit starves for other food, he is as much a prisoner as the woman sacrificed to useless gentility. Instead of division and ill-feeling was it not better for the pair of them to unite and struggle together for a more equal share of the diverse aspects of living?

She wiped her breath from the pane where it had clouded and obscured her vision. Had Ralph come to her now she would have fallen upon him and asked his forgiveness for sins he had never suspected her of committing. What opportunity had he had to amuse and allure her as his brother had done today? Leisure is needed to learn to philander and he had had little of that. She renounced her sympathies for Charles; she was contrite and a wiser woman would wake in her stead tomorrow.

At Carnow, Charles was innocent of any notion of how Theo's thoughts were running or of the violent interview between his father and Ralph. He had not gone home after leaving the Farnabys, having been invited by an old acquaintance to attend a smoking concert in the back room of an inn at Bridport Harbour. The evening had been raucously convivial and he did not return until Mr Carnow and Ralph had been lying sleeplessly in their beds for some hours.

Unlike Theo, whose rest was disturbed by self-recriminations, he slept like the just but the effects of his junketings did not induce him to rise early. By the time he had brought himself carefully to the breakfast table and was eyeing the kidneys with disfavour, the house was empty of all except the servants and Ettie. He had not been alone with Ettie for more than a few minutes together since his arrival from Canada and, deciding against food, he carried his coffee into the drawing room and prepared to observe her.

Ettie was sitting by the fire, working a pair of velvet slippers to give to Mr Carnow at Christmas. Her needle moved back and forth with precision and although she was leaning against the back of the low lady's chair in which she sat she gave the impression that she and it touched only by the coincidence of their mutual uprightness. She nodded to Charles as he came in but did not speak or change her expression. As he set his cup on a table and took the chair opposite hers, he compared the different atmospheres conjured by two women at two firesides in as many days, and felt that this one was not conducive to friendship.

He crossed his legs and stared at Ettie to put her out of countenance but she was not a girl to be ruffled by such a procedure and she countered him with a look of such adult awareness of his mischief that he gave up the attempt.

They sat for five minutes without conversation. There were no sounds in the room but the occasional snip of Ettie's scissors and an abrupt hiss from the grate as gas escaped from a coal. Beyond the door, maids could be heard going up and down the stairs to set the bedrooms to rights and carry the water and night-soil outside. From further away still, the noise of the mill could be heard unaffected by the absence of its new clerk.

The slippers that Ettie was sewing were crimson. She had one of the front pieces in her lap and was covering it in flamboyant foliage and flowers. Purple peonies, emerald ferns, mazarine lilies grew under her remorseless hand. She was not daunted by her flora's departure from nature and her thread did not catch or break. Watching her, Charles was again struck, as he had been on seeing her after the passing of ten years, by how little she resembled any of her three possible parents. There was nothing of her soft, doting mother about her. She had inherited no pretty ways, no female frailties and winning languishments from the lovely adulterous Mrs Trent; neither was she the nonentity that her legal father had been in Charles's eyes, nor a reminder of himself. He felt sure that she was a definite individual but in what direction her individuality lay he could not yet tell.

'It's a cold morning,' he remarked. He was puzzled as to how to draw her into conversation and hoped that the English habit of discussing the weather would tempt her.

'It is,' she agreed. 'I'm surprised to see so thick a frost after the evening we had.'

The subject did not appear to be of absorbing interest to her but Charles was pleased to hear that she did not answer in the monosyllables of a schoolgirl.

'The cloud had quite gone by midnight,' he said. 'As I was coming home the sky was as clear as glass. There was ice on the roads.'

He looked at the window as he spoke. The sudden fall in temperature had been severe and the panes were still as white as the muslin under-curtains. The warmth of the fire had not yet reached the far side of the room and the sight of such coldness close at hand made it all the more agreeable to be where he was.

'Are you comfortable here?' he asked.

'Thank you.' Ettie chose another silk and tried it against the one she had been using. 'This chair suits me.'

'I meant are you comfortable living in this house with the Ca – with my family?'

She threaded her needle. Picking up her work she began another leaf whilst considering what to say. The question was impertinent and she wondered what his motive was in asking it. From her observation of him since his return, she judged it unlikely that he was concerned for her welfare. His own happiness was of importance to him but he would not wish for it in others unless it would bring some benefit to himself.

She did not like him. His actions, manner and words were all of the type most abhorrent to her. She was not impressed by his smile, his lingering eyes, his elegance or his anecdotes of his travels. Despite her youth, her memory was too good and her reasoning too clear for her not to see, as Ralph and Louisa saw, that selfish idleness had taken him away from Carnow and poverty had brought him back. Although she had not said so, she was entirely behind Ralph in his resentment of the belittling of his years of endeavour and by the ease with which Charles had reinstated himself with his father. It was fortunate that her own behaviour was habitually so undemonstrative that Mr Carnow had no inkling of her attitude. She was aware that her sedateness, unnatural as it was for her years, made people believe her cold, but they were mistaken. She could give deep and loyal love to those whose merits deserved it, but she would never be captivated by breathing in the trailing smoke of charm. It pleased her that Charles did not think it worth exerting himself to fascinate her for she would have found the attempt tedious.

'I'm very comfortable here,' she said.

Charles was curious to know how true that was. Even after ten years, any normal girl would surely grieve for the mother who had not watched her grow and would be too ashamed of that mother's suicide and her father's crime to feel completely at home with those her father had cheated. Unless she cultivated humility – which Ettie patently did not – there must also be ill will against Mr Carnow for ordering Trent's arrest, however guilty she believed him to be. Of course, he thought, leaning his elbow on the arm of the chair and smiling behind his hand, if, as is likely, she is my daughter she may have inherited an excellent talent for her own preservation. Gaining a place in a wealthy household may seem worth losing poorer parents. I wonder who she intends to marry.

'Do you remember me?' he asked. 'From before I went away?'

'I do,' Ettie laid down her sewing. 'It's odd. I wouldn't have recognized you if I'd passed you in the street without being told your name but now that I do know who you are I have memories from when I was very small.'

The tone of her answer disconcerted Charles. There were a number of episodes from when he and Helen Trent had thought her too young to be dangerous which he would prefer her to keep forgotten.

'And your mother?' he said. 'A beautiful woman.'

'Yes, indeed. I've sketches of her that my father made. I think she would have been disappointed that I don't favour her.' She spoke matter-of-factly and again Charles was taken aback. That a fifteen-year-old should speak of her plainness with neither bravado nor wistfulness showed a striking degree of self-possession.

'Is it possible to speak of your father?' he asked.

'All things are possible,' she said. 'If you mean is his name taboo in this house I must say that Mr Carnow rarely mentions him – and then never without an injured sadness and a caress for myself – for fear I'll feel the sins of the father are being visited upon the child. Occasionally I've news of him from Mr Ralph. I'm prepared to speak of him freely.'

'News of him?' Charles was startled. He tried to disguise it but the momentary display of shock did not escape Ettie's notice.

'Twice yearly Mr Ralph receives a report of him from the prison governor. It's our only contact. He – Papa – has refused absolutely to communicate with me by letter or visit. He wishes people to forget whose daughter I am. Although he maintains his innocence, he's aware of the stigma attached to the family of a convict. I think his decision was mistaken. People will always gossip; their opinions are of no concern to me.'

Ettie spoke with her usual composure but she had been touched on a tender place in her heart. Throughout his banishment, she had cherished a silent love for Trent. He was a pair of arms that had swung her to his shoulder, a waistcoat-pocket full of candied cherries, a large hand and soft voice that led her through the water-meadows on summer evenings and told her of journeys that brought the flax and hemp. Her memories of him and the recollections of those who knew him did not lead her to believe that he would succumb to the temptation of crime. She felt a lack in her life and character because of his loss and though she was not one for useless repining she would have chosen his presence in her youth had the choice been there for her to take. It interested her that Charles was obviously shaken and baffled by her words.

'Reports from what prison governor?' he said. 'He was given a well-deserved twenty years transportation. Some Botany Bay road-gang should be having the benefit of his counting-house abilities.'

'As, indeed,' said Ettie, calmly, glancing at the clock, 'our counting-house should be having yours.'

He recrossed his legs, smoothing the cloth over his raised knee.

'Do me the honour of explaining yourself,' he said.

'My father,' she said, watching him closely, 'was not physically strong, as you will recall, and he was certainly not used to being herded amongst felons. He fell ill of a fever during his trial and was not deemed fit to leave for the port. By the time he had recovered, the governor of the gaol had seen his superiority to the usual run of prisoners and kept him back for secretarial duties. He's never left the country.'

Charles met her eyes. To all appearances he was again master of himself.

'So he is now – ?'

'He's in Dorchester gaol. We're neighbours.'

Charles, whose morning was proving increasingly disturbing, had been the only member of the Carnow and Farnaby households, apart from Ettie, who had slept well. At Allington, Theo's night had been racked by reproach of her folly while Louisa had lain wondering whether the niece she had believed to have intelligence was to be brought to grief by bad judgement. She knew Theo to have fierce emotions and she was concerned that they would gain the whiphand over her reason long enough to draw her into rash acts that she would long regret. Although she disliked Charles, she could see that he could exert a particular charm that people susceptible to oblique flattery could not resist. She strongly suspected him of having supported himself over the past ten years by using this vampire talent to part fools from their money. He was plainly practising it upon his father and Louisa did not doubt that, unless Theo was soon betrothed to Ralph, he would decide that the acquisition of a rich wife was easier and more profitable than trying to regain the mill.

She was still considering what was best to be done when Ralph abandoned the idea of being able to achieve anything constructive at the mill without having seen Theo. He had his horse saddled and, leaving a message of his whereabouts for his father, rode out through the white meadows towards Bridport.

It was bitterly cold. Hoar-frost as thick as snow coated the hedges, unstirred by any wind. In a farmyard, where cattle stood huddled in a cloud of their rising breath, children, wrapped crossways in shawls, slid on a frozen pond. Ralph's horse slipped on the icy road, stumbling almost to its knees, and he checked it, stroking its neck and speaking calmly until it was soothed. It was not yet ten and the pale sun, hanging low in the colourless sky, was giving no heat to the earth. A woman carrying wood to her back door called to him that it was a bad day for riding and he touched his hat and said that it was.

He wanted Theo. The argument with his father the day before had wounded him. The threat implied in Mr Carnow's words that the wealth of the mill would be used for Charles's benefit showed such a dismissal of the value of Ralph's own efforts that he wanted to cry out with pain and rage. He had never expected appreciation from his father but to be cast aside with such thoughtless speed was beyond endurance.

Lying sleeplessly in his bed the night before, feeling the cold increase, it had not assuaged his hurt and anger to know that Charles had been alone with Theo throughout the afternoon. He did not suspect Theo of succumbing to Charles's tawdry fascinations but it left a foul taste in his mouth to think of his brother enjoying her attentions while he had been, as always, at his work. It disgusted him to hear Charles's stifled laughter and unsteady steps along the corridor in the early hours. To take second place to an extravagant idler, who could not hold his wine, was not to be borne with passive patience. He needed Theo as his staunch ally and support; he wanted her sympathy and tenderness for his heartache, her hot indignation for his grievances; he wanted comfort from holding her in his arms. It was not possible for him to restrain himself longer. This morning he would ask her to be his.

He rode into the stableyard and left his horse with a lad whose soft hat was tied over his ears with a strip of red flannel. Discovering from the boy that the ladies were at home, he presented himself in the house and was taken to the drawing room where Louisa was sitting by a bright fire planning the week's menus. She set aside her writing-desk and motioned to him to sit down. The sight of his set face and rigid posture in the chair warned her that there had been further disturbing events at Carnow.

'I can see,' she said, 'that all is not well at home.'

Ralph inclined his head towards her.

'I've been told,' he said, 'that my attitude towards Charles is not what it should be. I'm uncharitable, inhospitable and unchristian. If he should absent himself again it will, indubitably, be my fault. Furthermore, the money derived from the mill is my father's and he will give it to whom he chooses.'

'It's as bad as that?'

'It is.'

Louisa put a pen that had rolled on to her lap on the table beside her. The expression on her face was serious. She did not underestimate the foolishness and injustice that the favouritism of a parent could lead to.

'Your mother and I both thought at the time', she said, 'that when Charles was given his share of the inheritance the rest should immediately be made over to you. It would've looked reckless to an outsider to see such a young man in a position to dominate his father – or ruin him – but we both foresaw a situation just like this. Has he changed his will?'

'Not to my knowledge.'

She looked across the room to the windows where condensation was glistening on the panes.

'There's little we can do except hope that Charles will make some wrong move that will open your father's eyes. I've missed your mother a great deal over the years but I don't think she was ever needed more than now. Though whether she could have made a difference, I couldn't say. No one can make a man treat his sons fairly. Still, it would have been something for you to have someone in your home on your side.'

It was a similar thought concerning a different woman that had brought Ralph there that morning. While he thought of Theo he saw Louisa smile at him.

'If the worst should come,' she said, 'remember that you have friends who love you. It's not only your father who has a mill. I have one and so has Theo. In one way or another you'll be a master in your own right.'

He was touched by her concern.

'You've always been generous to me,' he said. 'I hope you won't misunderstand if I say I'd rather be master through my own efforts than through the kindness of my relations.'

'Which,' remarked Louisa, 'is what makes you superior to your brother – but, my dear, if your father should make disastrous decisions remember what I've said. You can do for my mill what you've done for his. And, of course, if you marry Theo everything of mine will be left to the pair of you.'

He tightened his hand on the arm of the chair.

'Where is Theo?' he asked. 'I hoped to speak to her.'

'In the summerhouse. She wanted to paint the frost. Go to her now if you like to. She's quite alone.'

Out in the frozen summerhouse, Theo had not attempted to paint. She had had no real intention of doing so. Her mood of contrition had remained when she had woken from her restless night and she had made her art an excuse to be alone to indulge her remorse. It was an unusual sentiment for her and she was not good at it. Even as her heart yearned for Ralph, she could not help thinking that any clergyman or writer of improving works for young ladies would have looked on her at this moment as the very model of what the female should be.

She was pacing slowly from one end of the summerhouse to the other. It was so cold that when she turned and her long earrings swung against her neck, a shock ran through her as if she had been brushed by ice. She was wearing a dark blue velvet gown and mantle that she had brought back from Paris, with black lace thrown across her head. The effect was plain but more sumptuous than was normally seen in the town by day. In the still white light of the frost-encrusted glass, she looked like the queen of a northern tale. Pine-woods should have stood beyond her door.

For the first time in her life she felt that she could not go to Carnow. The thought of her ease with Charles still sent the blood into her face, which was pale with tiredness. She wanted to see Ralph but she was ashamed to seek him out, knowing that he was sure to have been told of her afternoon. What must he think of her? She dwelt on and exaggerated her disloyalty. The thought of meeting Charles at his home alarmed her and she was angry that this restraint and fear should have been brought into a situation that had been so simple before he had returned. Her anxieties over her feelings for Ralph were forgotten in her reaction against Charles and, again for the first time, she suffered a longing for things to be as they were in earlier years.

The weak sun had risen over the garden wall and was spreading a translucent glow through the pattern of ice crystals obscuring the glass of the pavilion. It filled the bleak room with a radiance that changed its aspect to glimmering invitation. Her spirits quickened with the increase of light. Opening one of the folding-doors, she looked out over the flowerbeds and paths.

There was no warmth in the sun. The white garden stood untouched by thaw. Rime coated every branch and trellis so that each rosebush, each fruit-tree, the very piles of straw protecting tender plants, seemed carved in intricate statuary and lit with the glittering brightness that snow and marble share. The pool, where she had trailed her fingers in September strolls with Ralph, was solid now with withered rushes captive in the ice. A thrush beat an old snail-shell upon a stone and the sound rang in the stillness. It seemed impossible that peaches should ever have hung plumply by these shining walls or the luscious scent of heliotrope stifled the heated air.

A sound from the house startled her. Ralph was coming down the steps that led into the garden. She drew back into the pavilion, shy of meeting him in her present condition. Since he had begun to love her, she had always had the upper hand because her feelings had been less strong than his. His longing had given her power and control but today, abashed and sensitive, she was unprotected. She watched a stranger walk towards her and, though she had wanted foreignness in a man, she was both attracted and diffident. The memory of being held to him in the wood enveloped her and again she was torn between the desire to yield and to run.

Retreating from his purposeful approach, she waited at the far side of the summerhouse. All awareness of the cold had left her.

She pulled back the lace from her head to cool herself. 'A thousand little shafts of flame were shivered in my narrow frame. O Love, O Fire!' Once more, she thought, my mind flies to a verse of eager acceptance. If I had listened to its first cry when he kissed me; if I had not fled then – He was entering the pavilion. She reached out, her hand against the wall, as if she could not stand alone.

Ralph hesitated as he came into the room. The object of his call was beating back and forth in his thoughts, stirring hopes and dreads that confused the simplicity of what he wished to ask. He had seen her withdraw from his sight as he crossed the garden and now she stood holding herself against the furthest corner as though she sought to be distant from him. There was a flush on her white skin and her eyes were wide. He found her so lovely that it caused him pain not to go forward and press her to him. His chest grew tight and his breathing rapid. He had blamed Charles for his cloistered hours with Theo but finding her in this way, apprehensive and on guard, he suspected her actions. Jealousy and hurt tempted him to think her guilty. The urge to hold her was mingled with the need to accuse.

In the strange glow of the icy light, he felt the restrained passions of desire and hatred flood his spirit, possessing his faculties so that reason and gentleness slid out of his grasp. What had she said to Charles in the privacy of their darkened afternoon? What had she done? A primitive urge to shout 'You're mine, mine. How can you be kind to my rival?' overwhelmed him and was barely suppressed. He knew he was acting without sense but there seemed so little reward in the world for virtue that his rational being could not assert itself. When he spoke his voice was harsh and his own words enraged him.

'Is my brother good company?' he asked.

Theo straightened and took her hand from the wall. A spasm of anger that her tenderness for his injuries should be bruised by suspicion disturbed her zeal to look up to him. Her mood would have made her susceptible to a dignified entreaty or a return to their old relationship of adult and child but his aggression riled her. She had never known him to be crude and she made no allowance for what had led to the vulgarity behind his question.

Tiredness, shame and resentment provoked a rash defence where a mature sympathy would have smoothed their paths.

'He is my cousin,' she said. 'Surely I may sit with him if I choose?'

'Do you choose?' Having begun foolishly, Ralph felt himself swept on. 'I'd hoped you were closeted with him against your will but if it was an affair that gave you pleasure – '

Theo clasped her hands, then, throwing them apart as if they repelled each other, began twisting her heavy bracelets as she had done before Charles.

'He did amuse me,' she said. 'We roasted chestnuts. Not an occupation which usually brings accusation in its train.'

'I accuse you of nothing. Perhaps I should do so. I do accuse him.'

'Of what? Of recounting tales of his travels to his family? I've heard of worse offences.'

'Have you? Have you, Theo?' There was the same bitter dryness in his voice that there had been with his father. 'Then consider his absence. Do you think an unattached man of his type entertains himself in the same way as young women and their aunts? He's told you the pretty stories – ask him to tell you the rest.'

She turned away abruptly. Her acquaintance with the ways of the world, though greater than her female contemporaries, was small and it shocked her to have them brought to her attention in this manner. It seemed barbarous that her compassion for Ralph should be met with coarse suggestions. In her innocence, she had suspected Charles only of selfish idleness and visions of depravity were too alien to her modes of thought to be accepted. Disgust aroused by the notion made her react in Charles's favour.

'What do you know of him that makes you say that?' she asked.

'I know his character and the temptations there are for men like him who have money to waste.' Ralph was aware that he was at a disadvantage. He was certain that Charles had lived a reprehensible life but he had no facts to put forward. Even had he had evidence, he would not have told it to Theo. He wanted to protect her from contamination by the grossness of the world and he could not talk to her of sordid actions.

She rounded on him. 'But you have heard nothing definite?'

'No.' His answer was reluctant but he was too proud not to be truthful.

Turning her face contemptuously from him, she made no reply. Her breath was white in the freezing air but the heat within her made her skin burn. Her disappointment was so strong that she felt she could do violence.

Ralph tried to calm himself. He was sickened by his stupidity and lack of tact. It would be better now to apologize and withdraw but the hunger for her love and loyalty that had brought him here and caused his jealous outburst would not let him go.

'I've begun wrongly,' he said. 'I hardly know what I'm saying.'

She did not move and he came closer to her.

'Theo, in the wood . . . '

Seeing her bend her neck and colour, he was encouraged to stand beside her.

'In the wood you asked to be private a little longer but your privacy is my solitude and I've great need of you.' He took one of her hands. She let it lie in his but did not return his clasp. 'My dearest,' he said, 'I love you. Will you make me wait? Be my wife.'

There was silence when he had spoken. The sunlight filtering through the icy glass was still as keenly dazzling, the frosted garden, seen through the open door, was just as motionless and glacial but Theo was not as she had been when she had come to look on them. His softer words were a balm to her anger but soothed only the surface of the gall he had induced. Excited and indignant, her mind reached for the understanding she had had of him in the night and could not hold it.

'I can't. I can't.'

She pulled her hand from his and raised it to her face. Her eyes were stricken but the blow she had delivered was too savage for him to interpret them. Again there was a silence between them.

'I thought you warm,' he said, at last. 'Warm and loving but you're as cold – as cold as – '

He struck the window suddenly with the side of his fist. Shards of ice shattered and fell to the stone.

'I won't take your no,' he said. 'I won't have it. One day you'll come to your senses.'

She swung sharply around, her back towards him. He could not see that she bit her cheek to keep back tears, and in a moment she heard his footsteps walk away.

Chapter Seven

'Who was that at the gate?' Louisa, handing her finished menus to a maid to take down to the kitchen, heard the sound of the recalcitrant side gate into the stableyard being thrust open with unusual violence. 'I must remember to speak to Blake about the hinges.'

The maid went to the only window from which that entrance could be seen and, wiping the condensation with the edge of her apron, craned against the glass for a glimpse of who had passed through. The front of the garden was empty but, between the wrought-iron frets of the half-closed gate, she could just see a figure striding vehemently back and forth as if he could not wait to have his mount fetched.

'It's Mr Ralph, ma'am,' she said. 'He d'seem in a rare taking to be away.'

Louisa looked up sharply from the pens she was putting into their case. 'Mr Ralph? Alone?'

'Yes, he's – oh – ' Hasty footsteps on the frozen path diverted her and, moving to a window facing on to the flower garden, she took on the aspect of a setter that has seen a quail. 'Miss Theodosia's coming up the – oh, ma'am, she d'look flurried as a hind-deer.'

Louisa rose and joined the maid in quick strides. Theo was approaching the house in obvious distress, and although her agitation was plainly as great as a hunted doe it was fiercer than the description implied. Louisa began walking to the door. Her heart moved within her at what this scene meant and the pain it must bring to Theo and Ralph. Inwardly, she cursed Charles and his blandishments.

Turning back at the door to speak to the interested maid, she tried to seem composed.

'Heat a negus,' she said. 'Miss Theo has taken cold from the frost. And bring in her paints.'

With these injunctions, which fooled no one in the kitchen, she left the room and went across the landing. As the maid slipped past her and down the backstairs, she saw Theo come blindly into the hall and put her hand on the banisters.

'Theo! Oh, Theo, my dear.'

Hearing her aunt's sympathetic voice and the rush of her skirts as she ran down, Theo shuddered and began to climb as if she had been ill for weeks. Louisa reached her and held her closely as she had done when Theo was a girl.

Theo laid her head on Louisa's shoulder. It was a momentary refreshment to be again in the position of a comforted child but the time had gone when Louisa's arms were enough to protect her from her sorrows.

'He asked me,' she said, 'but I can't. I told him I can't.'

Her breathing was as rapid and rasping as an exhausted runner but her words came not with the high tremor of hysteria but the anguished firmness of one who has accomplished a grim but necessary task.

Louisa bowed her head and rested it against Theo's. She clasped the shivering woman more tightly, feeling the coldness of the air outside rising from her clothes and hair. Exclamations poised on her lips but she forced them back. She was certain that Theo's refusal of Ralph would not be to her happiness but it would do no good now to be contentious. Her disappointment was acute. She knew Theo to have a need to love and be loved and that the years when their old family affections were enough were past. It seemed that the girl she had nurtured had grown only to be adrift on storm-wracked seas. The parent's fear for the safety of her child made her want to urge Theo to reconsider but she knew that only harm would come of arguing for a marriage that Theo did not joyfully seek for herself. It was mortifying to remember that it was she who had interrupted the burgeoning attraction between Ralph and Theo by taking her niece abroad to learn her own mind. The thought of the young man returning, heart-sore and rejected, to the home where he was not valued made her blame herself. She did not doubt that it was Charles who had unsettled Theo and it was a vexation that Theo's head could be turned so easily by fool's gold. The desire to console her dear girl was tempered by a wish to shake her.

Theo raised herself from Louisa's shoulder. 'I'll go to my room,' she said.

Her voice was low and her tone implied that she was not to be questioned. Her outburst had been the only display of her wretchedness there would be. Grasping the banisters again, she began to climb. She felt as drained as if she had dug a ditch and Louisa reached about her waist to support her. They gained Theo's room without being seen by a servant and Theo sank awkwardly on to the bed. Unfastening her mantle, she let it fall behind her.

'I can't think why I'm so tired,' she said. 'And,' she gripped the coverlet as she felt a spasm of nausea, 'I must be unwell.'

Louisa knelt and unlaced Theo's boots. A crust of frost, softened by the warmth of the room, slid from the leather and melted into the carpet. Drawing the boots off, Louisa rubbed Theo's small frozen feet.

'Lie back and rest for a while,' she said. 'The sickness will go when you're calmer. I'll have a hot brick sent up.'

Theo stood gingerly and Louisa undid her waist-ties so that she could step out of the heavy whale-boned petticoats that would have prevented her lying comfortably.

'Would you like me to stay?' Louisa asked.

'No.' Theo settled against the pillows as her aunt covered her with a shawl. 'I'll be better alone.'

Louisa bent and kissed her on the forehead. Their eyes met for a moment and Louisa thought she saw both defiance and shame in Theo's. She straightened.

'I'm going to the mill this afternoon,' she said. 'I need to discuss the arrangements for the Prince's exhibition. If you're able I'd be glad to have you with me.'

An invitation to view a manufactory is not the most common way to console a young woman distressed by an offer of marriage and at first it did not enter Theo's thoughts. When ten minutes of nauseous misery had passed and the negus, having been drunk and kept down, was spreading its medicinal properties through her veins, she began to review the scene with Ralph. An oppressive weight seemed to lie on her chest, hampering her breathing, like an incubus that crouched there whispering, 'Regret'. The desperation that had overcome her on her father's death was with her again. She felt that all connection with Ralph had ceased and his loss made the power of their attachment apparent. How was it possible to live without his love? In all its changing forms it had always been the background of her existence and to be without it was to walk naked through the world. She could not bring herself to be his wife but could she watch him turn from her to take another?

She rose from the bed, unable to be still. He had said he would not take no for her answer. There was that hope. He had said that he would wait until she came to her senses. At this remembrance a surge of anger went through her. Who was he to accuse and patronize her as he had done? Even though she had succumbed to Charles in her mind, there had been no action on her part to make her deserving of Ralph's suspicions and vulgarity. Her humiliation remained but in her outrage she deliberately gave herself up to enjoying her reaction to Charles. She clasped it to her as a drunkard clutches his bottle. The protection her resentment gave her against repining made her fuel her temper as if she could drive back the night with a ring of fire.

Taking her loose skirts in her fists, she threshed them back and forth. If she had been capable of renouncing her sex at this instant she would have done so without hesitation. The restrictions of womanhood that hindered every movement wound about her holding her fast. She would be brazen. It was not wrong to refuse to give up her name and soul and property to a man who spoke to her as though she were a child. She was not responsible for his pain. He had brought it upon himself. Let him witness that she was no nursling, and learn humility.

Pacing the floor from bed to window, from window to bed, her inhibiting gown dragging behind her, she turned her envy of Ralph's active life into a determination to emulate him. Her occupations did not satisfy her. To take part in business was unfeminine but she did not covet the female role. If the aunt was a heretic in these matters then why not the niece? There was much to learn but if her mind was filled with enquiry perhaps she would be less conscious of her heart.

'Good God! Have the markets failed?'

Moore was sitting beside the newly built-up fire in Ralph's office waiting to discuss the orders for the spring run to Newfoundland. It was unlike his friend not to be punctual and, having been told that Ralph had ridden to the Farnabys', he was filling his time with plans, confident that he would not be delayed long. The sight of Ralph's white and haunted face startled him.

Ralph stared at him as if he saw an apparition. It had not been his original intention to return to Carnow. Solitude or the presence of a trusted companion were more beckoning than routine. So far as he had been able to think in his first furious disappointment, he had thought of seeking Moore out but the possibility of having to make conversation with others he might meet in this endeavour gave him pause and he had turned for home. A long absence from the mill for unexplained social calls would give rise to comment from his father and brother and he had no wish for his proposal to be guessed and made the subject of pity or ridicule.

The frost still lay on the earth as he rode slowly back, sounds still rang with strange sharpness across the frozen fields but the cold they carried did not seem as chill as the world to which he was returning. He had told Theo that he would not accept her answer but she had made his hopes barren and he could not see beyond her rejection of him. In his anguish, he saw again her stricken eyes as she refused him. What had he done to make him so repellent to her? He had only loved her and spoken of his love. Had he not been patient and faithful? Did he not have a right to jealousy? It seemed to him as he wrestled to govern himself, that he would rather destroy her than see her with Charles.

The mill had not excited him as he rode into it. Its noise and industry did not stimulate him as it had always done, summoning his wits and strength to its aggrandizement. As he left his horse in the yard, he had allowed himself the bitter picture of Theo as the wife of his brother and Charles as inheritor of the mill. Louisa's generosity would make him a master but the thought was as ashes in his mouth. What was his life without Theo? He did not wish to be a slave to labour all his days with no private attachments to give his efforts meaning. Business was not enough.

He had entered his office absorbed with these reflections and barely recognized the friend he had wanted to see. The memory of what he had arranged for that morning returned to his distracted mind and he closed the door in no fit state for an interview.

'Forgive me,' he said. 'I'd quite forgotten – have you waited long?'

Moore got up and indicated his chair. 'Here,' he said. 'Come by the fire. Where's your wine?'

'The corner cupboard.'

Ralph threw his gloves on the desk and hung his greatcoat on a hook on the wall. He sat tensely and stared at the flames as Moore filled a glass with sherry and brought it to him.

'You ought to have rum for this weather,' said Moore, crossing the room and coming back with a glass for himself in one hand and a chair in the other. 'There's nothing like it for heating the blood.'

'It isn't my blood that needs heating.'

'Oh?' Moore settled himself close enough for confidences to be exchanged. Since the arrival of Charles, he had seen which way the wind was blowing and it was not difficult to add together Ralph's appearance and the knowledge that he had been with Theo to realize that a crisis had been reached. Not having been told of Theo's previous prevarication, he blamed her inconstancy entirely upon Charles and it grieved him that it should have been his ship that had brought the miscreant home.

Ralph did not reply immediately. The words he wished to use were so full of scorn and rage that, even in his desperation, he knew them to be unjust. He drank his wine in one and sat hunched forward, rolling the glass between his palms.

'This is between ourselves,' he said eventually.

'Of course.'

'I offered to play the part of a husband this morning and – I was not found worthy.'

It was what Moore had expected but hearing it spoken changed it from possibility to fact and a swell of sympathy rose in him as he contemplated the wrecking of Ralph's hopes. The ease with which his own courtship was progressing only made his friend's plight more poignant.

'Did she give you a reason?'

Ralph laughed. 'I don't think we need look far for that. No – she gave me no reason and no mercy.'

'But did she seem certain of her mind? A woman doesn't always accept at the first asking whatever her inclinations might be.'

'She was unequivocal. She said "I can't" – there isn't much to mistake in that.' Ralph set down the glass whose stem was in danger from his vehemence. 'But I'll persevere. I may not admire her judgement as I did before, I may not think her quite the prize she was, but I'll persist. When she comes to her senses I'll be waiting. I told her so.'

Moore raised his eyebrows. 'We all want our wives to be dutiful,' he said, 'but do you think it was wise to put it so plainly?'

'Am I to be criticized by you now?'

'You know that I support you. I'm merely suggesting that she may wish a more flattering approach. It's obvious that she's susceptible to blandishment.'

'I won't hear a word against her.'

'Perhaps if you took a leaf from Charles's book.'

'I'll be damned if I will!'

Ralph shut his eyes. Profanity was so rare from him that it jolted them and, for a moment, it seemed that the voices in the office beneath were being raised in protest at his oath.

The sounds of argument increased. They could not hear clearly enough to tell what had caused the quarrel but the high tones of a boy were asserting his innocence of some deed of which older men were accusing him. There was an element in the boy's declaration which reminded Ralph of Theo's passionate 'I can't!' and he rose abruptly, knocking over his glass, and strode towards the door.

'This behaviour here!'

He descended the stairs with Moore in his wake and entered the head clerk's room.

'What is this conduct?' he demanded before he noticed the presence of Mr Carnow in the agitated group assembled there.

His father met his eyes defensively. Despite his favouritism and anger over Ralph's attitude, a hint of guilt had disturbed him as he had lain awake repeating their last conversation in his thoughts. He was glad that their first meeting since his threats should be in circumstances which deflected attention from their personal relations. Seeing Ralph take command in this manner impressed upon him the contrast between the lives of his two sons and he wanted to show Ralph by his actions that the best interests of the mill were his goal.

'We have the thief,' he said.

A clerk gave the boy a push and he stumbled forward to stand facing Ralph and Moore, with a crescent of reproachful faces around him. His protestations had subsided as Ralph appeared and he stood, wide-eyed and awkward with adolescence, a hair's breadth from tears.

'Gilmore?' said Ralph, surprised. 'Surely not.'

'The marked coin was found in his desk,' Mr Carnow said. 'I was there. I saw it myself.'

Ralph addressed the miserable boy. 'Have you an explanation?'

'No, sir,' Gilmore's voice, already uncertain in pitch, was shaking. 'But I didn't take it, sir. Please, sir, believe me, I swear I didn't take it.'

'No one knew we were putting the marked coin amongst the petty cash,' said Mr Carnow. He indicated the chief clerk. 'Even Bryher wasn't told until he reported another loss just now and we began a search. And, as you saw, the mark was slight – not enough to be noticed by another thief and slipped into the boy's possession to incriminate him.'

'May I see?'

Mr Carnow passed a half-sovereign to Ralph who examined it. The row of three nicks above the queen's head were there, minute but indisputable to those who knew where to look.

'This is the second time in as many weeks there's been a theft,' Mr Carnow said. 'I won't stand for it. You – ' he prodded Gilmore on the shoulder, 'you wretched, ungrateful boy. I hired you for your father's sake. He was an honest man when he was alive. What would he think of you now, eh?'

'Sir, I didn't — ' To his shame, Gilmore began to weep and could not continue.

Bryher turned away in distaste.

'By rights,' Mr Carnow continued, 'I should put you in charge. The assizes would soon knock the villainy out of you.' He paused to let the boy's imagination work. 'Well, I'm no friend to a thief but you're all your poor mother has, God help her. You're dismissed. Don't let me see you here again.'

The boy gazed blindly about the room as if seeking some hitherto concealed source of support but finding none, fled through the connecting door into the counting-house. His judges could hear him stumbling as he collected his outdoor clothes and left the building. There was silence when he had gone. Although not strikingly intelligent, he had shown a willingness and good humour that had made him liked and the shock of his fall was greater because of it. There was an air in the room of not knowing how to resume normal life.

'Go back to your business, if you please,' Mr Carnow said and a general movement began.

Watching the men return to their stools, Ralph was struck by an absence that was growing more common. 'Where's Charles?' he asked.

Mr Carnow looked uncomfortable. It would have strengthened his case for his elder son if he had been found diligently at work on his accounts.

'He carried a message to your aunt's mill,' he said. 'No doubt she's delayed him there. These matters always take longer than we expect.'

'That would depend,' said Ralph, drily, 'on what our expectations are.'

With a glance at Moore, he turned on his heel and, carrying an atmosphere of contempt with him, left to discuss the safer storms of the Atlantic Ocean.

Mr Carnow had been mistaken in supposing that Charles had been delayed at Louisa's mill for, at the time that he had suggested this to Ralph, Charles had not yet begun to think seriously of carrying out his errand. During the dismissal of the unfortunate Gilmore, Charles was seated comfortably in the back parlour of the Bull ordering chops and had no intention of removing himself from his retreat until the chance of returning from Bridport before the day's work had ended was gone.

He was not feeling as satisfied with life as he had been the evening before. What he had seen as his success with Theo had distracted him from his predicament but the malaise following the previous night's festivities and the disconcerting revelation that Trent, whom he had thought securely in Australia, was barely a dozen miles away had had a lowering effect. He told himself, as he leant back in the settle, that Trent's proximity was of no importance but the element of the unexpected was unnerving. Beyond a fleeting mention by his father of the financial difficulties which had followed the fraud all those years ago, there had been no reference to Trent and Charles searched his memory for a hint in his mother's letters of there being a question in anyone's mind that the clerk had been guilty. None was to be found and he was confident that even had Trent been declared innocent no suspicion could have rested upon himself.

Nevertheless, discontent was beginning to work within him. Although he had spent more hours away from the ledgers than with them during his week of employment, the prospect of years of application to business was seeming increasingly dreary. An indulgent father who could be trusted to supply a stream of reasons for leaving the confines of the mill, as he had done this morning on discovering Charles in need of fresh air, was all very well but it did not provide the leisure of a gentleman. It was remarkable how a short period of freedom from anxiety could enlarge a man's desires. A month and a half separated the Charles who had sat in the inn at St John's drinking hot brandy with Moore and the Charles who was stirring the same spirit today, but the fears of the former could no longer be entered into by the sleek and rested figure of the latter.

He put one foot up on a chair near him and considered it. The memory of casting aside his boots on the first night of his voyage home with the certainty that his father would soon provide him with new remained with him and he smiled complacently at how right he had been. Mr Carnow had urged him to equip himself with all the necessities for English life and charge them to the family accounts. He had not needed to be told twice and articles from the lengthy lists taken by delighted tradesmen had begun to decorate his person. His smartness was now not the result of unceasing effort but was achieved carelessly by lifting the lids of tailors' boxes. Yet this transformation was not enough. Scrutinizing the foot upon the chair only served to feed his dissatisfaction. It was, he thought, a provincial boot. A boot which, while able to hold its own amongst the country gentry, would not care to be seen in the Row. With an irritable sigh, he recalled that there were gentlemen who would not accept his company, however he was shod, because of his connection with the mill. As an absentee owner he would find old money willing to turn a blind eye to how he came by his income but the active part he was expected to play in the industry would cut him off from the society he wished to have.

His musings continued throughout his chops and cheese and by the time he set out for Louisa's mill an idea he had begun to toy with the previous afternoon was growing increasingly attractive. The mill was on the riverside in the heart of the town and so he left his mount at the inn and went on foot through streets alive with the trade he despised. In the pale afternoon the fires in the netmakers' cottages threw warm light on tableaux of work scenes unchanged for centuries, except in details of furnishing and dress. Wagons, whose noise irritated him here as at Carnow, rolled past bearing finished ropes that would survive the Equatorial sun or the frozen spume on Greenland whalers. Great horses, their hoofs spiked or wrapped in sackcloth, breathed white smoke from gaping nostrils as they drew the wealth he coveted over cracking ice. He wanted power over this world but not to be part of it.

Entering the mill-yard, he asked at the outer office if Miss Farnaby was there, and on being told that she was in the netting shed he strolled unhurriedly across to it. He was bringing nothing more than a request that the manager would visit Mr Carnow, which could as well have been sent by a servant, but he felt no shame that his father should have given him such an excuse to waste his day and he had deliberately enquired after Louisa instead of Mr Wykeham in the hope that meeting her would lead to news of how he had affected Theo.

The noise inside the shed was distracting. In two rows of ten, twenty Jumper looms were braiding the cord made in the line-walk at the far side of the yard. Men, stony-faced with concentration, jumped rhythmically upon the treadles, compressing the springs that formed the slip-knots, and at the sight of Charles they exchanged glances with resignation or wry humour according to their temperament. The shuttles passed back and forth;

the completed fifty-yard pieces were carried to the lofts to be fitted and rigged. Charles walked down the rows, calculating more ably than he had yet been seen to do in the counting-house.

He saw the Farnabys before they noticed him. They were standing at the far end of the shed talking to Mr Wykeham and a braider, who was making intricate movements with his hands as if he were explaining a netting technique. Charles was surprised to see Theo for he had not suspected her of having an interest in manufacture. Her intensity as she watched the braider was startling. It was incongruous to see her here amid machinery and the stench of oil, standing with her shoulders braced as though she must brave an unwelcome duty and her gloved hands clenched upon a pocket-book.

The manager was the first to observe Charles's approach. His eyes met Charles's without giving an opinion and he said a word to Louisa. The braider stopped his explanation and the two women turned towards the newcomer. It gave Charles a start of pleasure to find Theo's face so white and tense. It flattered him that the previous afternoon should have had such an effect on her. Although she did not move, her posture seemed to show that her impulse had been to retreat from him and that she stood motionless against her will. That was, thought Charles, as it should be. It encouraged him in the plan he had been dwelling upon at the inn. He liked a woman to be drawn to him in fearfulness and it was useful that this one should be both passionate and malleable. The simplest solution to his need for money and leisure would be to take Theo for his wife and her possessions for his own. It could be done; her desire would make her too headstrong to listen to her aunt's advice and a husband who could not mould a girl to his whim with the advantages the law gave him was a poor man indeed. There was also the fillip of giving his brother pain.

He smiled as he reached the waiting group and made his greetings. Taking Theo's hand, he raised it with a continental flourish.

'My dear cousin,' he said, 'I can't tell you the benefit that this meeting confers on me.'

Chapter Eight

The Farnabys and Carnows did not keep Christmas with their usual gaiety. That Theo had refused Ralph was known only to themselves, Louisa, Moore and Maud – who was capable of keeping a secret confided to her by her lover – but the coolness between the pair was obvious. They behaved civilly towards each other in company and twice danced together at the festivities of friends, when not doing so would have excited remarks, yet there was an edge to their conversation, their tone and glances that made observers lean towards each other and talk behind their fans.

Theo was more wounded by their encounter in the summer-house than she let herself believe. She felt that she had lost Ralph's good opinion and it startled her to find how much that loss hurt despite the injustice of its cause. Her resentment did not lessen but she deliberately kept her anger alive to protect her from regret. She accepted that circumstances might have goaded him into more violent words than he would normally have used but it demonstrated thoughts that were not what she wished for in a husband. He did not think her his equal; he assumed that given the opportunity to fall from virtue she would take it.

It pleased her to see the acerbity that was beneath his urbane manner when they met. She wanted her independence to provoke and punish him. During the first week after her refusal she had sought to avoid his presence but she found that she had a strange compulsion to be near him. Their antagonism turned him into the stranger she had longed for months ago and, although if he were to offer again she would still decline to be his wife, she found him more alluring. Her excitement confused her desire to chasten him. She knew that she was behaving badly but the stimulating effect of her rebellion gave her a feverish energy and she steeped herself in the intricacies of the business whose profits had thrust her idle life upon her. The world that Ralph inhabited, but which had rarely entered the drawing room, began to be revealed to her and this too made him foreign. The curious combination of long hours of tedious administration, the frustrations of late payments, lost orders and delayed delivery of materials urgently needed to meet deadlines, the element of gambling, the responsibility for so many people's livelihoods, and the triumph of far-reaching trade intrigued her. She wondered why she had never joined Louisa in this adventure before. The disapproval with which her acquaintance watched her unfeminine investigations was more than compensated for by the interest it gave her and its destruction of her self-pity. She could not avoid concluding that, in a society which caged its women, it was better to be born into her own inactivity than into the life of a factory girl.

Her new appreciation of her own privilege did not give her a puritanical view of Charles. She did not realize that he was acting with discretion when they were together because he considered that restraint during these first months would be the best way to deceive and win her. His circumspection only seemed to make Ralph's accusations more odious and, to Louisa's alarm, she stubbornly fostered the idea that he had been misjudged by all except Mr Carnow. The memory of the undercurrents during the afternoon when they had roasted chestnuts was resolutely suppressed and she allowed herself to be entertained by him for the joint purposes of amusing herself and annoying Ralph.

If she had known how far beyond annoyance Ralph's emotion was, she would have thought twice about her conduct for she was not naturally malicious. There was a darkness in his spirit that had never been released before. His early disappointments, struggles and envies had not touched him as did the fear of losing Theo. Even his mother's death, which still grieved him, had not taken the salt from his meat nor made the progression of years the blank to him that it now was. He could not reconcile himself to the thought that she might not be his. The pain of wanting her when she did not want him held him in a maelstrom of vicious sensation so that, to appear normal, every action of his days needed the concentration of one who steers a storm-driven ship.

The jealousy aroused by seeing her conversing with Charles did not blind him to the fact that his brother was behaving courteously towards her and this made him afraid. He was not naive enough to think that Charles had a new appreciation of family life which was governing his manners. Even the little work that was expected of Charles must be galling to one of his habits and Ralph did not doubt that he had cast about in his mind for an easier way to become wealthy and decided upon one of the oldest methods. To Ralph, Theo was the beating of his heart but to others she was a mill and a bank deposit. The capturing of this particular prize would appeal to Charles above all others for, at one stroke, it would provide him with an appealing heiress, injure his brother beyond endurance and gladden his father, who still had ropeworks in his own gift.

There would be no use in warning Theo of his suspicions as she would think only that he was prejudiced. It was plain that she gained excitement from consorting with Charles and from spurning him. If she accepted Charles in a rash moment, he was sure that pride would keep her to her word and she would be lost to him. He had too active a character to wait patiently for her to realize what Charles was about, and, indeed, he no longer trusted her to do so, but he did not know how to go forward. He was too incensed by her behaviour to have control of himself when he was near her. A sharpness pervaded all his dealings with her and worsened his torment. He longed to need her less but her disdain served to make her more attractive and they began the new year with the bonds between them altered but unweakened.

The personal affairs of the masters might be in chaos but, close at hand, love-in-a-cottage was progressing steadily despite the handicap of one of its participants being oblivious to its existence.

It would have been unlikely that Barclay Hyde could have withstood the entreaties of any woman who had offered to work for him, so it was fortunate that Sadie Holman had applied to him first. The exchange of housekeeping for instruction had been just such a bargain as would interest him and Sadie was now firmly established in his home. Although she was not living in, she was spending more time at the schoolhouse than either of them had anticipated. She was fulfilling all his practical domestic needs from breakfast to supper while still caring for her family. He had grown to expect her presence and, if she was not there, was always half-consciously listening for her step on the path.

The lessons he gave her took place in the evenings when she returned from giving dinner to her brothers and sisters. In the early weeks she had been nervous and would sit listening to him with her hands folded in her lap and her eyes fixed upon his face, so that he blushed whenever he looked up at her, but as they became less of strangers they grew more easy with one another. The hours she was giving to his work were taking her from her braiding and gradually they came to sit together in the kitchen, the range open to give them firelight, with her nets spread over the floor. Her fingers moved the wooden needle back and forth amongst the twine, forming knots with mesmeric regularity, as her soft 'There now!' punctuated his tales of Roman heroes. If she were required to write, she would set aside her tools and grasp the pen, bending over the paper with such laboured concentration that the nib would splay like a deer's foot.

Barclay did not suggest she use a child's slate. Her eagerness for knowledge touched him and he did not want to humiliate her by any suggestion of incompetence. He had found his niche in teaching pupils at the school but they, like all children, did not see why they should be studying when there were games to be played and money to be earnt. It was a special pleasure to return to warm, quiet evenings with a young woman who thirsted for all that he could tell her.

He was happier at this time than he had ever been before. His isolated position of being neither a master nor a hand and the disrupted state of the Farnabys and Carnows meant that he had little society but it did not discourage a hope that he cherished within him. Since the day he had seen Maud walking through Bridport with Mrs Parris he had been infatuated by her. Her demure and delicate appearance was exactly what had always filled his romantic dreams. They had met several times in the lanes and once at her home when her parents had invited him to drink tea, and her kindness to him contrasted favourably with the daughters of his old colleagues. He was so unused to thoughtfulness towards him from women that he misinterpreted it, taking it for a far stronger inclination for his company than it was. His confidence had not yet increased enough for him to approach her with affection but week by week it seemed more possible. Unaware of Maud's yearning for wild seas, he dwelt upon the day when his mother's workbox would be opened by her hands.

He did not realize that much of his new boldness was being given to him by Sadie. The first sight of his helplessness had pulled at her heart as a child pulls its mother's skirts. Throughout her nineteen years she had not understood that she wanted someone to rely on her completely but when the call came she recognized it. The impulse that had drawn her to Barclay's gate on the afternoon of his arrival had not led her astray. Her wish for the joy of learning and her need for someone to be dependent upon her came together in the gentle tongue-tied scholar and she deliberately began to make herself indispensable to him. She wanted him for her own and it seemed too natural a desire for the difference in their station to deter her. Her family were old enough to do without her now, and the way seemed open for her to insinuate herself so deeply into Barclay's life that he would come to be unable to contemplate her absence. She was not daunted by his idolatry of Maud, whose very name turned him crimson, for she was aware of Maud's attachment to Moore. The thought of the pain he must suffer when he realized the truth distressed her and she filled his house with an atmosphere of love that nurtured him without being obtrusive.

On a windy morning in late January, she had set the schoolhouse to rights and, having returned to her own home to fetch it, was carrying her father's bread and cheese to him in the hackler's shed. The mill-bell rang at noon for work to stop for dinner but it was customary for a bite to be taken at ten and Holman liked his daughter to bring it to him. It was a raw day with the threat of rain and she walked quickly, her shawl about her brow and her pattens ringing on the stones. She did not notice the roar and drone of the mill for she had always lived there and it was the Sunday silence which seemed strange. Men were stepping out of doorways, bread in hand, looking at the weather and retreating inside with shrugs and a shake of the head. They called to Sadie as she passed, offering to relieve her of her basket, and she replied with sure saucy comments that were no part of Barclay's teaching.

Turning a corner beyond the warehouse she went into the room where her father spent his days. The wheelbarrow he used to fetch his materials was inside the door piled with white, glinting Italian hemp and he was bending over it drawing hanks of tow out of the tangled mound.

'Time for your old dad, have 'ee maidy?' he said, good-humouredly. 'A moment spared from that schoolmaster o' yourn?'

She pushed the shawl back from her hair and set down the basket. 'Maybe I can bring 'er to 'ee tomorrow or maybe not. That'll depend on how I d'feel about your nonsense.'

Holman laid the hanks across the rest of the hemp and rubbed his palms down the sides of his legs.

'Be my pot warmed? I be so cold as a frog.'

She took a cloth bundle from her basket and unwound the wrapping to reveal a stone bottle which she handed to him. He pulled out the cork and began to drink the hot cider with relish. His shirtsleeves were folded up, showing muscular forearms on which the hair was standing upright from the chill in the room. Setting the bottle down on his bench, he wiped his mouth with the back of his hand and reached for the onion she was passing him.

'Gal,' he said. 'Can't 'ee wait till I be a-sickening for summat afore 'ee go doctoring I?'

'I ent got the hours to be running about nursing of 'ee,' she said, firmly. 'There bain't nothing like a boiled onion to keep from—'

As she was talking, the door opened and she broke off as Ralph entered. She made her bob and Ralph nodded at her and her father.

'Is this the new consignment?' he asked, pointing to the hemp in the barrow. 'I came to see how well it cleans.'

Holman tossed the bitten onion back to Sadie, who caught it and returned it to the basket.

'That's the first of 'un,' he said. 'I were drawing out the hanks when 'twas ten, master, and Sadie come with my bread.'

'I won't keep you from it long,' Ralph said. 'Do one strick so that we know the quality.'

Holman lifted a hank from the barrow and stood behind the larger of two boards on his bench. Tall metal pins had been hammered through it at intervals and he began to beat the hemp against the wood, drawing it through the teeth so that the short stalks and debris were combed out. When the strick ran easily through the pins without needing to be wrenched, he moved across to the second hackling-board whose smaller teeth were as close as pine needles. The hemp flashed to and fro, catching the light as it grew clean and smooth, until Holman was satisfied and laid the finished strick along the bench for Ralph's inspection.

'A good buy, I think,' said Ralph, stroking the fibre and rubbing a strand between his fingers.

'Better'n the last,' Holman said. 'Less rubbish in 'er by half. That was best you changed the order, master. This'n will spin lovely.'

'Good. I'll leave you to your refreshment. Send word if any of the other parcels are not of this standard. I'll be at my desk all afternoon.'

Knowing that the new consignment of hemp was to be tried that morning, Mr Carnow had gone to the offices to consult Ralph on the subject and accompany him to the hackler. He was not entirely happy that their material had been ordered from another supplier for, though the efficiency of the firm with which they usually dealt had declined since it had passed to the nephew of their old merchant, he was suspicious and indecisive in the face of changes in trading practices. He had not stood in the way of Ralph's experiment but he wished to soothe his mind by visiting him to grumble about risks. Not having warned Ralph that he wanted to be present, he entered the building only to be told by a clerk, who was braving the elements in the doorway to eat his slice, that Mr Ralph was not in and had not said where he could be found.

Uncertain what to do now that his purpose had been thwarted, Mr Carnow hesitated in the corridor. He could hear the other clerks taking their few minutes' break in the counting-house and, without any clear reason, he decided to have a moment's conversation with Bryher. Not wanting to disturb the men at their rest, he did not go through their room but walked slowly along to the door into Bryher's office through which Ralph had come on the day of Gilmore's dismissal. He was more breathless than usual this morning and a tenderness in his calves had begun to be troublesome. Absorbed in his annoyance with these ailments, he pushed open the door and was met, not by the rising of Bryher meticulously wiping his pen, as he always did on transferring his attention to his employers, but by Charles who was closing the lid of a cash-box with one hand as he placed something in his pocket with the other.

'Good morning, sir,' said Charles, blandly. 'I found myself short of the ready. I needn't leave a note as I've told you.'

Mr Carnow eased himself into a chair and laid his fist against his chest. He felt a little disorientated by the scene. That the petty cash was reserved for business was almost a sacred matter and had served to prevent confusion over the years. It was unheard of for even himself or Ralph to take money from it for private use and he was disconcerted to find Charles helping himself in this casual way. Against his will, unsavoury questions came into Mr Carnow's mind and were pushed away.

'A note?' he said.

'Naturally I would have left a line saying what I'd taken. Bryher would be upset if he thought he'd made a mistake.'

'That – that was considerate of you, my boy.'

There was no trace of guilt or embarrassment in Charles's demeanour. It was true, thought Mr Carnow, that Charles had been from home so long that he might have forgotten the rules of the mill, or he may not have believed them to apply to the family. He had taken as grave a view of the previous – of the thefts as his father and brother had done, which showed him to have a proper appreciation of the serious nature of unauthorized appropriations. No, it was plain that his behaviour was innocent.

'I don't want to criticize, Charles,' Mr Carnow said, uncomfortably, 'but if you needed more money couldn't you have come to me?'

'That's generous of you, sir,' Charles looked his father directly in the eye, 'and so I would if I'd known where to find you in a hurry.'

'You wanted money quickly?'

'I ran into some old friends last night and they asked me to join them for lunch in the Greyhound at noon. We made rather an evening of it, going over reminiscences, and when I got up this morning you'd left the house. A man must have something in his pocket if he isn't to look foolish.'

'Then you haven't worked today?'

'No, sir,' an appealing consciousness stole over Charles's face. 'I have to admit that I was carried away by the pleasure of meeting men I'd known when we were lads together. They were happier days. I forgot myself. I hope you'll forgive me for it. I'll send word that I can't meet them.'

Mr Carnow rose heavily and put his hand on Charles's arm.

'No,' he said. 'All work and no play makes Jack a dull boy, eh? Maybe it's hard for you to change your habits all of a sudden. I don't hold it against you for wanting to talk over your memories. I'll ride in with you and say how d'ye do to your friends.' He laughed uncertainly. 'I'll not stay, so you needn't look worried. I daresay the young men don't want the old ones hearing all their doings now any more than they did in my youth. But, Charles, if you need money in the future you come to your dad, don't go borrowing.' He gave his son an awkward pat. 'We must think about raising your allowance. What I gave you can't stretch far and I'm sure you find uses for it. Come, the house is no place to be today. We'll go to town and take a glass before your friends gather.'

'It's as I found it when I returned, sir. There's almost two guineas missing and the door into the counting-house was locked. I leave the key in it during the day; anyone could turn it.'

Bryher spoke earnestly as he showed the cash-box to Ralph. His distress was obvious. There had been no incidence of dishonesty amongst the clerks, except the thefts by Gilmore, since the notorious forgery ten years before and, the miscreant having been dismissed, no new precautions had been taken to secure the monies that passed through the office. Having been promoted to his post after the arrest of Trent, Bryher was sensitive to any shadow that might be cast on his probity or wise management of affairs. He had hailed Ralph, as the latter entered the building, with a familiarity born of great anxiety and was displaying the rifled box with agitation.

'Do you suspect anyone?' Ralph's tone was severe but not

accusatory and it encouraged a garrulousness in Bryher that was not normally present.

'No. I came back to my room before the break had ended, as is my habit. There was no one here or in the corridor. I saw at once that my desk had been tampered with and discovered the theft. Naturally, my first thought was to question the clerks, which was when I discovered the locked door.' He set down the box and taking a handkerchief from his frockcoat rubbed the palms of his hands with it.

'The men showed no sign of being aware of anything untoward. They were as shocked as I. Morris had been standing at the outside door for a few moments but he'd seen no one but Mr Carnow and, of course, he would never – I blame myself. I do, indeed, Mr Ralph. After last time I should have made changes but with Gilmore gone . . . '

'You're not culpable.' Ralph was staring at the box as if its recent past was printed upon it for him to read. 'If anyone should have acted differently it was me. We were too hasty. I was a great deal surprised by Gilmore's guilt. It was out of character and yet I accepted the evidence. Well, we were mistaken and the boy's name is tarnished because of us. Unless we're the victims of a sudden rise of criminal behaviour, the thief is still amongst us. I think this has become a matter for the constables.'

A vision of upheaval, interrogation, and scandal caused Bryher a pang of distaste. He was a conscientious man and prided himself not only on the smooth running of the counting-house but on maintaining a personal, if limited, interest in his staff. It pained him to imagine suspicion resting upon them.

'I'm sorry to have to agree with you, sir,' he said. 'I'm reluctant to make the matter public but—'

A knock at the door interrupted him and, at Ralph's call, Ettie came in, a scarf neatly folded over her plain bonnet and her lips parted from brisk walking. She saw the situation immediately.

'I'm come with a message from Mr Carnow,' she said. 'It occurred to him, as he was leaving with Mr Charles, that the cash-box might cause puzzlement so he sent me to tell you that Mr Charles has borrowed from it with his sanction.'

There was a moment of eloquent silence as the men absorbed her words. The news was as shocking to them as discovering Charles in the act of taking the money had been to Mr Carnow and it had the addition of fresh humiliation for Ralph. The son who did not deign to work was the one whose peccadilloes were winked at. Ralph grew white at the temples and Bryher, aware of the implications of the scene, looked fixedly at his inkstand in embarrassment.

'Puzzlement,' said Ralph. 'Aye, he might well say puzzlement. Life is a quiz to us all.'

Ettie was standing with her hands demurely folded in front of her. She made a slight movement to retrieve Ralph's attention and he saw in her eyes that she had more to tell.

'I won't keep you from your business,' she said. 'Will you be lunching at home? There'll be only the two of us. Mr Carnow has gone into town with Mr Charles.'

Two hours later Ralph was at the dining table hearing Ettie's account of his father and brother's return to the house after the morning's incident. He had been brooding upon Charles's action and his mood was dark and decisive. Ettie had also drawn conclusions from her observations and, as she was in accord with his judgement, was not oppressed by the atmosphere he had carried into the room.

'I can go further,' she said. 'Mr Charles and I were alone for an instant while Mr Carnow changed his gloves. I asked him outright. "Did you take it before?" and he replied, "I never take what isn't mine."'

They looked at each other over the cloth. Ralph had dismissed the maid and they had the privacy of waiting upon themselves.

'What a girl you are for plain speaking,' said Ralph, coolly. 'I wonder if he knew that you would understand him.'

'Or that I'd repeat the remark to you. It's hard to say. He may be so confident of gaining the mill that he's already becoming careless but I think not. I doubt if he'd believe that a young female would have wit enough to see through him.'

She drank a spoonful of soup as she finished, the picture of docility, and Ralph laughed shortly. It was the first time that they had spoken so freely on the subject of Charles and it gratified him to find a partisan living beneath his roof. He knew that she was not to be swayed by her emotions; any opinion she held would be the result of scrutiny of the object in question and it made her words all the more pleasing.

It was as well, he thought as he reached for the salt, that he had found this comfort, for life at home could hardly be more irksome. It had long been the custom for springcleaning to begin early in the household and the disruption it caused was today added to the strained relations of the family. For reasons lost in the recesses of time, the disturbance was heralded by a simultaneous invasion of chimney-sweeps, workmen making general repairs and, oddly, the piano-tuner. It was partly the resulting turmoil that had driven Mr Carnow to grasp the excuse to flee into town and Ralph was not sorry he had done so.

If his father or brother had been present he could not have controlled his temper. On the occasion of the theft which had led to placing the marked coin in the cash-box, his suspicions had immediately flown to Charles but he had dismissed them as petty. Despite the low esteem in which Ralph held his brother's character, it had seemed to him beneath even Charles to stoop to pilfering, especially so soon after his return when their father's purse was open to him. Now the episode was made more squalid by Ralph's certainty that Charles was not only the thief but had used his knowledge of the trap to cast blame upon an innocent boy. He had, of course, no proof and must restrain the impulse to accuse Charles to his face. No, his next move should be different.

I am, he told himself as he rang for the mutton, grateful to Charles for showing himself to be so despicable. It needed such an act to rouse me from my patience. What have I been about? I should have defended my right from the time we knew he had come to settle.

He raised his head to look at Ettie. His place had been set at the side of the table where it had been since Charles's return and she was opposite him. The hall was full of the clattering of poles and brushes as the sweep was hushed and directed away from where the master was eating, but inside the room there was no sound. Ettie recognized the creative nature of his brooding and did not wish to distract him by questions. She had decided it was time he grew less passive and she was not to be disappointed.

'Will you carry another message to the counting-house?' he asked.

'Yes. What shall it be?'

'Tell Bryher that I'll be away for an hour or two. Nothing more.'

'And what is the something of which I may tell him nothing?'

He leant back in his chair. 'I intend to visit the Gilmores and reinstate the boy.'

Ettie nodded.

'You must be careful of what you say to them and to your father,' she said.

'Oh, I shall be more careful of myself and my words in future than I have been recently.' He reached into his pocket. 'And on that subject – is there a man from Scott and Brindley here today? I believe I saw their cart.'

'There is. He's seeing to the scratch on the bureau.'

'My aunt was saying to me only last week that she regretted having advised me to give up the head of the table to Charles; she thought it would be temporary – a gesture to a guest. And, indeed, I'm tired of the new arrangement.' He withdrew his hand from his pocket and opened the penknife he had brought out. Only a narrow cloth had been laid upon the table, wide enough to accommodate two people. He laid the point of the knife on the shining mahogany that flanked the linen and drew it towards him, scoring a long groove through the surface, then twisted the blade, driving it back so that the wood was gouged out. Calmly, he closed the knife and replaced it in his coat.

'There's been an accident,' he said, 'which will take a deal of repairing. More than can be done at home. Instruct Scott's man to take this table back to the workshop and let the round table from the library be brought in here!'

Chapter Nine

The March winds were not living up to their reputation as Theo rode out of Bridport towards Charmouth but there was enough movement in the budding trees to make the day lively. Despite the spikes of green in the hedgerows, there was not yet a feeling of spring in the cold air and the winter-bournes still ran noisily in courses whose summer dryness could not be imagined.

Theo was paler than she had been last autumn and there was a harder expression in her eyes. The mare she sat seemed to be in empathy with her rider for there was a nervous eagerness to increase her pace in her movements, a tendency to surge ahead and to react skittishly to slight alarms. Theo often rode alone now. Ralph no longer called on her or asked her to ride out and, when she was not deep in what she called her apprenticeship to the loom, the house seemed too confining. Life was bleaker than it used to be. It did not hold the comfortable family relations that had been unappreciated but sustaining, nor offer the choices for the future that had been too easily within her grasp to be attractive. She was lonely and because of it had become more brittle and aloof.

This morning she was acting as if there had been no loss of intimacy between the Farnabys and Carnows. Although there was not the easy communion between the households that there had been before Charles had returned, they still dined together regularly and Louisa visited to discuss business. It had grown increasingly apparent to the women that Mr Carnow's health was not what it might be but he had steadfastly refused to admit it and, his sons being too occupied by their antipathy to notice how much he was weakening, they had decided to take matters into their own hands. Mr Carnow's snorting derision of the idea that he should be examined by a doctor was to be overruled and ignored.

With a note from Louisa inside her habit, Theo had ridden to the home of their physician half an hour before, intent upon persuading him to pay an uninvited call on her uncle. His housekeeper having given her the alarming news that he was 'a broken leg in Chideock', she was riding in his wake with the hope that she could waylay him on the road as he came back.

Her endeavour was rewarded. She was holding in her mare, who was curvetting past a field gate in an attempt to take fright at the swaying elder that overhung it, when she saw the doctor's gig coming towards her. On being hailed, he stopped obligingly beside her.

'Dr Lloyd,' she said, 'I'm here purposely to meet you.'

He was calculating her health as she spoke. She was not as hearty as he wished her to be but he knew the gossip of the town and that her pallor came from a cause he could not cure. He had attended all her childhood fevers and considered her strong enough to survive troubles of the heart.

'Well, Miss Theodosia?' he asked, resting his whip across his knees. 'Are you a mump, a measle or an ague?'

'None of those.' She reached into her breast and brought out Louisa's note. 'I'm a conspirator. My aunt and I are set to bend you to our will.'

She leant down, holding out the letter, and, remarking that his good name would be worth nothing if he were found in clandestine correspondence with young women, he broke the seal and read it. Mr Carnow's symptoms and Louisa's belief concerning them had been put in a few lines and the doctor's acquaintance with the family led him to accept that there was reason for her concern. He knew that Louisa was not a fussing woman while Mr Carnow was a man whose sense deserted him in crucial areas of life. Though too forthright and bantering for the more tremulous of his patients, Lloyd was a humane man, and not one to deny such a request as the Farnabys were making.

'Did you plan to take me with you now?' he asked.

'If you'd be so good. Your housekeeper had no other call for you.'

'Then,' he said, '"lead on Macduff". And you must come into the mill to find our victim. It will be so much harder for him to refuse if you're there to report to your aunt.'

The news that the doctor had been seen entering the house with his bag and accompanied by Miss Theodosia spread rapidly through the mill. The health of the owners was naturally a matter of concern to the employees, and speculation, exaggeration and enjoyable pessimism embroidered the bare fact that Mr Carnow was closeted with his leech. By the time the story reached the brothers it was almost bordered in black.

Charles was the first to hear it as he sat on his stool in the counting-house and he immediately affected an anxiety which drove him to leave his task and repair to the house for information. Although he had not become a conscientious worker, he had been spending more time at his desk since the incident with the petty cash. He was aware that he had taken a false step in helping himself again from the same source and put this foolish move down to a recklessness born of boredom. It had amused him to make the first theft, knowing what consternation it would cause, and to slip the marked coin into the belongings of a boy who had not been sufficiently deferential to him, but it had not been worth the diligence he had had to feign since his father had caught him out. It was true that he had been able to pull the wool firmly back over Mr Carnow's eyes but he was aware that Ralph was not deceived, as the reinstatement of Gilmore showed. Ralph had not challenged him on the matter and the clerks had been told only that Gilmore's innocence had been discovered but there had been a sea-change in Ralph's behaviour that left Charles in no doubt that they were now active enemies.

In all aspects of their life, Ralph was behaving with an undeclared confidence that had not yet taken any particular form but existed as a subtle difference in their relations. As they sat at their round table, to which, by Ralph's private orders, joints were being carried already carved, there was a current of silent struggle to dominate the other diners and Charles did not deny that it could no longer be said who was sitting at the head.

Charles, himself, had grown more ambitious. He was behaving with circumspection because of the cash-box and his desire to win Theo's approval, but he was quietly altering his intentions. It would be well to marry an heiress but even better to have his father's mill as well as Theo's. Surely it could be done. If his father was still so besotted as to accept that there had been no guilt attached to Charles in the most compromising of positions, it was likely that he could be persuaded to let his favouritism bloom to a gratifying degree. Charles was biding his time to gamble for high stakes once more.

At the house the doctor and his patient were in Mr Carnow's bedroom – the one asking plain-spoken questions as he made his examination, the other answering in aggrieved and irascible tones – while Ettie poured tea for Theo in the drawing room. It had become rare for Theo to be there in her riding-habit. She had dropped her old custom of calling in casually, preferring to avoid complications by having Ettie come to her, and entered the house only to dine. Sitting as she was, with the scent of fresh air and leather caught in the folds of her dark cloth skirts, she was reminded of former days. Her boots and chamois trousers made her feel more alive and active than the satin slippers and low gowns she wore as a dinner guest. This sensation, coupled with her anxiety for her uncle, which seemed to have more cause now that it had been translated into the actual presence of a doctor, made her restless. She was fingering the fringe of the table-covering beside her when Ettie brought her cup.

'I'm sure there's no need to be agitated,' said Ettie, eyeing the nervous movements of Theo's hand. 'Mr Carnow may not be as flourishing as we would wish but no doubt Dr Lloyd can give him a tonic.'

'I hope you're right.' Theo took her teaspoon and began stirring unnecessarily, lifting it at intervals as if dredging for the sugar. 'Waiting for someone's good health to be confirmed brings all kinds of imaginings forward. And we must simply sit here alone and twiddle our thumbs.'

'We're unlikely to be alone for long,' Ettie had seated herself again and was attending to her own wants. 'The word of what's happening will have spread by now.'

'And you think my cousins will be concerned enough to come?'

Ettie set down the teapot and reached for the cream. 'Mr Ralph will be concerned and come if he can. Mr Charles will be glad to leave his desk.'

Her answer annoyed Theo. A more malicious remark from someone who was given to gossip could have been shrugged off but Ettie's clear judgement and practice of keeping her own counsel made her implied criticism damning. In her present state of mind, Theo would have preferred her companion to share her own confused and fevered attitude towards the brothers.

'You see more of Charles than I do,' Theo said, restraining her urge to reply snappishly. 'Hasn't your opinion of him softened at all?'

Ettie took up her cup.

'Strictly speaking, I couldn't be said to have had an opinion before his return. He was a legend to me; nothing else. But it's curious, the longer he stays the greater the strength of my memories of when I was very young. I dwell on them against my will and there seems to be – I hardly know how to describe it – a something which is just outside my grasp.'

It was so unusual for Ettie to mention her early years that Theo was startled.

'What kind of thing?' she asked. 'Does it involve Charles?'

'I couldn't say. It eludes me. I feel it's the key to a mystery but as there's no mystery to solve I'm no wiser.'

The sound of steps approaching the door prevented Theo from enquiring further. The oddity of the remarks from the level-headed Ettie intrigued her and caused her to look at Charles as he came in with a scrutiny he found encouraging.

He had assumed an anxious expression as he entered the house and, adjusting his voice to the slightly hushed accents of one who is showing courage in the face of unknown illness, he asked after his father without pausing to greet the women. His attitude was nicely calculated and he thought it becoming. Theo, whose irritation at Ettie's censure of him and interest in the girl's reaction to his presence had given her a readiness to find him beguiling, agreed. She explained the circumstances in a few sentences to which he listened, first with attention and then contrition.

'I should have done this myself,' he said. 'It's quite wrong that the burden of decision should have been on your shoulders.'

'It was principally my aunt.'

'Nevertheless, the ladies of a family shouldn't be wearied by these considerations. It was my part to take the responsibility.'

Theo mentally raised her eyebrows at the thought that she or Louisa might be overcome by the strain of summoning the doctor but Charles's discreet manner towards her during the past months was paying its dividend in biasing her towards him. She took his scruples as affectionate protectiveness and his first consideration being her comfort, not his father's, as a flattering compliment. It pleased her that, after years of neglecting his relations, he was taking his duties seriously. She glanced at Ettie but her face was a mask.

'Of course, one always thinks of one's father as so much stronger than oneself,' he said. 'That's my only excuse. It's impossible to think of a parent dying.'

Ettie turned her head slightly to look at the miniature of Mrs Carnow that hung on the wall. Charles affected not to see her.

'There's been no talk of dying,' Theo said. 'We were just made anxious by his breathlessness.'

The abrupt mention of death alarmed her but her wish to be kind made her voice calm.

Charles went abstractedly to the fireplace where he stood leaning on the mantel, gazing into the crackling flames, one foot raised on the rail about the hearth. He gave the impression of being absorbed in contemplating his father's mortality and indeed he was, but not in the fashion Theo believed.

He had not given his father's well-being any thought. It was true he had noticed Mr Carnow's ailments but only to find them tedious. He disliked having to dawdle beside his father when they walked together or being forced to listen to the gasps that afflicted the sufferer after any effort but he had not considered that these annoyances were more than changes to be expected with age. His own hopes and plans, resting as they did on Mr Carnow's emotional weaknesses, had occupied him too much for him to consider that illness might deprive him of his one sure haven.

As he stared at the glowing coals, he blamed himself for having made such slow progress towards financial security since his return. Theo was receiving his attentions willingly but he was not yet certain of her. If his father were to die it would be difficult for him to continue to court her for neither Ralph nor Louisa was likely to give him a home or income and he had no means to provide himself with either in the area. It would be prudent to begin to be more ardent in Theo's company and to cajole his father into altering his will.

He was cupping his chin in his hand and thinking how he could proceed when the sound of steps approaching was repeated and Ralph entered.

Ralph had heard the news of the doctor's visit from Bryher when the customer with whom he had been discussing dates had left his office. Bryher had divested the information of the dramatic details it had been gathering as it passed through the mill but the bare fact was enough to cause consternation. Despite his father's follies, Ralph had a sincere love for him and he was ashamed that the provocation Mr Carnow had been offering him over Charles had prevented him from giving a proper importance to the symptoms of failing health. Occasions when he should have suggested medical advice sprang into his mind to accuse him as he hurried, set-faced, to the house. Not knowing whether Mr Carnow had simply felt himself in need of reassurance or if a crisis had occurred, he arrived at his home in dread of what he might find. Following the voices, he hastened into the drawing room and discovering the family group instead of his father and the doctor could not tell if this were a good or bad sign.

'My father,' he said. 'How is he?'

'That,' Charles lifted his head from his hand and spoke sorrowfully, 'is what we're endeavouring to find out.'

Ralph addressed himself to Theo. 'Why are you here? Has there been an accident?'

The implication that she would call uninvited only because of catastrophe reinforced the disquiet she had felt earlier with the memories of her old easy association with this house. She disliked being reminded by him of their changed circumstances and took refuge in privately objecting to the shortness of his manner to her. Wilfully, she exonerated Charles, who had shown such a pretty concern for his father, and blamed Ralph for having left the fetching of Dr Lloyd to Louisa and herself.

'I'm glad to say,' she told him coldly, 'that there hasn't yet been any alarming incident. My aunt and I arranged this consultation in order to prevent one.'

'Then Dr Lloyd has come only to make an examination?'

Theo nodded. Charles wishing to see Ralph take enough rope to hang himself remained silent.

'Is it necessary?'

Even as he spoke, Ralph could have bitten off his tongue. He recognized the brusqueness of his tone and senseless nature of his question but he could not stop himself. They were the manifestation of an absurd hope that she would say 'No, we're all play-acting'. It was plain from Theo's expression, however, that she did not view them in this light.

'It would not have been necessary,' she said, 'if someone from my uncle's own household had thought to seek reassurance from Dr Lloyd sooner. It's extraordinary that no one's found his condition worth noticing.'

Despite the general condemnation in her remarks, it was obvious to her listeners that they were directed at Ralph. His self-criticism did not improve his temper in being taken to task in front of Charles and he sat down angrily in an armchair, crossing his legs as if delivering a blow to the air. He was aware that Charles was enjoying his discomfiture.

'Whatever mistakes have been made,' Charles said, 'at least we can now unite in attending to his welfare. That should improve upon his past circumstances.'

'Those who have harmed his peace of mind so severely in the past,' Ralph said firmly, 'would do well to improve.'

Not wishing to have this remark pursued in front of Theo, Charles did not reply immediately and was saved from having to find another approach by Dr Lloyd giving brisk orders to a maid in the hall, before joining the family in the drawing room.

'May I ring for fresh tea?' Ettie asked him.

'If it's for yourself, missy,' Dr Lloyd sat comfortably on the sofa. 'I'll take a little of my patient's fine sherry.'

'And my father, sir?' said Ralph, as a glass of wine was procured.

Charles took a seat close to Theo.

'We're most concerned about him,' Charles began, but having received a glance of undisguised scorn from the doctor decided not to continue.

'I found a slight dropsical condition,' Dr Lloyd accepted a sweet biscuit from Ettie. 'A man of Carnow's age and full habit may expect a certain weakening of the heart and the problems it brings. His lungs are congested and so he is breathless; his tissues are congested and dropsy begins to declare itself in the limbs. There—'

'Is the disease fatal?' Charles, anxious for his future, was unable to stop himself interrupting. Theo approved of the level of anxiety in his voice.

'Allow me to finish, sir,' Dr Lloyd again glanced meaningly at Charles and returned his gaze to Ralph. 'The malady is not yet dangerous and there's much that I can do to prevent it becoming so. A preparation of digitalis would reduce the enlarged heart and cause it to beat more properly – this would empty the lungs and tissues.' He paused to take an appreciative mouthful of wine and Theo felt a rising of relief that seemed to lighten her own heart. 'However,' he went on, 'I've met with an obstacle that often impedes me with gentlemen used to good health.'

Ralph uncrossed his legs and sat forward. 'He refuses treatment?'

'He does indeed. And I know how it will end. Without what he's described to me as the sweepings of the apothecary's floor he will worsen until he admits his need and I must begin my work upon a far weaker frame.' He turned to Theo. 'A man needs a wife, my dear, to govern him in these matters. What can any of us do when the ladies are against us?'

'My aunt and I will do what we can,' Theo said. 'And Ettie will be here – but, Dr Lloyd, can he be persuaded to nothing that will help him? Uncle Carnow is not usually—' Remembering that he had been foolish on occasion, she stopped short.

The doctor smiled at her confusion. 'None of us likes to admit that we're becoming frail. It's hard to hand ourselves into another's keeping. But I've begun my campaign with a suggestion that he has a change of air. The seed is planted and if he does try a resort or take the waters it may benefit him by the rest or confirm in his thoughts that he's ill and ease him towards treatment. Either result is to the good. And now,' he put down his glass and stood up, 'you and I, Miss Theodosia, will call on your excellent aunt.'

Although she had learnt that her uncle was sickening for a failing heart, Theo was freed from the vague fears of fatal disease that gather before a diagnosis is made. She was cheered by Dr

Lloyd's faith in the efficiency of digitalis and his confidence that Mr Carnow could be brought to take his dose before many weeks were out. As she and Louisa had sat listening to his reassurances, she had realized the weight of the barely admitted worry that had burdened her, and in her release from it was able to experience some excitement for the project that was on everyone's lips.

It was a topic which was being discussed, not only by the Farnabys and their visitor, but by much of the world. 'The Great Exhibition of the Works of Industry of all Nations' was now only six weeks away. An extraordinary structure of glass and iron was rising in Hyde Park to house the cornucopian variety of ingenious artifacts expected and exhibitors were waking up to the notion that what had been a dispute in the newspapers, a series of letters and applications and a conferring with their workmen and railway officials over the best methods of moving their prized manufactures was becoming an event liable to cause crowded excursion trains.

The Farnabys and Carnows were both sending equipment and products to the Exhibition. Louisa had entered the netting machine that Theo had stared at blindly on the day of Ralph's proposal and the tools and products of rope-making were to glorify the Carnows. Both families hoped that the resulting orders would make them bless Prince Albert's name.

The refreshing effect of the ending of suspense and the enlivening plans to visit London in order to admire their own possessions made Theo wake the next morning more like her old self than she had been for months. In her softened mood she remembered Barclay Hyde. Riding back to Bridport beside the doctor's gig the day before, she had heard the children chanting their tables as she passed the school and had felt guilty that she had not taken a more active interest in what was her own creation.

She was engaged until she had lunched but in the early afternoon she set out on foot for the mill. Louisa had already called on Mr Carnow and returned with the news that he was a little shaken by having a name put to his malady but adamant that he did not need physic. Having received this information, Theo did not intend to go to the house and hoped to be undisturbed by either brother.

There was less wind than there had been on the previous day and the road was beginning to dry after the rains of the week before. She gathered a bunch of the wild daffodils and primroses that grew in the hedgerow as she walked and bound them with a long stalk of periwinkle. It had been plain when he had been unpacking that Barclay liked his home to be ornamental and she thought that flowers would be welcomed.

She had almost reached Carnow when she saw Maud loitering towards her and, discovering that her friend had no purpose other than daydreaming out of doors, invited her to come on her own errand. Their knock at the schoolhouse was answered by Sadie, who told them that Mr Hyde was at his blackboard and who stood watching them as they went through the garden with a degree of calculation that puzzled them.

Barclay's services were required for the mill children only in the mornings and the women were confident that they would not be interrupting a lesson. Knowing from past experience that the great latch needed both hands to lift it, Theo passed her flowers to Maud to hold as she wrestled with the entry to learning. She was commenting over her shoulder to her companion as she entered that the door fastening was unsuitable for infants and it was not until it was too late to retreat that she turned her head and saw Ralph standing beside Barclay.

There was an initial similarity about the men as they first saw their visitors. An unguarded hunger lit their eyes but, though Barclay remained in a state of adoration obvious to all except its object, Ralph had drawn shutters over his feelings before Theo had taken another step. He would have preferred not to meet her today. Her pointed remarks about no one in his father's home summoning medical help rankled. He was pale from a night of anxiety and self-castigation but each time he thought of her blaming words, justifications of his conduct rose up. In the dark reaches of the night, when the doctor's optimism seemed groundless, he remembered bitterly the hopes he had had of Theo becoming his comfort and solace. Now, seeing her again, he wanted her no less than he had ever done but he despised himself for it.

He had come to the school that afternoon out of courtesy to Barclay, who, he was sure, would have heard the doom-laden rumours concerning Mr Carnow's health and whose gentle soul would need to be put at ease. Like Theo, he felt guilty that he had not paid Barclay more attention and the sentiment had not been decreased by finding how genuinely sorry Barclay had indeed been to hear that there was illness in the family. The scant attention bestowed on him by the Farnabys and Carnows had appeared great to the lonely young man and had seemed a strong bulwark between himself and his solitary past. Both Theo and Ralph would have been surprised to realize how happy Barclay was at that moment with them both calling upon him amongst the desks where his talent was thriving, with Sadie close by in his home and Maud, demure and sweet, smiling at him over the bright flowers she carried.

Finding the company unable to begin a conversation, Maud held out the posy, still cool and fresh in its brilliance, to the large-eyed Barclay. She was so absorbed by Moore that she was the only one who had not noticed the affection Barclay harboured for her and her behaviour towards him was always of kindly innocence.

'These are for you, Mr Hyde,' she said. 'To bring the spring into your parlour.'

In her sensible walking-costume, she was not quite the vision she had been in her tear-drop bonnet but to Barclay, as he took the flowers with shaking hands, she could have been Aphrodite. His shyness prevented him from expressing his gratitude as fully as he wished and his thanks alerted Theo to his belief that they were from Maud without enlightening Maud herself. He touched his face to the blooms for their faint, green scent and closed his eyes.

'Should we find water for them?' Maud asked.

'Yes,' Barclay roused himself, 'we should, Miss Parris, if you would . . . There's a can of water, a jar . . . ' and talking incoherently of twigs, catkins and drawing from life he led Maud to the corner where the necessities for instruction on botany and art were stored.

'Do you think,' said Theo softly when the pair could no longer hear her, 'that love and reason can ever exist in the same person?'

There was a jolt in Ralph's heart; a physical sensation of hope. It seemed to him that her question was an acknowledgement of her own caprice; a recognition of how unwise she had been to encourage his brother and refuse himself. The harshness he had cherished for her fled from his mind. He wanted to gather her to him but a tenderness for her in the difficulty of her revelation made him cautious.

'No,' he said, gently, 'I don't think it can. It's too much to ask. We've simply to trust that we're forgiven for the follies we commit in love's name.'

His voice was low and his words undisguisedly directed at their own tribulations. They were, to all effects, alone for the couple at the far end of the room had turned their backs for Barclay to show Maud the route to Newfoundland on the globe. Theo shivered at the sudden intimacy that had come upon them. He had not asked for her forgiveness but he desired it and she was shocked by the warmth it gave her to know he felt himself in the wrong. Her resentment did not clear as his had done but she was willing to be spoken to further in this vein.

'Should we ask outright to be forgiven?' she said. 'Or should those we've injured see our meaning and reach out their hand to us?'

'Theo, I—' Ralph was moving to be nearer her when the door was drawn open and the privacy of all four was shattered. Sadie entered. Her eyes, confident but wary, went first to the navigators, who left their travels and came back towards Theo and Ralph, Barclay carrying a glazed jar filled with flowers.

'I d'come to see if you'rm bringing your callers to the house, sir,' she said, addressing Barclay. 'If you'rm wanting any refreshment.' She glanced about the shadowy schoolroom. 'There bain't no comfort for 'em here.'

Chapter Ten

The Great Exhibition, which was enthralling the world with its imminence, served as a diversion even to the Farnabys and the Carnows. They could not be said to be living in harmony but the pervading excitement in the town and the arrangements for their parts as exhibitors and excursionists kept their conversation, if not their thoughts, from more dangerous matters.

There had been a threat of thunder in the air when Mr Carnow had suggested that Charles, instead of Ralph, should travel up to London before the opening to supervise the setting up of the family machines. He was afraid that Charles was finding his work tiring and thought that being amidst the bustle of preparations at the very heart of the venture would be stimulating for him. Charles, although tempted to put his brother's nose out of joint in this way, felt that too many unavoidable and tedious labours would stand between himself and the pleasures of the city for the journey to be worthwhile. He declined the offer before Ralph needed to become firm, saying that his knowledge of the business could not rival Ralph's. Mr Carnow thought his decision graceful.

Ralph's immediate action on returning to Dorset was to call on the Farnabys. His excuse was a need to assure Louisa that her exhibit had been successfully put together but the truth was that he wanted to see Theo. Since their conversation in the schoolroom, his optimism about their future had begun to revive and he hoped for a reconciliation. He told himself that it was slightly to his shame that he was prepared to forgive her previous behaviour on so small a pretext as an oblique apology but the fact was that her words had been the spark that starts the forest fire. The renewal of expectation had been like the daze of first love and he had been moving towards a declaration with caution. He recognized how difficult Theo's admission must have been and he was afraid that a clumsy enthusiasm for her contrition would embarrass her into a second withdrawal from him. When they met, he was more gentle towards her but had not yet spoken out.

Today, the news he brought of the tumult in London carried them over what awkwardness still lay between them.

'And will everything be ready?' Louisa asked. 'Is it going forward as planned?'

'Our exhibits are there,' said Theo. 'That should be quite enough to quicken the world.'

They were sitting in the drawing room, which was so bright with April sunshine that one of the blinds had had to be lowered.

'The leak in the roof has been attended to,' Ralph said, 'or rather the commissioners have said that its extent had been exaggerated. We may make of that what we will. The painters are painting again and the carpenters carpenting, so the building may be finished. They struck work when their break for tea was cut from an hour to a half. But it'll be a miracle if all the objects are unwrapped by Mayday. The place is chaos. The makers of packing-cases must be happy men from here to Timbuctoo.' He helped himself to another slice of walnut cake. 'May I have another cup? I haven't lunched.'

'Didn't Ettie have something waiting?' Louisa asked, as she poured. 'That isn't like her.'

'I haven't been home. My horse was left for me at the station and I came straight here.' He glanced at Theo as he took his cup. 'I thought you would want to hear that all was well.'

Theo busied herself with the spirit-lamp that was keeping the water hot. She was flattered that he had come there before Carnow but she did not want to meet his eye when his meaning was so obvious. Although she could not forget the assumption of superiority there had been in his reaction to her refusal, she had softened towards him since he had acknowledged himself at fault. She was no longer eager to hurt him as a punishment for his suspicions of her, but she could not return the depth of feeling that was now once again showing in his face. It puzzled her that since that day in the schoolroom he had made no further attempt to win her and she was vexed to find herself disappointed despite a continuing wish for independence. She was glad that they were nearer to the friendship they had had before love had disrupted their relations. It was useful that the Exhibition was happening at this time for it gave them a bridge over the quicksands of their ordinary speech. She used it now to avoid commenting on his last remark.

'Are the exhibits wonderful?' she asked. 'What did you see?'

Ralph would have preferred a more tender reply to being told how he had hastened to be with her but he appreciated that they were chaperoned and could not express themselves freely. She was at least showing an open interest in his activities which she would not have done a few weeks earlier.

'There were wonders,' he said. 'What kind would you have? I saw trees under the glass roof that looked no taller than orchids in a hot-house. There's to be a crystal fountain that – no. I won't describe the building to you. Let that be a surprise. I saw an electric telegraph wire from Birmingham a mile long – the greatest length ever drawn – and a jar of honey from Mount Hymetus. There's iron from the forests of Sweden and a piece of native gold from a Russian prince that weighs more than six pounds. There are more marble figures with less clothing than can be imagined – and that reminds me.' He paused to take the cream that Louisa was handing him. 'I heard a most unfortunate thing. There was a decorator in St James's Street – and being so near he must have thought there'd be no problems with transportation. He'd just finished a fine specimen of his art on glass in gold and arabesques for the Exhibition and had it placed on a van to take to Hyde Park, but before it could be tied down a gust of wind lifted it quite off the van and dashed it on the pavement. One of the great panels was smashed into a hundred pieces.'

'Were you told what he said upon the occasion?' asked Theo.

'I wasn't but no doubt it was educational.'

'I think my vocabulary would have nothing strong enough for such an occurrence.'

'That,' said Louisa, 'is as it should be or I've failed in my duty.'

Theo leant back in her chair, biting small pieces from a finger of biscuit. She was infected by the common excitement of being at the hub of the world that was gripping her countrymen. It stirred her to be with one who had just been amongst the clamour and animation of the final preparations, as she had been stirred by Charles's tales of his travels. She felt that Ralph had brought the tumult of the city back with him to hurry her blood.

'Did you make sure of our accommodation?' Louisa went on.

'Yes, I checked the booking directly I arrived,' he said. 'And it was as well we wrote for the rooms months ago. Beds are like gold-dust. It would do us no harm to be in the hotel business at the moment.'

'I wish we were going for longer,' said Theo. 'It doesn't seem enough time.'

'Speaking for your uncle and myself,' Louisa joined Ralph in a second piece of cake, 'one day walking round will be ample for our feet.'

'And it will be open until October,' Ralph said. 'If you wanted to go again I could take you. I'd like to show you how much there is to see.'

Theo did not want to encourage him but the prospect of their expedition made her smile as if she welcomed his offer.

'Let's look forward to our present venture first,' she said. 'I think it will be a day to remember.'

The Exhibition was opened by the Queen on the first of May with striking pomp and pageantry and the following week saw the Carnow and Farnaby party take the London train to view the assorted marvels of the world. They were to pass two nights in the dark and comfortable family hotel known to their grandfathers in order to have an entire day to enjoy the spectacle. The group assembled, with rather more anticipation than elbowroom, in the first-class carriage consisted of Theo, Louisa, Ralph, Charles, Mr Carnow, Ettie, Barclay and Maud. The last three appreciated their good fortune in being taken as guests for, despite the reduction in the price of entrance to the Crystal Palace from a sovereign to five shillings, the overall cost of the jaunt was considerable. Barclay, particularly, was delighted by Theo's kind remembrance of him and harboured a suspicion that it had been Maud's prompting.

Theo was surprised by her own light-heartedness as they left the hotel the next morning. It could not, she thought as she climbed into the first of the four-wheelers they had ordered, be simply the change in their surroundings for she had no argument with her home beyond the strained affections that had entered it. Her spirits were always raised by travel but a single day in the city would not normally be diversion enough to make her so pleased with the world.

She was sitting with her aunt, uncle and Ralph. They had not set out for Hyde Park until shortly before ten for Mr Carnow had felt the journey to London more than he had expected but, even with the late start and concern for its cause, the mood in the vehicle was cheerful. It must be the occasion, she told herself, which is making me so easy in my mind. Our usual constraints and antagonisms have been put aside for this excursion. We smile at each other and speak pleasantries; the relief is invigorating.

Behind her, in the second carriage Charles was not sharing her contentment. It was a torment to him to be in London without the freedom to occupy himself as he chose. He felt degraded by their old-fashioned accommodation and by jolting through the crowded streets to a glorified fair in the company of two great girls and a besotted youth. The effort he had been making to deceive Theo with patient discretion was working but he was bored and tired by it. He was not yet sure that she would accept him if he offered and the thought of the persuasions he must use before he could secure her income made him sour. It irked him that the previous months of exertion must be followed by weeks more, but it must be done. The diagnosis of his father's complaint had concentrated his mind upon the need to secure a competence. The realization that Mr Carnow might die before putting his regard for his elder son into legally bound benevolence had brought back some of the fear of the future he had felt in Canada. He had intensified his friendliness towards his father, demonstrating a touching concern at every opportunity, but the proper moment to suggest a change of will had never come. It was imperative that he should provide for himself without the necessity of sitting in the counting-house and he had decided upon this day as the beginning of the change from agreeable companion to lover in Theo's eyes.

The annoyance at having to go to such lengths for his fortune was making him reckless. He was uniformly civil and considerate when with Theo or his father but spite was showing itself in his attitude to others. Despite his downfall in New York, he had not sufficiently learnt the lesson that a disguise must be worn at all times if it is to be effective. Seated in the dusty carriage, out of sight of those he wished to impress, he felt no need to make a pretence of good humour.

His three fellow travellers paid no attention to his silence. Neither Maud nor Ettie had been in London before and were occupied in seeing all that they could through the small windows of the vehicle. The glass had been let down and the sounds of the traffic, the street-sellers calling their wares, the altercations between barrow-boys and the drivers whose way they blocked came clearly to ears unaccustomed to such mobbing and activity. Barclay, who had explored the city as a student and who had been taken, when a boy, to the zoo by his guardian in the hope that the curiosities there would give him an interest in shooting, was able to answer eager questions put to him by Maud about their route. Her smiles and exclamations were a tonic to his shyness and her hand upon his sleeve as she pointed out to him the flags and gaieties of the scene astonished and transported him.

Ettie sat more quietly than Maud. Alert and observant, she was leaning forward, one hand on the rim of the window, in order to absorb as much of the scene as she was able but it was not her nature to be as demonstrative as a young woman whom life had never injured. Nor was she completely engrossed by the novelties about her. The strange sensation of being within the grasp of the key to a mystery that had been growing in her mind since Charles's return was strongly upon her this morning. She could smell violets and though this scent had never troubled her before, today it was raising a confusion of memories of her early childhood. Images of her mother came into her thoughts, snatches of summer afternoons charged with fevered and unexplained expectancy, of whispers and shut doors, of a soft, female voice saying, 'Hush now, it was only a dream'. This rise of remembrance disturbed and intrigued her. She did not struggle for the meaning of the flood but, like the pike lying poised amongst the streaming weeds, she waited for the flow to bring her what she sought.

Beside her, as they drew near Hyde Park and the carriages crawled more slowly amongst the congestion, Charles could barely restrain his irritation. The nervous excitability arising from his proposed usurping of Theo's affections made him more than usually intolerant of naive conversation and the sight of innocent love. It was impossible for him to sit calmly enduring the pleasure of the other three without showing that he despised them.

'I wonder,' he said to Maud, when she turned from the window to ask Barclay another question, 'what Moore would think if he could see you flirting now?'

The remark froze Maud's query on her lips. Her eyes showed her to be startled and distressed by this interpretation of her behaviour. Barclay, too, was taken aback. Knowing only that Moore was a friend of Mr Parris, he was not cast down by the coupling of the captain's name with Maud's but he resented the implication that there was something improper in what was being said. He was afraid of Charles's sleek self-confidence but he was not prepared to leave Maud undefended. Blushing deeply, he said, 'Sir, you're offending Miss Parris. I must ask you not to . . . '

He was unable to frame a suitable conclusion to his request and his words were left hanging a little lamely. Maud and Ettie, however, appreciated how much the effort had cost him and united silently in his favour.

Charles inclined his head sarcastically.

'I wouldn't offend a school miss for the world,' he said. 'And, after all, we're among friends. We're a family party. Or part of a family.' He faced Ettie. 'What a shame your father couldn't be with us. But we could send a souvenir to the prison. I saw a "Moral and Religious Guide to the Exhibition" advertised.'

Ettie returned his gaze coolly. 'Would you recognize such a guide?' she asked.

Charles raised his eyebrows. He had not expected his jibe to be met with such sang-froid and did not have a ready answer. It was Ettie who spoke next.

'Are you wearing violet pomade?'

The question disconcerted him. He was, indeed, wearing the preparation in his hair and had chosen it for that day from pure devilment. It had seemed to him an excellent joke to array himself for the charming of Theo with the scent he had worn to disguise his affair with Ettie's mother. Under Ettie's steady gaze, he felt absurdly guilty and wondered just how good her memory was. The care he and Helen had taken to hide their secret from adult eyes had not been extended so scrupulously where the infant Ettie had been concerned. If she remembered enough to put two and two together it would be disastrous for him. The revelation of his past intrigue was the last thing he needed with Theo unsecured – but, no; it was ridiculous to think he had been discovered. He became conscious that all three were staring at him.

'I am,' he said. 'Do you have an objection?'

She did not reply. Turning as if to resume her observation of the street, she dwelt on her own question. She had always associated that scent with her mother. Her mother's shawl which she had brought with her to her new home with the Carnows, where it had been folded away as too fine for a child, had been so strongly perfumed that for several years the air became sweet with violets whenever she laid back the tissue to look at it. The Bible with her mother's maiden name inscribed inside had the fragile flowers pressed between the thin leaves, yet neither plant nor scent, wherever encountered, had awoken the tumult of reminiscence that had come today. She let the puzzle sink into her mind to be mulled over.

In the first carriage, Theo felt a mounting excitement. The street was so crowded that the horses were walking more slowly than she would have done herself on a clear footpath. They were passing families, in Sunday clothes that were too warm for the bright morning, weaving their way through the increasing press of food- and trinket-sellers, obviously bound for the same destination. The smell of fried fish and hot mutton pies hung thickly in the air. A woman mopped the jacket of a boy crying over spilt gingerbeer, lifting her face to her husband to mouth words that were plainly to the effect that they were not even there yet and look at him! Flags were strung gaily across windows and the sound of a distant band was heard above the din.

She felt ready to admire everything and like everyone. Ralph was sitting opposite her, watching her as much as their route, and she smiled across to him more naturally than she had done for months.

'I think,' he said, 'that if you lean out you could see the building from here.'

Sliding forward on the leather seat, she put out her head to crane over the jostling multitude that hampered them. When she drew it in, her eyes were full of amazed delight.

'It is,' she said, gazing around at all three. 'It is a crystal palace!' She looked at Ralph again with mock accusation. 'And to think you said nothing of it. Not a word.'

'If I had,' he said, 'it would have been no better than a newspaper description. I really couldn't have pictured it for you, could I?'

'It might be made of ice,' she said, wonderingly. 'Or fire where the light is dazzling.'

An omnibus forcing a passage between them and the park railings ended her view until they had drawn to a halt. Ralph climbed down and handed the party on to the road. Encouraged by Theo's mood, his own spirits were high. He hoped that this excursion might mark the beginning of a new and open love between them by removing them, for a time, from the tainted atmosphere of home. It was his intention to keep her to himself and have the pleasure of guiding her to all he knew would interest her most. A heavy pressure on his arm distracted him from these thoughts and he collected himself to see his father having difficulty with the step.

'Take my other hand as well, sir,' he said, offering it. Mr Carnow grasped it and lowered himself awkwardly on to the ground. He had woken that morning more exhausted than he had thought possible after a day's travel and the erratically paced journey to Hyde Park had made him breathless. Hours of parading past exhibits in the heat of a glasshouse seemed a feat beyond his endurance but he was too embarrassed by his weakness to admit it. Mentally he cursed Dr Lloyd as if the physician had caused his condition by diagnosing it. Taking off his hat, he fanned himself with it while still holding one of Ralph's hands.

Louisa, who had been shaking out her crushed skirts, looked at him keenly.

'Are you quite well?' she asked. 'Would you rather go back to the hotel?'

He shook his head emphatically. At that moment there was nothing he wanted more than to be sitting quietly in a cool room, but he would not admit it.

'No, no,' he said, with a forced smile. 'The heat of a closed carriage – a little exercise and air.'

The arrival of the rest of their party prevented a detailed enquiry into the true state of his health. Maud rustled to his side in such a shower of exclamations and thanks to her hosts for bringing her to witness the spectacle that Mr Carnow was able to ignore his family's concern in complimenting her on her exuberance. There was a general feeling amongst the visitors that her unqualified enthusiasm was the proper attitude on entering the Exhibition. The throng moving towards the main door began to carry them with it and the atmosphere of amusement was so great that Charles was able to gather himself under its cover before his relations had noticed that he was unsettled. He glanced at Ettie as he followed Theo but she was concentrating upon the remarkable building and gave no sign of being aware of him.

The air of festival and holiday imbued Theo as they went into the main hall. She had been so relieved by the lessening of tension amongst them that, unconsciously, she was shielding herself from anything that might detract from her felicity. Her back had been to her uncle as he was helped from the carriage and her ears had been too full of the babble of voices, the hum of machines, the strains of music and flashing of water for her to notice the conversation behind her. As she stood in admiration, gazing at the creeper-hung galleries and the great crystal fountain that glittered with prismatic spray, her eyes dazed by the sharpness of the sunlight glinting through the vast glass roof, it did not seem unnatural that Mr Carnow should be holding the sleeve of the son he did not value.

She wandered with her group towards the Machinery Court to see their own exhibits, too struck by the noise and number of people and objects to walk purposefully or take in what she saw. The artifacts were equally lost on Barclay. Maud, who did not want to impose herself too much upon the Carnows and Farnabys and who was touched by his defence of her in the carriage, had accepted the offer of his arm. She was strolling with a little affected bravado to show Charles that her familiarity with

Barclay was so innocent that she could display it to the world. To Barclay, it seemed that life had nothing more to give.

They stopped so often to comment on novelties that the morning was gone before they had examined their presentations and basked in the remarks they overheard. Despite the obvious success of their manufactures, their satisfaction was not complete. Louisa and Ralph were concerned by Mr Carnow's laboured breathing, which his protestations of good health did nothing to hide. It had been necessary for Ralph to support his father on their slow promenade and his intention of pairing with Theo had had to be set aside. He accused himself of selfishness in his disappointment but it was consoling to know that Theo must see that he was tending to Mr Carnow as she would wish. She could not criticize him for neglect as she had done when she had summoned the doctor.

Charles was also discontented. He looked out of place amongst the implements of trade and, as he walked in the wake of the group, his determination to use Theo to remove himself permanently from the proximity of cog-wheels hardened. There had not yet been an opportunity to draw her away from their party but he stalked her, alert for his chance.

It came as they returned to the central avenue in search of refreshment before exploring another section. Theo, who had wondered slightly that Ralph did not seem to have the zest for pointing out curiosities that she had been expecting, was drifting behind Barclay and Maud in a hot and dreamy state. Her head was swimming from the commotion of machinery and press of visitors. Because of the crush, she had not raised her parasol but at that moment the sun seemed so glaring that she stopped to open it. The catch was awkward and she was left a little behind the rest as she stood still to attend to it.

Mr Carnow, too, was feeling the heat. Try as he would, he could not seem to take in enough air and his swollen legs were painful. His replies to enquiries about tiredness had become testy and the arm that had merely lain along his son's to steady him was now dragging at Ralph like a dead-weight. As they emerged into the main hall and the thought of the further exertions before him struck home, he felt bile rise to his throat and a giddiness overtake him.

'Must sit down,' he said to Ralph in a whisper. 'Don't alarm – must – '

He was subsiding as he spoke. They were at the foot of a flight of stairs to a gallery and Ralph, a pang of fear in his own heart, grasped his father firmly by the waistcoat with his free hand and turned him so that his bulk was lowered gently on to a step. Louisa came forward, removing the silver top of her sal volatile bottle to hold to his nose as Ralph undid his cravat. Ettie began to make a breeze with her pocket-book and beckoned to Maud, whom she knew to have a small fan. All was done with silent rapidity and caused no stir amongst the flow of visitors.

Charles, looking over Barclay's shoulder, saw the colour coming back into his father's open-mouthed face and the vagueness go out of his eyes as he smelt the salts. It was not then, he decided, a catastrophe. Indeed, quite the reverse for it would occupy the others long enough for him to remove Theo without exciting remark. He strode quickly to where she had mastered the folding-stick of her parasol and was opening the silk canopy. Standing to prevent her having a clear view of the stairs, he asked, 'May I show you the arts? The others are going on to the chemical substances. Or perhaps the civil engineering. They don't know which to do first.'

A glance at what she could see beyond Charles and the people passing between them and her family showed their party in a huddle apparently discussing where to proceed. Neither of their choices held much fascination for her and the notion of going to a display which involved less noise was attractive.

'We can all meet again at four,' said Charles, 'as we agreed.'

It had been arranged that they were to gather where they had come in if they became separated and mentioning this seemed to add force to his suggestion, as though dividing into different groups had been expected. Thanking him, she took his arm and he led her resolutely through the crowd. Within minutes, they were out of sight of the staircase and as much alone, in the myriad strangers, as if they were marooned at sea.

It seemed to Theo that their situation was more intimate than any they had been in since the afternoon of the chestnuts. Walking at his side, with her glove pressed between his arm and body, she felt conscious of every movement of her limbs as if she were learning to skate on ice. Lost in the crowd, they were free of the knowing eyes that followed them on their home ground, recording each nuance of their meetings to pass on into the web of gossip that wraps about a town. She did not like Ralph's acquiescence in this liberty. It aggrieved her that he had not objected to her being with Charles in this way and, against her will, a degree of sourness entered her good humour and made her compliant to Charles's direction.

Charles's own pulse was swift. The months at Carnow had not exercised his faculty for cunning and duplicity to the full. His immediate acceptance by his father and the mild manner with which he had been lulling Theo had been too easy to satisfy him. At this turning-point in his relations with Theo, there seemed to be a surging in his blood as he prepared to mould her to his will. Confidence excited him. Memories of old deceptions heightened his expectancy and enlivened his face. He did not yet change the restraint of his manner towards her but when she looked at him his eyes seemed narrower and more piercing than they had been before.

Theo let herself be led and he guided her on a route that he had chosen to put distance between themselves and their party but which seemed to be a thoughtful tour of the best of the sculptures. He paused before a block of marble dug from the quarries used by Phidias and repeated anecdotes of ancient Greece that had always served him well as a display of culture and sensibility. He was sprightly beside a figure of Puck and reverential under the electroplate brilliance of a silver Iron Duke. A bronze lion, with paws turned out like a dancing-master's feet, made him frivolous. Knights in shining armour brought a nostalgia for the days of chivalry. To remind her of their shared appreciation of Italy, he lingered amongst the works from Milan and admitted to a painful emotion at seeing them exhibited as Austrian. It caused him regret, he said, for a country to which Europe owed so much to see her genius in art, her chief glory, appropriated with her territory by conquest. No one could enter the Milanese sculpture room without a sorrowful feeling and the same sense of injustice – sentiments which, had Theo not been made soporific by heat and tiredness, she would have recognized from a newspaper description only three weeks before.

In the course of time, they found themselves in a transept in the dappled shade of elms. There were open courts around the trees where fountains played in marble basins and goldfish swam in the glittering waters. Tables were set out for picnics and Theo sat at one as Charles went to fetch lemonade.

It was quieter here. The couples and families resting beneath the leaves spoke in sporadic murmurs as they sat. A green light flecked with brightness flooded the ground and its stillness puzzled Theo until, looking up through the mounting branches to glimpses of the glass roof, she remembered with a smile that there would be no wind to stir it. She slid her thin silk shawl off her shoulders so that it rustled down to trail upon the floor. It would not do to uncover her head in such a public place but she undid the ties beneath her chin and, taking off her gloves, leant to dip her fingers into a pool and touched her cool, wet hand to her throat.

This place seemed secret and separate from the turmoil all around. The noise and bustle encircled the sanctuary but the spreading shade was an oasis of restful calm. Theo relaxed into the atmosphere of tranquil leisure; there was a feeling of duty done in having seen so much and a deserved reward in being seated here. She suspected that there had been an element of performance in Charles's flow of conversation but it did him no harm in her eyes to be exerting himself to please her.

And he did please me, she thought. His company was amusing. There were no undertones to his words, no unspoken criticisms or demands hovering at my head. Perhaps it is because he is straightforward that people are set against him. Our age is not, as he complained, a time of tournaments and ladies' favours worn upon a lance. Frankness is seen only as concealment for base intention. I cannot join in condemning my own cousin for mistakes made ten years ago.

Her reverie was broken by Charles's return and she flushed as if she expected him to read her thoughts. He set down two glasses of lemonade. 'I don't know whether I'm a felon for bringing these out of the refreshment room,' he said, gaily. 'I crept out when the girls' backs were turned.'

'I would have denied all knowledge of you if you were caught.'

As she spoke, Theo found that her placid enjoyment of the scene had fled with his arrival. Her throat had tightened so that her voice was forced and the consciousness of her body that she had had as they walked was with her again. She noticed that two women, who had been sitting in slumped attitudes on the edge of a tank, had straightened and were exchanging comments behind their hands with their eyes fixed on Charles. It was not the first instance she had seen of his power to draw a gaze but it unsettled her. To be near him where nothing was known of his past and no disapproval was carried in the glances seemed to make him stranger and she saw herself with him as passers-by must see them – a man and woman alone in the throng with all the implications of intimacy in their situation. It was not so many months since she had longed for a stranger and she could not hide from herself that, in this moment of revelation, she found him attractive. His easy elegance and world-weary manner that fitted so badly in a counting-house showed to advantage in the city. She felt that he was different today. It was as if an engine concealed within a polished casing had been set in motion and, though its working was invisible, vibration troubled the air around.

'You're hard on me,' Charles said and Theo, forgetting her last words, again felt that he could read her mind and the colour rose higher in her face.

I have her, Charles thought. She puts her fingers to her throat as if there is a constriction there. Her head lifts because I am watching her. She has trailed her hand in the pool and put it to her neck. Drops of water cling to her skin. They gleam as she breathes. She is a prize worth the winning. I would marry a plain, mincing miss for my freedom and be master of her in a moment. She would cause me no disturbance but this one may disturb me in other ways. It will be luxurious to have such a woman eager for my attentions; to see her enthralled by my compliment, that head lowered, those dark eyes filled with tears at my rebuke. She will seek to indulge me for she will learn to fear the harshness of the withdrawal of my love. And when I tire of her, there will be her – my – money and always, always, as she walks upon my arm, there will be Ralph looking on.

'I'm so grateful for these hours,' he said. 'There's been a sweetness in them which I can't explain to you.'

'A sweetness?' Her heart beat faster as the simplicity of the afternoon fell away.

He leant forward. His face was barely an inch closer to hers but she shrank against her chair.

'We're in town but can you smell the forest? The woods where flowers grow?'

Alarmed and fascinated, she did not reply.

'Your face,' he said, 'your hands – they are so white and all about is green. You are the lily of the valley and the scent is sweet.'

He held her eyes for an instant that seemed long to them both then lifted his glass and held it as if he would make a toast. Mesmerized, she raised her own but he only touched his to hers and sat back. They drank in silence, the glasses cold and slippery with condensation, the rhythmic sounds of the machinery all about them felt but not heard.

When their glasses were empty, he stood up and came over to her. Reaching down, he drew up her shawl and draped it carefully across her shoulders. As he arranged its folds, his finger brushed her cheek and she started as he had meant her to. In the shadow of the leaves, her eyes were wide and revealing.

'Come,' he said. 'The others will be wondering. We must make our appearance.'

Chapter Eleven

'Naturally I believe you didn't know what was happening but if you ask me to think the same of Charles you must be disappointed. It would be too much of a coincidence for him to have chosen that moment to take you away, otherwise.'

In a low-ceilinged bedroom at the hotel, Theo was brushing her hair with defiant strokes as Louisa paced the uneven floor.

'Would it?' said Theo, her silver-backed brush gleaming in the candlelight as it moved firmly up and down. 'I think a coincidence – however unlucky – more likely than the hardness of heart that would be needed for him to use his father's collapse as a diversion. Is he a monster? What has he ever done that you believe him so devilish?'

It would have gratified Charles, who was now lying on his own bed, with a novel in one hand and a cheroot in the other, to know that the circumstance that had led to his unnoticed capture of Theo was still working to his advantage. She had suspected nothing against him when they had reached the entrance and found only Barclay, Ettie and Maud waiting for them. Their tale of how Mr Carnow had been taken so faint that Ralph and Louisa had felt it necessary to help him back to the hotel had shocked her. She was distressed by the idea that she had been giving herself up to pleasure whilst her uncle might have been breathing his last. Ettie's calm reassurances that his weakness had not been judged so ominous that it was proper for the entire party to lose the benefit of the exhibition had bolstered her a little but her nerves, pulled taut by Charles's manipulations, did not allow her to be optimistic. She chided herself for selfishness and Charles's pretty concern for his father and anxiety to go to him quickly had served only to keep her emotions at a high and unsettled pitch.

She hurried from the carriage and was relieved to hear the news that a sleeping draught had been administered to Mr Carnow by a physician who had thought him overly exhausted by the journey, but the evening had not been relaxed. The effort to keep up an easy conversation at the dinner table had been too much for them all, suffering as they were from a variety of loves, disappointments, cares and hopes. The unfamiliarity of their surroundings – the crowded dining room, the bustling waiters bearing trays over the heads of guests calling for extra porter, the gusts of smells, savoury and sweet, that flourished as the kitchen door opened – seemed to make them more tired and they were conscious of their feet as they ate their cutlets.

Theo had been glad to go up to her room. The day, with its assorted alarms and excursions, had taken more out of her than she had bargained upon. She found herself wishing that she could go home but, as she undid her hooks and laces to fold her clothes inside the camphor-ridden wardrobe, she was honest enough to recognize that it was not because she needed the comfort of her own belongings about her. It was because Charles had revealed that his feelings were not brotherly and, though his fascination had been compelling and lingered in her mind as the scent of fruit hangs in sultry air, she wanted to run from him as she had run from Ralph. She did not think her reactions commendable and, as was her habit, where she blamed herself she exonerated others. If she had been proud of her behaviour, she could have judged more clearly of Charles's.

It was into this readiness to absolve Charles that Louisa, who had been sitting with Mr Carnow until dinner and had not yet been able to talk to Theo alone, had come to be told her niece's account of the afternoon. Theo had unlocked her door reluctantly, standing behind it as she drew it back so that no one in the corridor should see her state of undress. She did not want to be questioned. Her mood was one in which her sense of having done a wrong that she could not specify would make her stubbornly defensive. Although she considered it reasonable that Louisa wanted to hear what had occurred, it was only with an effort and a grudging manner that she was able to tell her tale. Its reception surprised and irritated her. Louisa's immediate conclusion that Charles had seized the opportunity caused by his father's indisposition to spirit Theo away for his own purposes had not occurred to Theo. The idea disgusted her. The development of the afternoon had persuaded her that Charles had not separated her from the others simply to show her sculpture but the notion that he could have been as callous as Louisa suggested was too repugnant for her to consider. It strengthened the view that Charles had been carefully fostering in her that he was the victim of prejudice.

Louisa, in her turn, was disturbed and angry. Since Theo had refused Ralph, she had feared for her niece's future. It was plain that Theo's reason could be overruled by her feelings and she could not be trusted to see traps laid for her if they were hidden in the correct way. For months, Louisa had watched Charles's circumspection with Theo and was sure that he was making a calculated attack upon her by playing on her susceptibilities. She had hoped that when he began to display his intentions more obviously Theo's eyes would open but tonight she found them determinedly shut. The danger such foolishness could lead Theo into made Louisa rage inwardly against both her and Charles. Her skirts whisked behind her as she walked to and fro, suppressing the urge to take Theo by the shoulders and shake her.

'I do believe,' she said, 'that he has a monstrous capacity for cold cruelty.'

She stopped pacing and stood at the foot of the bed, the fingers of one hand clenched on the brass rails at its end. Theo was standing with her back towards her, using the mirror on the chest of drawers for her vigorous brushing, and did not turn round.

'It is a pity,' Louisa went on, 'that you were a child when he left his family. You were too young to see the pain his leaving caused.'

Theo laid down her brush. She stared resentfully into the glass at her aunt's reflection.

'It's natural for a man to make his own way in the world, isn't it?' she asked. 'Or was it written in letters of stone that he was to be wedded to the mill?'

'If he was, he took his bride-price with him. You recall that he was hardly asserting an adventurous independence. He cajoled his doting father into giving him a sum of money that all but ruined the rest of the family. But I leave that aside. It was selfish enough but the real cruelty came later.' She paused. Men's voices were heard in the corridor; boisterous laughter broke out amongst them and was hushed noisily as they passed towards the stairs. Overhead, footsteps crossed the room above. 'Think of the years he was away. How would you have acted if it'd been you who had gone? Would you have written three or four uncommunicative letters in the first months and then let silence overtake you?' She waited until Theo petulantly shook her head. 'No – because you'd have some understanding of the heart-ache you'd caused. I saw how the loss – no loss in my mind – how the loss of him affected his home. I saw your aunt ashamed and unfairly blaming herself for the wrong road her elder son had taken and bitterly anxious for the burden it would throw on her younger. I sat at her bedside as she died longing for the sight of her first-born. Ralph was there but where was Charles? At which pleasure resort? And all this time – for a decade – as Ralph has worked his youth away, I've seen your uncle grieving and yearning for his favourite, gradually teaching himself not to have hopes of the post, afraid that his boy was dead – for why else should he write nothing? – and puzzling, puzzling, racking his poor, bewildered mind for an explanation of his desertion.'

She stopped to draw breath. Theo was standing perfectly still. Her head was up but her eyes were downcast and Louisa could not see the expression in them.

'And now,' said Louisa, 'he's returned. He has no money but we're not to suggest that there's a connection between those two facts. He's come back out of affection. All is roses. Except that his little brother has grown up and won't let the mill be plundered again without a fight and he finds himself obliged to work – however perfunctorily – for his living. He finds the situation uncongenial and is looking about for another position. Are you aware what it is?'

Theo cast a burning glance at Louisa. She had no experience of seducers; she lived amongst men for whom an open interest in a woman was followed by marriage and part of her alarm at Charles's change towards her had been because she believed it was leading to a proposal. In the hours since they had left the Exhibition, she had not had the peace she needed to dwell on her reaction to the possibilities that had arisen but, in the startled and disjointed thoughts she had had, the notion that he was pursuing her for her wealth had not entered her mind. She dismissed it now. Their close family connection made it inconceivable. Even in this moment of disgust at her aunt's opinion of his intentions, she admitted to herself that there was no logic in her faith but she did not give it up.

'I see from your face,' said Louisa, more gently, 'that you understand me and reject my interpretation of what he's about. My dear, be on your guard. There are snares and delusions in this life. Temptation must be enticing or it isn't tempting. I know that he has an attraction when he sets himself to use it. He's come here with all the glamour of a stranger but still has the familiarity of a cousin. He brings novelty and new conversation. He's a handsome man. But ask yourself how much he's really told of what he's been doing these past ten years. Where has his fortune gone? Why did he neither write nor return until he was impoverished? And why,' she reached for Theo's hand and held it, unresponsive, between her own, 'does his preference fall upon an heiress – and one loved by the brother he hates?'

Theo withdrew her fingers from her aunt's. She was shaking, though it was not from cold, and she lifted her shawl from a chair and wrapped it around her. As the folds enclosed her, she remembered Charles's brief touch as he had covered her that afternoon and a sensation of stifling heat pervaded her.

'Perhaps,' she said, 'it's because alone amongst his family – except his father – it's been she who's welcomed him, she who's been prepared to judge him for what he's become not what he used to be.' Drawing the shawl closer about her, she stood mantled like a Roman matron to hide her tremors. 'And that's how I'll continue my estimation of him. I'll judge by what I see and what I hear from him, as I'd wish to be judged myself, and old enmities will have no place in my reckoning.'

The pleasure-party was English enough to conceal its tumultuous feelings as it journeyed home, and would-be travellers who opened the door of its railway carriage at the various stations to Dorchester could not guess at the ferment beneath its calm exterior. Disappointed of a seat, the new passengers hurried down the train thinking only how those already in possession of a compartment might well look calm.

Although the excursion had not been the triumph hoped for,

it had been a success for half of its participants. Maud had enjoyed the sights in a straightforward manner. Ettie, joining her in this, had also been intrigued by the repercussions of Charles's peculiarities and by the character traits displayed in the party all the previous day. Barclay was so far into heaven after defending Maud and squiring her, almost unchaperoned, for an entire afternoon that it was a struggle for him to be concerned for Mr Carnow. The only one amongst the four who were glad they had gone to the Exhibition whose satisfaction was not innocent was Charles.

He had been reviewing every detail of the hours spent with Theo and they made him complacent. Her readiness to come away with him, the ease with which he had amused her, her dilated eyes, quick breath and shrinking silence under the trees pointed to her being his for the asking. As he sat watching the countryside rush by with its procession of meadows, waving children and riders contending with startled horses, he congratulated himself upon his campaign. The past months had been tedious but the reward was rich. Literally rich, he thought, with a smile that did not go unnoticed by Ettie. Images of Paris and the Mediterranean passed through his rejoicing mind. And this time, he told himself, there will be no anxiety over bills, no necessity to pretend friendship for the weak. My mill will coil out my wealth as it coils out its ropes. My nets will trawl an unending catch of leisure.

He looked across the carriage to the source of his felicity, who was apparently absorbed in a magazine whose pages she was not turning. Her dark hair, swept back into a heavy chignon, gleamed in the sunlight and emphasized the paleness of her cheek. The ornate gold earring closest to him swung with the movement of the train and stroked her white neck. Her wide, silk skirts spread about her, overlapping Barclay's leg and displaying the narrowness of her waist. The desire to possess not only her money but her person invaded him again as it had done in yesterday's shadows. He had been celibate since the unfortunate affair in New York and was weary of it. His eyes travelled to his brother and his appetite for Theo was sharpened by his relish of the agony its slaking would cause Ralph. He knew from the strength of his own hatred how savage Ralph's jealousy would be.

Ralph's eyes were shut. He was fully awake but he wished for privacy – an uncomfortable desire when elbow to elbow with relations for a hundred miles. He could sense Charles's exultation and the urge to take him by the throat was as powerful as it was unwise. Louisa had told him that Theo had been ignorant of Mr Carnow's collapse and, knowing her affection for her uncle, he believed her but he was hurt and bewildered by her choice of companion. His dream of slipping away with her had been vanquished by the reality of an afternoon in fear for his father's life. There had been no question in his mind of whether he should attend to Mr Carnow but, as he supported him in the hastily summoned cab and sat beside him in the darkened hotel room, watching the sick man's sleeping face with anguished tenderness, the knowledge that Charles had usurped his plan tormented and goaded him.

It was a frame of mind which did not leave him in the days that followed. Good had come out of the anxiety as Mr Carnow had been frightened by the evidence of his increasing ill-health and agreed, with mutterings, to be dosed by Dr Lloyd. Using this news as an excuse to call on Theo, for he no longer felt able to visit the Farnabys without a reason, Ralph rode over two days after their return, hoping to hear that there had been some reluctance on her part to be escorted by Charles or that the time spent alone with him had been distasteful to her. He was willing to hear his brother's name reviled, but arrived to find the house empty of both cousin and aunt. Moore's ship had reached harbour the evening before, after making a fast passage to and from Newfoundland, and, it having been carrying Farnaby products as well as Carnow's, the maid informed him that Miss Theodosia was gone on board and the mistress was at her mill.

Ralph had business of his own with Moore and had arranged to meet him that afternoon but he could not bear to wait longer before he saw Theo. Accordingly, he turned his horse's head towards the bay and followed her. Whither thou goest, he thought a shade bitterly, there go I. What a virtue is loyalty.

An hour before, Theo had also set out alone for the harbour and on horseback. It was no more than a mile to the sea but she had deliberately chosen to ride because she felt that her habit, being formed of the most masculine articles of her wardrobe, was suited to her errand and would give her confidence. A passerby, who could read her thoughts, would have looked on her trailing skirts and veiled hat and been hard-pressed to say where her lack of femininity might lie. There was, however, not merely a similarity in colouring between the black and white of most gentlemen's dress, and her habit, but it allowed her an ease of movement not found in the usual garments of a lady. It's a curious thing, she said to herself as she walked her lively mare down South Street, to be a prisoner of one's clothing. When I'm not in the saddle, I can't walk without my legs being hampered by the weight of layers around them. I can't roll up my sleeves or throw my gown over my head if it rains, as a working-girl would do. I can't breathe deeply or bend comfortably for the tightness of my lacing. If I run, the fastenings fall from my hair.

A sailor was sauntering along the pavement in a holiday mood and she considered his wide-legged trousers and knitted jersey. There's more than fashion in the way we're dressed, she thought. Is it a coincidence that a gentlewoman is believed indecent, a disgrace to her class and sex, if she doesn't encumber herself with styles which prevent her being active? I go to do what the world expects to be done by a man and feel unfit for it in my usual guise.

Her task was not difficult nor did it require any attribute that the world might believe to be properly male. She was calling upon Moore to discuss his success with her ropes and nets. Their conversation would be as it had often been before. The difference lay in it taking place by appointment at the harbour and not in the course of a social meeting in a drawing room, with Louisa to ask any pertinent questions which he had not covered. Her apprenticeship was progressing well and her head – that same head that her father had told her was too pretty for business – was full of the striving and venture, the monotony and risk that made up the industry that fed and housed her. It made her feel alive and at the hub of activity but as yet she was like a child taken on board ship to stand at the helm between the steersman's arms. Today was the first time she had undertaken any duty without her aunt or Mr Wykeham, who managed her mill as well as Louisa's, at her side and it gave her purpose.

It was a fine, bright morning. An occasional wandering breeze rustled the new leaves that hung over walls but the sun was warm enough to have brought the women of the terraced cottages on to stools in their doorways to braid their nets. Theo greeted them as she rode past, commenting on the day and the arrival of the ship. As she left the centre of the town the houses became larger and the netters were replaced by tradesmen carrying baskets to the servants' entrance. Halls stood open to welcome the spring air and an upstairs window was lowered for a hand that flapped a duster.

On the low ground half a mile before the bay, tall Georgian houses had been built, with gardens running down to the meadows that bordered the river. Their whiteness was a dazzling contrast to the clear, blue sky that was streaked with cloud far to the east. Between the houses, Theo could see geese picking their awkward way over the grass to the reeds. Beyond them was the glinting sea and the crumbling, sandstone cliffs that rose on either side of the harbour.

Noise increased as she approached the shore. Seagulls were squalling over a bucket of refuse that had been flung from a lugger, swooping and rising with arched, forward-beating wings, necks outstretched and yellow beaks open to parry the threats of the first-comers. Their screams rebounded from the quay. On the shingle beach children played arduous games with mounds of pebbles while their mothers and nurses called warnings of the waves. A man in a straw hat rode solemnly by on a balding donkey, lost to the ribald encouragement from three loitering seamen. Salt cod was being unloaded from Moore's brig to the accompaniment of shouted orders and was carted to a nearby warehouse.

Moore was standing in conversation with a customs officer. His face was animated and, despite the early season, already darkened by sun reflected from cold waters. The sound of saws and hammering in his father's shipyard was a background to the stir of his own crew. Hearing the scrape of her mare's hoofs on the cobbles, Moore turned to see Theo. The officer executed an old-fashioned and military bow in her direction and walked smartly away as Moore went to join her. She slid down from the saddle and took his hand.

'You've made a good speed with your crossings this time,' she said. 'We didn't expect you so soon.'

'I couldn't have asked for better winds and the ice was barely troublesome. If every voyage were as free from problems, I'd be a happy man.'

She drew the reins over the mare's head to lead her. 'I don't believe you would. You'd grow bored and pine for something to tax you.'

He raised his head to look across at the masts of his brig and smiled. 'You're right. I'd be hiring myself out to a whaler to keep my blood moving. Life must have action to be worth the fight.'

Theo wondered what her next step should be. She did not know how to introduce the subject of business nor whether Moore would change when spoken to on matters that were not social. Would he resent her presence and reveal her ignorance and inexperience of what was the heart-beat of the town?

'Will you come over to the yard?' Moore asked. 'I've taken the ledger and receipts to my father's office.'

It was his practice to use his cabin for such purposes but he had foreseen Theo's unease and did not want to expose her to the interest or the language of the sailors and dockers. An inn would have been little improvement but she had often been to the shipyard and he judged that she would not feel out of place. He was used to discussing cargoes with Louisa and did not share the common view that women should stay in the home. Just as he approved of Maud's eagerness to sail with him, so he was pleased to see Theo choosing to take part in her trade. It was inconsistent of him that where he would have found severity the quickest, and therefore kindest, way to teach a youthful seaman his craft, he was gently smoothing Theo's passage.

Gratefully, Theo turned the mare and they walked over to the shipyard. It was older than much of the harbour, most of which had been built twenty years before when it had become a bond-port and needed a custom-house and other additions suitable to its raised status. Moore had Napoleon to thank for establishing his family's fortune and enabling him to be master of his own brig at so young an age. In the first decade of the century, when Trafalgar had seemed glorious but a focus of fear, eighteen men-of-war had been built at Bridport and his grandfather's yard had changed from a small and struggling enterprise to a solidly prosperous concern. It was alive today with the sounds of carpentry and the resinous scent of the planks greeted them as they went through the gates.

The office was panelled in Norwegian pine and smelt of sweet, dry sawdust. Men in white aprons passed the windows with chisels hanging from their belts and planes protruding from their wide front pockets. Moore drew a chair back from the desk for Theo and moved one for himself.

'Will you take a glass?' he asked. 'Or shall I send out for tea?'

'Don't trouble. When in Rome – I'll have wine.'

He unlocked a cupboard and held out a bottle. 'Your aunt would drink Madeira,' he said.

'She's always been shameless. I'll do the same.'

'Well, if I can't tempt you to rum . . . '

He put two glasses on the desk amongst the papers and poured.

'Did you carry this?' she asked.

'I did. The vintners give part of their payment in kind.' He stoppered the bottle. 'Though why Madeira should go around the world or three times to Newfoundland before it's mature, is more than I can say. It's profitable, mind. I've a new layer of casks lying in the hold now.'

They slipped unobtrusively into their business. When Ralph rode into the yard and tied up his horse next to Theo's, he entered the office to find Moore refilling the ink-well while Theo made notes on his transactions. She had not expected to meet Ralph there and, glancing up from her work to find him in the doorway, she smiled shyly. There was a spontaneous warmth between them.

'I've never seen a Manchester man I've liked so well,' Ralph said, coming in.

She laid down her pen. 'I'm a novice. I must look strange.'

'On the contrary. It suits you.'

He sat down across the desk from her. Moore pointed to the wine and, at Ralph's nod, poured a measure into another glass. The memory of how, on the day in the wood, Ralph had also said that fast riding suited her came into her thoughts, as did Charles's assertion that beautiful women were born to do nothing. It did not act in Charles's favour. Despite her previous indignant support of Charles, she felt a sensation of shame that she should have experienced such a strength of attraction to both brothers. Sitting in this office, stimulated by her occupation and her easy acceptance into what had been a male province, with Ralph behaving towards her without disapproval or superiority, she could not understand how she had succumbed to Charles.

The jealousy he had suffered since the Exhibition faded from Ralph as the three sat talking. His hopes, which rose and fell like spring tides, were high again. The look of pleasure that had crossed Theo's face when she first saw him had been as natural as it was unexpected and its balm brought him a reassurance that flooded his veins like strong drink. The tales of Indians and trappers that Moore had heard in St John's took the place of cod-lines and nets. White winters when the wind spoke to men crazed by solitude; long days in canoes gliding over unending lakes where the forest was reflected in stillness and peace; the call of the wolf, howling into the night – these held them rapt and drew out Ralph's reminiscences of trading voyages he had made to Canada, Italy and Russia. He had often sailed to Newfoundland before Charles had left, learning the ways of the industry that his brother did not want to know. Since Charles's departure, his travels had been made from necessity and in dread of what harm his father might do in his absence. There had been no possibility of leisurely tours and now that he had restored the firm to its success he longed to take Theo to share the sights he had seen, just as Moore yearned to have Maud at his side.

Moore had brought Maud a beaver pelt and a quart of maple syrup. Theo and Ralph teased him gently, united in the security of old friendships and forgetting for an hour the complications their changing feelings had wrought in their relations. It did Moore good to watch them. He could not help blaming himself for Charles's arrival in England and it was a relief to see the pair at ease with each other again. He spread the fur over the desk and as Theo ran her fingers through its softness he pulled the cork from the stone syrup-jar. Using the grog spoon from the wine cupboard, he dipped it in and lifted out a sample of the dark, aromatic contents, twisting the spoon to wrap the sticky drooping strands around it.

'Taste this,' he said to Theo, offering it to her with his other hand cupped beneath it.

'No,' she said, laughing. 'That isn't lover-like. You should keep Maud's gift for her.'

Her voice was as light-hearted as her mood. Moore looked from her to Ralph and back again.

'Try it,' he said. 'I think there could be sweetness for us all.'

Chapter Twelve

Although it was still May, there was a feeling of June in the air as Theo strolled through her garden two days after her appointment with Moore. It was early afternoon and, sustained by cold chicken and a custard, she had emerged from the house to anticipate summer in a wide-brimmed straw hat and a carefree mood. She was carrying a set of croquet hoops and was stopping at intervals on the lawn to drive them into the grass with the firm pressure of a white kid boot.

It was again bright, fresh weather and the tree-covered hillside beyond the high wall was the vivid, tender green of young leaves in sunlight. The day was made for cheerful thoughts and Theo was indulging in them as she prepared the game that reminded her of previous summers. She could not recall how often she and Ralph had roqueted each other into the shrubbery, giving and receiving no quarter, but she looked forward to a resumption of their sporting rivalry with a pleasure that had not seemed possible only a few weeks ago.

The last of the hoops in place, she straightened up to look at the field of play with satisfaction. She was on the long lawn behind the house and from there could see the roof of the pavilion in the burgeoning flower garden. She had not entirely reconciled herself to Ralph's behaviour during his proposal but she found that she could now view the scene of that shameful winter hour without the indignation that had since always risen in her breast at the sight of its pillars. The warmth she had been feeling for him, that had been reawakened by his apology in the schoolroom, had increased in heat in the shipyard. It had been an unlikely hothouse for forcing love but his acceptance of her in a guise that would have outraged most men and the atmosphere of activity and roving achievement, that was so markedly absent in the stifled lives of women, had excited her desire for him. The introspection that the disruptive emotions following Charles's return had brought to her was gradually making her grow in honesty with herself. She recognized that the sharp and fiery antagonism there had been between herself and Ralph after her refusal of his offer had been a perverted expression of the attraction she still felt for him.

Her sensibilities and judgement had led her so far astray over the past months that, although she acknowledged she was a depraved creature she did not wish to hide her face from Ralph. On the contrary, in her certainty that he was once more her lover, she longed to have him near that she might demonstrate the strength of her willingness to be joined with him. Oh, God, she thought – her eyes closed and her face upraised to the sun – if I had not run from him in the wood. Such cowardice, such vacillation as I have shown does not deserve a second chance but it will come and he cannot be more ardent that I. Her imaginings made her tremble; she put her hands to her neck, lost to her surroundings. I will never meet his advances coldly, she told herself, I—

'Miss Theodosia.'

She opened her eyes to find a maid standing before her, watching her speculatively. A flush covered her face as though she expected the girl to have seen her private thoughts exposed.

'The sun's warm today,' she said, patting her cheek to explain its high colour.

'That it is,' said the maid. ''Tis heartening to see 'un. I've a message, miss. A man's over from Carnow to find will 'ee drive out to the new meadows with the young master in half an hour? He's to take back your answer.'

Theo's breath caught in her throat. She clasped her hands to steady herself.

'I will go,' she said. 'Tell him to say to Mr Carnow that I'm ready for him now and will not keep him waiting.'

Although the message Charles had sent to Theo had not been delivered to her exactly as he had instructed, it had had the misleading effect that he had intended. It had been his particular order that his Christian name should not be mentioned in the invitation. Having heard that both Ralph and Louisa were occupied elsewhere that afternoon, he decided to strike while the iron was hot and lure Theo to a suitably romantic situation for a proposal. After his experience of her reaction to him at the Exhibition, he did not doubt that he would be accepted if he could entice her somewhere that would bring them no interruption, but, equally, her own recognition of her feelings while under the elms might induce a maidenly reluctance to be alone with him again. He had, therefore, asked the question in the name of Mr Carnow, hoping that she would assume that her uncle wished to take her out. The fact that the maid, knowing that the buying of the land at Loders had been Ralph's cherished project, had assumed that it was he who had sent the messenger had only served to work in Charles's favour.

He was confident as he drove the trap towards Bridport and drew it in outside Theo's gate. Calling the stable lad to him, he sent the boy to summon her, thinking that it would be more awkward for her, on realizing the mistake in his identity, to renege on her agreement to the expedition if she joined him in the street than if they had met indoors.

The skittish and showy chestnut saddlehorse that he had bought for himself with his father's money was between the shafts, shifting its weight from one leg to another under the resented harness, and Charles, regarding his turnout critically as he waited, was almost gleeful with admiration of his appearance and prospects.

The look that passed fleetingly over Theo's face when she saw him was slightly daunting but she had come out of the gate with such eagerness that he rallied, telling himself that she had merely been conscious that she was displaying her preference too openly. He offered her his free hand with something of a flourish and her instant of hesitation before she took it to climb beside him gingered him. It seemed that he would have to overcome an outbreak of diffidence and it made the afternoon more interesting. He became less obviously buoyant but his confidence did not diminish.

Theo was angry with herself for the mistake she had made. Her impetuous assumption that things were as she wished them to be had once again led her into a rash action. It would have been the work of a moment to ascertain which brother had sent the invitation but she was not one to look for facts where her feelings were involved. There had been no room in her mind for anyone but Ralph and so she had come to this pass. She did not blame Charles for what could not be his fault but she was acutely uncomfortable as they drove past the mill, knowing how her situation could be interpreted.

She became more easy as they left Carnow behind them and drove into open country. Charles was carefully keeping his conversation innocuous and she persuaded herself that being for once about his family's business, he had asked her to join him only for the pleasure of company in the trap.

It could not have been better weather for a drive. The sun and clear blue sky were bright but not glaring and the early summer heat was tempered by a gentle breeze. In the hedgerows the hawthorn blossom was turning brown as it withered and cast soft showers of petals on to Theo where the way was too narrow for Charles to avoid brushing the overhanging branches. She shook the flowers with their scent of sweet decay from her arms and lap, afraid that Charles would comment upon bridals but, though the thought came to him, he judged it unwise and kept silent.

They reached the farm without anything being said that could make Theo suspicious of Charles's motives. It was hotter in the yard amongst the byres where the air was still and Theo waited in the shade of a barn while Charles arranged the care of his horse. He had been vague to her about the purpose of his visit, saying only that he was to look over the land for his father. His sole reason for being there was to have Theo to himself but she had no inkling of it and stood in the shadows, watching hens scratching the dry earth, lost in the dreams of Ralph that had returned to her as she relaxed in the trap.

The horse having been delivered into the keeping of a lad, Charles led the way into the meadows and towards the river. The previous owner of the farm had agreed to sell on the condition that he could remain in possession until spring, when the house he was having built at Weymouth would be ready. The land had passed to the Carnows only three weeks before and it was this that made Theo so gullible about the necessity of Charles viewing the ground. There were alterations to be made to provide for the growing of flax and hemp and she had heard Ralph talk of the need to build a retting tank to soak the crops before the fibre could be separated from the stalks.

Men were at work in the fields nearest the yard. These were the first to be converted from pasture and hemp seed was being sown in their deep soil. The foreman, who was to live in the farmhouse, was overseeing the process. Noticing Charles and Theo, he hurried, hat in hand, to greet them and offer himself as a guide. He was an industrious, garrulous man, eager to please his employers in a position that was a rise in status and responsibility for him and it was with difficulty that Charles was able to dissuade him from accompanying them to explain the plans for every inch of land. Had he been by himself, Charles would have abandoned politeness in his refusal of the offered service but he did not want to offend Theo and they left the foreman, still lively with phosphates and warnings of mud, at the gate that took them into the untouched fields.

They strolled over the grass towards the river and made their way along the bank. They crossed a secretive meadow, bounded by high hedges of elder and brambles where butterflies flitted and danced above white saxifrage, and then another, thickly golden with buttercups that stained them with clinging pollen as they waded through the flowers. The narrow river ran smoothly at their side flowing silently through the valley to the sea. Climbing a stile, they found themselves in a bay a few yards wide, canopied by crab-apple trees, gnarled and old but still heavy with pink and cream blossom that filtered and altered the light as the elms had done when the pair had last been alone together.

Charles had not made a reconnaissance of the land but it seemed to him that nowhere on their path would be more conducive to romance than this scented, dappled bower. He loitered at the river's edge after handing Theo down from the stile and she, still unaware of his motives, stood by him, watching the shining water slipping smoothly over the stones. A part of him was contemptuous, inwardly mocking her, as he prepared for the simple victory that would deliver a fortune into his keeping, but there was no hint of it on his face. He had been perfectly open during their journey but now he let a suggestion of tension enter his manner as if he had been repressing words he could barely hold back.

He was silent but Theo was aware of a change in atmosphere. It was nothing that she could define and she almost scorned herself for her imaginings but she became instantly alert and wary. The warm, May-laden air seemed to grow thick and strange as it does before thunder. The small waves still rippled against the far side of the bay, the bees still moved softly amongst the blossom but they had grown sinister to her. She did not move. An attempt to leave would prompt a scene she was convinced was coming and she wanted to stave it off while she adjusted to the realization that she had been duped.

It might, she thought, be unfairly harsh to accuse him of deception. A man in love must use some excuse to gain the privacy he desires. That is accepted. He wished to see me alone and I've given him no discouragement. How could he tell I would not welcome it?

With her habit of defending him, she tried to see his tactics in the most generous light but today she had not had a net of charm cast over her and her aunt's plain warning that Charles intended to marry her for her money was present in her mind and no longer seemed ridiculous. To herself, she had called him a man in love but she did not sense love in the charged air. Standing quietly above the gliding water, she was poised to pluck the fuse from gunpowder.

'Can you think,' Charles asked, 'of anything more like heaven than this?'

He turned towards her, speaking seriously and with a slight wistfulness.

'It is a pleasant walk,' she said, guardedly.

'I've travelled to curious places,' he said, 'and seen fine sights – lakes, mountains and forests, the Louisiana bayous, the Mississippi, the New England fall but I think there's nothing that touches the heart like an English spring.'

It was on the tip of Theo's tongue to ask him why, then, he had not returned sooner but she did not want to release an answer that she believed would be smooth and sentimental. She did not feel herself to be alone with him; at one shoulder she had Louisa and at the other, Ralph, angry and accusing in the summerhouse, demanding to be told what she thought Charles had been doing on his travels. It was only a day since she had sat in the shipyard with men reminiscing of journeys whose purpose had no concealment in them and she found that Charles's stance as a man of the world did not touch her. She seemed to look at the moment from outside and saw herself standing with an undeniably handsome figure, who had engineered a tête-à-tête in a situation redolent of romance, but who was not affecting her as he assumed he would. The woman he had mesmerized under the elms had been left in the city; she found herself bored by him and conscious that the very clothes he wore to maintain his elegance had been earned by someone else.

Receiving no reply, Charles went on, 'I believed I was poor when I came back here. I was rich in experience, it's true, but I thought my lack of wealth meant poverty. During the months of my return I've realized that I was wrong. I am poor but it isn't gold that I need.'

He paused and Theo, even in her dread of what was to follow and her disgust at his pretence, acknowledged to herself that it was prettily done.

Turning more fully towards her, he fixed an ardent gaze upon her face. 'I've understood my spiritual poverty,' he said. 'I yearn for that which a man most desires, without which he is incomplete – the highest form of companionship he may aspire to enjoy.'

Theo had been watching the river as he spoke.

'What was your experience?' she asked.

'What?'

'You said you were rich in experience. What was it? How did you live?'

Charles was thrown off balance. He had expected a tender and agitated response.

'As a gentleman,' he said, with as much dignity as he could muster.

'I think that I can't be a lady,' Theo said, observing a leaf turning slowly on the water. 'Many would say that I'm not. We are, of course, in trade and I find, increasingly, that I glory in it.'

The contempt Charles had felt for her changed to malice. He was aware that her remarks were a jibe at him and meant to make her suspicions of him known. That she did harbour doubts was a new and unwelcome idea. It did not lessen his determination to have her in his power but it made him resolve to make her suffer for it later.

'If anyone belittled you in my hearing,' he said, 'they would pay for it.'

Theo felt the awkwardness of her position. Despite her anticipation of his offer, she could not turn it down until it was made and if she fled he would merely accompany her back to the farm, causing annoyance as they went. He was waiting for her to acknowledge his compliment. She inclined her head coldly.

It occurred to Charles, when he saw the effect of his words, that there would be occasions after their marriage when it would give him pleasure to strike her. He had seen her behaving imperiously to Ralph and it had been meat and drink to him but to find her daring to resist his attentions after he had had her trembling and wide-eyed amongst the fountains enraged him. For all that he coveted her wealth and body, he would not waste his respect upon her once they were in his possession. She would bring him advancement but she was only a woman and would learn to rue the day that she had not shown him reverence.

'But how can you suggest that anyone would question that you're a gentlewoman?' he asked. 'I can think of no one more worthy of the name. You're a grace to your sex and the man who wins you will be blessed and ennobled by your favour.'

Theo shuddered. The insincerity of his protestations and the memory of honest words of love that she had not valued revolted her. She touched her cheek as if she wanted to close her mouth against a reply, leaving a trail of pollen on her skin that gleamed dully in the subdued light.

Charles was encouraged. He saw that he had unnerved her. Inwardly, he sneered at how easily he had overthrown her defences. She was to be had by fulsome flattery and he hastened to press home his advantage.

'I've tried to keep my feelings from you,' he said. 'I've sought you out as a cousin because I believed I had no right to present myself as your lover. I'm not your equal nor ever can be. You are all that I desire to be myself.' He took her hand softly between his own. 'With all humility, I entreat you to become my wife.'

Theo raised her face towards the canopy of blossom that engulfed them. There was no movement in the air in this enclosed corner. She felt stifled.

'My lover?' she asked.

He drew her hand closer and held it to his breast. 'Upon my honour,' he said, 'I do love you.'

Her lips drew back from her teeth. Turning her head, she looked at him with scorn that was almost a snarl.

'Do you think I'm so foolish as to be unaware of what it is of mine that you desire?' She pulled her hand from its resting place but he tightened his grip on her fingers. 'Is it my character or affections? I refuse your offer. Now, enough! Release me.'

She had been too plain for him to persuade himself that there was any prevarication or hope of being coaxed in her mind. There was revulsion in her expression but the surprise that she should have seen through him did not quite conquer his conceit.

'Dearest,' he said, hurt and astonishment in his tone. 'What is this? I've admired and – yes – adored you since our first encounter on my return. You've been a revelation to—'

Unable to contain her anger, Theo interrupted him.

'Have done!' she said fiercely. 'Do you dare talk to me in this way? What else must you have ventured to be so easy in your lies?'

He grasped the wrist of her imprisoned hand. Her blood pulsed heavily under its constriction and a pricking numbness spread down towards her nails.

'Your aunt,' he said, bitterly, 'and my sweet brother. They've poisoned you against me, haven't they? What have they said? They must have been at work recently – it's no time since I had you breathless when I came near.'

The truth of this made her hot with shame. Seeing her flush, he smiled at her discomfiture.

'You are vile,' she said.

Her voice was quiet and venomous. He knew that he had lost. Wrenching her wrist, he threw her hand back at her and they stood facing each other, shaking with the violence of their loathing. If he could have obtained her fortune by killing her, he would not, at that moment, have hesitated to do so.

Theo turned away. With her good hand, she climbed the stile and began to retrace their path to the farm. She was sickened by his actions but too enraged to be afraid. In her heat, she felt that she could match his savagery with her own. She did not look round when she heard him come after her. He followed closely enough to have touched her if he reached out but he did not accost her. They did not speak and the sounds of orders being called in the hemp field came clearly over the hedgerows.

Charles quickened his step so that, as they emerged on to ground in view of the labourers, he appeared to be walking amicably at Theo's side. The foreman raised his arm in greeting to them and began to approach but Theo, occupied by her thoughts, did not see him and Charles affected not to. There was more than the loss of her wealth in her refusal of him; there was the prospect that Ralph would gain all that had been denied to himself. He could not endure the idea of it. If he could not have her, he would soil her for his brother.

With a sudden movement, he encircled her waist, dragging her back as he placed his free hand on her breast and kissed her. The assault was unexpected and swiftly past. He released her before she could gather herself to resist so that it seemed she had welcomed his embrace. He became conscious that they were being watched and, as the foreman halted, unsure whether to retreat, he lovingly murmured a foul name into Theo's ear and left her, in her shock and confusion, while he joined the men with the exaggerated calm of a lover who has been discovered in his passion.

Chapter Thirteen

'But she'll tell me nothing. I asked her "Why won't you speak?" and she just turned her head away. What am I to think?'

Ralph was roaming about the dining room at Carnow, fidgeting with one of Ettie's pens. She was sitting at the round table, that had never been ousted by the one Ralph had damaged, where she had been checking the butcher's bill and making out orders for provisions. Since she had told him plainly that she had seen through Charles, she and Ralph had grown into the habit of discussing family affairs with a directness that gave Ralph some relief from the feeling that his home had become barren.

'You have a choice.' She screwed the cap on to her ink-well. It seemed that Ralph's mood might lead to vigorous gestures and she did not wish her work to be wasted. 'You can think what Charles obviously wants you to and become sour and angry and fall out with Miss Theo. That, of course, would gratify him. Or you can keep hold of your sense and realize that Charles has done something insulting and it's too painful for her to tell you of it. To tell any of us but especially you.'

'If he's hurt her I believe I could kill him.'

'Which, no doubt, is much of the reason why she won't speak. If we lived a hundred years ago, you could have called him out but these are modern times. We must control ourselves or have the constables about our ears.'

Ralph lifted the lid of a soup tureen that stood on the sideboard and replaced it with a clang. The advantage of talking to Ettie was also its disadvantage. Her perfect composure let wisdom flourish but, although it is best to arrive at a rational judgement, a little temper along the way is satisfying.

As was obvious from his pacings, he was in a disturbed and puzzled frame of mind. Theo and Louisa had been expected to dinner the previous evening but a note had been received at Carnow cancelling their engagement without giving an explanation. This had been followed by a late visit to Ralph by Moore, warning him that rumours were spreading of Theo and Charles having been surprised in a compromising position in the meadows. It was being said that if Miss Farnaby did not marry the elder Carnow brother, then she ought to. Despite his own observance of Theo's familiarity with Charles, Moore did not believe that she would forget herself enough to be improper with him and his report was given in order that Ralph might not hear it in an embellished form from others and be led into rash actions. It was the behaviour of a friend and Moore had his reward in being there to restrain and calm Ralph.

Distrust of Charles and the insecurity of his own hopes had first filled Ralph with jealous suspicion. When Moore's common-sense had damped that fire, a violent need to challenge Charles to reveal the truth had overtaken him but Charles had absented himself, claiming that he had been invited to pass a few days with friends, without leaving an address. Until beyond midnight, when he had ridden away assured that Ralph would do nothing reckless, Moore had counselled caution and belief in Theo's innocence. Ralph's wounded heart had swayed him this way and that as he lay staring into the darkness but he had walked into the Farnabys' drawing room in the morning ready to take Theo's side.

He had found Louisa, anxious and exasperated. As they waited for Theo, she had told him how Theo had left the house the previous day with Charles but had returned alone and on foot, refusing to account for her distress or lack of companion. Louisa's contempt for Charles made her think him capable of any outrage and she had insisted upon questioning Theo, fearing that her niece's irrational impulses might convince her that whatever Charles had done had made marriage to him a necessity. She was relieved to find that Theo's independence had reasserted itself. A short, sparsely detailed description had been given her of how Charles had indeed proposed and, on receiving a refusal, had behaved in a manner which was gross and disgraceful but which had not put Theo in physical danger. It had been plain to Louisa that Charles had chosen to make Theo appear dishonoured as an act of vengeance and though his victim was unequivocal in her despisal of him, he had lodged a canker in her breast that could embitter her spirit. Louisa was furious that

Charles should be moving freely amongst them with his wickedness unchecked and when she had called him corrupt in front of Ralph and the pale and silent Theo, neither had contradicted her.

'My aunt says that she'll speak privately to my father,' Ralph said, turning back to Ettie with her pen still twisting in his fingers, 'and that in the meantime making a display of grievance will only serve to encourage the scandalmongers.'

'That's wise, as you're well aware. Not only for the sake of Miss Theo's reputation but also as she'll be more likely to open to you if she thinks it won't lead to your hands about his throat. She might gain a primitive excitement from that thought but she's too civilized to want its actual performance.'

'I can't answer for what I would have done if I'd heard of the rumours while Charles was by.'

'Then we must be glad that you have friends to put a barrier of good sense between you and the deed. And you can be grateful to Charles. One thing is certain. He has not only lost a wife and fortune in Theo – he has made an enemy who will look elsewhere for a companion.'

Ettie continued to sit at the table after Ralph had left her but she did not look at her work. She was thinking of Theo and Charles. It had been on the tip of her tongue to tell Ralph that Theo would look elsewhere for a husband but, as the words were in her mouth, it occurred to her that however scornful of Charles Theo might be, she would be unable to take the dispassionate view of his behaviour that would make her feel free to turn to another. There were rare occasions when Ettie wished that her early life had not stifled her own emotions but, when she saw how easily sensibility could steer a ship upon the rocks, she did not envy those who were at its mercy. If Charles had made Theo feel defiled, it was possible that she would hold herself aloof from both brothers.

It had not surprised Ettie to hear of yesterday's events. Since her question to Charles about violet pomade as they had driven to the Exhibition, her thoughts had not often left him. She found herself unable to see him without thinking of her mother. Images from her first years constantly appeared in her mind, arousing an intense sensation which the girl who was pitying Theo's susceptibility to feeling had not yet recognized as hatred, love and grief. There was an atmosphere of intrigue and mystery in her memories with overtones of menace and fear. Despite having few recollections of the Charles of that time she had a strange conviction that he had been part of her days; a conviction that was bound to an impression of times when she had been left alone in unfamiliar places until her mother had returned, flushed and with promises of treats if she said nothing of the rest they had had on their walk.

'Hush, now, it was only a dream.'

The soft voice inside her head was so real that involuntarily she lifted her eyes from the bill beneath her hand as if she expected to see someone in the room.

'Mama?' she said, experimentally, and the name seemed natural in reply to the voice. She closed her eyes, willing herself to remember the cause of the phrase that had come to her now, as it had come when she had smelt violets on Charles. Nothing revealed itself. She opened her eyes on to the figures on the bill and suddenly, with a vividness that startled her, she recalled a night when her mother had bent over her, pulling the sheets over her shoulders as she soothed and coaxed her. I was afraid, she thought, and was told it was only a dream. Why? What had frightened me? It was – I had woken in the dark and heard Mama crying in her bedroom beyond my door. She was pleading with a man and his voice was not my father's. I knew the voice and distrusted it. The man was laughing at her, assuring her that she would join him and live like a duchess. I didn't want her to leave. I climbed over the rails of my bed and felt for the door handle in the blackness. He said, 'It won't only be my inheritance the old fool gives me,' then I opened the door halfway and Mama ran and pushed me back so that I could not see in. She hushed me and when she left she turned the key. There was a scent of violets.

Ettie leant back in her chair. She found she was so rigid with tension that she was shaking. Unclenching her hands, she made an effort to recover. She did not welcome what her memory had disclosed, but she was not one to shy away from unsavoury truths. It seemed clear, from the snatches of remembrance conjured by Charles's presence and her observance of his character, that there had been a guilty liaison between himself and her mother. In the opinion of the world, that would be another disgrace for the daughter of a felon. But might it be the exchanging of one disgrace for another instead of an addition? Charles – and she did not feel the need to put a question mark to the name – had been anticipating money over and above what his father was to give him. Five hundred pounds had been stolen and never recovered shortly after Charles had disappeared. She had not ceased to believe in her own father's innocence. The conclusion that the theft had been carried out by Charles convinced her but she admitted that she had no evidence to support her theory and there were few who would accept the suspicion of a convict's child against the inevitable denial that would come from Charles if she were to accuse him.

She turned the matter over in her mind. Trent's imprisonment had been an accepted injustice to her – an affliction that was unfair but inescapable as if it were a cancer that had smitten him. Feeling the agitation within her, she thought that she had not gained by the revelation that had come to her. A relative peace of mind had been lost to a hope of her father's release which was unlikely ever to come to fruition. She could not begin to calculate how Charles had carried out the robbery and too many years had passed for an investigation to reveal what had really happened. Nevertheless, her suspicions must be laid before Ralph and in such a way that, even if they were not developed, good would come of them. She folded her papers into her writing-desk and placed it under her arm. After the experience of the previous day, Theo would believe Charles capable of treachery on this scale. She would go to Theo with her story, claiming to have a reluctance to be the first to speak of her mother's adultery to a man and ask her to tell Ralph. Theo would then be obliged to talk to him intimately and who could say what would come of that? Rising with resolution, Ettie went to fetch her hat.

Although he had admitted that he was not in perfect health, Mr Carnow would not agree that his condition was severe. With much grumbling, he was now taking the doctor's nostrums but had, if anything, increased his activities in an attempt to appear well. The following afternoon, while Theo was still digesting what Ettie had told her, he arranged to walk over to the flax-beds that lay along the river on the Beaminster side of Carnow with Mr Parris, before joining his estate manager at his home to look through the day-book. None of this was necessary work, as Mr Parris knew, but there was a certain collusion between Mr Carnow's family and senior employees to keep him from tasks that would involve concentration or strain. They had decided that if he would not willingly accept convalescence, then convalescence must be thrust upon him.

So it was that when Charles returned and asked for his father, he was directed over the meadow to the Parrises' comfortable brick house. He was not loath to have an excuse to stroll across the fields in the warm sunlight instead of going to his desk and made his way through the mill and over the weir while considering the best method of achieving his new end.

He had not been staying with a friend, as he had claimed at his sudden departure. He had no friends of the closeness that would allow him to arrive on their doorsteps unexpectedly and had found that a night at a hotel of the quality he preferred did not please his pocket. His mood was evil. He had believed that he had only to reach out his hand to grasp a fortune, and the violence of his fury against Theo for preferring to keep it in her own possession knew no bounds. The desire for wealth coloured all his thoughts and poisoned his judgement. He had no doubt that Theo would now accept Ralph and the thought of his brother controlling her riches and beauty caused his head to throb as if a garrotte were being tightened round it. His early inheritance was pushed from his mind and it seemed unjust that Ralph should have the enjoyment of mill and heiress while he was condemned to a counting-house stool. It was his regret that he had not shamed Theo more. She must now be soiled in Ralph's eyes but not enough to prevent him coveting her money.

There had been a moment the night before when, inflamed by the brandy with which he was quenching his disappointment, he had imagined himself returning to violate her. It was not in him to comprehend that Ralph might value her for different reasons than his own nor that in such an assault it is not the victim who is dishonoured. There was a satisfaction for him in thinking of her disgraced and rejected by a sickened and thwarted Ralph. It gave him a lewd pleasure to dwell on it but, whatever gratification there might be in debauching her, the risk of arrest would be great and, even if she were too crushed to stand up in court against him, his purpose would not be served in the long term.

His only road to wealth now lay through his father's foolishness. He had considered repeating the forgery that had been so profitable to himself and disastrous for the Trents ten years ago, but his investigations had early discovered that Ralph had moved the Carnow banking account to Dorchester, where those entrusted with the mill's transactions were now wellknown, and had hedged about the withdrawal and moving of monies with so many safeguards that another theft was impractical. If he were ever to be independent, he must persuade his father to make a new will. The share of his inheritance which he had been given must be looked on by Mr Carnow as forgotten, as it was by himself, and a new division must be made. Indeed, why should there be a division? Was he not the elder son and was not everything his by right? It was only his mother's interference that had secured any portion for the younger brother, who ought to have made his own way in the world. His mother was not living now and if he could not defeat the dead he was a poor champion for his prospects.

He walked across the meadow towards the Parrises' house with renewed determination. The grass was being left for hay and was fragrant with clover and fading buttercups that reminded him of the gold stain on Theo's cheek where she had put her pollen-drenched fingers. He was following a path that had been trodden through the grasses. His whip was still in his hand and he was absently drawing it along the stems, as a boy draws a stick along railings, leaving the feathery ears trembling behind. He had walked this path many hundred times before. It was as familiar to him as if he had never been away. In this meadow, he saw none of the small changes that had disorientated him on his return. The house ahead, the hills on the horizon, the very shape of the trees on the boundaries of the field were as he had left them. How often he had wandered beside the river as a boy, tickling frogs with a reed to make them jump, and how often he had ridden home from the hunt along the neighbouring lanes through winter sunsets that dyed the valley red, sullenly resenting the presence of the mill.

I made the wrong choice, he thought, twisting the flower from a tall daisy and shredding it with his thumbnail. It would have been wiser to stay. I should have worked on the governor to oust Ralph. I couldn't have got round Mamma but I could have persuaded the old man to have a secret will drawn up in my favour. There'd have been nothing she could have done; she wouldn't have known. Then, when she died, what a shock the little brother would have had. It's what I should have done. I could turn the dad about my finger in those days. We could have had a manager – or hired Ralph – and I would have had the income to do with as I chose. Well, there's time enough yet. It may even be more promising now. There may be a death in the offing and how sweet the fruits of that would be with a new document lying in the lawyer's box.

The confidence that had been restored during his months in this safe haven, that had burgeoned under Theo's blushes and suffered so severe a defeat from her refusal was seeping back into his veins. It flourished under the stimulation of wanting revenge. There had been nothing in his father's behaviour towards him since his return to make him think that he was no longer the sun in Mr Carnow's sky. The lenience that was shown him in his time-keeping, his place of prominence at table before Ralph's supposed accident with the knife, the freedom he had been given with the tradesmen of the town and, most of all, the ease with which he had escaped accusation over the thefts from the petty cash – thefts which it was plain from the reinstatement of the sacked boy that Ralph interpreted correctly – all showed that he was still his father's favourite. It should be possible to play upon the sick man's love and sense of duty for his elder son in such a way that he would be convinced that he had not dealt fairly with the one who ought to be his heir.

He could not deny, as he considered bending his father's will to his ends, that his belief in the success of his audacity was prompted by fear. With the loss of the security offered by Theo's wealth, the forlorn nature of his months in Canada pressed upon him and the pit of poverty yawned at his feet. He had thought himself recovered enough to venture alone into the world again if need be, but his readiness had been that of a man seated comfortably in an armchair who knows that his offer to go out into the wind will not be accepted. The idea of taking up his old life again, with its risks and perils, its struggles to seem affluent, its dependence on the turn of cards and smoothness of tongue exhausted him. He shrank from it. His confidence was desperation. It was the boldness of one sure that he can cross a tightrope because he dare not contemplate the chasm below.

Opening the wicket-gate, he crossed the lane to the Parrises' house. A small, hedged lawn separated the front door from the road. As he followed the gravel path to the porch he looked through the windows and saw that both Mr Parris's office and the drawing room were empty. The day was too fine for him to want to wait indoors with the threat of Mrs Parris appearing from some retreat to make forced conversation. Passing round the corner of the house without pulling the bell he strolled towards the rear garden, intending to find a restful seat but not averse to teasing Maud if she should happen to be there.

Hearing the crunch of footsteps on ashes beyond a screen of lilacs, he went in a slow pursuit of them. His feet were now on grass, that had recently been scythed, and made no sound. There were signs scattered at random that it was Maud, not her mother, who was in occupation of the garden. A basket-chair had been placed in the shade of a young copper beech and a girl's shawl lay over its back and arm. A book, which Charles suspected of being a sentimental novel, lay open on a small table beside the chair and a bluetit, eyeing Charles warily, hopped between two plates pecking crumbs. A trug, half-full of cloyingly sweet lilies-of-the-valley, lay on the edge of the border and an open parasol, that must have been bowled over by a breeze, had settled handle-up in a clump of late wallflowers.

It pleased him that this house and its grounds belonged to the Carnows. He liked the prosperity it indicated to have such a property for the use of an employee and it made him feel powerful, as he strolled down the winding turf path between the lilacs, to think how in future years he could make people tremble for their homes and work.

The path ended in a glade that had been contrived for the secluded enjoyment of one who had a romantic and flower-loving frame of mind. It was enclosed by scented shrubs and overspread by a cherry tree from which hung a swing, now entwined with honeysuckle. A small, octagonal summerhouse, strewn with blue and white striped cushions, was positioned so that an occupant could look out over the iron fence to the meadows or in to the lush privacy of the grove. The grass was mossy here and invaded by waves of forget-me-nots and scarlet poppies. Peonies with swelling buds and drooping crimson blooms were sumptuous in the sheltered warmth, and honesty hid amongst the bushes. The only formal ornaments were the china jars of purple irises that flanked the pavilion door.

Maud was standing with her back to Charles, absorbed in attaching a net to the rails of the fence. She looked defenceless and Charles, remembering how easily he had stung her in the London carriage, was prepared for amusement.

'You don't keep up with the times,' he said. 'This looks like something from the Ark. Don't you know that nature worship has gone?'

Maud started up, turning towards him, and he was gratified to see a look of timidity pass over her face.

'It is old-fashioned,' she replied, with an effort, 'but that's how I like it.'

'Are you an old-fashioned girl?'

'In some matters.'

He smiled disagreeably. 'I wonder which they are,' he said.

His voice conveyed suggestions that took her back to their journey to the Exhibition and she felt herself growing hot and awkward. She could not think why he was there. He never paid them social calls and if he had come on business to her father he would not have appeared alone in this way. She did not want him near her. There was a threat of danger in his presence that was unnerving and made her want to keep a distance between them. It was not that she feared physical harm from him but there was something in the twist of his words and glance of his eye that she could not define but which, even before his jibe in the four-wheeler, served to cheapen whatever was in his range. In her youthful love for Moore, she was sensitive to innuendo and Charles made her feel indecent and unworthy of her hopes.

Moore had not been far from her thoughts that day. His ship

had been unloaded and provisioned with an efficiency that had outstripped previous arrivals and he was to sail again that evening with a new cargo for the Baltic ports. He had been with her for an hour that morning and was expecting her to stand upon the quay at high tide to watch his departure, with her feelings written upon her face. When they were together she was sure of him and during his absences she felt no reason to doubt their future but when Charles was before her, with his sleek disparagement, she suffered a sense that the world was not all as safe as the part that she had seen and that unexpected waves could dash her against a rocky shore.

Charles was watching her expression with satisfaction. A sheltered girl was easy prey and he did not fool himself that being able to intimidate Maud was a token of the success he would have in dominating his father but, even so, he felt his own importance. He put out his hand to a peony and broke off a bud that was beginning to unfurl.

'I like to see a flower that's just opening,' he said; his eyes fixed upon hers. 'They hold such interesting promise.'

He fitted the bud into his buttonhole and walked over to the summerhouse. Maud tried to retreat but was prevented by the railings. He fingered the grey-green leaves of a rose that was trained against the trellised walls.

'Maiden's Blush,' he said, 'It used to have another name. "Cuisse de Nymphe". Thigh of the Nymph. That always reminds me of days that I have known.'

There was another footstep on the ashpath and he turned sharply. Sadie Holman was standing at the side of the glade, carrying a wooden box.

'Look yonder,' she said, indicating the field. 'Snakeweed. That d'always remind I of sommut an' all.'

She came forward, unconcerned by the anger that momentarily hardened his features, and laid the box beside the net that Maud had left hanging from the fence. Sweetpea seedlings glowed a clear, delicate green in the sunlight.

'There now, miss,' she said. 'That's nearly tied on. If you take that un and I take this, we'll 'ave 'er done in a trice.'

Maud turned away from Charles and began knotting the loose ends of cord to the posts. She was relieved by Sadie's appearance and envious of her indifference to Charles's provocations. It vexed her that she allowed herself to be discomposed by him. There was a childishness in her reaction that she recognized but could not yet vanquish. But, she thought as she industriously tightened her knots, he is here and so must be a guest of sorts and I have turned my back on him. I am discourteous and continue to be so because he deserves it. That must be a step towards maturity. What freedom there could be in becoming an old woman who insults everyone.

Beside her, Sadie looked unflinchingly at Charles before fastening the last length of twine. Since the party's return from London she had found herself constantly dispatched to Maud by Barclay with tokens of undeclared love. His modest cheerfulness and assiduous polishing of his mother's worktable told her that something had happened in the city to make him believe that his suit might prosper. Her own observation of Maud while on these errands and her knowledge of the purpose of Moore's visits informed her that Maud had not only given Barclay no encouragement but did not realize the nature of his friendliness towards her. The disappointment that was looming ever closer for the sensitive young man made Sadie's protective heart yearn to comfort him. As they had sat in his kitchen the evening before – he applying beeswax to the compartments of the worktable; she braiding the net she was tying now – he had wondered aloud why Maud had been so eager to borrow the volume of astronomy he had sent to her that morning and Sadie, aware of the reason for Maud's wish to learn navigation, had longed to draw him close to her and marry him herself for his own good.

Charles felt himself snubbed. He reverted to a moderate tone that gave Maud an instant's misgiving about her own behaviour. She was afraid that she had misinterpreted the intention of his previous remarks but the deliberate blankness of his eyes assured her that her distrust had been correct.

'I was looking for my father,' he said. 'He'll be tired after inspecting the flax-beds. I thought it best to walk him home.'

'Mr Carnow and Papa haven't come back yet,' Maud said coldly, congratulating herself upon her attitude. 'If you follow the river, no doubt you'll meet them returning.'

This was so obviously a *congé* that Charles did not feel he could stay unless he summoned his energy to make himself thoroughly disagreeable and he wanted that at his disposal for the opposite effect. He needed to woo his father, and his malice for the world was too near the surface of his being for him to be sure he could revert to charming Mr Carnow if he began seriously to torment a victim. Theo's refusal of him had been like an earth tremor that causes slight changes above ground but raises ancient secrets from their burial place.

Returning to the lane, he followed it down to the bridge and leant on the wall, absently watching the river flow beneath him. As he had left the garden, he had seen his father and Mr Parris across two hedges, moving slowly towards him, and, though they were now hidden, it had been plain that they had been drifting closer to the path that would bring them out at the gate beside him. He had no more wish to make conversation with the estate manager than he had wanted to encounter Mrs Parris in the house and he did not go to meet the walkers as they came along the riverbank. Lounging against the parapet, looking down at the weed trailing in the current, he tried to recruit himself for the manoeuvres ahead but the sight of the water glinting in the sunlight took him back to the afternoon with Theo and his heart jumped with a frustrated rage that did not prepare him for the mood he hoped to foster.

Too absorbed in his anger to notice the progress of the pair, he was surprised suddenly to find them upon him.

'Well, Charles, I thought you'd be away longer. Was your visit agreeable?'

Mr Carnow's voice was tired and he was walking with his arm through one of Mr Parris's.

'It was, sir.' Charles straightened and nodded to his father's companion, who returned his greeting with a courtesy that could be faulted in nothing but its coldness. 'They told me at home where you were. I thought we might go back together.'

Mr Parris did not need to have it put more plainly that Charles wanted to see his father in private. He turned his head to his employer.

'May I show you the day-book another time, sir?' he asked. 'There's nothing in it that needs reviewing urgently.'

His diplomacy gave Mr Carnow a pang. During the past two

hours, he had been unable to hide from himself that the task he had set for them both in looking over the flax-beds had been unnecessary. An unwelcome voice at the back of his mind had been pointing out to him that Ralph had all aspects of the business in hand. He was touched by the kindness that was being shown by those involved in the charade of protecting him from exertion whilst trying to make him feel needed but he was too exhausted not to suffer an unfocused resentment of the situation. He was not sure whether he was piqued by his ill health, Ralph's solicitude or the rising of the younger generation. A simultaneous desire to have the ordering of the mill in his own keeping and to be dozing in an armchair had hold of him.

'Yes, another time.' He took his arm out of his manager's. 'And now, my boy, I've leant on poor Parris enough; I must pass the burden on to you.'

'It's my pleasure, sir,' said Charles, going to his father's side, 'as I'm sure it was to Mr Parris.'

There was a smoothness in this remark that brought a flicker of distaste to Mr Parris's eyes but Mr Carnow felt a pathetic gratitude to his son for being so ready to be obliging. He had not begrudged Charles his unexpected stay with the anonymous friend but it had made him uneasy in a manner that could not be explained simply by it being the first departure Charles had made alone since his return from Canada. The warmth of his relief at seeing his son again made him realize how afraid he had been of another ten years' absence. He barely acknowledged Parris's farewell in his eagerness to have Charles to himself.

They went over the lane and entered the same meadow that Charles had crossed to the house, taking the worn path beside the river. It had grown warmer and Mr Carnow took out a sizeable silk handkerchief to pat his face and neck. His legs were more swollen than they had been previously and gave him pain with each step he took. They were walking at a snail's pace but the effort to move at all seemed too much and the drag of his weight on his son's arm was such that Charles was forced to support his elbow with his freer hand.

He's weaker that I reckoned thought Charles. That's hopeful for me. Playing the dutiful child is wearisome.

'I'm afraid you've overtaxed your strength,' he said.

'Not at – ' Mr Carnow began testily, then gave a faint laugh that was hardly more than a breath. 'Yes.' He squeezed Charles's arm slightly. 'I can tell the truth to you, can't I? You won't think badly of your old dad because he isn't what he was.'

'You're everything you ever were. That's what keeps me near you. But I have been worried that you're doing too much. I came to meet you for fear you'd come back alone after too long a walk.'

Fatigue and sentiment prevented Mr Carnow speaking. In the privacy of wakeful nights since discomfort had stolen his accustomed peaceful sleep, he had found that his tears were unusually ready to fall. He would lie thinking of the events of the day or forming mundane plans for the kitchen garden when, suddenly, his face was wet and his weary heart racked with unaccountable anxieties. This gentleness from his beloved boy made his eyes prick and throat contract. He could not trust himself to reply.

Charles did not miss the effect his words had had. He looked at the distance there was to the mill and calculated that, even with their current slowness, he could not be sure of saying all that he wished before they would be in danger of interruption. With his father in such a susceptible state, the chance to influence him was too good to let pass.

'You have been overtiring yourself,' he said, with a soft accusation that made Mr Carnow swallow. 'How would you have got home? Sit here and we'll rest a little before we go on.'

He led his father closer to the water, where a fallen tree lay with its bark polished from years of strollers stopping to seat themselves on it. A willow, that had once been pollarded but had since been allowed to grow long branches from its ungainly stump, shaded them as they sat down. Mr Carnow took off his hat and wiped his brow.

'It's hot,' he complained. 'I seem to feel the heat more than I did. There was that day at the Exhibition—'

'When you had us so worried. Are you faint now?'

'No, just weary. It's cooler here.'

Mr Carnow, who was more giddy than he cared to admit, laid his hat amongst the leafy twigs that were sprouting from beneath the fallen tree. 'Here's a new growth,' he said, folding his hands across his waistcoat, 'after all this time. Part of the root must be uninjured.'

'If the stock is good,' said Charles, 'there can always be a late flowering. It can lie dormant season after season and then, when it's least expected, the sap can return.'

'Yes,' Mr Carnow touched his son's leg briefly, 'and be very welcome.'

Charles took off his own hat and watched himself turn it round on his knees by the brim.

'Welcomed by some,' he said.

He judged himself to have got just the right degree of wistfulness into his voice and, indeed, Mr Carnow was instantly in the grip of an alarmed pity for such sadness.

'Has Ralph—' he began but Charles shook his head.

'I'm used to Ralph, Papa,' he said. 'I've had to learn to be and I don't hold it against him that he hates – that he wishes I hadn't come home. I'm not a saint myself.'

'Then who's hurt you? Surely Ettie has said nothing?'

Has she not? Charles thought. There never was a girl who was more eloquent in silence.

'Oh no. She's a credit to your generosity in making her part of your household. You're always generous, Papa.'

It pleased Mr Carnow that Charles had reverted to using his nursery name. The friendliness of it indicated that Charles felt his father had not been cold towards him. A doubt that was like a chill at the heart of his overheated body made him ask for reassurance nonetheless. 'And I? Have I done anything to wound you?'

Charles was not entirely clear in his mind how to greet this question. Naturally, if he were to lead his father into altering his will, it was necessary that he should provoke a sense of guilt, but it must be done in a cloud of affection if it were not to seem as though he were making harsh accusations. It was his present intention to use Theo's refusal to his advantage before any other version of the affair should reach his father's ears; prevarication would be the most useful course. He gave a melancholy smile. 'Women are the devil, aren't they, Father?'

Mr Carnow was relieved. The tiredness that suffused his being and throbbed in his swelling calves made him feel unequal to criticism of his actions or supporting even Charles in deep unhappiness. Charles's light remark made him hope that his son was merely cast down by a discouraging glance from a girl who had caught his eye. His prejudice in favour of Charles and his pride in his mill made him certain that no young woman would turn down such a catch when once she knew that Charles was serious.

'Are you in love?' he asked. 'I'm a blind old man. I hadn't noticed you hankering after anyone.'

'I've tried to hide it.'

'But, why? Any girl would be flattered. A handsome, well-travelled man with such an inheritance—' Mr Carnow brought himself up short and Charles, with a secret, malicious exultation at his own cunning, stared out at the far bank.

'Is that it?' Mr Carnow asked, slowly. 'Did you think you couldn't keep a wife on your allowance?'

'It's true that I've neither home nor income to offer but whose fault is that? Mine.'

'Neither home – ' Mr Carnow unclasped his hands and gestured with them helplessly. 'You have a home. How could you believe you couldn't bring a wife to it? Am I so unfeeling? Our house needs a mistress.'

'One who couldn't tell where her husband would get the next penny to give her? No, I've made myself unfit to seek a wife. That's been told me by the lady I had the presumption to ask and I can't argue with it.'

Charles spoke with a dignified resignation. He felt his father stiffen as he admitted the failure of his proposal, and it not only increased his confidence but warmed him to find himself so loved. If I were made otherwise, he thought, I would be softened by this and live for years upon the crumbs he threw me; I prefer to be master of the throwing.

'Forgive me,' he said. 'You're unwell and I bring you my troubles. I'll say no more.'

Mr Carnow put a hand on Charles's arm. He was overcome by compassion and haunted by fears that neglect on his part had driven his son from him a decade before and was now doing so again.

'My boy,' he said, 'who should you bring them to but me? In all those years you were gone – weren't there times when I ached to have you confide in me as you're doing now? What did I care how you came back – if you were ill or in debt or with what complications – if you would only return and lay your misfortunes on my breast for me to carry.'

Charles felt him shudder and covered his hand with his own.

'You choose your words better than you know,' he said. 'I miss my fortune. I used all that I had to travel and educate myself in the world. I believed the instruction it gave me was riches of another kind but it seems it has a different appearance. My hopes have been called mercenary because I couldn't match my lady's property. What can I say to that? A man should make provision for his future family. I didn't take her wealth into account but I accept that people will say it was that which I loved.'

Anger against the unknown woman who had wronged his son was making Mr Carnow tremble. His breathing was quick and shallow and did not satisfy his lungs. He had to make an effort to draw in enough air to ask: 'Who was she?'

Charles turned and looked him in the face.

'Theo,' he said. 'Or perhaps I should call her Theodosia now – or Miss Farnaby.'

'Theo said that? Theo accused you . . . ' Mr Carnow was aghast. He sat as if he had been stunned. A haze of midges formed above the water at his feet, hovered in their indeterminate dance and moved on. He felt that the ground was slipping from under him as the river slipped towards the sea. There was so much in his family that he did not notice. If only his wife were alive, she would have known and opened his eyes; he would not have been lost. The roar of the mill was a rhythmic background here. He gazed through the splaying willow branches to the roofs of Carnow. It had been the dearest wish of his wife and himself that there should be a match between Theo and one of their sons. It had been a gladness to him to find the attraction growing between his niece and Ralph. A simple happiness had seemed to be approaching but now . . . He could not dwell on the implications of the news he had heard. I am ill, he thought, I shouldn't have to hear this.

Beside him, Charles nerved himself to continue. He found their situation distracting; it was too like the scene of his refusal not to remind him of the failure that had robbed him of so much that he desired. His own audacity was intriguing and he drew upon his spite against Theo and his brother to make him bold.

'You'll understand why I tried to hide my feelings,' he said.

Mr Carnow forced himself out of his reverie and looked at Charles. A tear glistened on his son's cheek. It pierced the father's heart.

'You were too noble,' he said.

'At first. Who was I to come between Ralph and his love? But it came to seem that my love was warmer than his. I've already given up so much to him. And you'll have seen for yourself how I was received by Theo. I don't say that she's fickle but I was given hope.'

'And there's none? You won't try again?'

Charles smiled mournfully.

'Oh, no. My position was made clear to me. The insult rankles. No, she'll go to Ralph as it seems everything must. He'll have wife, mill – mills – most of your affection. It's the natural result of my youthful mistake and too late to be changed now.'

'Nothing's too late to change.' The fear of the consequences of having been too hard upon his boy returned to Mr Carnow and revealed itself to Charles.

'Perhaps you're right, Papa,' he said. 'I came home intending never to leave but it may be – I'm sure it is – better that I go and make a new life elsewhere. You have no place for me. There's room here only for Ralph.'

Chapter Fourteen

'You're quite sure that we can't be overheard? No one could listen at the door?'

Theo was standing in Ralph's office. It was the morning after Charles had waylaid his father in the meadows, and outside the window ropemakers were crossing to and fro as if no thorny events were happening to their masters. She had sent a messenger and had arrived before time.

'Nobody can hear us but I could lock the doors if you prefer.'

She nodded and Ralph went into the corridor to fasten the door at the top of the stairs.

'We're alone on this floor,' he said, returning and placing the keys on his desk.

'Then if we're discovered locked in my name will be worth even less than it is now,' she said, bitterly. 'Less than the sweepings of the street.'

'Your name's safe with me as it always has been. I'd do nothing to harm it. You used to lose patience with me because I was too keen to protect it.'

'So I did. I've learnt my lesson since. You know – I was an object of interest as I rode through the mill today. Men stopped to look at me. They laughed when I'd gone by. It wasn't the kind of laughter that I like.'

Ralph's face had grown severe.

'Point out to me anyone who treats you that way,' he said. 'I'll dismiss them.'

'No, let them be. Don't take away their livelihood for what Charles has done. I'll endure the slights as if I didn't see them and they'll soon pass. Some other fool will take my place.'

She sat down in the chair across the desk from his own. 'If you have any wine . . . ' she said.

He went to the corner cupboard to fetch it and poured her a glass. To force himself to be calm, he was mentally repeating the warnings he had been given not to show too violent a reaction to the insult Theo had received but his outward composure went against the grain. It cheered him that she had asked for this meeting and had not shied away from being tête-à-tête. Her intention to outface gossip was admirable and he wished that he had the right to protect her completely. He was glad that she was able to fight her own battles but would rather fight them for her himself.

As she raised the wine to her lips, he thought how few days had passed since they had sat with Moore in the shipyard. The thaw there had been between them as they talked then had warmed his hopes. He had brought himself to believe that they could take up their love where it had been interrupted by Charles's return. Now they were again amongst the trappings of business, in conversation over Madeira that had sailed the northern seas, and all was changed. The enticing softness in her friendship had disappeared once more. There were barriers about her as real as if they were forged in iron. Her face was determined and strangely mature but her eyes were hard with a hatred that he understood yet did not want to find there. He felt that a wild animal he had tried to tame had come to him of its own accord, with its wildness intact, and would stay only if he made no sudden movements. Sitting down at his desk, he waited for her to reveal the purpose of her visit.

Theo found herself unable to begin. Her mission was to put forward a theory of past happenings which was not merely delicate but involved scandal and crime. It had not been easy to make herself come. The difficulties ahead had appeared so vast and unsavoury that she had sent her message on the very date that Ettie had spoken to her for fear that, if she delayed, she would never send it.

How the world has rocked in the past two days, she thought as she looked out of the window at the heavy, summer treetops. A fruit I believed to be perfect and whole has split and shown me the maggots feeding on its flesh. Her hand went to her mouth for a moment as if her memories made her nauseous. It was tempting to retreat into the weakness that was expected of women – to fling her troubles at Ralph's feet and demand that he take the responsibility of solving them – but that was no longer possible for her. She could not take a passive part in dealing with

Charles. To discover that he had betrayed her trust by stalking her with restraint and traveller's tales as net and spear would have been sufficient to make her vengeful. Her eyes had been opened and she saw how he had insinuated himself into her favours by playing upon her sympathies and flattering her into a belief that he and she were set apart from the common run by their superior appreciation of – what? Of having been to Naples and back. She despised herself for having been taken in.

Well, she told herself holding her glass against her lips, my awakening was brutal enough to instruct me. I thought myself a revered and desirable woman but I'm merely a bag of gold. Her face darkened as she remembered the afternoon by the river and Ralph, covertly watching her, was alarmed by her expression. It had sickened her to recognize Charles's duplicity but it was his public debasing of her that made her loathing of him venomous. She had never before been touched so intimately. Having such familiarity forced upon her shamed and degraded her because of what he had said as he molested her. He had called her a harlot and she could free herself from neither the foul sensation of his hand upon her breast nor the vileness of the name. Reason told her to cast the accusation away as the meaningless obscenity of a disappointed man but the strange attraction she had felt for both brothers and her illicit excitement over their antagonism made her sure that she was, indeed, a tainted creature. If he had seen it, could she be certain that others had not? She shrank from the renewal of her desire for Ralph as if she were unclean.

'What I have to tell you isn't easy for me to say,' she said, at last. 'While you listen you must think of me as a man.'

Her first words had sent a chill through Ralph. They sounded like the introduction to a second and uninvited refusal until her request reassured him. There were many ways in which she might torment him but she was too hot-blooded to imagine that he could set aside his awareness of her sex in matters of the heart. He nodded, still wary of saying anything that would send her away.

'Ettie called on me yesterday,' she said, hesitantly. 'She'd come to a rather curious conclusion and she didn't want to be the first to speak to you about it. I suppose she thought it touched you too nearly. It isn't like her but, then, it throws dishonour on her family as well as ours.'

'Dishonour?' Ralph was sitting upright and attentive. 'You use strong terms. Has she discovered something new about her father?'

'No, she's as convinced of his innocence as she ever was. More so. If her memory's serving her correctly, he never was guilty – it's her mother who's to be seen in a worse light.'

Ralph thought back to the fragile and lovely Helen Trent. 'I've never known Ettie to be misled by her memory,' he said, 'but it'll take a deal to convince me that her mother could carry out a fraud.'

'Not her mother,' Theo twisted her empty glass on the desktop. A loathing of Charles and a belief that, if Ettie was willing to expose the Trents' disgrace, it was not for her to shy away from talking of the affair, did not make the relating of their conversation simple. 'This does concern the theft but – ' She paused and took a breath before continuing. 'Since Charles came home from Canada Ettie's found herself disturbed in her mind. She's mentioned it to me before. She said she felt he was a key to a mystery that she hadn't known existed. When he was by, her thoughts were flooded with remembrances of her early days; his scent troubled her but she couldn't decide why. Then yesterday morning the solution to the puzzle suddenly arrived. She said it sprang at her.'

Theo watched her fingers kneading the stem of the glass as she spoke. She repeated the tale Ettie had told her of unexpected suspicions, of violet pomade and the recollection of the night her mother had wept whilst a man had flaunted the prospect of wealth. Her throat grew dry as she softly related the adultery and treacherous crime that had stained the life of a child, imprisoned her father and turned her into a girl with a reserve and gravity beyond her years. Silence seemed to press about her words and cold invade the sunlit room. Her head was bowed when she finished speaking as if it would give Ralph privacy if she did not look at him. Outside, a laden wagon rumbled out into the road to cries of warning that it was too near the gates and they both stared at it sightlessly.

To judge by appearances, Ralph had received the news calmly but his composure was due to shock preventing any one of his conflicting feelings gaining the upper-hand. Despite the stealing of the petty-cash, he had not credited Charles with the dishonesty and baseness necessary for serious crime and he found it painful to learn the truth. He would rather have continued to despise his brother for selfish indolence than have this darkness enter his family. It was beyond his comprehension how Charles could have lived at ease with himself, knowing the destruction he had brought upon the Trents. Horror pervaded him at the thought of Helen's suicide and the long imprisonment of a decent and innocent man. He was disgusted but not surprised that Charles had persuaded Helen into adultery; it was like his brother to take his pleasures without concern for the consequences for others. He wondered how Charles could stay in the same house as Ettie when he had deprived her of parents in the cruellest manner and how he could boldly court the father he had robbed and cheated. A satisfaction that good might come of evil rose in him for, even though they must suffer the pain of revelation, this might mean the banishing of Charles and the freeing of Trent; but this optimism was immediately replaced by helplessness. There was no proof whatever that the events Ettie remembered had happened or that the remark she had overheard – 'it won't only be my inheritance the old fool gives me' – revealed Charles's guilt in the fraud. I'm no criminal, he told himself, I can't begin to imagine how he did it and it's so many years ago.

'You believe it, too.' Theo broke into his thoughts. She was leaning forward, her arm on the desk and what she said was not a question.

'I do. I wish I didn't. It sickens me.' He got up, unable to be still, and walked a few paces to the window. 'It makes my skin creep to think of him amongst us with his smiles and his – ' he raised both fists and touched the panes with them as if he must make some gesture of aggression, 'his violet pomade. He takes the shelter of the father he almost ruined; he sits at table with the girl whose mother he – he did ruin. Dear God, when I look on the sorrow and harm he's done! Is there no injury he hasn't caused? Wasn't his inheritance enough for him? We were almost bankrupt and Papa's heart broken. I've spent my youth in here, in this room, working and working to provide for the family.' He rested his forehead for an instant against the glass. 'But that's nothing. Can you imagine what Trent has been through? And Helen Trent is dead. She died in agony and shame and couldn't even be buried in consecrated ground. Her death is on his hands.'

He looked round at Theo and, even in his own rage, he was shaken by the vindictiveness he saw. Her eyes were those of a predator. Turning from the window, he grasped the back of his chair.

'And he hasn't done enough or had enough, has he?' he asked, bitterly. 'He wanted more. All this while, he's sidled around you with his compliments and elegance. So careful; so cosmopolitan. Lies and deception to have control of your money and – just as a secondary prize – of you. What would your life have been worth if you were in his power?'

'I will never be in any man's power. I'll hold my place in marriage as an equal – let the law do what it will.'

'It could do much. You tell me to think of you as a man but you're a woman and as his wife he could have put you in hell. And I would have been there with you.'

Again, she thought, I'm excited by their antagonism. I'm defiled and not fit for any husband. I want to rest against him to be comforted but I must be guarded and solitary.

'What can we do?' she asked. 'We must be rid of him but how? We have no evidence and Uncle Carnow won't believe such accusations. If we told him he'd call it spite and go on doting on Charles until the mill's handed over to him on a plate.'

Ralph pulled back his chair and sat down. He had seen how she had mentally retreated from his declaration on her behalf and it was another grievance to lay at Charles's door. But she is here, he told himself. She has come to me and, if it's not in the manner I wish, at least she looks on me as an ally.

'I don't know,' he said. 'I'm too angry to think clearly now. Most of this occurred so long ago that there'll be no trail to follow.'

'There's Trent.'

'Yes, that would be a beginning. He's always refused to be visited but I'll write to the prison governor to make an appointment. I wonder if he knew of his wife and Charles? There may be something he remembers that will point our way.'

*

While Theo was closeted with Ralph, another fraught interview was taking place in the Carnows' house. It was being carried out by Louisa and Mr Carnow but was being listened to attentively by Ettie, who saw no reason to reveal her presence in the current disturbed and interesting state of family affairs.

Ettie had been sitting in the breakfast room where the sunlight was cheerful, simultaneously improving her Italian and her knowledge of horticulture with a tedious volume of the reminiscences of an ardent and aristocratic gardener. The number of fountains this Tuscan lordling had ordered seemed to her excessive but he was sound on the manuring of the kitchen beds. She had been disapproving of his laying water traps that drenched his unsuspecting guests, when she had heard Mr Carnow hailing Louisa in the dining room. The folding-doors that connected the two rooms were slightly ajar and she could hear their conversation perfectly.

It had cost much for Louisa to come this morning. She was perplexed by conflicting loyalties and saddened by the rift she must cause but she was not one to hang back when an unpleasant duty was to be faced. It had been her conclusion that it was more necessary to protect Theo from further insult than to keep Mr Carnow from the shock of what she had to tell him of Charles's conduct. She was worried by the effect that the news might have on Mr Carnow's declining health but she reasoned that if all unsavoury incidents were to be accepted passively for fear of worsening his condition, Charles would already be in the position of tyrant without having to inherit the mill.

Neither Theo nor Louisa knew of the other's mission. Louisa had not been present when Ettie had related her suspicions and they had not been divulged to her. Theo had made the common mistake of youth in thinking that the older generation would not understand the strength of desire and greed that could lead to adultery and fraud. She believed that Louisa would find the accusation too far-fetched to be credible. Louisa, in her turn, did not wish to tell her niece that she could no longer come to the Carnows' home while Charles resided there until notice of this ultimatum had been given to the supposed master of that house. She felt that Theo might object on grounds of its drawing attention to herself if she knew of it beforehand but would accept the accomplished withdrawal with secret relief if it were undertaken behind her back.

As Theo recounted Ettie's memories to Ralph in the locked office, Louisa was sitting sombrely in grey silks across the dining table from Mr Carnow, shattering the attention he had been giving to winding the eight-day clock. Even before she arrived he had not been concentrating upon what he was doing. He was still distressed by the episode with Charles beside the river and he was wandering about the house, interfering with this and that, merely as a method of denying that he was feeling more unwell than previously. Louisa's appearance had been welcome as a diversion, not least because he was in need of familiar and reliable friends about him. He was aware that Louisa did not second his high opinion of Charles but he expected sympathy from her. It did not occur to him that she could think so badly of his elder son that she would not consider it fitting that Theo should marry Charles. Her fondness for Ralph might mean that she was not as eager for the prospective match as she would have been if Ralph had never declared his attachment but, surely – and, here, the doting father found that unexpected pinpricks of guilt on behalf of the younger brother prevented him from losing himself completely in his bias towards Charles.

He had noticed at once that Louisa was looking solemn and he took this as an indication that Theo had told her of her proposal from Charles. Her refusal would naturally have upset her aunt and it was his immediate assumption that Louisa had come to commiserate with him. He was not without hopes that Theo could be persuaded that she had made a mistake and he was glad to have this opportunity of discussing the matter. Having had his offer of refreshment turned down, he drew out a chair for his visitor and took one himself. He shook his head and opened his hands in a gesture of bewildered sadness.

'This is a sorry business,' he said.

Louisa was puzzled; she had anticipated a blustering defence of Charles.

'Well,' she said, 'it's easier for me that you know about it. I didn't want to have to tell you.'

'I heard yesterday.'

'Really? Ralph didn't mention that he'd speak to you. Somehow I thought he'd keep it to himself.'

'Yes, I can see that he would. To give him his due, he's never been one to crow over others' misfortunes. No, he's said nothing. Charles told me. It pleased me that he feels he can come to me with his troubles. I must have regained his trust.'

Light began to dawn for Louisa.

'Regain it?' she asked, sharply. 'What can you think you ever did to lose it? And what did Charles tell you?'

'Of his love for Theo,' Mr Carnow was surprised by her tone. 'Of how he'd been refused by her.'

'Indeed?' Louisa privately congratulated Charles on his strategy. 'He may have told you of the refusal but I find it unlikely that he fully explained the how or why. Nor, I daresay, did he describe the unpardonable liberties he took in order to publicly disgrace her.'

A sensation of drowning filled Mr Carnow. He did not want this new and rank complication. His tiredness seemed to swell within him as his mind denied the possibility of what he was hearing. Louisa leant across the table and put a hand over one of his.

'You and I are old friends,' she said, gently. 'Do you think I'd distress you if I could help it?'

He was gazing at her white, ringed fingers.

'I thought you'd come to comfort me,' he said. 'I thought we could sit over tea and decide how to coax Theo into accepting my boy.'

It went to Louisa's heart to see him so pathetically downcast. In spite of his follies, she had much affection for him and she condemned Charles for having put her in a position where she must hurt one or other of her family.

'My dear,' she said. 'I'm so sorry that I've had to come to you like this! It was clever of Charles to give his version of the story first. No doubt, he told you of a love he's striven to hide and a future laid waste by grief. I'm sure he was noble and restrained – it's how I'd choose to be myself if I was trying to be convincing with such a tale.'

'He's been hurt.' Mr Carnow had put his thumb over hers and was holding her tightly even as he rejected what she said.

'No, it's my girl who's been hurt. Her innocence and trust have brought her to be blind to her own cousin stalking her for money. She forgets that she's an heiress but Charles didn't.'

'He told me she called him mercenary,' Mr Carnow spoke angrily but still clung to her hand. 'Why should he care for her wealth? He'll have enough of his own.'

'What do you mean? He's already had his patrimony. Do you intend to give him more?'

He did not reply and she went on.

'Ralph told me some time ago that you'd threatened to leave the mill to Charles. Is that what you've decided?'

He released her and sat back, looking abashed and defiant.

'It isn't certain,' he said.

Louisa had thought herself prepared for this but, when it was upon her, she was astounded.

'So,' she said, coldly, 'all that Ralph has done is to go for nothing. He's to watch another have the reward he's worked for. You're taking your favouritism too far. Don't you remember how near you were to ruin after Charles had been given his inheritance? You know as well as I do who set this business on its feet again. It was because of Ralph that no man or woman of your mill lost their employment and your name didn't carry the stigma of bankruptcy. And it's all to go to Charles who was away doing who knows what in pleasure resorts?'

'He thinks there's no place for him here,' Mr Carnow said, pleadingly. 'If he isn't made comfortable, he'll leave again.'

Such weakness disgusted her but she forced herself to be calm. 'Now you've said a wise thing and will act on it foolishly.' She gripped the edge of the table. 'He'll stay as long as you pander to him. What does that tell you about the sincerity of his longing for you and home? He wanted Theo because marrying her meant that he could have his cake and eat it. He'd be rich without having to lift a finger or wait to inherit.'

'You want him to leave!' He tried to shout but the strain of taking enough breath was too much. 'You want him to go! You've always preferred Ralph.'

'Yes, I have. It's as well someone did. I've bitterly regretted having taken Theo abroad instead of letting her accept him, young as she was. I know that he would never have treated her as if she were a woman of the streets as Charles has done.'

Mr Carnow began to stand up. 'I'll hear no more,' he said.

Louisa met his eye and held him in his chair. 'What you don't hear from me,' she said, 'you will from another. It's common gossip and will be blamed upon Theo, as such slurs always are cast upon the victim. Let me tell you plainly that after Charles had been turned down by her, he followed her to a field where men were there to see the insult. He then kissed and embraced her, his – his hand firmly upon her breast. He deliberately made it appear that she welcomed these attentions.' She stopped to collect herself. Although her voice was steady, her own pulse was rapid with the pain of what had occurred and the shock she was administering.

'You'll understand,' she continued, 'that I can't allow Theo to enter this house whilst Charles is in it.'

'Little Theodosia?' Mr Carnow was aghast. 'She's had freedom here since she could crawl. Won't she come to my home? She used to be pleased to sit on my knee.'

'She's no longer a child. She's old enough to be prey for the likes of Charles.'

He put his hand to his chest and hunched himself over a sensation that was not quite nausea or pain but a mixture of the two. Seeing it, Louisa was afraid for him and silently cursed Charles.

'None of this is true,' he said, faintly. 'None of it.'

Louisa rose to her feet. 'I'll leave you to think on it,' she said. 'Remember that I came to protect Theo – not to make us enemies. It grieves me to see you in this anguish but I must say one more thing. If you leave your mill to Charles, I'll leave mine to Ralph. I didn't tell you of my decision before because I thought it might encourage you to be unjust. I'm telling you now to show you my belief that Ralph is the better man. Theo, of course, will have her own. Each of our three children will have possession of a mill. We shall see what comes of it.'

Chapter Fifteen

Having gained information from her eavesdropping, Ettie did not hesitate to pass it on. No sooner had Ralph seen Theo out of his office and sat back to brood over his brother's evil doings, than Ettie took her place. Like Louisa, Ralph had thought himself prepared for Mr Carnow to become so desperate to hold Charles that he would renege on the agreement over his younger son's inheritance, yet he found himself shaken by the potential foolishness being transformed into a strong possibility. He had suffered so much hurt and humiliation at his father's hands that these did not increase as he listened to Ettie relating the conversation she had heard. Instead of feeling isolated and discarded, he was warmed by the comradeship shown him by the three women, who were ranged upon his side. It was an encouragement to know that he was supported and he was immediately combative.

He had never really expected Mr Carnow to leave the mill away from him and the injustice of it roused him to set his cards upon the table in front of his father. Again, like his aunt he had been more guarded in his behaviour than he wished because of Mr Carnow's failing health. He was not, however, about to surrender the result of his years of struggle to Charles for fear of worsening what might be a temporary condition. Telling Ettie what had occurred between Theo and himself that morning, he wrote to Trent requesting an interview and dispatched her to the post office with it, before returning to the house in pursuit of his father.

He approached meeting Mr Carnow with dread. His plain speaking would be the most open breach there had been between them and he did not want to sever their bonds of affection. Determination carried him into the drawing room, where his father was nursing his agitation by the empty hearth, and steeled him against being deterred by the poignancy of the moment. It was tempting to water down his message, for the comparison between himself and the frightened, wounded man, who regarded him so piteously, made him feel vigorous enough to be confident of success if he started life afresh. Had it not been Charles who would benefit from the melting of his heart, he thought he would have bitten back his words once more but the unfairness of what faced him overruled his long habit of protecting his father.

He stood in the room that he had always known, which, in days to come, he would not enter as a friend if he were rebuffed.

'I'm not here to persuade you to change your plans,' he said. 'I won't coax or bargain with you. What you intend to do is wrong. It wrongs me. Cast your mind back over the years and ask yourself if that isn't true. I've given you more love and forbearance than was your right and I'll never break myself of doing so, whatever you may deny me. But, hear this. There's a pretence that I've helped to foster that there are two masters of this mill. There's only one and I am he. Your name is on the deeds and you can steal my birthright from me to give to your favourite, but if you do there'll be failure. My loyalties will be elsewhere. I'm tired of modesty and discretion. What you desire isn't just; it isn't honourable. Give me what is mine.'

'He wept. It was terrible to see it.' Ralph turned his head to look at Theo as she sat beside him in the trap. 'I'm sorry I'm repeating myself but it's marked me. He was so helpless – as if he were my child, not my father. If I'd watched him bleed it would have been easier.'

'And he still said nothing of what he'll do?'

'No, but I'm convinced that the shock of the past few days has made him reconsider. He pressed my hand as I raised him from his chair last night. I haven't ever known him be tender in his glances when he thinks he won't meet my eye.' He laughed a little bashfully. 'Hark at me. I'm like a girl blushing for her first love.'

'Girls aren't always so delicate,' said Theo. 'They can take attentions for granted. Uncle Carnow is the girl who couldn't appreciate what she had till it was gone.'

They were driving over the high downs, along the road to Dorchester that was barely less straight than if the Romans had never left their outpost. It was four days after Theo had told Ralph of Ettie's suspicions, and the weather had grown hotter. The sky was so mercilessly blue that Theo had tied an overlapping scarf around the broad brim of her hat to shield her eyes from the brilliance. The white dust rose behind them and hung in the still air before settling softly back into their tracks. To their right, beyond the sultry valley, the sea rolled calmly with an incoming tide.

Their purpose, hidden by a claim from Theo that she wished to visit certain shops, was to have an interview with Trent at the gaol. It was an appointment that, for different reasons, was causing them both disquiet. The complications Ralph had envisioned with his father had melted at his touch, only to be replaced by those raised by receiving a letter from the prison governor saying that Trent refused to see him or any other member of the Carnow family. Acting on her own suggestion, Theo had then written to him humbly requesting that she be admitted to see him. She remembered his character well, and basely, she thought, played upon his chivalry and fatherly feeling. Without mentioning Charles or the fraud for which Trent was suffering, she wrote that Ettie had told her of a matter of the gravest importance which made it imperative that she should meet him. She would not force herself upon him but entreated him to grant her this favour. He did grant it.

Her sheltered life had never before led her into a prison and she was apprehensive about what she would find. To walk into the gaol was to confront another aspect of the underside of life that had been thrusting itself upon her over the last few days. She put her arm over her breast to protect herself as she remembered the squalid revelations she had had. The sensation of Charles's hand forced on her still crept upon her skin. It was impossible for her to imagine herself ever being eager to be touched by a man and this further cause for hatred of Charles urged her to carry out this present venture.

Without this spur, she felt she might have shrunk from what she was about to do. Although she had known and liked Trent when she was a child, and despite her belief in his innocence, she was afraid to meet him. He might have grown brutal and coarse from years of associating with criminals. Even if he had not, how could she face a man incarcerated without cause by the misdeeds of her own cousin? What if he had not learnt of his wife's adultery and she must make him aware of his having been cuckolded, without being able to effect his release? But I must go on, she thought as she looked out over the sweep of the downs to the glinting horizon. I may hurt him in that way, it's true, yet he'll have the assurance that three of us are convinced that he's innocent as he's always claimed. And who can tell? He may hold some shred of information that was made nothing of at his trial but which will point our way to gaining his freedom and guarding Carnow from Charles. I asked the world to give me more than the safe monotony that's the usual lot for the wealthy of my sex. My prayer was answered and I won't cry that I don't like it.

They drove in silence, each thinking of their task and its reasons. The road dropped from the brow of the hill and ran through undulating meadows where sheep hung their heads beneath the harsh sun. In the shade of a copse that cast green shadows on a ring of standing stones, they lifted their faces to the air as if to drink the coolness to preserve them from the heat to come.

'When we arrive,' said Ralph, breaking suddenly into their settled abstraction, 'I can ask again if he'll see me instead. I don't want you to have to do this. It's no place for you.'

Theo emerged from her reflections with difficulty. She felt half-hypnotized by the motion of the journey and her concentration upon revenge. Like a young warrior about to be tested in battle, trepidation and excitement seethed within her calm exterior. She was ready to take offence at being thought incapable but the expression on his face checked her. He was trying to shield her from unpleasantness just as he had done in the time of their courtship when he had not wanted to expose her to gossip. She would have given much to respond to his kindness as a lover should, but Charles sat between them.

'No,' she said. 'He might take fright and refuse us both. Don't be anxious. I've more strength than you imagine.'

'I've never thought you weak.'

'You have – too weak to know my own mind. I did weakly swallow Charles's charm at face value but now I've discovered my strength with a vengeance.'

The road was pitted enough for Ralph to occupy himself with

guiding their horse through the less dangerous ruts. It was not easy for him to act as though he was her brother. Her reference to his foolish accusation when he had proposed embarrassed him. If there was a time in his life that fate would allow him to obliterate and have again, he would choose the afternoon when his arrogance had shattered his chance of happiness. She had admitted in plain terms that part of his judgement of her had been right but she spoke with an angry bitterness that warned advances away.

He dared not offer her the comfort that he longed to give. To suggest that he ask again to meet Trent was as near as he could venture to a protestation of love and it was not only for her sake. He wanted her to succeed but was afraid that, if she did, her realization of her independence would mean she did not need him.

They left the trap with an ostler at the King's Head and walked down to the river. The hangman's cottage, whose welcoming appearance contrasted so strangely with its tenant's occupation, was mellow beneath its old thatch beside the weir. Theo took Ralph's arm but did not lean on him and he could feel her tension in her grip on his sleeve. When they reached the gaol, she untied the scarf from her hat and handed it to him to keep in his pocket, where he twisted and pleated it throughout her absence until it was returned to her in a forlorn and useless state.

A turnkey was on watch for them and opened the gate at their first knock. It struck Theo how unaware he seemed of the solemnity involved in crossing the boundary of this place of captivity. Her palms were damp and her breathing quick but he smiled and made comments on the weather as he refastened the lock, as if they were stepping into his parlour. Familiarity blinds us to many things, she thought, but there's enforced death here and the sundering of families who will never meet again. Does he test the wind when the transportees are leaving and women weep beyond the walls? Are the crops his concern when he hears the gallows creaking?

In a courtyard beyond the entrance women were staring openly at them. One strolled slowly by carrying a mop and bucket; another was knitting with scarlet wool – her fingers working faultlessly as her eyes drank Theo in; a young girl, mouth open to the sun, slept propped against the cells; several sat on stools netting. This last activity was disturbing to Theo. It reminded her of how small the division could be between those at liberty and those confined. The free and the convicted woke, ate and went about their occupations but some had crossed a dark threshold and could not return.

Ralph was speaking to her and she dragged her attention back to him.

'The governor, Mr Plowden, is detained with the chaplain,' he said. 'He sends his apologies. The turnkey will escort you to Trent.'

'Where will you be?' She spoke casually but, now that the interview was at hand, the prospect of going forward alone did not please her.

'In the office here. You have permission to stay as long as it suits you and you'll be brought back.'

'You'll wait?'

'Yes, I'll wait.'

The turnkey stepped forward and waved towards the courtyard. 'Ma'am,' he said.

She left the shelter of the gates determinedly as if she were setting out to open sea. Everything about her from her ability to leave the gaol to her conspicuously well-made clothes made her self-conscious under the scrutiny of the women she passed. Even with the company of the turnkey, she felt exposed and defenceless and her sense of being a stranger in a foreign land increased when they reached the men's quarters. There was apathy written upon many who watched their progress but still there was enough unspoken threat to make her walk firmly with her head upraised.

The prison was constructed in six blocks around seven courtyards. Her protector led her to the main building, under one of the iron bridges that connected it to smaller blocks at its corners, and through an entrance where another gaoler sat reading a newspaper aloud to three men half-heartedly weaving baskets. All four got to their feet at Theo's approach and one prisoner sheepishly touched his forelock.

'Miss Farnaby to see Trent,' said the turnkey who she now regarded as her own.

One of the convicts looked sideways at his neighbour and winked.

'He's ready for you, ma'am,' said the gaoler, pointing down the corridor with the folded newspaper. 'In the end room. You'll have it private. Quiet as Easter Sunday.'

She followed the turnkey along the passage, her hands folded tightly together. They stopped where it turned to the right and he glanced through a grill in a closed door.

'This un's a visiting room, ma'am,' he said, kindly. 'You won't have to go in no cell. I'll sit on that bench yonder and you give I a shout if you need anything. Just you take your time.'

She nodded, her voice difficult to find, and he held open the door for her. An instant of panic overtook her as she heard it shut but she quelled it as quickly. A man was facing her with his back to the light from a barred window. The whitewashed room was empty except for a plain table beyond which he stood and two chairs drawn up to it. She did not know whether she recognized him. He seemed familiar yet with that unexpected quality of strangeness that a friend has when long acquaintance falls away and we see him as if for the first time. She could not say whether she could have named him if she had met him in the street.

'Mr Trent?'

'Miss Theodosia.'

Hearing him speak roused more memories than the sight of him had done and the import of their situation silenced her. He misinterpreted her intake of breath.

'I beg your pardon,' he said. 'I used the old term. Perhaps I should say Miss Farnaby.'

'No,' her fingers were still tensely entwined. 'I always think that's my aunt.'

'Is your aunt in health?'

'She is, sir.'

Theo was disorientated by their conversation. It had not occurred to her that the ordinary niceties would figure in it.

'Will you sit down?' he asked.

She pulled out the chair nearest to her and he sat opposite, his back still to the bars. His thinness troubled her. He was clean and dressed with sober decency but the lines on his face were too deep to be smoothed and his eyes looked at her from some far desert region.

'Ettie asked me to convey to you her loving greetings.'

Because she was ill at ease, Theo spoke stiffly as if she were repeating a lesson but Trent's face softened at the message.

'You call her by her pet name,' he said. 'Are you her friend?'

'More than that, sir. I regard her as a member of my family.'

The well-intentioned answer immediately removed the tenderness from Trent's expression.

'That doesn't please you?' she asked.

He regarded her with a cool, steady gaze. There were marks of his spectacles on the bridge of his nose and she remembered how he had always polished them on a green silk handkerchief.

'I didn't want to meet you,' he said. 'I agreed because you were so courteously pressing and because you're a Farnaby. You wouldn't be here if you were a Carnow. You may think me impolite. That's as maybe. I have good reason.' He leant an inch closer. 'I looked on your uncle as almost a friend. Not quite, naturally, our stations in life wouldn't allow it. He needn't have prosecuted me. I gave him my word that I was innocent and, after all my years of loyal and honest work, he believed me guilty. I was betrayed and it killed my wife. Do you think I can bear to be near a Carnow? Yes, they've saved Ettie from poverty and worse – for worse does come to girls the world shuns; this place has shown me that – but consider what it is for your child to be raised by those who wrongly stole your freedom and good name.'

The years that he had endured behind these walls gathered about Theo in the quiet room. He had been dead to her until today; a legend of the long past.

'I make you uncomfortable,' he said. 'Do you dislike to have the truth spoken of your uncle? Are you an affectionate and dutiful niece, Miss Theodosia?'

'I am, sir, but my love and duty don't prevent me seeing that my uncle isn't a sensible man.'

He inclined his head and rested against the back of his chair.

'If anything in this matter can be so described,' she said, emboldened, 'then it's fortunate you were never transported. Do you fare well in – this company?'

'A little mercy has been shown me,' he said, dryly. 'The Keeper – the governor – finds me useful for my secretarial abilities.' He smiled slightly. 'Not only those. It's one of his obligations to draw up accounts. I do them. He has more faith in me than the Carnows had. Every quarter they're audited by JPs, who never dream they're agreeing the records of a fraudster.' His eyes hardened. 'Are you surprised by my position?' he asked and his voice was like the oil poured on raging waters that keeps its calm despite the turbulence beneath. 'Do you begin to think that my punishment is not as harsh as you'd imagined? That things have not gone so badly with me, after all? I see you do. Then suppose that the gates aren't opened to let you home tonight. Nor tomorrow, nor for a hundred, a thousand tomorrows to come.

'I've never seen my dear wife's grave. My Helen, who died for shame of my shame. The years pass and my daughter grows up in the shadow of humiliation and grief. I must pray to be forgotten by her and all who knew me if she's not to be stained by my degradation. The world has been cruel to my family.' He held his bunched fingers to his brow as the permanent ache there worsened. 'My health is poor. I believe it unlikely that I'll live to be released and for that I'm thankful. I wait only for oblivion.'

Beyond the bars, there was laughter and jeering. The sound of several men in a half-violent, half-playful scuffle approached and retreated from the window. A turnkey called a sharp order and silence returned. The light fell on Trent's sparse hair making its whiteness seem transparent. I believed in the one who did this to him, Theo thought; he would have put me in another prison and as cold-bloodedly.

'You mistake me,' she said, her voice shaking. 'I know that you're innocent, as does the daughter who'll never cast you from her mind.'

Trent trembled visibly. Looking as though he had been struck, he covered his face with his hands.

'I've suffered despair, Miss Theo,' he said. 'I hope you may not learn the meaning of the word.'

'And there are two Carnows who can say where the guilt really lies. Ralph and Charles are both aware of your innocence.'

'Mr Charles has come back?'

'He has and his presence has roused memories in Ettie. I'll tell you what she recollects, sir. Forgive me if you find it painful. I repeat it only for the chance that it might make you remember something that can lead us to evidence that will release you.'

In gentle tones that faltered when she saw him crushed by what she said, she told him all that Ettie knew. He sat crouched on his chair, his back bent so that the cheap cloth of his coat strained between his hunched shoulders. It was no kind act to deliver such fresh sorrow and, as she spoke, Theo condemned herself, weighing what she saw against what Charles might yet do.

'I'm afraid this has been a shock to you,' she said. 'I'm so sorry, so very sorry. Perhaps I should have said nothing.'

He shook his bowed head with a slight, abrupt movement.

'No,' he said, in a sighing whisper. 'The man's a villain. God grant me some remembrance that can harm him.'

'But if it does no good!' Theo cried, her own throat full. 'I could have left you in ignorance of your wife's misconduct.'

He raised his hand in a dismissive gesture.

'Does Ettie know when he seduced her mother?' he asked.

'No, it impresses her as a constant background to her infancy.'

'My heart's been broken since I was accused.' His voice was stronger but he kept his face lowered. 'I think it would break again if Ettie isn't my daughter.'

A wave of nausea rose in Theo. It came upon her suddenly that the child they had all cared for with such magnanimity could be of their own blood and her naivety startled her. She had taken it for granted that Charles had debauched Helen Trent after Ettie's birth and the implications of this new possibility were sickening.

Trent looked up at her blanched face. 'It would be a fitting twist,' he said, 'if the girl Mr Carnow has been charitable towards was his granddaughter, wouldn't it?'

'I've seen nothing of Charles in Ettie,' Theo said. 'For her own sake, I can't believe she's his.'

'You've given me grounds to hate him. I can do it with ease; I've become well-versed in hatred – but something more than justice must have brought you here. Young ladies don't visit convicts in gaol because of a girl's unverified memory.' He watched her closely. 'You must be an heiress, Miss Theodosia. Did he try to marry you?'

She nodded, her lips compressed.

'No doubt he's run through his inheritance and the money for which I've paid. You must have seemed a safe haven.'

'He fooled me. I thought him ill-treated because he told me so.'

'I distrusted him when he was a youth. I didn't want him for my master. He was always one for honied words and bills of promise but I never suspected the degree of his depravity.' He slid his two fingers into the opening of his waistcoat and rocked himself as if over a spasm of pain. 'I believed my wife was pure. I can't bear to –'

He was unable to finish. The hollows beneath his cheekbones were livid in the uncompromising light.

'You're convinced by what Ettie remembers?' Theo asked.

'I am. If I'd lived a free man I'd have defended her virtue against all accusations but life has taught me what wickedness there is in the world. I'd rather have hanged than learnt of her vice but at least she'll have known my innocence. She was clever enough to have added two and two and the answer killed her. How could she have revealed her paramour's guilt? She had no more evidence than we. Ah, Helen.' He bent lower under his burden. 'You've brought me a bitter cross, Miss Theo. There's no greater gift than a strong and loyal love. I thought that I'd been given it.'

'You have it from your daughter, sir. She's never wavered in her belief in you. Is there nothing you can remember to substantiate her tale?'

He shook his head again, more slowly. 'How can there be? I wasn't in the bank when the fraud was done; I didn't draw the cheque. I had no reason to suspect your cousin until today. There's no hope for me.'

They sat in silence, facing the truth of his assertion. In the corridor the short-stepped tramp of shackled feet went by.

'Will you do me a kindness?' he asked.

'Gladly, if I'm able.'

'When Mrs Carnow told me of my wife's death, she said Helen had left my – had left Ettie a letter to be opened when she was twenty-one. I thought it would contain the wishes that any mother would have for her daughter's future or a justification of her suicide. Now I believe it will tell of Ettie's parentage. She could have been afraid rumours of her affair would leak out and wished to assure her girl that she wasn't base-born. Or she might have wanted her lover's child to know she wasn't fathered by a clerk. Is the letter secure?'

'I can't say. I'd forgotten its existence but if Aunt Carnow agreed to pass it on, I'm certain it will have been kept.'

He nodded. 'I've some respect left for Mrs Carnow, disgraced as I am. She did what she could amongst the wreckage and a woman's hands are often tied. This is the kindness I request. I may not live to reach the opening of the letter. If I do, ask Ettie to tell me its contents. Whatever they may be. I am already in pain; I want to die in knowledge.'

Chapter Sixteen

'I did remember it but it didn't come to mind in this connection. I've thought of it often but I suppose I expected an outpouring of sentiment, not any kind of explanation.'

There was a hint of emotion in Ettie's voice as she and Theo sat in the Farnabys' drawing room, waiting for Ralph to bring them Helen Trent's letter. The blinds had been closed against the sun and the pale, green light suited their conspiratorial air.

'Are you quite sure you want to read it now?' Theo asked. 'Aunt Carnow promised it would be given to you when you reached your majority or were to be married. We don't want you to feel pressed into going against your mother's wishes.'

Ettie stirred slightly in the upright chair she occupied. 'It seems Mama wasn't given to keeping her word. It's best we open it now.'

A stranger in the room would have thought Ettie perfectly calm but to Theo, who was familiar with the girl's normal habits, her small signs of discomfort were a clear indication that she was suffering severe distress. It was the day after Theo's visit to Trent and it was Ettie herself who, on being given an account of the conversation as soon as Ralph and Theo had returned, had suggested that they ignore her mother's instructions and read her dying message at once, in the hope that it contained evidence to incriminate Charles.

'Perhaps,' Theo said, tentatively, 'there may be something in it that Mrs Trent felt you could accept more easily when you were older.'

Ettie crossed her legs neatly at the ankle. In appearance, she had her usual composure but a tremor in her voice again betrayed her.

'If you mean that Mr Charles is my father,' she said wryly, 'that's impossible. If he was my sire, I'm illegitimate and, as a bastard, the law deems me "no man's child".'

Theo dropped her eyes, not knowing how to reply.

'But whatever the outcome is,' Ettie went on, 'I'll continue to call myself Trent and I won't claim you as cousin.'

Theo looked back at her young friend.

'My dear,' she said, gently, 'I'd be proud to know that we were kin but for your sake I hope that Trent's your father.'

'I spent a long time staring into the looking-glass last night,' Ettie said. 'I can't see a resemblance to either of them. Does anything strike you?'

'No, your features are your own but, now and then, while your – while Trent and I were talking yesterday, his manner of speech reminded me of you.'

'You say that to be kind.'

'I'm repeating what I thought.'

Outside a window, a bird flew up from a stem of ivy and cast a shadow against the blind. The sudden motion distracted them, throwing them into a restless silence. They expected Ralph's arrival but he had been unable to say exactly when he could join them. He, too, had remembered the letter when reminded of its writing and, searching his mind for where it might be, had decided that it was likely to have been stored in the mill's main safe with a packet of documents concerning his mother's private business. There had been no convenient moment the evening before for him to rummage in the safe but they had planned that he should remove it with a lease he needed to examine that morning and join them while Louisa was driving to Beaminster to lunch with the rector's wife.

'I hear him coming.'

Ettie started up at the sound of steps on the path and opened the door to listen for his knock. She leant out into the landing, holding her long hair away from her ear with her free hand. A few words passed between Ralph and the maid, then Ettie stood back to let him in as he came up the stairs.

Theo twisted round on the edge of the sofa to watch him enter. Her heart was rapid with anticipation and she had to restrain herself from running forward to greet him. United as they were by their common desire to oust Charles, she was able to be less awkward in his company than before she had told him of Ettie's recollections. Ettie's scheme to bring them together by her own pretended reluctance to expose her mother had worked to this extent but the ghost of Charles's touch still divided them. The image she had conceived on the evening of Charles's return, when she and Ralph had ridden back from the woods, of herself poised on the brink of diving, returned to Theo now. She could not give herself up to the rushing waters. As each brother had held and kissed her in their separate ways, she had felt trapped by different means and she feared physical powerlessness. She wished it was not so. As she had lain in her room last night, endlessly going over the events of the day, Trent's statement that a loyal love was life's greatest gift had recurred to her too often for her not to apply it to her own case. She knew that this gift was offered her and she had learnt its worth but still she dared not take it. None the less, her face was alight as Ralph turned towards her and a warmth spread in him as he saw his welcome.

Ettie closed the door after looking about the corridor for anyone who might overhear and came hurriedly to Ralph's side. Theo had also risen and the three stood together as Ralph reached into an inner pocket of his frockcoat and drew out the letter.

It was of yellowing paper folded into a square and sealed with red wax. A pale blue ribbon was tied around it and Ettie could not tell whether a faint scent of violets was only her imagination. She lifted her hands for it as if wine were to be poured into them and Ralph rested it delicately on her palms.

'Was it where you thought?' Theo found herself speaking in a hushed voice and he answered her in the same way.

'Yes, among my mother's packets. I had no difficulty bringing it away.'

They watched Ettie as she stood gazing at what she held. The muted sunlight softened the pallor that had come upon her and suited the tantalizing melancholy of the message from the dead. The direction in faded ink was inscribed with an elegant flourish that was not in accord with the crime and grief that had harrowed its writer as she prepared for her grave. Her penmanship was made for gaiety and the eyes that saw it now were afflicted by the poignancy of what might have been.

'Will you read it and tell us if there's anything that would help our case?' Theo asked, gently.

'No,' Ettie said. 'I will read it and then give it to you. There may be useful trifles that I'd overlook. I'm not myself.'

She turned from them and went to a chair beside a pedestal

table where a window shed a bright glow on the old paper. The ribbon was tied in a love-knot and she set it aside, smoothing it in a straight line with her thumbs. Ralph placed his penknife on the table and went back to join Theo on the sofa. Ettie slid the knife under the wax, which parted easily, and, with great care, unfolded the lines.

My dearest Henrietta, she read,

I write to you in the darkest torment of my soul, in ignorance of where or how you will receive this letter. I direct it to Mrs Carnow to give to you but I trust no one, saving my Edward, who suffers where I cannot reach him, even if I dared to look upon his face.

I shall have been long buried outside holy ground when you read these words. You will think of me as a wretch and your father as a thief, a felon. I beg you to clear your mind of blame to Edward and visit your condemnation solely upon me, for the guilt is all mine. Disgrace and degradation are justly attributed to me; vice and treachery are my practice.

Honour my husband for he is a good man; indeed, he is good. The fault was mine for falling prey to a seducer. My weakness has brought this trouble to us. Believe me, Ettie, that my wantonness was not for fleshly lust nor the coveting of the material favours of a wealthy man. My heart was truly given to this worthless, faithless creature, this base scoundrel whom I cannot, even now, expose for what he is. If I did so it would not help Edward. What proof have I? None, none. Oh, God, that I had died long since.

I cannot tell you who you are. My viciousness began before your coming and, of the two that knew me, there is no saying whether it is the pure or impure man who can claim you as his own. Perhaps I puzzle you. Perhaps no scandal but the death by my own hand, that waits for me this night, has reached you. I cannot let that be – for it will seem that I was driven to the ultimate and most lasting sin for shame of Edward's fall. The shame is mine.

I am weary, child, and my thoughts swim here and there. Bear with my lack of clarity. Let me state that I am, and have been since I was taken to wife, the whore of Charles Carnow. I did not intend to cheat the husband I respected but I was young and beguiled by a fair face and declarations. I have learnt in anguish and despair that all about this libertine is sham and counterfeit. I cannot say he stole my virtue for I gave it willingly; I can justly accuse him of committing the fraud for which Edward will be transported. He has boasted of it to my face, though I did not understand his meaning until the crime was done and he was lost to me. Charles is gone and leaves me no address. I do not deceive myself that his promise to send for me will be kept nor would I go to him, except to plead that he exonerate the innocent man he has destroyed. I know now why he was amused that his father would give him more than his inheritance; I know why he read to me certain cases of fraudulent cheques with such depraved enjoyment; I know that the money withdrawn by the false signature will be in his possession. He will have hired a boy to fill an office vacancy and sent him to cash the sum as his first – and only – task. There is a disappointed lad somewhere to be found and a man in irons. Is this not simple? And is it not horror? His father believed him across the English Channel before the theft was even committed. I am helpless; I can do nothing but remove myself from this vale of tears. I have lived in sin and must die in sin. I am afraid of hell but my wickedness condemns me to burn whether or not I do this final act. Forgive me, dear heart, and study to be a better woman than your mother was. The Lord keep you and preserve you from the fate that was mine.

In the room the silence grew; an expectant living hush in which Theo thought her own breathing too loud. Ettie's face was turned away from her watchers while she read and she did not move towards them as she held out the paper for them to take. They came to her and Theo held the letter for them both to see as they stood beside the motionless girl. Their fingers touched when Ralph took a corner of the letter that was shaking in Theo's grip and, in her pity for the past sorrow it contained, she laid her cheek against his shoulder. He put his arm lightly about her waist and it awakened her to the present.

Ettie was pleating the ribbon in uneven folds. It spilled out of its tucks as she pinched another crease and she threw it from her, so that it fell off the table to the floor. The sight was as shocking to Theo and Ralph as hysterics would have been in another and Theo leant over her, clasping her closely. Ettie pressed herself into her comforter and Theo felt her tremble with the effort to keep control.

'Oh, my dear, my dear,' Theo said. 'Don't try to be restrained. If ever there was a cause for weeping it's here.'

Ettie shook her head against Theo's breast and sat back from her.

'No,' she said, her eyes wet. 'What use is it? Better to retain your wits and act to some purpose. If Mama had indulged in foresight instead of emotion – '

She smoothed her disordered hair, adjusting the black velvet band that held it from her brows.

'I told you I wouldn't call you cousin,' she went on. 'And so I won't. There'll be no complication there.'

'Oh, love,' Theo said, touching her lips to Ettie's unseasonably cold hand.

Ralph bent and kissed the valiant girl upon the forehead.

'I'll claim you for my niece,' he said, 'whether or not Charles fathered you. I'll be private to save Trent further humiliation but you're of my family and I swear I'll repay the harm that's been done to you.'

'Can we begin from this?' Theo asked. 'We have a clue as to how the fraud was done.'

'We have our start,' he said. 'With Ettie's permission, I'll show the letter to our lawyer but I believe he'll say that the accusation of a woman about to die by suicide won't count as evidence. We can advertise around Bristol for the boy involved and send to London for details of how such thefts are committed. As Ettie says, we must act to some purpose and, yes, we can begin.'

Despite Ettie's determined retrieval of her self-possession, Theo did not consider her fit to return at once to Carnow, where she was likely to encounter Charles, and insisted she stayed in Allington to be petted. Ralph, therefore, rode back to the mill alone, his mind divided between the revelations of the tragic Helen and the memory of Theo's instinctive turning to him in her sadness.

The moment when she had rested against him rewarded him for having curbed his urge to interfere with her visit to the prison the day before. He had dearly wanted to persuade the authorities to have him shown in to Trent instead of her and it had needed much restraint to accept her refusal of his offer to try to change the course of their visit. Although it pleased him to see her taking an active part in their business, he admitted that he still had reservations about her ability to go about the world with the freedom of a man. That Theo was as capable as he, was a hard lesson for him to learn.

The sun was high as he rode back and his horse's neck lathered with sweat where the reins touched it. By the time he reached the stableyard, he was thirsty with heat and decided to go into the house to drink and cool down before going back to his office. Putting his head round the kitchen door to ask for lemonade to be brought, he sluiced his face in cold water in the scullery and went into the drawing room.

It did not please him to be met by the sight of Charles lying on the sofa with a cushion beneath his head and his feet crossed carelessly over one of its arms. A newspaper had been discarded on the floor beside him and a brandy bottle and soda syphon stood on a small table, conveniently to hand. It was plain that he had spent much of the morning there and he did not look about to move.

They were spared from greeting each other by the maid bringing in a tray for Ralph. He poured a glass of the lemonade, that was as sour as his opinion of his brother, and sat in an armchair beside the fireplace, where a large china vase of scented flowers brought the summer into the room. It was no relaxation to be in such proximity to Charles but he did not intend to be driven out of his own home, any more than out of the mill.

The familiar roar of the works drifted through the open windows and a bee wandered through the muslin curtains and hovered about the vase, before landing bulkily on a rose to squeeze between its inner petals. Ralph contemplated the recumbent figure of Charles. He expected to feel loathing when in his brother's company but he was surprised by the violence of repressed triumph that gripped him as he watched Charles affecting an exaggerated nonchalance. A primitive desire to wreak an immediate physical vengeance upon Charles for the injury to Theo deserted Ralph to make way for a confidence that, although the evidence needed to rout him was yet to be found, a more complete and lasting retribution could be had for the outlay of a little patience. He did not realize how much he was relishing his anticipation until Charles turned his head on the sofa cushion to reach for the brandy and noticed the manner in which he was being watched.

'What are you smiling at?' he asked, snappishly.

Ralph shrugged his shoulders. 'The day's so charming,' he said, pleasantly.

Charles grunted and filled his glass, splashing soda into the spirit unsteadily.

'I didn't know you were a nature lover,' he said. 'There seems a lot of it about. Well, I daresay it'll be a solace to you in days to come.'

The bee had emerged from the heart of the rose, powdered with pollen, and was performing acrobatic manoeuvres with its back legs. It lumbered into the air and wavered out into the June brightness. Ralph sipped at his drink, running the acid liquid slowly over his tongue. The image of a distraught and dying woman burned in his mind and granted him release from the bonds of brotherhood. A strange elation flooded through his veins and made his eyes distant and unnerving.

'I've been thinking of the Vikings,' he said. 'Was it the Vikings? Perhaps I'm wrong. I mean the Berserkers. Before they fought, they created a hatred of their enemy so uplifting that it was a divine madness. I believe I understand them.'

Charles stared at him. 'Are you drunk?' he asked. 'If not, you're mad and it's no wonder the superior Miss Theo won't lower herself to come here any more.'

'Ah, but then,' Ralph said, 'it's so much more enjoyable to meet her elsewhere.'

Charles raised himself on one elbow. 'You've been meeting her?' he asked, startled, before collecting himself and reverting to his goading tones. 'You'll have no luck there but I can see that you must try to provide for yourself; your future's so uncertain.'

Ralph swirled the pips around the dregs of his glass and set it back on the tray. He stood up and approached the sofa. The curious, far-away threat was still in his eyes as he looked down and Charles sank back, unsettled by his expression.

'Do you imagine I don't know what you tried with Theo?'

Ralph said, in a voice as soft and smooth as cream. 'I do know and will have an eye for an eye when I choose. You're lying here counting your chickens. Don't expect them to hatch. You'll never have Theo and you'll never have the mill.'

He put his hands about Charles's throat and Charles shrank down against the sofa as if he hoped it would part to let him through. Ralph smiled again and deftly tied the light cravat that Charles had loosened against the heat. He patted the finished knot and put his head to one side to admire the effect.

'There,' he said, 'all the appearance, if not the substance, of a gentleman. These things are so important, don't you think? What else is needed to make you complete?' He ran his fingers through his brother's hair. 'A little violet pomade?'

When Ralph had departed, the air of menace he had created lingered in the room and banished Charles's peace of mind. The tranquil indolence he had been basking in since his late breakfast was shattered beyond hope of repair, although he could not quite say why. There had been such a certainty in Ralph that Charles's thoughts were now hunting hither and thither for any event that could have caused it. He found none but the qualms remained and were the more alarming breaking, as they did, into the buoyant mood he had been in after playing upon his father's sympathy over Theo's supposedly heartless and mercenary refusal of him.

His carefully worded warning, as he and Mr Carnow had sat by the riverside, that he would leave if the terms of inheritance were not altered in his favour, had had the intended effect. Mr Carnow, tired and frightened, had assured him tearfully of his abiding love and agreed, with profuse and sentimental compliments, that the expectations of one of Charles's birth should not be affected by the rash mistakes of youth. It had been so gratifying a demonstration of paternal affection and regard that Charles had not felt it necessary to enter the counting-house since.

He had not, however, seen any sign of a lawyer being summoned or visited and Ralph's strange elation made him feel how much more comfortable life would be if his reinstatement as heir were put in writing as soon as possible. Accordingly, he rose from the sofa and neatened himself, smoothing his ruffled hair at the over-mantel mirror, in preparation for seeking out his father and discovering whether any legal move had been made.

Pulling the bell, he enquired of Mr Carnow's whereabouts and was told by the girl that he was resting in his room. He mounted the stairs and knocked loudly enough on the bedroom door to waken his father if he were sleeping. Hearing an answering call he entered and found Mr Carnow sitting, propped upright with pillows, his legs stretched out on the day-bed by the window.

The exhaustion Mr Carnow had been suffering had increased during the trials of the past days and this morning he had not felt equal to leaving his room. He was dressed as an invalid in his chintz dressinggown, cream kerseymere trousers and the resplendent slippers that Ettie had embroidered for him. The effort of eating a boiled egg and muffin had left him melancholy and seeing Charles advancing upon him did nothing to lighten his gloom. He mustered a smile that hid his reluctance to talk to his son and Charles brought a chair close to the bedside with the easy manner of one who knows he is welcome.

'I'm sorry to see you unwell on so fine a day, sir,' Charles said. 'Won't you come out and sit in the shade?'

'My legs are more swollen today. Look at these ankles – like pillars. I couldn't face the stairs.'

'Not if you leant on me, Papa? As I want you to?'

Mr Carnow shook his head. He found Charles's tone unctuous and was glad that his own poor health would hide any sign that his attitude towards his son was changing. His confusion over the startling conversations thrust upon him by Charles, Louisa and Ralph made him feel treacherous. He had been so used to doting unquestioningly upon Charles that it seemed like blasphemy to be critical of him or suspect his word but he was unable to deny that his trust was shaken. Now he was admitting to himself that Charles might be flawed, he discovered he had been suppressing doubts that had been raised by several aspects of Charles's behaviour. These misgivings had been presenting themselves repeatedly in his thoughts and his exhaustion was made worse by being unable to explain them away.

Much as he wanted to believe that Charles had not realized he had been taken ill at the Crystal Palace, he could no longer do so.

It was too striking a coincidence that Charles should have chosen that moment to remove Theo from their party and the watchful eyes of Ralph and her aunt as, indeed, it was that his return to the family home had occurred only after the mysterious dissipation of his fortune. The size of Charles's bills at tailor's and bootmaker's, after his rash invitation to make any necessary orders, had taken him aback. The discrepancy between Charles's protestations of wishing to take an active part in the firm and his actual practice in the counting-house, together with the incident of the petty cash – all these suspicions loomed in his mind and gathered force with the shocks of the past few days.

At the time that Charles had told him of Theo's refusal he had been convinced of his son's sincerity and had been willing to offer any inducement to prevent a second disappearance. Louisa's crisp assertion that Charles had so insulted Theo that their niece could not be safe at Carnow had distressed him with such severity that his memory of his talk with Charles had altered. The stealthy, yet urgent, dwelling upon the changing of his will to give Charles another share in the wealth to be inherited became prominent and was unsavoury enough to encourage the disappointed father to believe Louisa's tale. He knew that Louisa was just and clear-sighted and that Theo – who he had never imagined would ever be driven from his house – was not one to cry wolf.

Perhaps he could have closed his eyes to the truth that faced him even yet had Ralph not finally stated plainly that a wrong was being done. In all his fear of losing Charles, it had never occurred to him that he could forfeit Ralph. The realization of what his life would have been without Ralph, and what it might still be, came home to him. He saw himself bankrupt and bereft, sitting, on sufferance, at Louisa's hearth. An appreciation of the qualities of the son he had taken for granted was growing in proportion to the probability that Charles was a hypocrite.

He held up a hand and turned his splayed fingers from side to side, displaying the congestion.

'Look,' he said, 'my arms are swelling too. I can't get my ring on.'

Charles had no wish to examine his father's symptoms but Mr Carnow's unnatural fatigue and the turgid nature of his limbs made a hasty alteration to the will all the more desirable.

'Then, of course,' Charles said, 'you mustn't overtire yourself. Keep to your room. I can arrange that any affair you may want to see to is brought here.'

Mr Carnow looked out over the blossoming garden to where he could make out the top of one of the Carnow drays moving towards Bridport.

'There's no need,' he said, sadly. 'Ralph can manage without me.'

'But what of your private business?' Charles leant closer with a conspiratorial air. 'Aren't there matters better arranged out of Ralph's sight?'

A chill invaded Mr Carnow, despite the heat of the day. He turned back to his son and although Charles was smiling it was as if he were gazing into the eyes of a wolf.

'From the moment you were born,' he said, 'you were very dear to me.'

Too satisfied by the compliment to notice the reproach in his father's voice, Charles sat upright again.

'I'll have what I want?' he asked.

'My boy,' Mr Carnow said, 'you'll have all that you deserve.'

Chapter Seventeen

The shocks Theo had received in the prison and her own drawing room had increased her hatred of Charles but, as she ruefully admitted to her reflection on the second morning after reading the letter, had also had the salutary effect of directing her thoughts away from herself. Her aunt's warnings and her belated awakening of good sense had prevented her from becoming a victim of Charles's selfishness; but others had not been so fortunate. His insulting behaviour to her in front of the workmen was unmanly and offensive, but when she compared it to the injuries done to the Trents she was able to regain a sense of proportion. He had been eager to add her to those he had sacrificed to his own ends but as she had refused to give herself in marriage and she was no longer to visit the Carnows' home, his guns were spiked as far as she was concerned. She did not believe that he would assault her in any more serious way now that Louisa had made his actions known to the family, and free of personal danger from him she was able to concentrate on the havoc he had wrought in other people's lives.

Ettie's distress had touched her deeply. She was so used to the girl's composure that she understood how acute must be the pain that caused the small changes in her demeanour. They had spent all the previous day together, driving out along the coast and sitting on the shingle of Chesil Bank, listening to the soft growl of the glinting sea. The sun shone and the ribbons of their wide hats curled about their necks as they talked of suicide, adultery and theft. Ettie, whose quiet loyalty to her father had never been shaken, was horrified by how he had been used and by the manipulation of her mother's weakness. The naming of the betrayer and Theo's meeting with Trent had given reality to a tragedy that had become almost a myth and had opened old wounds. The idea that she could be Charles's daughter was abhorrent to her and she staunchly continued to call Trent 'Papa' as she mourned her early years with a degree of emotion that Theo would not have thought possible two days before.

They had sat until the stones bore the imprint of their bodies and the salt breeze had whitened their boots and dried their lips. If they were not related by blood as they drove back into the sunset, they were bound by loving intimacy. Like two shipwrecked swimmers who had supported each other to the shore, their existence had become merged by circumstance. Their empathy at this time of trial had been heady and inspiring. The girl renowned for her coolness and the young woman whose heart too often ruled her head returned with their friendship deepened by crime and death.

The pouring out of her loss had strengthened Ettie enough to recover the appearance of her old self and she had decided to resume her usual occupations in order not to give rise to comment. Although Theo thought this sensible, pity made her want to continue cosseting Ettie and she went out that morning to the bookseller, in search of a gift that would divert the girl's mind from her sorrows.

She was walking home with a volume of Arabian travels that the shopkeeper had described as both instructive and sensational, when she was brought out of her reveries by hearing her name anxiously called. Rousing herself, she found the Carnows' stablelad looming over her as he sat bareback on Charles's chestnut.

'Oh, Miss Farnaby!' he said. He was a sensitive boy and excitement and adolescence made his voice change pitch several times in this short exclamation.

'Yes?' Immediately, she was alarmed. 'Is anything wrong?'

'Mr Carnow, miss. 'Ee's took bad. The maid went up for to fix his bed and 'ee were lying on the floor a-gasping for breath and all swoll up like a turkey-cock. "Mercy!" says she and sets to pick 'un up but 'ee were too heavy for 'er and she d'run down to the kitchen and next thing I'm sent for the doctor and Mr Ralph.'

He stopped, astonished by the importance of this break in his routine.

'And where is Mr Ralph?'

'At Armstrong's, miss.'

The implications of what this could mean if her uncle had indeed changed his will passed through her mind but concern for him and those who shared her love for him were predominant. Her skin pricked and the heightened alertness that affects those who can cope in a crisis made her brisk.

'Go straight to Dr Lloyd,' she said. 'I'll fetch Mr Ralph. If the doctor isn't home, seek him out and make sure you tell him to his face that this is serious. Don't rely on messages.'

She turned about and began walking hurriedly back across the bridge to High West Street as the boy overtook her. Part of her mind was chanting a repetitive prayer for her uncle's recovery but her experience of her father's death had taught her that wishes do not preserve life and her heart went out to the foolish, suffering man. She did not want to give Ralph this news and, despite her quick pace, her feet felt heavy as she turned into the alleys that led out from the centre of the town. The familiar roar of the mills and rumble of heavy drays surrounded her here as she skirted the braiders who had come out into the fine weather to make their nets.

Passing the gates of her aunt's mill, she cut through an inn yard and emerged into an area of small ropewalks worked by the members of single families. It was quieter in these lanes but the air of purposeful industry was no less. Knocking at the open door of a red-brick shed, she received no answer and went in uninvited.

Inside the walk, three teams of ropers were at work. Despite the open windows, it was torridly hot and the familiar, heavy smell of the hemp made it seem airless. Returning the nod of the man nearest to her, who had looked over his shoulder briefly as she entered, she glanced round for Ralph and saw him standing with his back to her at the far end of the shed examining a finished rope. Tenderness filled her as she watched him going about his business, oblivious to the worry that lay in wait. Much as she wished not to be there, it felt right that she would be the one to tell him the news and be first with her ready sympathy.

Holding back her skirts, she made her way up the narrow passage between the wall and the nearest team. The long stretch of yarn that they were twisting ran beside her at waist height, supported by skirders that kept it from dragging on the floor.

Ahead of her, the lower-end man was cranking a jack whose three revolving hooks had already caused the loose hemp attached to them to bind into strands. Now the ropemaker was walking slowly behind the swivelling hook towards the jack, moving his grooved top along the strands so that the combined actions left a made rope after him. It was a process that Theo had seen all her life and it gave a soothing stability to a world that had changed too often for her liking in recent days.

Ralph had laid down his rope as she reached him and had put his hands in his pockets. She touched his shoulder lightly and, startled, he turned to her just as the most senior of the Armstrongs came through a rear door holding the ledger in which he recorded the outwork his firm did for the Carnows.

'Miss Farnaby,' Armstrong said, 'will 'ee step through?'

He pushed back the door with his elbow but Theo shook her head. 'Thank you, no. A word with my cousin here, if I may.'

Armstrong placed the book on the coiled rope and went over to watch the third team fastening new yarn on to their jack. All the men in the shed had noticed Theo and were watching her with eyes that flickered between her and their work.

'What's amiss?'

Ralph spoke tersely and she knew that her face was heralding what she had to say.

'Oh, Ralph,' she said, 'I'm sorry. You must go home. I met Lessing riding for Dr Lloyd and you. Uncle has got worse. He was found on the floor of his room.'

The colour left Ralph's face as he listened. When he had told his father that he would always give him more love and forbearance than was deserved, he had not been lying. The thought of life without being plagued by the old man's follies gave him a painful anticipation of grief.

'Is he alive?' he asked.

'Yes but struggling for breath. I know no more.'

'I'll go back now.' He took up the hat he had hung on a chair. 'Will you tell Louisa?'

'At once – and Armstrong.'

He went out of the end door and she heard the clatter of his horse's hoofs before she had joined the surprised ropers to make their excuses. She was oddly pleased by the lack of discussion there had been between them. They had known and trusted each other's reactions without the need for many words and as she walked through the town towards the uncertainty of illness, an old certainty that had faded under the fierce Italian sun, fed upon adversity and grew strong.

At Carnow, Charles was seated in the hall, ostensibly on guard for the first sight of the doctor but in reality drinking a cup of coffee while considering his prospects. It was not necessary to hide his excitement at what was afoot for it could easily be portrayed as natural anxiety and, as such, a credit to him.

He was feeling smug; a condition which did not lend itself well to the air of elegance he liked to cultivate. At this moment, the cat that got the cream could not have been more pleased with himself than was Charles. He was perfectly confident that he had not only persuaded his father to agree to give him a second inheritance but that the will had already been altered in his favour. Despite his infirmity, Mr Carnow had given orders that he be driven to his lawyer the previous morning and had returned, exhausted, instructing Charles that Ralph was not to be told and that no more was to be said on the subject. Having achieved this end, Charles was quite ready to let delicacy keep him silent but he had not denied himself the luxury of imagining the pleasures of wealth.

Leaning back in the basket-chair, he gazed out of the open front door at the constant movement in the road beyond the garden wall. The laden carts, the hackler with his barrow, the women going to collect their yarn – all gave him a sense of mastery and ease. He poured another cup from the coffee pot and stirred in a liberal helping of sugar. There were bridges to be crossed before he could come into his own, but this morning the world seemed full of promise.

There were light steps on the stairs behind him and Ettie came to the door. She walked a few paces into the garden to look along the road and, failing to see Dr Lloyd, returned to stand on the threshold.

'You're in my way,' Charles said.

Ettie turned.

'Then,' she said, 'I'm one of several.'

She came back into the hall and stood to one side of the entrance, where she could watch the road. Since she had unburdened herself to Theo, she had called upon all her hard-learnt self-discipline to regain her composure and she was not one to fail in anything she did. She would gladly have seen Charles hanged for what he had done to her family but no one could have guessed it from her face.

'Papa,' she said.

Charles set down his cup on the edge of the saucer and slopped coffee into his lap.

'Damnation!' He put the saucer on the table beside him and mopped at himself with a handkerchief. 'Why did you say that?'

'I was thinking aloud.'

'But why say "Papa"?'

'I have one. Mayn't I think of him?'

He stared at her, exasperated. She was too difficult for him to read. He threw the stained handkerchief on to the table.

'Ruined!' he said.

'Ruin can come so suddenly, can't it?' she replied. 'Or sometimes it can be slow and drawn out.'

Disquiet was invading Charles's peace. Of course, she can know nothing, he thought. How could she?

'You haven't asked after your own father,' she told him. 'I expect you're too worried.'

'Naturally, I'm concerned.' He fidgeted in annoyance. 'I assumed you'd say if there'd been any alteration.'

'There's none physically but he's getting more fearful. He sent me down to check the doctor hadn't come.'

'Good God, I'm here. Doesn't he trust me?'

Ettie continued to deliver her expressionless gaze. 'Sick men will have their fancies,' she said.

Feeling that he was becoming wrapped in an invisible web, Charles stood up angrily.

'Then take over the waiting,' he exclaimed. 'I'll go and change. I'm in no state to receive anyone.'

The sound of a trap being driven rapidly up to the gate directed their attention outside to where Dr Lloyd could be seen handing his reins to a passing roper.

'Ah,' said Ettie. 'We have company.'

*

For the next five nights Louisa slept at Carnow. Dr Lloyd was not happy with the worsening of his patient's dropsical condition. A nurse was brought to live in but Mr Carnow was so distressed by his deterioration that it was felt that a responsible member of the family should be at hand twenty-four hours of the day. Ralph's time had other calls upon it, Ettie had the necessary sense and willingness but not the experience and Charles was distrusted by all the household; Louisa's offer of her presence was, therefore, welcomed and her competence made the inevitable difficulties and anxieties less trying than they would otherwise have been.

It was one of these problems that she was talking of to Theo on the fourth morning after Mr Carnow's collapse. They were in the stableyard beside the house, and the boy who had first told Theo of the trouble was leading her mare into a cool stall until she should be needed. It was just before ten and was already hot enough for the two women to seek the shade.

Theo had not been into the house. Her uncle was not well enough to want the diversion of visitors and, as he was content to be asked after by his niece, Louisa had not wanted to invite the annoyance that might occur if she encountered Charles. Theo, however, had not been satisfied to sit at home, hoping for messages, and they had decided that she should stop at the yard during her rides and have her information from, as she put it, 'the horse's mouth'.

'You're looking tired,' Theo said, as she leant against the wall of the room where the harness was kept. A rich scent of leather and saddle-soap was drifting out of the window beside her to mingle with the smell of warm bricks.

'I've good reason,' Louisa reached up to her back hair and secured a pin more firmly. 'Much as I care for your uncle, I don't think he has the sense he was born with. We were all up half the night because of it.'

'What did he do?'

'As I told you yesterday, he hadn't been improving despite the digitalis. Then in the evening he grew much worse. He hadn't wanted to eat dinner – he'd only picked at it – and at about nine he began to vomit. That upset him and he was doubled up with stomach pains. Next he started getting extra heartbeats.' She paused to take breath, her palm on her chest as if her own heart were aching. 'Ralph rode for Lloyd and, thank God, he was at home and came at once.'

'He was able to ease the symptoms?'

'He was able to prevent them recurring. He had the intelligence to do what none of us had thought of – he counted the powders he'd left for the treatment.'

Theo was watching her intently. 'Good heavens!' she said. 'He wasn't still not taking his doses?'

'Oh, he was taking them. It transpired that whenever he was alone in the room he was struggling out of bed and giving himself an extra packet. Or two or three to judge from the number of papers that are missing. He felt he was making up for the medicines he'd refused before. It was poisoning him.'

A ginger cat was strolling across the yard, its coat bright in the brilliant sun. It sat down in the shadow of the mounting-block and licked a paw.

'The powders are locked away now,' Louisa went on. 'I should have done it from the first but it didn't occur to me that it was necessary. To give him his due, he's shamefaced.'

'But has he recovered?'

'He's weak but a great deal better than last night. He was sleeping when I came down.'

'And is Dr Lloyd pleased with the change?'

Louisa stroked her fingers over her temples and sighed.

'I think I'd say that he's satisfied there's been an improvement,' she said. 'But, my dear, we must accept that the treatment may not work. Your uncle's been strong in body all his life but now there is a possibility that his heart will fail.'

'And he would die?' This was the first time the thought had been put so plainly into words and Theo's voice held a plea that it should not be so.

'Yes, love,' Louisa said, gently. 'He may die.'

Theo raised her face to the sultry air.

'Do you know,' she said, 'the sky's clear but I think a storm is coming.'

Chapter Eighteen

The June days passed and although his health recovered from the setback he had given it, Mr Carnow did not improve enough to leave his room. As the roses that climbed to his window bloomed in white profusion and the full-leaved trees quivered in summer breezes, he lay against his pillows heavy and melancholy. Theo slipped into the house to see him, using the servants' stairs to avoid Charles, and would sit holding his hand as he dozed or read to him softly from books he had loved in his youth.

She had small expectation of finding Charles for he restricted his visits to a formal five minutes morning and evening and he was disliked enough in the household for no one to tell him that she came. It was not that she feared a meeting but her revulsion for him was too strong to be hidden and she did not want the irritation of his jibes. The consequences of an argument between them might cause harm to her uncle if he overheard it or had it reported to him by Charles. In this time of sickness, discretion seemed the better path.

During these weeks, she did not see Ralph as often as she would have liked. As his father's role in the running of the mill had been nominal, his work did not increase but so much of his leisure was spent with Mr Carnow, who had become pathetically eager for his company, that he had few hours to spare. When they were together, her heart went out to him for the anxiety in his eyes. Her uncle's illness had made her conscious of the fleeting nature of life and she longed to cling to those she loved. She was ashamed that thoughts of how loss could hurt her were intruding on her compassion for her uncle and had owned that she had felt a childish relief when her aunt had come home from her nursing. Louisa had merely laughed, and told her not to try to be a saint – the world, she said, is a dangerous and lonely place and it is natural to crave the presence of those who care for us.

It was at the beginning of July, when the sombre weeks of apprehension had lowered all their spirits, that Theo noticed an unwelcome change in her uncle. She was sitting at his bedside reading aloud from *Ivanhoe* as he lay watching the patterns the swiftly moving clouds cast on the wall. Her throat had grown dry and she was glad to be interrupted by the maid bringing in the tea-tray. Like most invalids who are just the wrong side of convalescence, Mr Carnow had an active interest in the small events of his day and took comfort from a routine that had his well-being as its reason for existence. At this hour of the afternoon, he liked to have a cup of weak Indian tea and two biscuits. It had become important to him.

Today, he greeted the advent of the tray without enthusiasm and after a single, half-hearted sip pushed the cup away.

'Is it too dark, Uncle?' asked Theo, who made her own tea strong enough to fell an ox and thought that she might not have added enough hot water for him.

'No,' he said, mournfully. 'I don't have the stomach for it.'

'Will you eat a biscuit? Then you might want to drink.'

'No, I want nothing.'

The maid had been drifting about the room making small adjustments to its tidiness and she came over to the bed.

'Now, sir,' she said, 'you didn't hardly touch your lunch and that egg for your breakfast come back to the kitchen with only a bite gone.'

Mr Carnow stirred, his swollen form massive beneath the light coverings. Since the nurse had been dismissed because having a stranger to see to his needs had unsettled him, he had been tended only by his relations and the house servants. The maids had served the Carnows for years and a degree of familiarity had resulted.

'I'm not hungry, Fan,' he protested.

'Then you d'ought to be, sir,' she said. 'Or leastways you should force summat down. You'll be that empty from last night.'

'Last night?' asked Theo. 'What's this?'

Mr Carnow avoided her eye.

'Didn't 'ee say, Miss Theo?' said Fan. ''Ee were took bad gone midnight. Brought up every last mouthful o' supper.'

Mr Carnow continued to stare at his feet but when Theo touched his hand to make him look at her, she saw that he was afraid.

'Why didn't you tell me?' she said.

He did not reply but only gazed at her as a child gazes at the mother he trusts to drive terrors away.

'Has Dr Lloyd called yet?' she asked.

'No, miss.' Seeing her master's condition, Fan replied for him. 'But 'ee's expected this evening.'

'Well,' said Theo, speaking calmly despite her alarm. 'My aunt will meet him and no doubt he'll set all to rights.'

Dr Lloyd was not as sanguine as Theo had tried to appear to her uncle. Over the next week, Mr Carnow sank a little every day and the threat of heart-failure grew more and more menacing. The doctor was puzzled. Although his patient had not been gaining strength, he had been stable and it had seemed to Dr Lloyd, who was acquainted with the undercurrents in the family, that the lack of improvement was due to mental not physical reasons. There appeared to be no cause for the sudden worsening.

'If I didn't have your assurance that my preparations were out of his reach,' he said on the eighth morning after Theo's discovery, 'I would say he was taking extra doses again. He shows distinct signs of digitalis poisoning.'

He was standing in the drawing room with Louisa, Charles and Ralph. Upstairs, Ettie was sitting with Mr Carnow with a concern that was not diminished by not knowing whether he was her grandfather.

'Not,' he went on, 'that he's capable of getting out of bed alone now. Is it possible that a servant could be smuggling the drug to him?'

'No.' Ralph, the marks of sleeplessness on his face, was emphatic. 'The packets are kept in a locked chest in my room. I keep the key on my watch-chain.'

'And the correct number are there?'

'They are.'

'Do you oversee the taking of them? He couldn't save an earlier dose to take double later?'

'Either Ralph or myself is always present,' said Louisa. She had returned to stay in the house during the crisis and was aware of the strain that was on Ralph.

Dr Lloyd set the sole of his boot on the hearth-rail and put his thumbs in his waistcoat while he thought.

'In one way,' he said, 'I'm sorry that such diligence is being shown. If only there was some method by which he was being given intoxicating levels, we could end it and all might be well. As it is, I'm afraid we must accept that this is nature and ready ourselves for the worst.'

There was a moment of silence as they absorbed this then Charles, who had been listening without comment, asked, 'Could it be that you're mistaken in the quantity of medicines he needs? Perhaps he can't tolerate what you've prescribed.'

The doctor raised his head with an anger that he instantly controlled.

'I'll put your question down to worry over your father,' he said, 'and take no offence. No, I have not miscalculated.'

'I ask,' said Charles, coolly, 'because you've withdrawn from your use of one potion you tried last week. If that was ill-advised, why not the other?'

'The diuretic was used, as I explained at the time, to reduce the water retention that was putting too much pressure on his heart. It had the desired effect, if you recall, of easing the congestion in his lungs and enabling him to breathe more freely. Unfortunately, as is always the danger when the treatments are used together, it caused a too rapid and irregular beating of the heart. That's why I stopped its use. It's all been normal medical practice in the circumstances.'

'Normal,' Charles said, 'but ineffective.'

Dr Lloyd had worked amongst the sick and their relatives too long to lose his temper at such provocation but it was difficult for him to conceal his distaste for receiving criticism from this quarter. He had learnt how to read whose anxiety was genuine and it was not Charles's face that excited his pity.

'Be quiet, Charles.' Louisa's voice brooked no disagreement. 'I assure you, Dr Lloyd, we're perfectly satisfied with what you've done. The shame is that, through no fault of yours, the treatment was delayed for too many months and then hampered by the overdose. We must pray that the attack is not final – and if it is, we'll know we spared no effort to prevent its sad end.'

Two nights later, Theo was again keeping watch at her uncle's bedside. She had not been there at this hour before but that afternoon she had found Louisa so wearied by previous vigils she had insisted that she and Ralph should stand sentinel by turns until dawn. It was almost twelve and she sat, tired and heavy, waiting for the clock to strike one when she was to be relieved by Ralph and driven home by a man-servant.

The room was almost dark. A single candle burnt before the oval mirror on the chest of drawers and its image was reflected by the ancient gilt-framed looking-glass that hung opposite. Surrounded by shadows, listening to the laboured breathing from the bed, Theo found herself subject to odd fancies. The point of light that gleamed in the old glass drew her eyes but she did not want to look in it for fear that she would see a face other than her own. The warmth of the summer night thickened air tainted with sickness until it seemed that it was her own breast that shuddered as it slowly rose and fell. At the edge of her sight the gloom writhed and beckoned until she moved her head and it was still. The curtains pulled half around the bed made the suffering figure indistinct and persuaded her now that a stranger lay in black seclusion, now that it was death.

The hours were long and she felt the headache and confusion that tormented her uncle when he woke had become hers. Her heart beat quickly with her imaginings and she softly left her chair to distract herself. Making no sound, she went stealthily behind the screen that hid the washstand. Dipping her hands into the jug, she pressed her wet fingers against her temples and neck. She was standing with her collar open, letting the drops of water trickle over her throat when she heard the door pushed gently back. Slight as it was, the noise startled her. She shook as she tried to fasten her brooch and told herself it was Ralph.

Before the intruder had crossed the room, an undefined alarm had gripped her. She knew Ralph's tread and this was not his. She bent forward so that she could look through the gap between the panels of the screen.

Charles was at the bedside looking down at his sleeping father. He held a wine glass of milk. It was an innocent pose yet Theo found it sinister. Her mind said that her uncle was not always watched, and knowing that Louisa was not on guard it was to be expected that his sons would want to assure themselves that he was safe – but Charles was no ordinary son and her flesh crept as he stood silently in the dusk.

The candle flames were flickering in the draught from the closing of the door and the darkness shivered and rearranged itself as they steadied. Charles went forward to the low cabinet where the basins and necessities of illness were arranged. He was hidden from Mr Carnow by the bed-hangings but Theo could see him set down his glass and, taking a paper from his pocket, pour a powder into it. Replacing the empty packet in the robe he wore over his trousers, he stirred the milk with a spoon he had brought with him and pulled back the curtain to reveal the pillows.

'Papa,' he said.

His voice was low but firm and Mr Carnow moved restlessly and looked about him as if he did not understand what he saw. Charles put his arm beneath his father's shoulders and raised him a few inches.

'Take a little milk, Papa,' he said.

Obediently, Mr Carnow drank, sucking at the glass with painful gasps. When he had finished, Charles laid him against the bed and wiped a smear of milk from the corner of his mouth.

'Sleep,' he said. 'You must rest.'

He waited a moment while Mr Carnow, who had barely been awake, lost consciousness again. Returning the hangings to where they had been, Charles moved towards the door.

Behind the screen, Theo was transfixed. The horror before her was too great for her to accept. Charles went out into the corridor and the recognition that her chance of proof might be lost roused her. She ran across the room and dragged open the door. A lamp was burning on the landing and shone upon Charles as he turned to see her in the doorway. For a moment they stared at each other, hatred naked on their faces, then arrogance slid over him like the drawing down of a blind and he passed on towards his room.

His confidence delayed her for an instant but the reality of what she had witnessed asserted itself and she went swiftly after him. An unfamiliar strength surged in her and she grasped him by the wrist, throwing him off-balance against the wall. The glass fell from his hand and rolled, unbroken, on the carpet as she grappled to pinion his free arm. He struck her across the cheek but her brooch was loose and she tore it from her throat, driving its pin into his palm as he raised his hand to hit again.

More arms came round her, reaching past her own to grip Charles. Unheard by her, Ralph, disturbed by the struggle, had come out of his room to be confronted by the unexpected scene. He did not wait to question the opponents. Seeing only that Theo was assaulted, he went to her aid. He twisted Charles's injured arm as Theo clung to the wrist she had not let go of and together they forced him to the floor. Doors were opening. Louisa and Ettie stood in their nightclothes aghast and baffled by what they found. Theo looked up, her fair falling about her wild eyes.

'His pocket!' she said and Louisa, a sudden suspicion taking her, bent and withdrew the paper from the folds of Charles's robe. A few grains of digitalis remained where the packet had been creased.

'I saw it,' said Theo, 'and will swear to it.'

Chapter Nineteen

It was Ralph's contention, when the women had restrained him, that he would have Charles hanged but Theo would not allow it. Much as she wished Charles to be punished, she believed that the shock of learning how little his beloved son had valued him would kill Mr Carnow. She was supported in this by Louisa and Ettie immediately and later by Dr Lloyd, who was summoned to try to counteract the poisoning and to confirm the contents of the drug-wrapping, and by Moore, home from the Baltic and free to remark that the northern seas were calm compared with life in Bridport.

After an initial attempt to claim a misunderstanding, Charles did not deny having given his father a series of overdoses during the course of a week. He realized that his chance of using Carnow to feather his nest was gone and the offer of some retribution other than the courts loosened his tongue. It gave him a perverse pleasure to disgust the family he despised. They were, at first, puzzled by how he could have obtained the digitalis and it amused him to reveal that he had merely removed the necessary amount from the stock kept in the house when it was discovered that his father had been taking too much of his own accord. It had been supposed that Mr Carnow had consumed all that was missing – nothing could have been simpler.

The revelation took place on Moore's ship while it lay at harbour with Charles securely locked into a cabin. All concerned in this imprisonment were aware that, on his release, Charles could assert that the circumstances had induced him to make a false confession. Before they were too troubled by their quandary, Charles's past rose to accuse him in the shape of the answer to Ralph's newspaper advertisements.

'This has been a strange business,' said Mr Frenton, the Carnows' lawyer, as he gazed upon Theo, Ralph, Louisa and Ettie, who were crowded into his small private office one afternoon shortly after the shocking event.

'In my profession one could almost say that the unusual is usual but, still, we must retain a form of innocence for we never expect such occurrences in the families of our friends.'

'It startled us all,' said Louisa, firmly.

Mr Frenton made a placatory gesture. 'Indeed, indeed. Of course, I meant no disrespect. How could any of us have guessed at Mr Charles's actions.' He inclined his head to Ettie. 'I may say, Miss Trent, that although I was rash enough to accept the verdict against your father, I had always found him to be an honourable and trustworthy man and considered his fall into temptation uncharacteristic. If the identity of the real culprit were not so distressing, my satisfaction in applying for his release would be unadulterated.'

Ettie bowed slightly. She had accompanied Theo to the gaol the day before and been reunited with her father. It was the third time that Theo had visited him for she had gone to him after they had read his wife's letter to fulfil her promise to give him the knowledge of its contents. He had asked that Ettie should tell him but he had not expected that it would be opened so soon and Theo had felt that the tale it contained was too grievous for a girl to have to pass on. Trent, who had stoically deprived himself of contact with his daughter for what he believed was her own good, was touched by her loyalty to him. When Theo had requested that Ettie should go with her to inform him of their hopes of his liberation, he had readily agreed. The careworn man and the dignified girl had sat across a table from each other in the whitewashed cell and Theo, grateful and glad, had seen their resemblance, not in feature but in movement, posture and way of thought. Apart, they had no shared lineament that could remind an onlooker of the other but together there was no doubt of Ettie's parentage.

'And do you think that release is likely?' Louisa asked. Since the night of Charles's unmasking, she had been told of what Ettie had remembered and how it had been acted upon. Her revulsion at Charles's perfidy had been the same as Ralph's and Theo's but she had also noted that Theo had chosen Ralph, not herself, as fellow conspirator and thought that her child had grown.

'I believe our case is strong.' Mr Frenton placed the fingertips of both hands against each other. It was a habit that he had begun as a young man in order to appear reflective and now could not shake off. 'My senior clerk returned from Bristol this morning after examining the Mr Andrews who answered the newspaper advertisement, with gratifying results.'

Theo glanced at Ralph, who raised his eyebrows as a signal of his surprise. They had not expected their enquiries to bring them the information they needed to prove Charles's part in the fraud. It was unlikely that any man would want it to be known that he had been so soundly duped as a youth and more than possible that he had sought work elsewhere. The letter that had arrived had gone beyond their most buoyant expectations.

A Mr George Andrews, writing from a good address in Bristol, had declared himself to have been the boy Charles had persuaded to cash the forged cheque as a probationary duty for the illusory office position. He described both the event and Charles in enough detail for his account to seem authentic. That he had not come forward during the investigation of the crime was explained by his ignorance of it having taken place. Immediately after his disappointment over finding Charles's offered post to be non-existent, he had become disgusted at his lack of success in his home town and had left to seek his fortune in Liverpool. Angered by his previous misadventures, he had thrown himself into the work of a shipping office and, determined never again to be made a fool of, had prospered vigorously. The previous year he had married the younger daughter of an owner of merchant vessels and returned to Bristol to ply her family's trade in that port. Shortly afterwards he had read of a fraud being perpetrated in the same fashion as Charles's and realized that he had been used as a pawn for committing a felony. 'Although I did not understand its import,' he had written, 'the incident stood in my memory as a curious annoyance.'

'Our witness,' said Mr Frenton, 'is a capable and respected professional man with a remarkable memory. My clerk showed him the sketches of young men at the age Mr Charles would have been ten years ago and Mr Andrews was able to identify his supposed employer at once. He's prepared to testify to the fact.' He picked up the notes he had before him. 'I may mention that it's an ill-wind that blows nobody any good. Mr Andrews has it that his later success can be attributed to the vexation caused him by the episode, coming as it did after sundry other less dramatic failures to find work. It acted as a spur. In his own words, he had been a "pudding of a boy" and the affair "shook him awake".'

'I hardly think Trent will find that a compensation,' Ralph said, 'but it's something. There's no saying what will follow when one life touches another.'

'That's quite true,' Frenton nodded and laid down his notes. 'In that context and considering the circumstances, Mr Ralph, I don't think it's betraying a client's confidence to tell you that the very day you came to me asking whether Mrs Trent's dying letter would stand as evidence, your father also called here. It seemed that he had been put under some pressure by Mr Charles to alter the will in his favour. Despite his earlier regrettable acceptance of a premature inheritance, Mr Charles wanted to become master of the mill. In his poor state of health, Mr Carnow wished to avoid the unpleasantness that would ensue if he revealed that he had lost faith in his elder son and he prevaricated. It would appear that Mr Charles believed he'd won the argument and, therefore, your father's death would have been of profit to him.'

'Believed?' asked Theo. 'Was the will not changed?'

'Why, no, Miss Farnaby. Mr Carnow was anxious that it should remain as it stood. He came to see me to make sure that if he died, Mr Charles would be unable to challenge it. I assured him that it was so.'

Again, Theo looked at Ralph. She had seen the tendons in his neck tighten as Frenton had begun to talk of the will. Now, his face relaxed and took on the expression of one who comes suddenly upon an alluring vista. She had put out her hand to clasp his before she remembered where she was.

'I think,' said Louisa, diverting Frenton from a scene which he would relate to his wife that evening, 'that we may turn our attention to the practical matter of obtaining Charles's confession.'

The business to which Louisa referred was accomplished smoothly, to the relief of all concerned. The reappearance of the boy who had inadvertently been his accomplice in the fraud, had been an unforeseen blow to Charles and made him realize the seriousness of his position more than either being caught in the act of poisoning his father or being confined on board ship had done. The family's reluctance to expose Mr Carnow to the knowledge that his own son had tried to end his life had been Charles's protection against standing trial. The sobering fact that both a reputable witness and a damaging letter could be brought to a prosecution of him for the forgery carried an unwelcome breath of the prison-house into his calculations. It was probable that, for the sake of releasing Trent, his relatives would be prepared for his father to suffer the lesser misery of seeing him accused as the real culprit. Alone in the airless cabin, Charles did not learn remorse for those he had hurt but, for himself, he knew fear.

He had not bargained for the softness of the hearts of his captors. If Trent was to be freed, it was necessary that Mr Carnow should be told the vile truth of Charles's actions ten years before but it was decided that he should be spared his son being sentenced. In the presence of Frenton, his senior clerk and Moore as well as Ralph, Theo, her aunt and Ettie, who might be thought to be prejudiced, Charles wrote and signed four copies of a full confession to the fraud. One of these, together with Helen Trent's letter, Mr Andrews' evidence and the prison governor's good opinion of his most unfortunate convict, was to be sent to the Home Secretary in confident expectation of gaining Trent's liberty.

For the private use of the family, in case they should ever need it, Charles was also obliged to confess on paper to the poisoning. In return, he was to be given a passage to Australia and a hundred guineas to set him on his feet when he went ashore. If he should ever again be seen in Britain, the second confession would be used against him.

Mr Frenton was not party to the spiriting away of Charles. It was felt that the strain upon his professional discretion would be too great if he were to be told that the prerogative of the courts was to be winked at in this manner. To spare him the embarrassment of the truth, it was declared that a momentary laxness by one of Moore's crew had resulted in Charles's escape. A letter from Charles, postmarked Dover and declaring that he was leaving for the continent, was received shortly afterwards and it was decided that it was not worth trying to track him down.

A week of anxious waiting followed Charles's departure from Bridport Harbour but on the eighth day Moore returned from London, having seen Charles into a berth on an Australia-bound ship and the ship safely out to sea. It had been felt that Ralph's absence from home at this time would seem too suspicious and Moore had readily volunteered to be Charles's guard on his last, ignominious journey on his native waters. To avoid the opportunities of slipping away that a train might afford Charles if he became less compliant, Moore chose to recruit a fellow captain and friend to assist him. The *Megan Lee* hove to in Lyme Bay and two passengers were rowed out to it in the darkest part of the night. The remembrance of his feelings of optimism and security when he had reached this shore from Canada had assailed Charles as he climbed the rope ladder on to the vessel that was taking him away. The pang had made him miss his footing and, as the sailors clutched him, Moore had looked into his eyes by lantern-light and seen an understanding of all that he had lost.

On the afternoon of his reappearance in Bridport, Moore was walking across the meadow from the Parrises' house towards the mill. There had been a shower that morning but the fresh breeze that had sped him to London was still agitating the hedgerows and had dried the ground. The bright, warm, scintillating day suited Moore's temper as he walked with a glowing Maud upon his arm. Their progress was hampered by her habit of resting her head against his shoulder and his of pausing to kiss her. This wanton and scandalous behaviour was caused by Moore having again asked her parents for permission to marry her and having been granted it. He was due to sail for Newfoundland the next day on the final run of the year and the betrothed pair were sauntering into town to give their news to Moore's father.

They crossed the bridge over the weir and began making their way through the hurry of the mill. When they were outside the Carnows' house, Moore stopped.

'I'll just look in on the patient,' he said, 'and bid him goodbye. I'd feel badly if I didn't and he took a turn for the worse while I was away.'

'Theo says that he's rallied well. You should find him on his feet in October but, of course, you'd better.'

'If you go on to give Hyde his book, I'll meet you there.'

The lovers parted and Maud strolled on, the volume of astronomy that Barclay had lent her in her hand. She did not notice her surroundings. Grey waves surged beside her and the aurora borealis coloured her skies. She stood at the wheel of the brig as the shadow of the masts fell on walls of green and groaning ice. In a year, she too would sail for Canada and already the deck rose beneath her feet.

Barclay was sitting in his parlour, preparing a lesson for the following morning. The window was open to let in the air and the sun was flowing through a jug of vivid beech leaves that stood on the sill. He could hear Sadie moving about in the kitchen and the shining results of her earlier work, as she polished around him while telling him the gossip of the mill, made the room cheerful and welcoming. As he sat at the small table in his shirt-sleeves, Barclay felt that all was well with the world.

He saw Maud enter the garden before she had reached the door. She was wearing white and the brightness of the day turned her into a dazzling vision for one who was besotted with her. He had risen from his chair and had ushered her in before she could knock.

'This is a pleasure, Miss Parris,' he said. 'Won't you sit down? Will you have tea?'

'I'll sit,' she said, doing so, 'but, as I'm only to stay a moment, I won't have tea.'

Suddenly aware of his state of undress, Barclay took his jacket from the hook where Sadie had hung it and began to put it on.

'Please, Mr Hyde,' said Maud, 'don't for my sake. It's much too hot to be mannerly.'

He let the jacket drop on to a stool and came to sit on the edge of a chair opposite to hers. She had stood on his path before and in his schoolroom but it was the first time she had sat in his house and it raised the contentment he had been feeling into a feverish hope. The image of her so much at peace in his own parlour, playing her fingers over the worktable he longed for her to use, troubled his affectionate heart and almost made him cast himself at her feet. Instead, he sat, rigid and speechless, grasping his knees.

Maud was too preoccupied to be observant and minutes passed before she noticed they were at a standstill. She cast about for a subject of conversation.

'You have an agreeable home here,' she said, at last. 'I trust it suits you.'

Barclay's head was throbbing and a great pulse seemed to be beating in his throat.

'It would suit me better,' he said, 'if . . . It lacks one thing . . . '

He drew breath, wondering if he was choosing his words correctly, and Maud, contrite, proffered him the book.

'Oh, yes, Mr Hyde,' she said, 'I'm so sorry. I know I should have brought it back before but I'd such an interest in it and such a particular reason for learning about the stars that I was remiss.'

Thrown off his stride, Barclay could only take the book in confusion.

'I can tell you now,' she went on. 'It was between ourselves before but . . . I wanted to learn navigation. I thought it would be useful for a captain's wife.'

She waited to be congratulated, but, as Barclay was plainly nonplussed, felt that she must make herself clearer.

'I am to be married to Captain Moore. It was settled this morning.'

From the kitchen, there was the sound of a step being made towards the door and then the room was quiet. Barclay had difficulty swallowing. There was an emptiness in his breast where his hope had been.

'The captain's a fortunate man,' he said, gently, 'and I'm sure deserves you as much as anyone could. No doubt he'll show you the four corners of the earth but wherever you go, my fond wishes will go with you.'

He had hardly spoken when Maud, affected by the nature of his compliment, had seen Moore outside and gone to join him. She left Barclay standing helplessly, feeling that the sun had grown colder. Sadie came into the parlour. The kindness in her eyes, that was always there for him, was strengthening and warm. She came up to him and touched his cheek.

'Well, then, my dear,' she said. 'Miss Parris is a proper, fine lady but she baint for thee. That ent no good a-hankering after she. It d'make my heart ache to see 'ee sad and I'll tell 'ee what we'll do.' She took his hand and held it between hers. 'Thee and me shall put up the banns for I d'ave enough love for the both of us. I'll see it d'come right. Now,' she pulled him gently to his seat, 'do 'ee sit there and think on.'

Although Theo had told Maud that Mr Carnow was rallying, his health did not begin to make his family easy until July was over. The strain that had been put on his body by the poisonous levels of digitalis would have been hard enough to recover from without the depressing effect of the shock it had been necessary to give him. The family had hoped to keep the truth hidden until Mr Carnow was in a better condition to sustain it, but he became so agitated by Charles's absence it was felt that it was wiser to risk telling him than to let his imagination run amok.

This lesser of two evils caused Mr Carnow violent pain but also had positive results. Having his eyes opened to Charles's crimes, confirmed his growing suspicions and made the loss of his son's presence easier to bear. The deep shame he felt for having believed that the loyal Trent had committed fraud – a shame worsened by learning of Charles's seduction of Helen – made him fear to face Ettie but she, mature and firm, bore him no malice and pointed out that few men would have given the daughter of a convict, who had harmed them, a comfortable upbringing under their own roof. Most of all, the knowledge made him appreciate the patient love of Ralph, who had uncomplainingly supported him for so long.

Nevertheless, it would have been too much to hope that he would not suffer a melancholy that would lengthen his convalescence and this proved to be the case. The turning-point came when it was heard that the Home Secretary had been both prompt and merciful and was prepared to offer Trent a pardon. Although this was a second-rate method of obtaining freedom, Trent did not stand on ceremony and embraced his chance of walking out of the walls that had been his world for a decade.

In his desire to make reparation, Mr Carnow insisted that the discovery of the real culprit should be reported in the local newspaper. He was adamant that Trent's name should be cleared, however unpleasant the nine-days-wonder might be for them all, and he wrote to Trent expressing his sorrow for the ruin that Charles had brought about. At first, Trent's bitterness made him reluctant to have any contact with the Carnows but Theo and Ettie persuaded him to the invalid's bedside. Once there, Trent's own experience of suffering softened him to the broken man, who was in torment for sins that were not of his committing. He accepted a position in the counting-house and the lease of a cottage nearby, for, apart from not wanting to separate Ettie from those to whom she was attached, he preferred to confront boldly the lingering questions in the minds of his old acquaintance than to endure the inevitable rumours in a strange place.

The release of Trent and his grudging forgiveness marked the beginning of Mr Carnow's recovery. He would never again have the health he used to enjoy but although he was delicate he was not infirm. Delivered from the pressing anxiety of his illness, his family were able to think of other things.

One August Sunday, Theo and Louisa walked over to Carnow to spend the afternoon. It was a day of drowsy heat and they went slowly, holding their parasols between themselves and the cloudless sky. The lane was hard and white and the hedgerows, unwashed by rain, were pale with dust. They passed two lovers wandering hand in hand; the girl dropping red petals from a garland of poppies that lay on her fair hair. When they reached the bridge at Carnow, they paused to look down into the clear waters of the stream and to say a few words over the wall to a blissful Barclay, who, with pegs and string, was marking out flowerbeds for his Sadie.

At the house, there was the same appearance of tranquillity. They went out on to the terrace and down the stone steps to the lawn. Ralph and Ettie were playing croquet in a desultory fashion and the sound of their mallets as they hit the balls was loud in the silence of the sleeping mill. In the shade of a chestnut tree, Mr Carnow and Trent were sitting in two of the collection of basket-chairs, with a table of jugs and glasses beside them.

Abandoning their game, Ralph and Ettie came to join the newcomers and accompanied them to the tree. Trent rose to his feet as they approached, lifting his hat, but Mr Carnow contented himself with the convalescent's privilege of grasping the arms of his chair late enough to be urged not to get up. Ettie busied herself pouring fruit cup and cucumber water, adjusting the set of her father's replaced hat as she took his glass.

There was little conversation. The day was so warm and hushed that the sounds of wood-pigeons in the elms beyond the orchard, the creak of basketry and the chink of Theo's heavy bangles as she plied her fan were enough to occupy them all. Across the grass, scarlet geraniums were ranged against tall delphiniums and the rose that climbed to Mr Carnow's window was still in bloom.

Theo sat beside Ralph, her hand a few inches from his. Her outward calm matched the peacefulness of the scene but, unknown to her companions, her heart was beating rapidly. She had come with a purpose that she had not mentioned to Louisa and an unusual trepidation made her strive to subdue tremors of expectation.

It was a year since she and Louisa had returned from the continent and she did not recognize herself as the girl that she had been. She had gone abroad to gain experience and had believed her travels had given her maturity but the events of the past twelve months had shown her that she had been mistaken. It occurred to her that if she had not been brought up to make choices and want more than a submissive marriage, she would not have almost come to grief. A spirit of independence opens the doors of the world but it must learn to recognize what is good if it is not to lead to sorrow. A conviction that she could tell true from false had brought her here today.

Feeling that he was watching her, she turned her head to look at Ralph.

'A perfect afternoon,' he said.

She quivered as if someone that she had not seen had touched her in the dark. He spoke lazily but his eyes were not quiet.

'It's too still,' she said. 'Will you walk with me?'

He got up and offered her his arm. They left the wide shade of the chestnut tree and passed the laurels that screened the orchard. Amongst the old apples, the pears, the plums and cherries that had been planted long ago but yet bore fruit, they had privacy and the living silence of summer. The garden closed around them; its twisted, lichened branches were a canopy of heavy leaves and swelling harvest; its high walls drew warmth into their russet bricks and held the heat, shimmering at the boundaries of the grass. They walked in anticipation, secret and hidden.

Theo's breath was shallow and her throat moved as if she wanted to speak but could not. She had removed her gloves and the cloth of Ralph's sleeve beneath her hand made her acutely conscious of the arm she held. The ground was uneven and, at times, when their footing was unsure, she swayed against him to steady herself.

When they had reached the centre, where a seat had been built around the gnarled trunk of an apple tree and honeysuckle climbed the stakes that held the ancient boughs aloft, she stopped.

'I have a mind to be married,' she said.

Ralph's heart convulsed within him. He took her hands in his.

'Oh?' he said, his voice as soft as if they were overheard. 'Do you know who to?'

She raised her face to him; the shadows of the leaves falling across her pale skin like a veil.

'To a man who has given me that most precious gift – a strong and loyal love – and who deserves mine; who will see me for his equal and recognize my right to be part of his world; who has known the winds blow coldly and has a hunger for my warmth.'

He grasped her hands more tightly.

'There was a man once,' he said, 'whose love gave him unfounded suspicions. His jealousy made him say harsh and foolish things. He was older than his lady and it made him too protective. He hadn't understood her worth. He's learnt her talents now.'

Theo drew her fingers out of his and reached into the folds of her skirts. She brought out a spray of wild rose leaves and brushed it over her lips.

'I was once kissed against this briar. Do you remember?'

'I remember.'

'I ran then, but today that season's past and I'm less inclined for running.'

'I remember,' he said again. 'It was like this.'

He gathered her to him and the silence of the garden enfolded them and was undisturbed. The rose leaves dropped from her hand and lay unheeded amongst the grass but, above them, the fruit was ripening and all about there was renewal and there was hope.